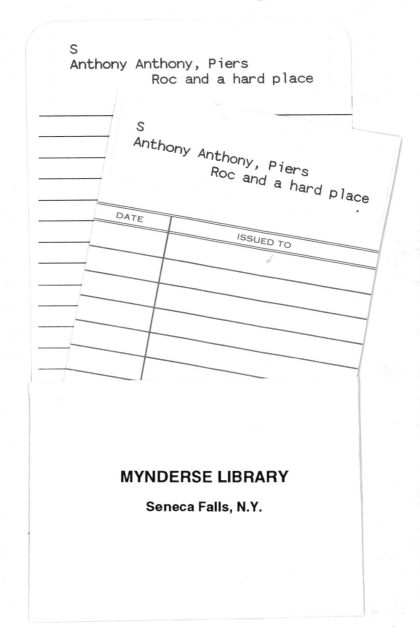

S
Anthony Anthony, Piers
        Roc and a hard place

S
Anthony Anthony, Piers
        Roc and a hard place
                    .

DATE	ISSUED TO

MYNDERSE LIBRARY

Seneca Falls, N.Y.

PIERS ANTHONY

ROC AND A HARD PLACE

TOR ®

A TOM DOHERTY ASSOCIATES BOOK

NEW YORK

ROC AND A HARD PLACE

Copyright © 1995 by Piers Anthony Jacob

This book is printed on acid-free paper.

A Tor Book
Published by Tom Doherty Associates, Inc.
175 Fifth Avenue
New York, N.Y. 10010

Tor Books on the World-Wide Web:
http://www.tor.com

Tor® is a registered trademark of Tom Doherty Associates, Inc.

Library of Congress Cataloging-in-Publication Data

Anthony, Piers.
   Roc and a hard place / Piers Anthony.
       p.   cm.
   "A Tom Doherty Associates book."
   ISBN 0-312-85392-0
   1. Xanth (Imaginary place)—Fiction.   I. Title.
PS3551.N73R64   1995
813'.54—dc20   95-30306
                                               CIP

First edition: October 1995

Printed in the United States of America

0 9 8 7 6 5 4 3 2 1

Contents

1.   PROBLEM 11

2.   SIMURGH 30

3.   MYSTERY 47

4.   THRENODY 67

5.   CURSE 86

6.   CONTEST 103

7.   AISLE 120

8.   MUNDANIA 137

9.   DEMON DRIVER 156

10. BOOK OF KINGS 175

11. CHENA 193

12. SCRAMBLE 217

13. MPD 235

14. PROSECUTION 256

15. DEFENSE 277

16. VERDICT 294

     AUTHOR'S NOTE 313

1
PROBLEM

It was a nice castle, with high turrets, solid walls, a deep moat, and an elevated office suite whose picture window overlooked the nearby community of nymphs. Fire cracker plants grew around the wall, useful for starting fires in the mornings, and the crackers tasted good too. The connected orchard had pie trees of the most sinfully delicious varieties. The mistress of the household was exactly as beautiful, devoted, and accommodating as her husband desired. A man could hardly ask for a better situation.

Except for one or two small things. "Where is your worser half?" Veleno muttered, looking apprehensively around.

"Don't worry," the Demoness Metria replied with a smile as her scant clothing shimmered into nothingness. "I sent Mentia off to see the Demon Grossclout about our other problem."

"Other problem?"

She pretended not to hear. "Grossclout's such an intractable cuss that it should take her days to pry any kind of an answer from him."

"That's a relief!" he said, looking more than relieved. "It's not that I want to be critical, but—"

"But Mentia is slightly crazy," Metria finished. "And you married me, not my worser half. But because she did fission off from me, being disgusted by my new goody-goody attitude after I got half your soul, we can't keep her away. She's the half of me you naturally don't like—the soulless half, dedicated to making your life half-muled.''

''Half-whatted?''

''Horsed, equined, donkeyed, asinined—''

He kissed her. ''I think I could fathom the word if I concentrated. Let's make hay while the sun shines.''

She looked perplexed. ''Hay? I thought you had something else in mind.'' A tantalizing wisp of strategically placed clothing appeared.

''I love it when you tease me,'' he said, picking her up and carrying her to the master bedroom.

She assumed the form of a nymph. ''Eeeeek!'' she cried faintly, kicking her marvelous bare legs in the nymphly way. ''Whatever am I going to do?''

''You're going to make me deliriously happy, you luscious creature.''

She inhaled, enhancing what hardly needed it. ''O, sigh, how can I escape this hideous fate?'' she wailed cutely, kissing him on eye, ear, nose, and throat.

They fell together on the bed, in a tangle of limbs, faces, kisses, and whatnot. ''You are the best thing that ever happened to me,'' Veleno gasped around the activity. ''You're just the most wonderful, beautiful, lovable, exciting, fantastic person in all Xanth!''

''You damn me with faint praise,'' she muttered, clasping him with such ardor that description would be improper.

Another demoness popped into the chamber. ''Oh, there you are, Metria!'' she exclaimed. ''No wonder I couldn't find you around the grounds. I have brought you what you most vitally need.''

Veleno stiffened, but not in the way he desired. ''Oh, no!''

Metria looked up from what was occupying her. ''At the least opportune time, of course. Do you mind, worser half? I happen to be busy at the moment.''

Mentia peered closely. ''Oh? Doing what?''

''Making my husband deliriously happy, of course, as only a demoness can.''

''When not being annoyingly interrupted,'' Veleno muttered.

Mentia peered again. ''Sorry. I thought that was a grimace of pain on what's-his-name's face. Are you sure you are doing an adequate job, better half?''

''Of course I'm sure!'' Metria said indignantly. ''He has not complained once in seven hundred and fifty times during the past year.''

''Oh? What about that groan he groaned just now?''

''That was when *you* appeared!''

''Well, if you feel that way, I'll just depart with what I brought, and never never return.''

''Oop, no!'' Metria cried with alarm. ''I need it!''

Her husband, somewhat bemused by the interruption, put in two more words. ''Need what?''

''Never mind,'' Metria said. ''It's a soldier matter.''

''A what matter?'' he asked.

''Secluded, cloistered, isolated, remote, detached, obscure—''

''Private?''

''Whatever,'' she agreed crossly.

''But what could be private from your husband?'' he asked somewhat querulously.

''Yes, whatever could you be suspiciously concealing from your trusting spouse?'' Mentia echoed.

''Can't we have this discussion some other time?'' Metria demanded, frustrated.

''Of course, dear,'' Mentia agreed. ''I'll pop back in during the next century.'' She began to fuzz out.

''No, wait!'' Metria cried. ''Now will do after all.''

''Why, how nice,'' Mentia said, smiling with something more than good nature. ''But don't you think you should introduce us first?''

''Whatever for? He knows who the mischief you are, from ever since you returned from that madness with the gargoyle.''

''Yes, but he may have forgotten. I've been away a whole hour, you know.''

''That long?'' Veleno inquired with resignation.

Metria gritted her teeth. There was nothing half so annoying as half a demoness! But she knew her worser half would not give over until she had her half-baked way. ''Veleno, this is the Demoness

Mentia, my soulless worser half, who represents what I was like before I got half-souled, except that she has no problem with vocational.''

"With what?''

"Idiom, language, speech, expression, locution, utterance, articulation—''

"Words?''

"Whatever. Instead, she's slightly crazy.''

"Yes, it's my talent,'' Mentia agreed proudly.

"And, Mentia, this is my husband Veleno, formerly a nymphomaniac, but he hasn't touched a nymph since I married him and took half his soul.''

"Yes, but hasn't he looked at nymphs out the window, with a glint in his—?''

"Pleased to meet you,'' Veleno gritted, drawing free a hand and extending it. "Now will you begone?''

"Charmed, I'm sure,'' Mentia said, forming a pair of pincers on the end of her arm.

"Ixnay,'' Metria murmured warningly. "Mortals are protected from harm in this castle.''

"Oh, that's right,'' Mentia agreed, disappointed. The pincers became an ordinary hand, which shook Veleno's hand. "That was one of the conditions of the restoration. Well, now that your mortal man and I have been properly introduced, I will give you what you most need, Metria.''

At last! But Metria still wasn't easy about this. "Veleno, dearest, why don't you take a little snooze for the moment?'' Metria suggested dulcetly, covering his eyes with her hand.

"But what could you need that I have not provided?'' he asked, frowning.

"Yes, I'm sure he will be really, truly interested in this very important secret matter,'' Mentia said, sitting on the edge of the bed, so that her thigh touched Veleno.

"Oh, all *right*,'' Metria said, really crossly.

"Have no concern, dear, I will explain it excruciatingly clearly,'' Mentia said. "What I bring is information to help abate your incapacity, so you won't be a failure anymore.''

"What incapacity?" Veleno demanded. "My wife has made me deliriously happy almost continuously since we married."

"That is the problem," Mentia said. "She has helped you with the chore of summoning the stork seven hundred and fifty—" she peered again "—and a half times this year, and more times during the prior year when I was too busy to be with her, unfortunately, and yet the stork has not gotten the message. She is clearly inadequate in this department."

Veleno pondered, slowly realizing the truth of this statement. "That hadn't occurred to me," he said. "I was too delirious to think of the stork. But how could it fail to get the messages?"

"That is precisely what Metria wants to know," Mentia said. "Whatever could be wrong with her to bomb so badly in so many attempts? Whatever could make her such a sore loser? Especially when I could so readily have—"

"Nuh-uh!" Metria and Veleno said together.

"So she sent me to ask the most intelligent creature she knows, the Demon Grossclout, for advice," Mentia continued without concern, "and he instantly delegated me to convey that essential advice to her. Naturally I delayed not half a whit to honor that stricture. Her failing is simply too serious to permit any delay."

"Thank you so much, Worser," Metria snarled.

"You are so welcome, Better. I knew you would want to attend to your washout without delay." Mentia's form fuzzed, and assumed the likeness of a giant lemon, then a cooked turkey. "I am thrilled to have been of so much help."

"You haven't been of much help yet," Metria said grimly. "What did Grossclout *say?*"

"Oh, that. He says you should go ask Good Magician Humfrey."

"But Humfrey charges a year's service for a single Answer!" Metria protested. "I don't want to pay that! That's why I went to Grossclout."

"Grossclout did add a few words," Mentia said. "I believe those words were *mush-head, cheapskate,* and *serve her right.*"

"That's Grossclout, all right," Metria agreed. "He still holds a grudge just because I chose to sand my nails in his dull magic classes at Demon U."

"Actually, that was I who did that," Mentia said, smiling reminiscently. "Back when we were inextricably bound together as alternate aspects of a single demoness. Those were the days! But I did not see fit to remind the Professor of that." She paused reflectively. "I might be able to remember a few more of his words, if it's really important," she offered helpfully.

"Thank you so much, no," Metria said. "I think I have fathomed his altitude."

"His what?"

"Manner, disposition, temperament, bent, inclination, penchant—"

"Attitude?" Veleno inquired.

"Whatever," Metria said crossly.

"From the height of his eminence," Mentia agreed. "Well, if you need no further assistance or advice on technique—"

"None!" Metria said.

"Too bad." Mentia faded out.

"You want the stork to deliver a baby?" Veleno inquired as Metria resumed activity.

"Yes. It's what married couples do. Raise children."

"But demonesses don't get babies unless they want them."

"Precisely. I want one." She looked away. "I suppose I should have told you, and I can't blame you for being angry."

"But I'm not angry."

"You aren't? But it might interrupt the delirium, and give you the solid obligation of raising a child."

"Exactly! I want a family, now that it occurs to me."

Metria gazed at him with adoration tinged substantially with relief. "Wonderful!"

Now he was thoughtful. "The stork must figure that our signals aren't serious."

"Which is ironic, considering how strong we have made them. I've just got to get the stork's distention!"

"The stork's what?"

"Observation, mindfulness, notice, focus, application—"

"Attention?"

"Whatever. What do you think I should do?"

He considered. "I think you should go to ask the Good Magician."

"But then I would have to leave you alone for a year."

"Surely you could return on occasion. It might mean you could make me deliriously happy only three or four hundred times in that year, but I think I can survive that deprivation. After all, I want you to be happy too."

"You dear wonderful man!" she exclaimed, and proceeded to do the impossible: to make him twice as delirious as before.

But before she went, she checked around the premises, debating with herself, because her worser half had decided to unify for the occasion, now that there was a chance her life would become interesting again. 'Do I really want to do this?' Metria asked herself.

'Why not? It isn't as if you have anything important to do around here.' Mentia had fissioned off in disgust when Metria married, got half a soul, and fell in love, in that order. Her worser half claimed to have been on a grand adventure with a gargoyle, and helped save all Xanth from madness, but that was surely an exaggeration. She had merged as soon as Metria stopped being nauseatingly nice to her husband.

'If you had half a soul, you would have a different alti—attitude.'

'Praise the Demon X(A/N)th that I have not been corrupted with any portion of a soul,' Mentia agreed. Their dialogue was silent because it was internal; no one else could overhear it. She pointed with their left hand. 'There's a sand worm; step on it.'

'I will not,' Metria retorted. 'That wouldn't be nice.' She lifted the worm carefully with their right hand and inspected it. It was, of course, made of sand; if direct sunlight or water touched it, it would powder or dissolve away. So she put it back in a dry shaded section, and watched it wiggle off.

'Disgusting,' Mentia remarked to no one else in particular. 'But you can redeem your demonly nature by squishing that June bug.'

'No way. Kill a June bug and the year loses its most romantic month.'

Mentia grimaced with the left side of their face. 'I'd rather have you half-bottomed than half-souled.' She looked around, using Metria's left eye. 'I see that go-quat tree is fruiting.'

'So is the come-quat tree,' Metria agreed. 'Veleno likes them, when he's coming and going.'

'Which is he doing when he's alone with you?'

'The opposite of what he wants you to be doing.'

But Mentia could not be shamed. 'Here is my favorite: the grapes with an attitude.'

'Sour grapes,' Metria agreed. 'Your kind.'

'So why are you dawdling around here, instead of getting moving to the Good Magician's castle?'

'I'm just not sure it's right to leave my husband on half rations.'

'There's all the food he needs, growing right around the castle here.'

'Half rations of delirium.'

'Oh.' Mentia looked around again, until the left eyeball was oriented completely to the side. 'Let's make it easy, then. See that winged nut tree?'

The right eye swiveled. 'Of course. The nuts are almost as nutty as you are.'

'If the right wing nut flies first, we stay right here. If the left one flies first, we pop over to see the Good Magician.'

'That would be a crazy way to make such an important decision.'

'Precisely. Agreed?'

Metria sighed. It was as good a way as any. 'Agreed.'

They watched the two nuts quiver. The right one spread its wings. Then suddenly the left one lurched into the air and flew across to the nearby bolt tree. 'How romantic,' Mentia said, amused by what the boldest bolt did with the nut.

'Why don't you find it romantic when Veleno and I—'

'Once is amusing. Seven hundred and fifty times is droll.'

'Not when you're in love.'

'I'm glad I'll never be in love. Let's be on our way.'

Metria couldn't dawdle any longer, even if it did seem somewhat nutty or screwed up.

* * *

The Good Magician's castle looked ordinary. Its wall and turrets were set within a sparkling circular moat, which in turn was inside a ring of mountains. Neither would be any problem for a demoness to pop across.

But Metria was unable to pop across. When she tried, she bounced off an invisible barrier. 'Darn, I forgot!' she swore. 'The old fool has a shield against demonly intrusion.'

'That's what you consider swearing? That's not even worthy of the Juvenile Conspiracy.'

Worse, she was unable to fly or dematerialize in this vicinity. Obviously the Good Magician had improved his defenses in the past century or so. 'We'll have to plod across the way mortals do.'

Metria plodded. As she approached the ring of mountains, she saw that they were in the shape of huge loaves of sugar. Fortunately the slope was not too steep to prevent her from climbing. It was a pain, having to leg it instead of pop or float it, but she wasn't going to let it balk her.

She crested the mountain—and abruptly lost her footing and slid helplessly down toward the moat. Here the sugar was loose and granular, offering no purchase. Soon she was unceremoniously dumped into the moat.

And promptly booted out again. She sailed back over the mountain and landed on the ground beyond. The grass hopped out of the way before her derriere struck; it was the grass hopper variety.

''That's boot rear!'' she exclaimed aloud. ''The moat is filled with it.''

'I think I begin to see a pattern here,' Mentia remarked. 'I think I'll leave you to your challenges.'

'Oh no you don't!' Metria retorted. 'You talked me into this nuisance; you'll help me see it through. Besides, I don't trust you with my husband while I'm away. You might promise him heaven, and give him hell, and I'd get the blame.'

'Curses! Foiled again.'

Metria tackled the mountain again. From the outside it was solid sugar, easy to climb. As she approached the crest, she trod extremely cautiously, but found no break in the steep sandy slope. The moment she stepped on that, she would be dumped into the moat with a kick.

This was definitely a challenge. That meant that not only would she have to struggle to find her way past this one, there would be two more beyond it. "What a pity!" she swore in frustration.

'What a pity!' her worser self mimicked. 'That half soul has denatured you.'

'So it made me into a nice person,' Metria retorted. 'So what's wrong with that?'

'It's undemonly. I'll bet you can't even say poop.'

'Of course I can say peep!'

'Point made.'

'Well, if you're so demonly, how do you propose to get us across this sweet mess?'

Mentia considered. 'The mountain is sweet, but the moat isn't. It likes to kick donkey.'

'So it boots rear. That's its nature. Tell me something I don't already know.' Metria rubbed her booted rear; if she weren't a demoness, that would really be smarting along about now.

'Maybe if we made it sweet, it wouldn't have so much of a kick.'

'Make it sweet? But how—' Then Metria saw the point. 'Let's get busy.'

She formed her hands into scoops and began scooping loose sugar down the slope. Soon she managed to start an avalanche. Sugar slid grandly down and plunged into the moat.

After she had scooped as much of the mountain into the water as she could, she found that she was able to descend without sliding. She had taken the edge off the slope. She went down and stood at the bank of the moat, which now looked somewhat soggy. She poked a finger into it, and tested a drop of soggy water on her tongue. There was only a little bit of tingle. Sure enough, she had pretty much denatured its kick.

However, the moat was now a mass of sickly sweet muck. The mere touch of her feet in it was enough to make her feel somewhat sick, as if she had overeaten or overimbibed. Since demons neither ate nor drank, she knew this was more magic. She would be very uncomfortable if she waded through all that, even if she didn't get her rear booted out.

So she walked around the edge until she came to the drawbridge, which was in the down position. She had not been able to reach it before because the steep slope had dumped her where it chose to in the moat, but now it could not stop her from reaching it. She had surmounted the first challenge.

'This becomes dull,' Mentia said. 'I'm going to take a nap. You handle the next challenge, and I'll handle the third, okay?'

'Okay,' Metria agreed. She wasn't concerned about her worser self, as long as she knew where Mentia was.

She set foot on the planks of the moat—and something buzzed up before her, barring the way. It seemed to be two dots, like an incomplete ellipsis, except that they were up and down instead of across. "What in tintinnabulation are you?" she demanded.

"I don't understand: What in what?" the dot formation asked.

"Bells, ringing, music, jangle, discordance, melody—"

"Try again: None of those words make sense," the dots said angrily.

"Damnation, hell, abyss, underworld, hades, inferno, perdition—"

"Let me guess: Tarnation?"

"Whatever," she said crossly.

"You think you're cross?" the dots demanded. "You're positively sweet, compared to me: I'm as angry as anything gets."

She peered at the dots. "Just exactly what *are* you, BB brain?"

"I'm an angry punctuation mark: an irritated colon," the dots said. "And I am going to make you pause before you continue."

"How long a pause?"

"Just this: As long a pause as it takes."

"As it takes to what? To refresh?"

"I thought you'd never ask: As it takes to make you give up and go away."

"I get it! You're another challenge."

"Too much of a challenge for you: Give it up."

Metria tried to walk around the nasty colon, but it moved over to shove her into the moat. She tried to jump over it, still being unable to fly, but it sailed up to intercept her, its dots glowing fiercely. She tried to crawl under it, but it dropped down and made a pooping sound that warned her back. There was just no telling what it might do. She tried to push straight through it, but it got positively spastic and she had to desist.

"How am I supposed to get past you?" she demanded, annoyed.

"Either go away or bring me some relief: Those are your options."

"Relief?" she asked blankly.

"From my syndrome: I am not irritable by choice, you know."

"But how can I bring you relief?"

"This is for you to figure out: Cogitate, you infernal creature."

"Do what?"

"Think, ponder, consider, contemplate, reflect: Work it out yourself, Demoness."

Metria thought, pondered, considered, contemplated, reflected, and cogitated, though that last made her a bit queasy. But it baffled her. "It's an edema to me," she confessed.

"Speak plainly, demoness: A what?"

"Puzzle, maze, riddle, conundrum, mystery, paradox, poser, problem, confusion, obscurity—"

"It didn't sound like any of those things to me: Try again."

"What did it sound like to you?"

"Enemy, energy, eczema, enervate, Edam: enough of this nonsense."

"Enema?" she inquired sweetly.

"Whatever: It hardly matters." Then the colon did a double take, its dots vibrating. "Enema: Maybe that's the answer!" It flew off to a private place to seek relief.

Metria quickly marched across the bridge. She had conquered the second challenge.

'Your turn, Worser,' she told her worser half.

'Good thing you couldn't think of the word "enigma." Sweet dreams, Better.'

'Demons don't dream.'

'I was being facetious.'

'Being what?'

'Humorous, droll, amusing, comical, funny—'

'I was being funny too, idiot!' Metria snapped, and retired from the scene.

Mentia stepped off the bridge and came to a pile of blocks. "What are you?"

"We thought you'd never ask," they replied. "We are building blocks." They moved, clomping along to form a square around her. Then more blocks climbed on top of the first ones, and others climbed on top of those.

"What are you doing?" Mentia asked, bemused by this activity.

"We are building blocks, of course. We are building a building for you."

"But I don't want a building. I'm just passing through."

"That's what you think!" the blocks chorused as they reached a level above her head, then started crossing the top, forming a dome.

"Hey, wait a minute!" she protested.

"Construction waits for nobody, blockhead!"

"Who are you calling that?" she demanded indignantly. "I'm an airhead, not a blockhead." Her head fuzzed into vapor.

But the blocks were silent. They had shut her in.

She realized, belatedly, that this was the third challenge. First the boot rear moat, then the irritable colon, now the building blocks. She had to get out of this sudden chamber.

She pushed at the wall, but it was firm; the blocks had locked into place. She checked the ground, but it was hard rock. Ordinarily nothing like this could inhibit any demon, but the ambient spell around the castle made her resemble an (ugh!) mortal. She discovered that she did not have a lot of experience handling purely physical things. But her memory of being sane and sensible in the Region of Madness the year before gave her the assurance that she could adjust to this problem, too.

She explored all around the chamber. Dim rays of light filtered in through the crevices between blocks, so that it wasn't completely dark. She tried to squeeze through a crevice, but she lacked even this power now. It was most frustrating.

'I wonder what Gary Gargoyle would have done?' she asked herself. 'He was a massive powerful stone creature who was transformed to a weak fleshly man for his adventure, so he had a real problem.'

'Will you be quiet while I'm trying to rest?' Metria demanded crossly.

Mentia thought, pondered, considered, contemplated, reflected, and cogitated as Metria had, and finally came up with a feeble notion: Maybe she needed to think differently. She knew there was always a way to handle the challenges, and usually it required ingenuity rather than strength. So she should use her mind rather than her body.

But that was what she had been trying to do, without getting far. What use was it to think endlessly, if the only notion it produced was to think some more?

'Not more, differently,' she reminded herself.

She considered the chamber again. She had pushed at one block and it was firm—but maybe there were others that were loose. She might push one out and crawl through the hole.

She put her hands on one block near the bottom. It was firm. She tried another. It was firmer. ''Poop on you!'' she said, berating it, but the block wasn't fazed.

She continued to check, but all the lower blocks were firm. This evidently wasn't the answer. She remained completely sealed in.

She sat down, leaned against the wall, and gazed at the dust motes dancing in the thin beams of light. The motes seemed to have a current, moving across the chamber. Where were they going? She focused closely, forming a very large and powerful eyeball, and traced their progress beyond the rays of light. But her effort was wasted; they didn't go anywhere. They just brushed up against the wall and slowly settled down toward the floor.

Then she had a brighter notion. The question wasn't where the motes were going, but where they were coming from! What was making that gentle draft? She traced that way, and discovered that the air was coming from one of the blocks in the ceiling dome. How could that be?

She put her hand up to that block—and her fingers passed right through it without resistance. It was illusion! She had given up too soon; had she pushed against every single block, she would have discovered that. This was the way out.

She put both hands up into the hole, then hauled herself up. In a moment her head was outside the building. She scrambled and got out, then rolled head under heels to the ground. She had navigated the third challenge!

"Why hello, D. Mentia," a voice said.

Startled, Mentia got to her feet. There stood a rather nice young woman. "Do I know you?"

"I think so. You brought Gary Gargoyle here last year. I'm Wira, Humfrey's daughter-in-law."

"But I never came up to the castle," Mentia protested. "How could you have seen me?"

Wira laughed. "Not with my eyes, of course. But Gary spoke well of you."

Mentia felt that she was getting in over her depth. 'Metria! Wake up. We're in the castle.'

Metria joined her. 'Just like old newspapers,' she remarked, looking around.

'Like old whats?'

'Ages, eons, epochs, eras, centuries—'

'Times?'

'Whatever. It has been nigh ninety years since I managed to sneak in here.'

"Hello, D. Metria," Wira said.

Both of them jumped. "How did you know me?" Metria demanded.

"Father Humfrey said you would be arriving with your other self. Now I will show you into the castle."

'That girl's eerie,' Mentia muttered.

'She must have developed other senses,' Metria agreed.

"True," Wira agreed.

The two selves ceased their dialogue and followed the girl into the castle. There they were met by a woman of indeterminate age. "Mother MareAnn, here is the Demoness Metria and Mentia," Wira said.

'Mother MareAnn?' one of them asked silently.

"I am Humfrey's fifth and a half wife," the woman explained.
"I am taking my turn with him this month. I was his first love and
last wife, because of a complicated story that wouldn't interest you.
My husband will see you now. Wira will take you up to his study."

Maybe a half wife was like a half soul: enough to do the whole
job.

"This way, please," Wira said, showing the way. She moved up
a narrow winding stair without faltering; obviously she knew the
premises well.

The study was a gloomy little chamber crowded with books and
vials. 'This hasn't changed a bit in ninety years,' Metria remarked.

"Of course it hasn't, Demoness," Humfrey grumped from within.
"Neither have you, except for that split personality you recently
developed."

"Nice to meet you, too, again, Magician," Metria said. "You
don't look much more than a day older, either." Of course, she knew
he had elixir from the Fountain of Youth, which he imbibed to keep
himself about a century old.

"Enough of this politeness. Ask your Question."

"How can I get the stork to take my summons seriously?"

"That will be apparent after you complete your Service. Go to
the Simurgh."

"Go where?"

"Your mind may be addled, Demoness, but not your hearing.
Begone."

"Now, just a urine-picking instant, Magician! You can't just—"

"Please, don't argue with him," Wira whispered. "That only ag-
gravates—"

"Pea," Humfrey said.

"I certainly will not!" Metria declared. "Demonesses don't have
to, and even if I did, I wouldn't—"

"As in vegetable," Wira said. "Pea-picking. Now, please—"

"But he hasn't Answered me!" Metria protested. "And no one
can fly to the Simurgh, not even a demoness. I demand a proper
Answer!"

"After the service," Humfrey muttered, turning a page of his giant tome.

Mentia made a sudden internal lunge and took over the body. "Yes, of course," she said, and followed Wira out of the study.

"You're so much more sensible, Mentia, even if you don't have half a soul," Wira remarked.

"I am more sensible *because* I don't have half a soul," Mentia replied. "My better half is befuddled by love and decency. I am practical, especially in crazy situations like this. We'll just have to walk to Mount Parnassus and see what the big bird wants."

"But she isn't there," MareAnn said, overhearing them as they reached the foot of the stairway. "That's just her summer retreat, when the Tree of Seeds is fruiting."

"But then we don't know where to find her."

"Ah, but I can summon an equine who knows the way."

"That's her talent," Wira explained. "She summons anything related to horses, except for unicorns."

"Why not unicorns?" Mentia asked.

"She once could summon them too, but when she went to Hell and married Humfrey she lost her innocence." Wira blushed, for it was indelicate to refer openly to matters shrouded by the Adult Conspiracy. There might be a child in the vicinity. "Now they ignore her. It's very sad."

Mentia had little sympathy. "My better half never cared about innocence until she got half-souled. She can't get near a unicorn either. So summon a horse who knows the way."

MareAnn led the way out of the castle and across the moat, which now looked quite ordinary. She stood at the edge of an ordinary field that was where the sugar mountain had been. Already a group of things were galloping across the plain.

Mentia stared. There were four creatures, each with only one leg. Two had narrow heads, and two had thin tails. Their single hoofs thudded into the dirt in irregular order, clop-clop, clop-clop, stirring up clouds of dust behind. "What are those?"

"Quarter horses, of course," MareAnn said. Then, to the horses: "Whoa!"

The four clopped to a halt before her. Each quarter had a silver disk on the side, with ribbed edges. On the front two disks, heads were inscribed; on the rear two, big birds with half-spread wings.

"Fall in," MareAnn said.

The four creatures fell together, and suddenly were revealed as the four quarters of a regular horse, now complete. Wira stepped up to pet him, and he nuzzled her hand until she produced a lump of sugar. "Too bad you can't ride Eight Bits," Wira remarked.

"That's his name?" Mentia asked. She was a little crazy herself, but this was more than a little crazy. "Why not?"

"Because he doesn't trust strange adults. He just falls apart and scatters to the wind's four quarters. But he does know the way, so you can follow him."

"Maybe he should just tell us where to go, and we'll go there ourselves," Mentia said.

"No, he can't speak," MareAnn said. "He can understand simple directions, but that's the limit. Anything more puts a strain on him, and—"

"He falls apart," Mentia finished, resigned to a tedious journey.

But Metria pushed to the surface. "No, there's a better way. How does Eight Bits feel about children?"

"Oh, he likes children," MareAnn said. "Especially if they are a quarter the size of adults. But—"

Metria dissolved into smoke, then re-formed as the cutest, sweetest waif of a child anyone ever beheld. Even Wira was surprised, realizing that something was different. "I know Mentia and Metria, but who are you?"

"I am Woe Betide," the waif said. "I have a quarter soul—half of Metria's—and I love horses, and I will just be so pathetically sad if I can't ride this one that I'll dissolve in pitiful little misery." She wiped away a huge glistening tear with one cute sleeve.

MareAnn exchanged half a glance with Wira, because it was one way: The sightless young woman had no half to return. "Maybe so," she agreed. She lifted the tyke to the four-quartered horse.

"Oh, goody-goody!" Woe Betide exclaimed, clapping her sweet little hands together. "Let's go."

But Wira wasn't sanguine about this. "We shouldn't send a little child on such a wild ride alone," she said.

"I'm not really a—" the tyke began, but then one of her selves stifled her before the horse could hear the rest.

MareAnn nodded. "Perhaps we can find an adult companion for her. I think there is a demoness who also knows the way, who still owes Humfrey part of a Service."

"A demoness!" Woe Betide exclaimed. "They aren't trustworthy!"

Again half a glance was exchanged. "You are surely in a position to know," MareAnn agreed. "But when performing a Service, a person is bound to do it properly. She will not be released until you are safely there."

The child's face made a cute grimace of resignation. "Oh, all right. Who is it?"

"Helen Back."

"Helen Back!" the child cried. "O woe betide me! She's the worst creature in demondom. Do you know what she does?"

"Yes," MareAnn agreed. "But she will be bound not to do it for this mission."

"I hope you're right," the child said, looking truly woeful.

MareAnn snapped her fingers, and smoke formed. It swirled before her. "Am I released?" it inquired.

"After you accompany horse and rider safely to the Simurgh," Wira said.

The smoke oriented on the pair. "That's no horse—that's four quarters. And that's no child—that's—"

"Woe Betide," MareAnn and Wira said firmly together.

The smoke sighed mistily. "So it's like that. Okay, let's hit the trail."

Woe Betide squeezed the horse's sides with her precious little legs. "Go, Eight Bits," she said.

And suddenly they were off, in a cloud of dust that left the two standing women coughing.

2

SIMURGH

T he quarter horse ran like the wind, but there was evidently a long way to go. The Land of Xanth whizzed by in the manner land did, moving back magically fast nearby and slowly farther out, because distant regions felt less urgency about such things. Woe Betide didn't know enough geography to tell what direction they were going, and was too young to really care.

"I wish I had a lollipop," she said.

The cloud of smoke appeared, floating beside her and keeping the pace. "What flavor?"

"Mustard gas."

A hand formed, bearing a yellow pop that was giving off vile yellow fumes. "Done."

The child snatched it and sniffed its fumes. She coughed and retched, and her darling little face turned blotchy purple. "Perfect!" she wheezed. "This stuff would smother an army."

"So what did you ask the Good Magician?" the cloud inquired. "Not that I care."

"How to make a signal the stork will heed," Woe Betide said as her voice crept back into her ravaged throat.

The horse's ears twitched. Fracture lines appeared along his body, as if he were about to come unglued.

"Because when I grow up in an umpteen million years, I'll need to know!'' Woe Betide exclaimed. ''Of course, right now I'm still a cute innocent little child, so am protected by the Adult Conspiracy, and wouldn't ever even dream of knowing anything like that. So the Good Magician hasn't Answered me yet, but when the time comes, he will.''

Eight Bits relaxed, and the fracture lines faded. All creatures of Xanth knew the importance of maintaining the Adult Conspiracy; no child could be allowed to learn the secret of summoning the stork so that it would bring a baby. Or the Words of Evil Power that would scorch vegetation and burn maidenly ears red. Or anything that was Too Interesting for a child's own good. Of course, children didn't much like the Conspiracy, but such was the magic of its nature that the instant they grew up, they joined it. Demons honored few rules of decent behavior, but they liked conspiracies.

The cloud of smoke that was Helen Back seemed to find the situation amusing. ''Are you *sure* you're a child?'' she inquired. ''It seems to me that I almost remember you in some other form, much older—''

''And what did *you* ask Humfrey?'' Woe Betide asked quickly.

''Where to find a summer salt,'' Helen answered. ''I collect exotic salts, and I have winter, spring, and fall salt, but could never find summer salt. I looked all over, from here to—'' She paused. ''But of course, I can't use that word before an innocent little child.''

And Metria couldn't reveal her true status while riding the quarter horse, lest he sunder into fourths. The demoness was teasing her as only such an infernal creature could, trying to trick her into betraying her age. Fortunately she already knew about such travels: The demoness had gone from here to Helen Back. And she always brought what was most needed, at the least opportune time. Or what was least needed, at exactly the right time. Woe Betide had tried to mess that up, by asking for a horrible flavor of lollipop, but it hadn't worked, and she had had to eat the awful thing.

''So after you finish with me, the Good Magician will tell you where to find that salt,'' Woe Betide said. ''Then you can sit below the salt and be a creature for all seasons.''

''Something like that,'' Helen agreed. A face formed in the cloud. ''You certainly seem mature for an itty bitty innocent child.''

"It's all illusion. I'm not what I seem."

Helen couldn't argue with that. They continued for a while in silence as the scenery went by. Far mountains shifted grandly, showing first one side, then another. Forests sprang up, grew tall, then quit. For a while they followed a paved road. Every time it came to an intersection with another road, it puffed itself up into double the size, trying to impress them. But it didn't work, because the other roads did the same. Sometimes the crossing roads contested for power, throwing out masses of curving lanes. The object seemed to be to touch the other road where it couldn't touch back, but evidently the roads had been at this contest for a long time, because every lane connected. Some intersections looked like diamonds, and some like cloverleaves, and some like masses of spaghetti. Sometimes a road chickened out and tunneled under the other, or bridged over it, but often there were still confusingly outflung lanes trying to score.

Helen got bored with this, so resumed dialogue. "What does the Good Magician have to do with the Simurgh?"

"Wish I knew. Where exactly does she live?"

"I thought you'd never ask. She lives in Qaf."

Woe Betide was puzzled. "In what?"

"Qaf. It's a mountain range that encircles the Earth."

"A mountain of earth?"

"Not exactly. It's made of a single emerald. It's pretty."

"I suppose so. The Simurgh must like pretty things."

"The Simurgh likes the whole of everything. But since she already has everything she needs or wants, what could you do for her?"

"I wish I knew," Woe Betide admitted. "Maybe she's getting ready to replace the universe again."

Now the cloud was startled. "What—with all of us in it?"

"Well, maybe it gets dull for her, after a while. Or dirty. She might prefer a fresh new one."

"But what would happen to all of us?"

"Maybe we'd all be squished into nothingness. Does it matter?"

Helen considered. "Probably not. But the human folk might mind." Then the cloud stretched. "I'm going to take half a snooze.

Wake me if anything interesting appears.'' The cloud settled into a featureless blob.

Woe Betide was left to her own thoughts. This really was a pretty easy trip. In fact, it hadn't been all that hard to get into the Good Magician's castle. True, Humfrey had grumped at her, but he had always been grumpy. Had it been too easy?

The more she pondered, the more the suspicion grew: Humfrey had *wanted* her to get in to ask her Question. Because he had something for her to do. Maybe he owed the Simurgh a favor. Maybe the Simurgh had asked for the services of a demoness. So Metria was it.

She sighed. So be it. She would do what she had to do, so she could prevail on the stork to deliver a baby to her. It was probably a fair deal.

The horse slewed to a halt. There was a massive chain across the road, so that they could not pass. Woe Betide was tempted to float over it, but feared the horse wouldn't understand. So she dismounted and stepped forward to inspect the nearest links.

Each one was in a flat oblong shape, with printing on it. In fact, each had a single letter of the alphabet. Woe Betide walked along beside the chain, reading the letters. They spelled out: THIS IS A CHAIN LETTER. IT HAS BEEN THREE TIMES AROUND THE WORLD. BREAK THE CHAIN AND YOU WILL BE SORRY. JOE SCHMOE BROKE THE CHAIN AND NEXT DAY HE CAME DOWN WITH CROTTLED GREEPS. JANE DOE PRESERVED THE CHAIN, AND SHE WON GREAT WONDERFULS. REMEMBER, YOU MUST PASS THIS CHAIN MAIL ON WITHIN 48 HOURS, OR ELSE.

Woe Betide considered. Was this interesting enough to wake Helen for? The demoness would be really annoyed if she missed something good. This seemed good. So she decided to let Helen sleep.

Still, she needed to get past this chain. She didn't have anything against it, but it was in her way, and she had a mission to attend to.

Could she go around it? She looked to either side, but the chain extended as far as she could see. That was because it went around the world three times. Could she climb over it? Maybe so, but Eight Bits couldn't. Could she squeeze under it? Again, she might, but the quarter horse would probably fragment with the effort.

She shrugged. She doubted that a chain belonged across the road anyway, whatever it might claim. She also doubted that this was one of the Good Magician's challenges. It was probably just routine mischief. So she would break it. She formed her little hands into big firm pincers and clamped them on half a link. She concentrated her demon strength. The key was to use the magic of narrowness: a really thin edge could cut through the most solid substance, if pushed hard enough.

The letters on the links changed. Now they said ooooowww!! But she continued her pressure, until she crunched through her link.

Then she went after the other half link. It tried to wiggle away, but she cuffed it hard enough to stun it. Cuff links: She remembered that advice from somewhere. She set her pincers and started crunching.

YOU'LL BE SORRY! the letters spelled. WHO BREAKS THE CHAIN IS DOOMED. AAAAAAHH!!

The half link snapped, and the chain fell apart. The way was clear. "What's this?"

Woe Betide jumped. There was the cloud, with a horrendous head of hair on it. "Nothing interesting," she said. "What are you wearing?"

"My Hell Toupee, of course. I picked it up on one of my trips to—never mind. I saw what you did: you broke the chain. You had better put on protective headgear too, before that chain gets organized to dump a century's worth of bad luck on you."

"What kind of toupee?" the child inquired, interested.

The cloud did a hasty reconsideration. "A Heck Toupee. That's what I said, I'm sure."

"Let's just get out of here," Woe Betide said, knowing she had put Helen on the defensive. As long as she remained in this child form, the other demoness was at a disadvantage. That was wonderful!

She mounted Eight Bits and zoom! they were off again. She

glanced back and saw the chain writhing angrily, but it couldn't catch up with them. She had broken the chain and gotten away with it. That gave her demonly satisfaction.

They passed a big fisin' plant by a river, surrounded by electrici trees. The plant was busy hauling old-dim and nuclear fish from the river and using them to fertilize the trees. Some of the trees extended out across her route, so she slowed. They hummed with power, and that made her a bit nervous; what were they up to?

She saw a huge fat boxlike creature trundling along beneath the trees. She sought to guide her mount past it, but it blocked her way. "Child, you are too small to be riding a big horse like that," it said from its monstrous peg-toothed mouth. "You should go home."

"Why don't *you* go home?" Woe Betide asked boldly, because there was something about this creature she didn't much like.

"Because I never follow my own advice. I'm a hippo-crate. I tell others how to run their lives, but none of that applies to my own life."

That confirmed her dislike. She wanted to get away from the creature, but it still balked her. Then she saw a smaller animal hopping along. It had long legs and was extremely furry. She recognized it as a hare. They were very popular with bald folk. So she extended one arm infinitely long and grabbed it. She plopped it on her head, so that it made her aspect entirely different. In fact, it made her look like a hairy little troll.

The hippo-crate had been looking around. Now it looked back at her, and did a double take. "What happened to the innocent little girl I was lecturing?" it asked.

"How would I know? I'm not innocent."

Disgruntled, the hippo waddled off, looking for the child, because it was much easier to tell children what to do than trolls. She was free to ride on.

After a further interminable ride and float, they came to a huge green mountain. It rose from the plain in a series of faceted cliffs, each one glinting brightly.

"Well, this is it," Helen said. "Qaf. Climb to the top and there will be the Simurgh. I've done my bit, and will begone." The cloud vanished in a dirty noise.

Woe Betide dismounted. She went to inspect the surface more closely. It did indeed seem to be pure emerald. The mountain was one big jewel.

The sun came out from behind a cloud. Suddenly all the facets reflected dazzling beams. One struck Eight Bits. The horse, startled, fragmented into quarters, and the quarters galloped off in at least four directions.

Woe Betide sighed. She was on her own.

She pondered, and concluded that since she no longer had the quarter horse, she could resume her adult form. She puffed into smoke, and re-formed as Metria.

She could simply pop up to the top of the mountain, but she suspected that the Simurgh would not appreciate that. The same went for flying up there. In Xanth, the Simurgh forbade all flying in her vicinity, and it was probably the same here. So the ascent would have to be done the tedious way.

Metria formed her hands and feet into big sucker disks. Then she applied these to the flat surface of the nearest facet and began to climb. The suckers popped as she pulled them free, and squished as she placed them higher. It was another type of magic: Suckers clung to polished flat surfaces. At this rate a few hours would get her to the top. Then she would find out what all this was about.

She heard a rumble. She extended her neck, making it swanlike, and rotated her head to look backwards.

There was a floating shape, and it didn't belong to Helen Back. It was Fracto Cumulo Nimbus, the worst of clouds.

She knew this was significant mischief. Fracto was a demon himself, who had specialized in meteorology, and had a sure nose for trouble. If someone had a nice picnic, Fracto came to wet on it. If someone had an important mission requiring him to travel rapidly, Fracto came to turn the forest trails to slush ruts. If someone camped out on a warm night, Fracto came to bury the landscape in colored snow. And if someone happened to be climbing a sheer emerald cliff, Fracto came to make the surface slippery and blow that person away.

Of course, there were ways of dealing with the evil cloud, and Metria understood them well. She could become a cloud herself, and

float impervious to the weather. She could even generate some lightning bolts of her own to shoot back at him. But she wasn't sure that
wouldn't count as flying, which would annoy the Simurgh. Fracto,
of course, didn't care whom he annoyed—or rather, *did* care, so as
to be as annoying as possible. But he wasn't here to ask any favors
of the big bird. So that was out. Once she had turned herself into a
stink horn, which had exploded in Fracto's midst, rendering him
even more insufferably stinky than usual. But again, that would require her getting into the air, and it didn't seem to be worth the risk.

She could avoid the storm entirely by becoming so diffuse that
she could float through the substance of the mountain. But again,
that might be construed as a type of flying. So the safest course
seemed to be to stick to what she was doing: laboriously climbing
the slope, hoping she could hang on despite the cloud's worst efforts.

Fracto was happy to accept this challenge, knowing that she was
pinned. He puffed up voluminously, crackling with lightning and
thunder. His center turned so dark, it was like swirling midnight,
and his edges swelled outward like gross blisters. The whole of him
was like a giant face, with two patches of glowing eye-clouds and
a huge round mouth which blew out icy drafts. "Iiiii've gooot
yoooou!" he howled, blowing smoke at her.

Rain splatted on the cliff, and water coursed down past her. It
was cold, and soon would turn icy. Her sucker hold was firm, but
how would she be able to make any progress up the slippery rest of
it?

Now Fracto huffed and puffed, and blew a gale at her. It was
tinged with sleet. She pulled in her head so as to protect it, but then
couldn't see where to go.

This was no good. Before long Fracto would succeed in dislodg-
ing her, and then she'd be falling, and she would either have to fly
or crash. She couldn't actually be physically hurt by a fall, but it
would be an embarrassment that would hardly be kind to her pride.
She had to find a way to nullify the ill wind.

She glanced again at the inky depths of the center of the storm,
and got a notion. What she needed was a light—a night light. The
kind that folk used when they wanted to conceal their nefarious
activities.

She extended her head and formed it into a lamp with a dark bulb. She turned on the bulb, and darkness radiated out from it. Her night light was in operation.

She turned up the power. The darkness expanded. Soon it covered the entire facet of the mountain she was on. She was hidden within its obscurity.

Fracto realized what was happening. The storm turned furious. But Fracto could no longer see her, so didn't know precisely where to blow most fiercely. Oh, he was getting frustrated!

The cloud tried another ploy. He turned the draft so cold that the coursing water became a sheet of ice, overlaid by slush. But under the cover of her night light she formed her nose into a prehensile snout similar to that of the mythical Mundane elephant monster and made a hard hammer at its end. She tapped at the ice and cracked it away, making a clear place for her sucker foot. Now the wetness didn't hurt; in fact, it made the seal secure. The cloud couldn't hear her tapping, because of the almost continuous rumble of thunder.

She made it to the edge of the facet and crossed the slight bend to the next. The storm still raged, but her night light protected her. When a gust of wind touched her she hunkered down and waited for it to pass, then resumed her tapping and moving. Fracto could not stop her.

At last the evil cloud got disgusted and stormed away. She had beaten him, again, and it was just as much of a pleasure as ever. She dissolved her night light into smoke, and resumed better progress.

The sun ventured to show its face again, no longer fearing the wrath of the storm. The emerald mountain dried, forming pretty mists all around it. They rose like unicorn tails, shining in the slanting sunlight of the closing day. She paused to appreciate the beauty of the scene, and realized that before she got half-souled, she had never had that experience. Now she could enjoy things for their art, instead of for what she could use them for. "If I could get rid of my soul right now," she said aloud, "I wouldn't do it." And that was one remarkable confession, for a demoness. She felt wonderful.

'Disgusting,' Mentia muttered, awakened by the feeling coursing through her. Then she tuned out again.

The peak turned out to be a mere foothill, part of a larger mountain. And, amazingly, the larger inner segment of the mountain wasn't green. It was light blue, definitely a distinct shade, beautifully complementing the green rim. She had understood that the whole thing was emerald, but either she had misunderstood, or those who said it was all emerald hadn't seen the inner mountain. Asthetically, this was even better, so she wasn't complaining.

Metria had to work her way down into the cleft-valley between peaks before starting up the next. And there she paused. She had heard something. More mischief?

No, it was a woman or a girl, a human being, lying between the slanting green and blue facets of the cleft. She had groaned, faintly.

Metria considered. Though she had used the night light, she preferred to climb by daylight, and there was not a whole lot of day left. Should she get involved with this human being, and perhaps get delayed too long?

'Of course not,' Mentia said. 'You have already wasted enough time discouraging Fracto. You don't have all day left, you know.'

That decided her. If her worser half was against it, it must be the right thing to do. She walked over to the woman. "Can I help you?" she inquired.

The woman lifted her head. Long dark hair framed a lovely face. "I hope so," she said, wincing. "I sprained my ankle, and don't think I can walk alone."

'I knew it! She's an albatross. If you help her, you'll never get to the top of the mountain.'

Metria ignored her worser self's objection, with an effort. "Maybe I can help you get home. Who are you, and where do you live?" She put her hands on the woman's shoulders and helped lift her to her feet.

"Thank you so much. I'm Mara. I was out bird-calling, and got lost in a storm and some sort of weird darkness. I fell, and couldn't get up, and when it cleared—well, I don't know where I am now."

So it had been Metria's fault, because the storm had been after her, and she had used the darkness to oppose it. She certainly had to help Mara find her way home. Her conscience would allow nothing less.

'If you hadn't gotten half-souled, you wouldn't *have* a conscience!' Mentia griped.

"Maybe I can help you cross this green foothill mountain, so you can be on the plain," Metria suggested. "I'm a demoness, you see, and—"

"A demoness!" Mara cried, affrighted.

"Don't worry; I have half a shoe."

"Half a what?" Mara inquired, looking down at Metria's feet.

"Footwear, leather, tongue—" She paused. "I mean essence, characteristic, quality, animation, spirit—"

"Soul?"

"Whatever," she said crossly.

Mara was reassured. "Oh—then you have a conscience, and can be halfway trusted."

"Yes. If I were an unsouled demoness, I wouldn't have bothered with you at all."

"True. What's your name?"

"Metria. D. Metria."

Mara extended her hand. "I am glad to know you, Demoness Metria. But I don't live on a plain, so I don't think going over that green mountain will help. I normally do my bird calls in the forest and glade, where they are comfortable. That's my talent, you know."

'Fat lot of use doing bird calls is here,' Mentia sneered.

Metria made another effort to ignore her. "Then maybe if we walk along the crevice here—"

"I suppose," Mara agreed dubiously. "But I'm sure I didn't walk far before I hurt my ankle."

Metria supported Mara, enabling her to walk reasonably if wincingly well. They followed the cleft around the slow curve of the mountain. But all they saw was more mountain. "I don't think this is the way," Metria said.

"I think you're right," Mara agreed sadly. "I don't know how I came to be here. I must have gotten caught in a magical vortex or something. Maybe you had better leave me and go on about your business."

'Take her up on that!'

"No, that storm and darkness were because of me, so I should help you get unlost. All I can think of is to bring you with me to the top of the mountain. Maybe the Simurgh will help you."

"The Simurgh! Isn't that the big bird who has seen the universe die and be reborn three times?"

"The same. I have to perform a service for her. So if you don't mind coming with me—"

"Oh, I don't mind! I'd love to see the Simurgh. It would be the experience of my life. But—"

'There is always a "but"!'

"But you'll have trouble climbing," Metria finished. "Lets see what I can do about that. Suppose I form myself into a long ladder against the slope; could you climb that?"

"I suppose, if didn't have to hurry, so I could favor my ankle . . ."

'I knew it!' Mentia said silently. 'This will take forever minus half a moment.'

Metria feared she was right. But her half conscience wouldn't let her go. She formed herself into an extendable ladder, and extended herself up the sloped blue facet until she reached a ridge she could hook on to. She formed a mouth at the foot. "I'm anchored. Come on up."

Mara put her hands and good foot on the rungs, taking hold. Then she tried her weak-ankled foot, winced again, but was able to put some pressure on it. Her hands took up enough of her weight to make it feasible.

Fairly reasonably soon Mara reached the top and looked around. "Why, this is just another foothill," she exclaimed. "There's a yellow mountain beyond."

Startled, Metria formed an eyeball on a stalk and looked. It was true: This was just another crest, higher than the green ridge, but lower than the yellow one ahead.

She formed a mouth and sighed. "Hold on."

She drew up her latter section, and extended her foresection, so that the ladder disappeared behind and appeared before, leaving the top section, where Mara perched, unchanged. When she reached the blue/yellow cleft, Mara turned around and made her way down the rungs. Then Metria shrank the ladder, and got ready to extend it up the faceted yellow slope. It was now getting close to dusk.

"We'll never make it up before nightfall," Mara said. "You had better leave me and go alone."

'Listen to her, dope!'

"No, it wouldn't be right." Then Metria had a notion. "Suppose I make an escalator?"

"A what?"

"A moving structure, automatic increase, dangerous clause, elevator substitute, forming steps—"

"Stairway?"

"Whatever. So you could ride up faster."

"Why, that's a wonderful idea! But do you have the strength to carry me like that?"

"I think so. It's just a matter of leverage."

So Metria extended herself to the next crest, hooked on, and Mara got onto the bottom of the ladder. Then Metria moved her rungs up, and hauled the woman fairly rapidly to the top. "This is almost fun!" she exclaimed.

But when they looked from the top, there was another mountain ahead. This one was pink. It was very pretty, but dusk was closing.

They got more efficient. This time Metria simply whipped her rungs over the top, and Mara almost slid down the other side. Then they mounted the pink slope—and encountered a white, almost colorless one beyond.

"I hope this doesn't go on forever," Mara said. "I fear I have become a real burden to you. Maybe you should just—"

'Listen to her!'

"No," Metria said firmly. "This would have been as long a journey alone. We're much higher than we were." Indeed, they could see the yellow, blue, and green ridges below, like so many shelves, though they hadn't been able to see the higher ridges from below. "It has to end somewhere."

"You are very kind."

'You are very foolish!'

They went on. Beyond the white ridge was a deep red one—and

this was the final one, because they could see its rounded peak, atop which perched a giant bird, silhouetted against the fading light. The Simurgh, at last!

They escalated down the white slope, and up the red one. But as they came within hailing distance of the big bird, the bird spread her wings and flew to an adjacent peak rising from what they now saw was a very long mountain range. Of course it had to be, to circle the world. The Simurgh had never even noticed them!

Metria focused an extended eyeball on the distant bird. Then she looked down at the endless colorific ridges below. It would be an awful job to descend and traverse all those, and then to ascend to where the bird now perched—and what guarantee did they have that the Simurgh would wait for them? To her, they were just insects.

"Maybe if I did a bird call," Mara said.

'Oh, great! Now we'll just serenade the birds!'

"Well, whatever you wish," Metria said, dispirited. She seemed to be on an impossible mission, because she couldn't even get the attention of the one she was supposed to perform a Service for. Had Humfrey sent her on a wild swan chase?

'Wild what?' Mentia asked.

'Waterfowl, heron, egret, gannet, crane, albatross, canvasback, duck—''

'Gander?'

'Whatever.'

Meanwhile, Mara did her bird call. She made a series of melodic, sweet, piercing, chirping sounds. She was really quite good at it; it sounded just like some exotic bird.

The Simurgh took wing and flew directly toward their peak. WHO CALLS ME? her powerful thought came.

Metria formed a mouth so it could drop open in amazement. Mara's talent wasn't to imitate bird calls, but to call birds—and she had just called the Simurgh herself!

"Uh—I—I—" Mara began.

YES, OF COURSE. BEGONE.

Mara vanished.

"Hey!" Metria exclaimed. "That isn't right!"

'Shut up, fool!'

BY WHAT DEFINITION, DEMONESS? Now the giant bird loomed close. Her feathers were like veils of light and shadow, and her head bore a crest of fire. The beats of her enormous wings were like waves of mist. She was an overwhelming presence.

Metria was seldom cowed by anything in the natural world, but this was supernatural. She dissolved into smoke, and re-formed in her approximately natural approximately human shape. "I was trying to help her. You have no right to banish her just like that! I don't care who you are, it isn't right."

YOU QUESTION ME? Now the great bird came to light on the tip of the red peak, her mighty talons digging into the glossy stone as if it were wood.

'Let it go, idiot!'

"Yes! Bring her back!"

THERE IS NO NEED.

'Silence, imbecile! She'll destroy you.'

"Yes!" Metria cried, responding to both the Simurgh's query and her worser half's warning.

The enormous head turned, one eye bearing on her. BE AT EASE, GOOD DEMONESS. I ACCEPT YOU FOR SERVICE. THE GOOD MAGICIAN CHOSE WISELY.

'Last chance, stupid! Stifle it.'

But Metria was beyond sensible restraint. "Well, I'm not ready to give service! Not to any creature who does that to an innocent person. Mara never harmed you; she wanted only to go home. I was trying to help her, because—"

The Simurgh twitched one wing-feather. Suddenly Mara was back, exactly as she had been before. "Let it be, Metria; I'm done here."

"You're safe?" Metria asked, half-stunned.

Mara smiled. "As safe as a figment can ever be." She vanished again.

'See? She doesn't really exist. You irritated the big bird for nothing, moron!'

NOT SO, WORSER SELF, the Simurgh's thought came, this time stunning Mentia, who had thought her thoughts were hidden. HER CONSCIENCE HAS SERVED HER WELL.

Parts of this were beginning to settle into haphazard place. "This was all a—a test? The woman, the storm, the chain? Like the Good Magician's castle?"

HE GAVE YOU TOKEN CHALLENGES, BECAUSE HE WANTED YOU TO PERFORM THIS MISSION. I VERIFIED YOUR FITNESS IN MY OWN FASHION, AS YOU NOW UNDERSTAND. I REQUIRE A PERSONAGE WHO IS INVENTIVE, DETERMINED, AND COMPASSIONATE.

Metria worked it out. "First a mere physical obstruction or two, of no particular consequence. Then a personal threat that needed to be dealt with. Then a small trial of conscience. Just to make sure I could do the service you require."

EXACTLY, GOOD DEMONESS. I AM CAREFUL ABOUT THOSE TO WHOM I ENTRUST IMPORTANT TASKS. I REQUIRE ONE WITH THE POWERS OF A DEMON AND THE CONSCIENCE OF A SOULED PERSON. YOU WILL DO. DO YOU HAVE ANY QUESTIONS BEFORE COMMENCING?

'Don't ask any, dunce!'

"This mountain—I thought it was supposed to be one big emerald, but—"

YOU ARE OBSERVANT, GOOD DEMONESS. IT *IS* EMERALD, OR MORE CORRECTLY, BERYL, THE TYPE OF STONE OF WHICH EMERALD IS BUT ONE SHADE. THE WHITE IS ORDINARY BERYL, THE BLUE IS AQUAMARINE, THE YELLOW HELIODOR, THE PINK MORGANITE, AND THE RED BIXBYITE, THE RAREST BUT FOR ONE.

"One?" Metria asked somewhat stupidly.

BLACK BERYL. The Simurgh twitched her head, and a bag appeared in her beak. TAKE THIS. The bag dropped to Metria's involuntarily outstretched hands.

She opened the bag. It was filled with glistening black disks. "What am I supposed to do with this?"

THESE ARE SUMMONS TOKENS. YOU WILL SERVE ONE ON EACH PERSON OR CREATURE OR THING NAMED, AND WILL GUIDE THOSE WHO NEED IT TO THE NECESSARY SITE.

Metria had never felt so stupid in her existence. "Necessary site?"

THE NAMELESS CASTLE. THAT IS WHERE THE TRIAL WILL BE.

"Trial?" She still had not caught her mental balance.

ROXANNE ROC HAS BEEN INDICTED AND WILL BE TRIED BEFORE A

JURY OF HER PEERS A FORTNIGHT HENCE. YOU WILL SERVE SUM-
MONSES ON ALL PARTICIPANTS: TRIAL PERSONNEL, WITNESSES, JURY.
YOU WILL SEE THAT THEY ARE PRESENT AT THE CORRECT TIME. THAT
IS YOUR SERVICE TO ME.

"But Roxanne's a decent bird. What did she *do*?"

THAT WILL BE MADE EVIDENT IN THE COURSE OF THE TRIAL.

"And how do I know whom to serve the summonses on?"

EACH BEARS THE NAME OF THE SUMMONEE.

"But suppose they don't want to come?"

THAT WILL NOT BE A PROBLEM. EACH PERSON MUST KNOWINGLY
ACCEPT THE SUMMONS, AND ACKNOWLEDGE THIS TO YOU BEFORE
YOU DEPART.

"But—"

'Give it a rest, dope! You are trying her patience.'

TRUE, WORSER SELF. The great eye oriented on Metria again. YOUR
INFORMATION IS NOW SUFFICIENT. PERFORM YOUR SERVICE, GOOD DE-
MONESS.

Metria realized that she had been dismissed. She started to change
into her ladder form.

YOU MAY POP ACROSS TO XANTH.

"Thank you," she said, relieved, and popped off, carrying the
bag of tokens.

3

MYSTERY

Metria popped across to Xanth, to her home castle, where she made her husband deliriously happy enough to leave him in a trance for several days. Then she considered. She realized that there could be a good many summons tokens in the bag, and it might take time to use them all up, so she had better get them efficiently organized. She opened the bag and spread the glistening black beryl disks on a table.

Sure enough, there were thirty tokens, and each was inscribed with a name. Most of the names were familiar, but some were obscure, and some amazed her. For example, her old nemesis Demon Professor Grossclout was on a chip. What in Xanth could *he* have to do with this? She turned over the disk, and on the other side it said JUDGE. Oh, of course; that was the perfect role for him. Another chip bore the name of the Simurgh herself; on the back it said WITNESS. She could have served that token at the outset, saving herself a difficult trip. Then she reconsidered: She might need to consult with the Simurgh if she couldn't find one of the people to summon, so she should save the Simurgh's own token as a pretext for that occasion. So she put that one at the end of the line.

One token was blank. That was interesting. Whom was it for? Or was it a mistake?

Then she got marginally smarter, and turned over all the tokens, classifying them by assignment. There was one for Prosecutor, and another for Defense, and others for Bailiff, Special Effects, and Translator. Translator? She turned that one over. It was Grundy Golem. That figured; he could translate anything spoken by any living thing, including plants. Who was Special Effects? The Sorceress Iris, mistress of illusion. That figured too. Someone had chosen these roles well. Since it must have been the Simurgh herself who marked the tokens, this was no surprise; she was, after all, the wisest creature in all Xanth.

But why did she want Roxanne Roc put on trial? Metria's limited direct experience with the Simurgh suggested that she was a fair-minded creature, and Roxanne was a good bird, quite loyal to her mission. In fact, she was doing a service for the Simurgh herself, in the Nameless Castle—where the trial would be. Was this the way the Simurgh rewarded her? That didn't seem to make sense.

Well, there was one fast way to find out. She would serve Roxanne's summons first, and ask her. Then she would go after the other important participants in the trial, and finally the Jurors, who were the biggest category and would probably be a nuisance to run down. Her schedule was coming clear.

She put the tokens back in the bag, and formed a knapsack to hold the bag. Then she popped over to the Nameless Castle.

This was a quaint medieval edifice begirt with towers, parapets, turrets, battlements, embrasures, moat, glacis, pennants, and all the standard accouterments. There were only one or two things different about it: It was made of solidified vapor and it floated high in the air. In fact, it was built on a cloud, which seemed like an island in the sky. From the ground it looked just like an ordinary cumulus. For some reason, few folk knew of it.

She walked up to the main entrance and knocked on the door, because it wouldn't be polite to enter unannounced, and besides, there was a spell that prevented unauthorized demon entry. In a moment there was a loud questioning squawk from the interior. "I'm the Demoness Metria," she answered. "Here on business."

The door creaked open, and she walked in. The interior hall was elegant in the usual manner, with finely set cloud stones for the floor, and carpets hung on the cloud walls. Though the Nameless Castle was made of vapor, it was surprisingly strong, and could withstand all the things a castle was expected to withstand. Enchanted cloud-stuff was light, not weak.

She came to the vast central chamber. There was an enormous nest of marbled granite, and on the nest sat Roxanne Roc, a bird so big she could swallow a normal human person without chewing. Just about the Simurgh's size, in fact, but not as authoritative or beautiful in plumage. Roxanne was mostly shades of brown. She had been assigned by the Simurgh several centuries ago to hatch a special stone egg, and was still at it.

Metria floated in. "Roxanne, I have a summons for you," she said. "But I'd like to know—"

The big bird opened her beak. "**Squawk!**"

Oops. She couldn't understand roc-speak. She could give the big bird the token, but that wouldn't satisfy her; she wanted to know what this trial was all about. How could she talk with the roc?

The question brought the answer: Grundy Golem. His name was on a token, as Translator. So she should summon him, and use him to translate for the roc.

"Be right back," she said, and popped off to the Golem residence.

Grundy Golem, Rapunzel, and their seven-year-old daughter Surprise lived in a tree house, actually a cottage industree. They were a small family, because Grundy could be picked up in one ordinary human hand, and Rapunzel could assume any size she wished, so preferred to match him. Surprise did too, for now. So Metria matched their scale, so as to fit in their residence.

"Why, D. Metria!" Rapunzel exclaimed, spying her, exactly as if glad to see her. The truth was that just about nobody was glad to see a demoness, but Rapunzel was beautiful in body and spirit, an ideal complement to the mouthy golem. Her distinguishing trait, apart from her niceness, was her infinitely long hair, which assumed various colors as it coursed down across her body toward the floor. "To what to we owe the pleasure of this visit?"

Rapunzel had succeeded in doing what was almost impossible: She made Metria feel guilty. So she hedged. "Um, could I talk to Grundy?"

"Of course." Rapunzel lifted her long hair out of the way and called, "Dear! There's someone here to see you."

Grundy walked into the room. He was a fully living creature, but still bore the aspect of his origin as a rag and wood construction. He spied Metria. "That's not someone!" he snapped. "That's Metria, the most mischievous nuisance in Xanth, who can't even get a word right."

This was more like it. Metria affected a serious mien. "Grundy Golem, I have an enjoin for you."

"A what, you ludicrous excuse for a spirit?"

"Bid, request, invitation, proposal, solicitation, petition, demand—"

"Summons?"

"Whatever," she said, smiling as she handed him his token. "Take that, you little crawl."

This time he chose to ignore the miscue. "What am I being summoned to?"

"The trial of Roxanne Roc."

"That big bird? The worst thing she ever did was annoy the Simurgh by innocently flying too close to Parnassus. Why is she on trial?"

"That is what I would like to know. Come with me and we'll ask her."

Grundy nodded, not really annoyed by the situation. "Bound to be an interesting story here," he said. "It should be fun translating for whatever weird creatures get hauled in. But what about my wife? I don't like leaving her out of it."

"I have a disk for her too," Metria said, producing it. "She's up for jury duty." She handed it over.

"But what about Surprise?" Rapunzel inquired as she studied her token.

"She's not on my list. Maybe this concerns something adult, and she's underage."

"But I could become overage," the little girl said brightly. "If I had to."

"No, dear," Rapunzel said immediately. "You must save your magic for when it's really needed, and not waste it for something that would probably bore you. You can stay with Tangleman while we're gone."

"Goody!" the child agreed. Tangleman had originally been a tangle tree, transformed into a jolly green giant man in the course of a censored chapter; his vegetable mind was somewhat simple, so he got along well with children.

"Actually, the trial is a fortnight hence," Metria said. "So the Jurors don't have to report to the Nameless Castle until then. But I'd like to have Grundy come to help me talk with Roxanne now."

"You got it, Demoness," Grundy agreed enthusiastically. "Say, didn't you get married or something? Why are you involved in this?"

"I got married, got half-souled, and fell in love, in that order," Metria agreed. "Now I'm trying to get the stork's attention. But Humfrey sent me to the Simurgh, and she's requiring me to do this. I pop back home every so often to make my husband deliriously happy."

"I know how that is," Grundy said, glancing briefly at Rapunzel, whose hair formed momentarily into a heart shape framing her body as she winked back at him. "Well, let's get a wiggle on. Take me to Bird Brain."

Metria picked him up and popped back to the Nameless Castle in the sky. She could do this now, because the castle door remained open, making a small hole in the protective spell. They arrived at the same spot she had vacated in the central chamber, before the nest.

"Roxanne Roc, I have come to serve you with a Summons," Metria said formally.

As she spoke, Grundy squawked. Actually he didn't need to, because Roxanne understood human talk. It was others who couldn't understand her. The roc's near eye widened. She squawked back.

"She says she can't go anywhere," Grundy translated. "She has an egg to incubate, and mustn't let it get cold. It is due to hatch any year now. Simurgh's orders."

"This summons is *from* the Simurgh," Metria said, and Grundy squawked. She flipped it at the huge bird.

Roxanne caught it in her beak, displaying surprising dexterity. She set it down on the rim of the nest before her, and focused one eye on it. Then she used one monstrous claw to flip it over, and perused the other side. She squawked.

"What's this about being the Defendant?" Grundy translated. "She says she hasn't done anything wrong. In fact, she has hardly been out of this room in almost six hundred years, and has guarded the egg faithfully throughout. Is this a cruel hoax, Demon Smoke?"

"All that with one squawk?" Metria asked, bemused. "Those were her exact words?"

"Well, I sanitized what she called you. It was actually—"

"Never mind." Metria was familiar with the golem's propensity for stirring up trouble. Roxanne had probably spoken politely. "You mean she doesn't know why she's to be assayed?"

"She's to be whatted?"

"Attempted, endeavored, ventured, exerted, wielded, judged—"

"Tried, fog-brain?"

"Whatevered. It must be something horribly serious, to get the Simurgh herself involved. Doesn't she have any hint?"

There was an exchange of squawks. "No hint," Grundy reported. "She has been here, just doing her job, as she said. There must be some mistake."

"The Simurgh didn't act as if there were any mistake," Metria said, remembering what the most knowledgeable bird in all Xanth had THOUGHT to her. "And the words on the token are clear. Roxanne will be put on trial, here, in a fortnight."

Grundy translated. The roc shrugged, remaining perplexed. She would be here, because she would not desert the egg, regardless.

So Metria walked out, closed the door, and popped back to Grundy's home. "I'll fetch you next time I need you," she told him. "Just make sure you and Rapunzel are there for the trial."

"We will be," Grundy agreed. "Rapunzel will make herself tall enough to reach that cloud, and put me on it, and then I'll haul her up after me as she changes back to small size. I wouldn't miss this trial for all Xanth."

"Neither would I," Metria confessed. "There's something awfully anomalous going on here."

"Awfully what?"

"Peculiar, odd, irregular, unusual, curious, bizarre, queer—"

"Strange?"

"Weird," she agreed crossly.

"For sure. If it were anyone but the Simurgh behind it, I'd suspect it of being a joke."

"The Simurgh doesn't joke."

"She doesn't joke," he agreed.

Still pleasantly mystified, Metria popped next to the only other entity on her list who might know about the trial: Demon Professor Grossclout. It would be an unholy pleasure, serving *him* with a summons.

He was teaching a class at the Demon University of Magic. She appeared in the back of the chamber, suddenly suffering a fit of apprehension. Grossclout had always intimidated her, though she had always denied it. His aspect was horrendous, even in demon terms, and small horns glowed red when he made a strong point. His face was so ugly that he could have walked without notice among ogres. But the worst of it was his overwhelming knowledge: If there was anything he didn't know, it was hardly worth knowing.

"And therefore," he was saying, "we can conclude that the fourth principle of responsive magic has not been violated, and there is no paradox." He paused, his eye glinting. Every student in the class trembled, fearing that the Professor was about to make an Example. "What are you doing here, Metria?"

Suddenly she was Woe Betide. She hadn't changed intentionally; there was just something about the professor that turned her spine to mush. This had never happened to her before. "Nothing at all, Your Greatness," she whined, a big frightened tear rolling down her cute little cheek.

"Most students come here with heads full of mush," he remarked. "You have a spine of mush. You couldn't have crashed this class without help. Come here, gamine. Out with it: What are you up to?"

Woe Betide took one dread step after another toward him, unable to help herself. "I—I—have something," she peeped.

"Give it here," he said with such ultimate authority that the rafters vibrated.

She handed the token to him. "It—it's a summons, sir."

"**What?**" Now the ground shook, and plaster and silt sifted down from the ceiling. The students cowered.

"To appear at the Nameless Castle a fortnight hence, to preside over the—"

"I can see that!" the Professor roared, and now the walls began to crumble. The students flinched as much as they dared. "Why is this trial occurring?"

"I—I thought you would know."

He glowered. "I shall certainly find out. Begone, mush-spine!"

And Woe Betide Metria was begone, involuntarily. She hadn't learned anything.

'I wouldn't have taken that from him,' Mentia remarked. 'You didn't either, before you got your soul.'

Metria couldn't deny it. There were times when a soul was a real liability. 'I should have let *you* serve him that summons,' she said.

'Let me serve the next one. Who is it?'

Metria checked her bag. 'Magician Trent and Sorceress Iris.'

'Um. You take Trent; I'll take Iris. I just had an adventure with her.'

She had arrived at her home castle. She went inside to check on Veleno, but he was still floating in a sea of delirium, a smile glued on his face. He would hold for another day or so. So they popped over to the Brain Coral's Pool, where Trent and Iris were supposed to be. But she didn't see them there.

She squatted and poked a finger into the water.

What do you want of me, Demoness? It was the pool itself.

"Where's Magician Trent?" she inquired.

He is not here. He took the Sorceress Iris on a second honeymoon, fifty-three years after the first. They like each other better this time, both being much younger than before.

"A honeymoon!" Metria exclaimed. "You mean I have to go all the way to the moon?"

That is what I mean.

She sighed. "Well, thanks anyway, Pool." She popped off to the moon.

She landed in a pile of moldy cheese. "Ugh!" she swore, sailing up and shaking off her feet. She had forgotten that the two sides of the moon differed; the one that faced Xanth had long since degenerated into cheesiness, because of what it saw. Only the far side remained unspoiled.

Once she got her feet cleaned off, she flew around to the fair side. Now she saw the surface of milk and honey, where newly married couples lolled in a reasonable approximation of the kind of delirious happiness she routinely provided for Veleno. Of course, it wouldn't last for those others, because they couldn't remain on the honey moon forever.

She gazed across the idyllic landscape, and spied a lovely fountain of firewater, with the smoke rising to form a backdrop of pastel-hued clouds. That was obviously illusion, as the moon didn't have clouds. She made for it, and sure enough, there was the Sorceress in her youthened state, a girl in her mid-twenties, idly indulging her fancy while Magician Trent snoozed.

She approached Trent. "Remember me, King Emeritus?" she inquired.

He woke and glanced at her. "Oh, hello, Metria. We once almost meant something to each other, in a vision of Mundania."

"True," she agreed. "That experience caused me to try marriage myself, as you remember. Now I'm on a mission for—well, here's your summons." She handed him his token.

He turned it over. "I am to be the bailiff at a trial? That's a novel notion."

"And this is the novel," She agreed, yielding the body to her worser self.

"And yours," Mentia said, approaching Iris. "We shared the madness, where I was sane."

"I remember," Iris agreed languidly. "I was youthened for that, and I appreciate it." She accepted her token. "Special Effects?"

"I don't know what that means any more than you do," Mentia said. "Maybe you're needed for illusion pictures of things that they can't conveniently bring to the Nameless Castle."

"The Nameless Castle!" Trent exclaimed, amazed. "The trial is there? Isn't that where that roc is?"

"Roxanne Roc," Mentia agreed. "She's the one on trial. You wouldn't happen to have a notion what for, would you?"

"I can't think of any reason. That is one dedicated bird. This isn't some elaborate spoof?"

"That's unlikely," Iris said. "Look at these summons disks. They are made of black beryl—one of the rarest stones in Xanth. No one would fool with them."

He nodded. "I should think not. Well, our stay here was about over anyway. When do we have to report for the trial?"

"In a fortnight," Mentia said. She looked around. "Oops, I feel some craziness coming on." She dived into Iris' illusion fountain and splashed in the rising water, sending droplets splattering against the backdrop.

Then the water changed to fire, and the fire changed to water, so that she was splashing in a column of fire. "Hoo!" she cried as it singed her derriere. "That's hot!"

"Well, you shouldn't mess with illusion," Trent remarked mildly.

'That's a hint we should get out of here,' Metria advised her worser self. 'They may want to conclude their stay here in style.'

'You would think of that, you married creature.' But Mentia obligingly popped back to their home base in Xanth. 'Who else do we need to serve?'

'Half a slew,' Metria said, checking. 'But only two more actual Trial Personnel. Grey Murphy and Princess Ida.'

'Not Grey and Ivy? That could be real mischief, especially if Ida gets a notion.'

'True. But of course, the Simurgh wouldn't do anything like that.'

'No more than she would put an innocent loyal bird on trial,' Mentia remarked.

'Well, if Ida did get a notion, we could sprinkle her with Lethe elixir to make her forget about Grey,' Metria said.

'Great idea! That could completely restore her talent, too, since the Ideas she makes become real must come from someone who doesn't know her talent.'

'That's a crazy notion,' Metria said.

'Thank you.'

'So where is Grey Murphy at the moment?'

'Use the token, blockhead! How do you expect to locate the rest of the names?'

'Oh.' Metria took out the token marked GREY MURPHY and held it up. Sure enough, it seemed to tug in one direction. It wanted to do its duty, and if the summonsee wouldn't come to it, it would go to the summonsee.

She floated, letting the stone disk show the way. She made herself smoky light, so that it was able to tug her along. Soon she was traveling at a respectable speed, through trees, boulders, houses, dragons, and whatnot. The general direction seemed to be northwest.

In due course she came to the coast, but the tug didn't stop. ''He can't be out in the sea!'' she muttered. But that was the direction of the tug.

A see monster lifted its huge eye and peered at her. She ignored it. See monsters didn't bite, they just looked. Of course, it was important not to let them see too much, because they got really smug when they suc-see-ded. When the big eye threatened to look down the front of her blouse, she changed it to a tortoise-necked sweater. When the monster tried to look up under her skirt, she changed it to slacks, eliminating any possible view of anything interesting. She could have changed form to a bird, or faded out entirely, but she preferred to tease the thing. Disgusted at not being able to see the color of her panties, the monster sank back under the sea surface.

She was now floating over the Golf of Mecks Co. She had to watch out for flying golf balls, because this was their natural home. They sailed in from all over, plunking into the water where they chortled as they sank forever out of sight. She couldn't blame them; it meant that they would never again be clubbed by irons.

The shoreline, discovering she was leaving it behind, set out to do something about it. She continued to fly in a straight line, but it curved around until it intersected her course. Then the sea made an effort, and pushed back under her, but the land would not be denied, and shoved forcefully across until it was going west, and hung on despite the sea's best efforts. She had not before realized how competitive these two elements were.

But by this time she was just about there. She was right at the westernmost fringe of Xanth, about to pass across the fringe of magic. Since she didn't know what would happen to her if she went beyond the magic, she came down to earth. When human beings left the magic, they lost their magic talents but were otherwise pretty much the same. When partly magical creatures crossed the boundary, they became Mundane creatures, unbearably dull. But demons were wholly magical, and they might simply cease to exist. She preferred not to risk it.

Yet the token still tugged ahead. She walked right up to the scintillating curtain that separated most of Xanth from Mundania, and stopped. The token tugged one way, and then another. What was going on?

'Buffoon!' Mentia said. 'Don't you remember—the river beyond moves about constantly. It's very mobile.'

'Mobile,' Metria agreed, remembering. 'It's always in a hurry to be somewhere else. The people who live by it have to keep moving too. But why would Grey be out there?'

Mentia considered. 'This is a crazy thing, so perchance I understand it better. I think maybe Grey is not out there. We're getting a reflection from the magic Interface I helped recompile; it's stronger than it used to be.'

There was that crazy claim again, about visiting Xanth's distant past and saving everything from encroaching madness. But maybe her worser half was right about one detail. Metria turned around and held up the token. Sure enough, now the tugging was stronger, from the east. So she left the crazy moving region behind and proceeded toward whatever Grey Murphy was up to. She was relieved; she could handle a river or place that was mobile, if she had to, but she didn't want to go any closer to drear Mundania than absolutely necessary.

The direction steadied. Possibly the mobile terrain beyond had caused ripples in the curtain, so that the reflection moved despite having a still source. Now she was orienting on Grey directly. She floated up and moved faster.

She came to a sign: YOU ARE NOW APPROACHING PENS COLA.

'What's Grey doing in a pen?' Mentia demanded.

Metria didn't answer. She spied a fence ahead. Each post was a very large writing pen, of a particular style. One was a feather quill, another a metal-tipped stake, and a third jetted colored water into the air.

'Oh, a fountain pen,' Mentia said.

Ropes were strung between the pens to complete the fence. The fence curved slowly into the surrounding forest. On each standing pen was a single printed letter. 'There's something familiar about this,' Mentia muttered.

'I know what it is!' little Woe Betide cried. 'I saw letters on a chain. Just walk along and read them.'

"Out of the mouths of babes and sucklings . . ." Metria muttered. She walked along, reading the letters. They formed a repeating series: COST OF LIVING ADJUSTMENT.

Metria couldn't make much sense from this. She stood and gazed at the fence, wondering whether to fly on over it. Was that what the fence was penning?

Suddenly the pens uprooted themselves and jumped to new holes beside the old ones. Metria could tell from the direction and curvature that the fence now enclosed a bit more territory than it had before. It had gotten larger. There were old filled-in holes inside the penned region, showing that this had been happening for some time. But who cared?

'I can't read those big words,' Woe Betide complained.

'Just use the first letters, dear,' Mentia suggested. 'C O L A.'

'The pens spell COLA?' she asked.

'Pens COLA,' Mentia agreed. 'And it seems it keeps expanding.'

Metria shrugged. 'Maybe that makes sense to you, because you're a little crazy, but I'm going to fly on by it now.' She lifted higher and followed the tug of the token on across the fenced region.

At last she caught up to Grey Murphy. He was just standing in place, looking puzzled. "What's up, man from Mundania?" she inquired, shifting to an appropriate outfit for the occasion: very short tight skirt, vaguely translucent very full blouse, voluminously flowing black hair with embedded sparkles, and a complexion so clear that one might almost see one's reflection in it. There was just something about men of power that intrigued her. He had been betrothed to Princess Ivy ever since he arrived in Xanth, and it seemed that he should have done something about that by now. She doubted that she could actually tempt him, but it was worth a try. A girl just never could tell about a human man. Especially a Magician.

Grey looked up. "What mischief are you up to this time, Metria?" he inquired.

"I have something for you," she said, inhaling.

He refused to be bluffed. "What is that?"

She leaned slightly forward, vanishing the top button of her blouse so as to expose more heaving scenery, but he didn't seem to notice. "A summons." She proffered the token.

He took it and turned it over. "I am to be prosecutor at a trial? I don't know anything about that."

"It's the trial of Roxanne Roc, at the Nameless Castle. I can help you find your way there, if you wish."

"No need. What did she do? I thought she was on a mission for the Simurgh."

"She is. But the Simurgh wants the trial. It's a mystery why. So you will have to prostitute."

"Have to what?"

"Indict, arraign, persecute—"

"Prosecute?"

"Whatever." She was ruining the good impression she was trying to make.

He shrugged. "Who else will be there?"

"Professor Grossclout. Magician Trent. Sorceress Iris. Princess Ida. A bunch of Jurors. Nobody important."

"The Demon Professor Grossclout?" he asked, brightening. "I've always wanted to meet him. He'll be the Judge, of course."

"Of course."

"I'll consult with him. He'll know what to do." He looked around. "But first I have to finish what I'm doing here."

"What *are* you doing, Grey?"

"I am looking for Re."

"Who?"

"A girl called Re. Humfrey said she would be here, in the region known as Ality, but I can't seem to find her."

"What's the matter with her?"

"She got confused, and is in trouble. Humfrey said her talent turned against her. So I'm here to nullify it, to get her out of trouble. My talent is the nullification of magic, so I should be able to handle it. She'll owe the Good Magician a year's service, of course. But there just doesn't seem to be anything here in Ality." He looked frustrated. "How can I nullify something when I can't find it?"

"Maybe I can succor," Metria said, intrigued.

"Maybe you can what?"

"Aid, support, deliverance, assistance, service—"

"Help?"

"Whatever," she agreed crossly. Why did her impediment always get worse when she least wanted it to?

"Since when do you try to help anyone, Metria?"

"Since when I got half-souled."

He reconsidered. "That does make a difference. Very well: How do you propose to help?"

"Well, this seems like a slightly crazy situation, so I'll see if my crazy worser half has any insight." She turned the body over to Mentia.

"Hello, D. Mentia," he said. "I don't think we've met before."

"Fortunately," Mentia agreed. "Kiss me."

"Why?"

"Because I'm the half without soul or conscience. I demand payment for my services."

"Kisses for help?"

"To start." She turned slightly so as to give him a better view of her profile. Metria had had the right idea with this outfit, but simply lacked the crazy cunning to exploit it properly.

"I'd be crazy to agree to a deal like that. Suppose Ivy found out?"

"That's what makes it interesting."

He pondered a moment. "Okay."

She was startled. "You agree?"

"One one condition. I do the kissing."

"Sure. One kiss for each helpful thing I figure out."

"Agreed. What have you figured out?"

"Go away and come back here."

"What?"

"Just do it, handsome. Craziness doesn't make sense until after the fact. You don't have to go far. Turn twice when you do it, too."

Grey looked baffled, but complied. He turned and walked away. Then he turned again and walked back. "What does this prove?"

"Have you turned and returned?"

"Yes."

"So if you came to Ality before, now you have come to Re-Ality."

He frowned. "I suppose. What's the point?"

"You have to re-do things to reach Re. Now that you have re-considered and re-turned to Re-Ality, you are closer to finding her."

"That's crazy!"

"Yes. Pay me."

He looked annoyed, but also thoughtful. "Very well. Come here."

Mentia stepped close to him and raised her face. But he took her head in his hands, turned it down, and kissed the top of her head.

"Hey, that's not what I meant," she protested.

"I kissed you. Nobody specified where."

"But that's—"

"Crazy?"

Mentia realized that she hadn't made precisely the deal she thought. Or maybe Grey Murphy was smarter than she thought. She shrugged. That simply made it more of a challenge. "Now, I think that Re has this power of re-doing, and maybe she got mixed up and re-jected herself. So you must search and re-search to find her."

"But I have already searched!"

"Right. Do it again. You have merely re-hearsed it so far."

He nodded. He went through the motions of searching, again. "Okay, I have re-searched. I still don't see her. What now?"

"Re-pay me."

"Oh." He took her right hand and kissed it. But this time a pair of lips appeared on her hand, and kissed him back.

"Now look around again," she said. "Examine and examine again."

He looked around twice. "Okay, I have re-examined the region. What now?"

"Pay—"

"Not until you produce something more positive."

She sighed. He was too canny to make this game really fun. "I think we must be very close to finding her now. Call her—and call again."

He nodded. He cupped his mouth with his hands. "Re!" he called. Then again: "Re!" He had re-called her.

There was a faint sound, almost like a female moan. "Quick, orient twice," Mentia said.

Grey focused on the area where the sound seemed to have come from, then re-focused. "I am re-orienting," he said.

"Do you feel anything?"

"Yes, there is something here," he agreed.

"Say it again."

He said it again: "There is something here."

And with that re-statement, a form appeared faintly. "Move her," Mentia said. "Twice."

He put his arms around the shape and moved it. Then he moved it again. The form became firmer.

"This has to be Re," he said. And again: "This has to be Re," he re-peated.

The form clarified. "Yes!" she breathed. "Help me! Help me!"

"Now I can use my own magic," Grey said. "I can nullify her magic." He put his hand on her head. "Verse. Re-verse."

The re-sult was encouraging. Suddenly the complete woman was there. She was re-asonably young and pretty. "Oh, you have saved me!" she cried. "It's such a re-lief. I'm so re-ally grateful!" She flung her arms about him and kissed him several times on the face before he could re-act.

"Ahem," Mentia said. "It seems to be that you let a number of payments go by, and now you're paying the wrong person."

Grey smiled ruefully. "You're right. You have been very helpful, Mentia." He disengaged from Re, took Mentia in his arms, and kissed her soundly on the mouth, twice. There was magic in his kisses that nullified her craziness.

"Wow!" she said, dizzied. "Wow!"

"Well, you did earn it," he re-plied. "In your slightly crazy way."

"I will re-frain from further demands," Mentia said, and gave the body back to Metria. She had been teasing him, but his magic had more than nullified her effort, and she needed to re-cover.

Grey turned back to Re. "What happened to you?"

"I was trying to re-build my house, and I paused to re-flect," she re-lated. "Something distracted me, and I accidentally re-pealed myself. The last thing I was able to do was re-lease a plea to the Good Magician to help me; I wasn't sure he would re-ceive it, but it was too late to re-vise it. Then you came and re-pulsed my own magic that re-mained re-pressing me, and re-juvenated me. Thank you so much, from the re-cesses of my heart! Normally I am more re-served, but—"

"Well, you know you will have to give the Good Magician a year's service before this is re-solved," Grey re-minded her. "He sent me to re-animate you."

"Yes, I am re-conciled to that," she said. "But I feel re-vitalized, and I really do re-spect the Good Magician."

"There is a magic path near here that will lead you safely to his re-constructed castle," Grey said.

"Thank you." Re organized herself and set off down the path. She had a long way to go, but her re-cent experience evidently gave her courage.

Grey turned to Metria. "Now I can go to the Nameless Castle. Where is it?"

"In the sky. Can you enlist the help of a roc bird to carry you there? You're too heavy for me to carry, much as I'd like to try."

"Yes, there is a roc who owes Humfrey," he said. He paused. "You know, you—or your worser half—have been so helpful that I no longer re-sent your presence. Your acquisition of a soul does seem to have made you a better creature."

Metria found herself blushing, something she never used to do in the old days. "Thank you. But I'm just trying to complete my own service to the Good Magician so I can re-produce."

"Oh?" I thought demonesses could do that when they chose to."

"Yes. But apparently it's much harder the second time. So now I need help to get the stork's re-vision."

He didn't challenge her miscue. "You summoned the stork before?"

"Yes, about four hundred and forty years ago, give or take a couple, but who's counting? It was a bad business, I now realize."

"There is surely an interesting story there," he said. "But I'd better call that roc."

" 'Bye," she agreed, and popped off.

She arrived at Castle Roogna. There at the two prominent corners of the roof were Gary Gar and Gayle Goyle, spouting water into the moat. It wasn't raining, so Metria wasn't certain where the water was coming from, but it was a nice effect. The moat looked quite clean, which wasn't surprising, because the gargoyles' job was to purify the water they spouted.

'I'll handle this,' Mentia said. 'I know them.' She moved up to take over the body, then addressed the two winged monsters. "Hello, you ugly brutes! Remember me?"

Both gargoyles swallowed their water so they could talk. "Demoness Mentia!" Gary cried. "We haven't seen you in a year."

"True. I've been with my better half, trying to figure out what her strange new life is all about. But now I have two summonses for you. You are to be Jurors at the trial of Roxanne Roc."

"Who?" Gayle asked.

"A big bird who is hatching something for the Simurgh."

"All right," Gary said. "We'll be there."

Mentia tossed a token up to each of them. They caught them in their mouths. Two more served.

She went on inside the castle, returning the body to her better self. Princess Ida came to meet her. "How nice to see you, Metria," she said, in very much the way Rapunzel had. But Ida never said anything she didn't believe, because she believed what she said.

Then Metria stared. There was something floating past the Princess' head. "Ida—there's a big bug about to land on you!"

Ida smiled. "That's not a bug. It's my moon."

"Your what?"

"Planet, globe, orb, heavenly body, orbiting fragment—"

"But what are you doing with a little moon?"

"It just came to me, and it was so cute, I couldn't tell it to go away. It's really no harm."

Apparently not. It was just a tiny blob that slowly swung around her head. "It does look sort of sweet," Metria admitted. "Will it grow up to be a big planet someday?"

"I hope so." Ida smiled. "What can I do for you?"

"You can accept this summons to participate in the trial of Roxanne Roc."

"Why, of course," Ida agreed, accepting the token. She was a very agreeable person. "And I see I am to defend her. I shall surely do my best."

This was almost too easy. "You're not worried because you don't know what you're defending her from?"

"I'm sure I will soon find out."

Metria decided not to argue. She had too many tokens still to serve to waste time. "And you can find the Nameless Castle?"

"I'm sure I will."

And if she believed it, she probably would, because Ida's talent was the Idea: Whatever she believed would be, would be. Except that the Idea had to come from someone who didn't know her talent. That limited it considerably.

But it was clear that Princess Ida did not yet know what this trial was all about. Metria's main vice had always been her curiosity, and now it was becoming almost painful. Why should there be such an enormous effort because of one big bird who seemed never to have done anyone any harm? The mystery intensified with every step Metria took.

4
THRENODY

M etria returned home to stoke Veleno up for a few
more hours, then assessed the remaining tokens.
Most of the names seemed straightforward, and she
thought there shouldn't be any problem locating them. But one name
she dreaded, because that person was bound to be uncooperative.
What would happen if she managed to serve every summons but
one? Would the trial be delayed, and would Metria then fail in her
service and be denied what she most desired? That would perhaps
be fitting, but she sincerely did not want it to happen.

If she was going to fail, this was the name that would fail her.
So the sensible thing to do was to tackle it next. Then if it went
wrong, she wouldn't have to bother with the other names. Unless
she got a release from the Simurgh. This was, after all, just one of
the Jurors, and there were more than a dozen of them; some would
be eliminated at the trial itself. But she rather thought that she had
better get all the names, if she possibly could.

So she lifted the token for Threnody, the half demoness wife of
Jordan the Barbarian. It tugged, and she floated where it led.

Deep in the jungle near the slowly diminishing Region of Madness, she caught up to Jordan and Threnody. They were eating a
freshly picked pot pie. It was, of course, shaped like a pot, and was
rich in iron.

Metria turned invisible and floated quietly up to them, knowing that a certain amount of discretion was in order. But it didn't work. Threnody lifted her nose and started sniffing. She was a lovely black-haired black-eyed dusky sultry beauty of comely aspect and statuesque proportion; in fact, she looked good, considering her age.

"Fee fi fo fum," the luscious damsel said darkly. "I smell the bod of someone's mum." She glared.

'You never could fool her, you know,' Mentia remarked for no particular reason.

Metria sighed and turned visible. "I really wish you would let bygones be bygones, Thren."

"Corpulent chance, Met! Go away."

"You know I've changed recently."

"Well, change into nonexistence, Demoness."

Jordan Barbarian continued eating, seemingly not interested in the dialogue. He was a rough-hewn primitively handsome man of middling age who took justified pride in his ignorance of civilized ways, but he had learned not to poke his nose into his wife's business, lest she cut it off. However, his crude male eye did explore the crevice of Metria's decolletage and the projection of her posterior, as was expected according to the Barbarian Code.

It was clear that this was going to be difficult, "I have something to give you."

"You have already given me more than enough," Threnody said, showing her teeth in unfeigned fury. "Now give me what I most crave: your total absence."

"Right after I give you this handsome engraved disk." She held it up.

"That looks like black beryl," Threnody snapped. "That's a summons from the Simurgh."

"Yes. For you. To be a Juror at a trial."

The woman brightened momentarily. "Are they finally trying you for treason against Xanth?"

"No, this is for Roxanne Roc."

"Then I'm not interested." Threnody faced away.

Metria had been afraid of this. The woman simply refused to take anything from her, or to give her anything other than anger. So she tried with Woe Betide.

The winsome little girl appeared. "Please, your delightfulness, if you will only accept this token, I will go away forever minus a few minutes." A big tear formed.

Jordan glanced at the darling tot. His eyeball did not sweat in the same manner as it had for Metria's tight-fitting adult configuration, but he had a certain interest in children, because their simple minds were parallel to his own.

"Don't tease me with that old act, you rotten brat!" Threnody gritted, impressed not half a whit. "I'll not accept anything from any of your deceitful variations, because I know it's the same soulless bitch of a demoness inside. Now, are you going to get far away from me, or do I have to start singing?"

Worse yet. Threnody's songs were always so horribly sad that Metria couldn't stand to hear them, and had to flee. "No, please don't do that!" Woe Betide cried, another big tear welling out. "You must take this token!"

Threnody started singing. Woe Betide clapped her little hands over her little ears, but the excruciatingly sad melody insinuated itself past them and into her head. She couldn't stand it. She lost cohesion, and reverted to Metria—who still couldn't stand it. It was Threnody's ultimate weapon against her, always effective.

She retreated until the sound became faint. Then she formed heavy earmuffs to dull down the sound so that the dirge was only faintly agonizing. Now she could stand it—but she wasn't close enough to plead with Threnody about the summons.

Still, she couldn't quit, because that could mess up her whole mission. It was just barely maybe possible that Threnody was suffering the merest slightest tiniest little suggestion of a hint of softening, and might on some impossibly far-fetched chance change her mind eventually. So Metria remained where she was, in sight of the dusky woman and the barbarian.

But Threnody was having less than none of it. She consulted inaudibly with Jordan; then the two of them walked away. It was clear that they would not gladly remain in Metria's sight.

So Metria floated after them. When she got too close, Threnody resumed her song of lamentation and drove her away again. So it was an impasse: Metria could not approach Threnody, or make her accept the summons token, but neither could Threnody make Metria leave her entirely alone.

In fact, just to make it interesting, Metria formed a diaphanous gown and teased the barbarian with it; that much mischief she could do from this distance. Naturally Threnody was not unduly keen on having her man entertained for too long in this manner, but unless she cut out his eyeballs they could not be prevented from straying. This was the nature of the features of barbarian men; it was involuntary.

Threnody abruptly turned and walked in a new direction. Metria realized that she was heading directly into the nearby Region of Madness. That was an extremely chancy thing to do, as Metria well knew. Obviously Threnody was prepared to risk it, in the hope that Metria would not follow.

'She's got a surprise coming,' Mentia remarked.

Indeed she did! For though the madness caused strange things to happen, and messed up the minds of ordinary folk until they became acclimated, it made Mentia sane. Because Mentia's normal state was slightly crazy, so her abnormal state was opposite. Mentia could handle the Region of Madness.

The fringe of madness came into view. It was a mere shimmer of unreality, suggesting the dissolution beyond. Most folk avoided it with horror, but Threnody was plunging on in, half dragging Jordan along. Metria floated in their wake, maintaining the compromise distance between them. She wanted to keep them in sight, because she wasn't sure the token would accurately track Threnody within the madness. It was impossible to be sure what would happen there.

Then for a moment they paused. There was a man, looking bewildered. His features were indistinct, as if he wasn't quite sure himself who he was or what he was doing here. He seemed to appeal to Threnody for assistance or advice, but she brushed him off and plunged on, still towing Jordan.

Soon Metria caught up to that place. "Hello!" the man cried. "Can you help me? I'm lost."

'Keep on moving, or you'll lose them,' Mentia advised.

But Metria's half conscience wouldn't allow it. She formed herself into a nonprovocatively garbed woman. "You don't want to be in this region," she said. "You're heading into madness."

"I surely am!" he agreed. "Where am I?"

"Pretty much dead center of southern Xanth. Now if you go back that way, you'll get into ordinary territory and should be all right." She pointed away from the madness.

"Xanth? I'm in Xanth?" He seemed amazed.

"Where else? Now, I must be on my way." For Threnody and Jordan were almost out of sight, their images fuzzed by the lunacy of the deepening madness.

"But I can't be *there*!" he cried. "It's not possible."

"Well, you'll have to settle that for yourself," Metria said, moving on.

"No, you don't understand," he said, following her. "I—I'm from—from Mundania."

"That's your misfortune." She forged on, watching the pair ahead.

"But this makes no sense," he said, pacing her. "Xanth isn't real. It's a story."

"Suit yourself. But if you don't reverse in a hurry, you're going to be out of Xanth proper and into madness, and I don't think you'll like it."

He shook his head. "I must indeed be mad. Or maybe this is all a bad dream. The last thing I remember is—" He shook his head. "Then I was floundering around here." He peered at her more closely. "If I may ask—who are you?"

'I think I know what's happened,' Mentia said. 'I'll take over now, before the madness drives you crazy.' Then, assuming the body, she spoke to the man. "I am D. Mentia."

"Dementia?"

"Close enough."

"I am Richard Siler."

"Richard? I know a Richard from Mundania."

"They call me Billy Jack."

Mentia was on the verge of her sanity as she entered the madness, so was able to make sense of this. "A nickname."

"Yes."

"I think I had better take you to the other Richard. He understands about Mundane visits."

"Thank you."

"But be prepared: This is about to get strange."

"Stranger than it already is? I doubt it."

"Suit yourself."

They came to a chair. There was a rock in it. "What's that?" Billy Jack asked.

"Obviously a rock in chair. Leave it alone."

But he was already removing the rock, out of some foolish sense of the nature of chairs. Immediately the chair tilted forward, causing him to stumble over it, and he landed sitting in it. The chair tilted back so swiftly that he flew out of it to land in something else. Meanwhile the chair tilted violently forward again, catching Mentia so that she, too, fell into it, and was similarly hurled back. She found herself in an invisible swing, swinging wildly back and forth. She felt wonderful as it swung high, and awful as it swung low.

"What *is* this?" Billy Jack cried as he swung past her. "I feel great—terrible—great—terrible—"

"It's a mood swing," Mentia said, figuring it out. "I told you not to mess with that rock in chair! Now it has rocked us right into trouble."

However, she was a demoness, so didn't need to submit to the antics of warped furniture. She dissolved into smoke and floated out of the swing. She crossed to Billy Jack, caught on to his swing, and held it still so that he could jump out.

"You were right," he gasped. "It is getting stranger."

"Just stay close to me and don't touch anything." The forms of Threnody and Jordan were dimly visible ahead; they had probably been slowed by something similar.

They ducked past the mood swings and hurried on. Suddenly they almost collided with a stout pillar. It seemed ordinary except for the whiskers.

Before they could pass by it, the pillar transformed into a big cat. "Growr!" it growled, and pounced.

Mentia became a splat of cold water. The cat struck the water, screeched, and turned right back into the pillar.

"What—" Billy Jack asked.

"Cat or pillar, obviously. Get out of here before it changes back."

"This is really weird!"

"No it isn't. We're only partway into the madness; these are fringe effects. Let's hope we can avoid the really weird things."

Suddenly something swept past them. It was like a metal ball, with arms, legs, mouth, and eyes sprouting from its surface. "Mine!" it cried, picking up the pillar.

The pillar changed back into the cat, screeching. But the ball sprouted more arms and caught on to all its extremities. It threw the cat into a pit. "Mine! Mine!" it cried.

Mentia turned cloudy and floated over the pit. It was half-filled with precious things ranging from jewels to golden coins. It was a treasure pit.

Mentia formed a mouth in her underside. "But what do you want with a cat?" she asked.

"It has two cat's-eye gems!" the ball replied, grabbing for the cat's eyes. It changed hastily back into the pillar.

"What is this?" Billy Jack asked, stepping up to the edge of the pit.

"Don't get so close!" Mentia cried.

She was too late. The edge gave way, and the man fell into the pit. His feet came down on top of the metal ball.

Then there was an explosion. Gems, coins, and creatures were hurled out of the pit. Mentia jetted across to intercept Billy Jack in midflight, became a huge soft pillow, and cushioned his crash landing.

"What was that?" he asked dazedly as everything settled.

She resumed her normal form as he got off her. "Obviously a mine. Didn't you hear it yelling, 'Mine! Mine!' as it collected things? But mines are very touchy, and you made it detonate. Now, stay out of trouble until I get you where I'm taking you!"

"I'll try," Billy Jack said contritely.

They went on. Now they came to a glade with a single acorn tree in it. The tree looked healthy, but seemed to have suffered recently. "That's Desiree's tree!" Mentia said. "Now I know we're on course."

"She owns the tree?" Billy Jack asked.

"Not exactly. She's the nymph of the tree. Hiatus should be close by." For she had been here before. She raised her voice. "Desiree!"

A rather pretty nymph appeared by the tree. "Who calls me?"

"The Demoness Mentia, halfway sane. I was here last year."

"Why, so you were," Desiree said, remembering. "With the sorceress and the gargoyle and the child. You brought me Hiatus."

"Yes. I'm just passing by this time." She glanced at the man. "This is Billy Jack, who I'm taking to see Richard White." Then, to Billy: "This is Desiree Dryad. If her tree suffers, she suffers."

"So nice to meet you," Billy Jack said politely, evidently somewhat bemused by it all.

"Did you see a man and a woman pass by here shortly ago?" Mentia asked.

"Yes. They had a quarrel with a timber wolf, but managed to get away." She gestured toward a nearby tree that looked a bit bedraggled. "It's normally very shy, and will raise a human cub if it finds one orphaned, but with the madness it sometimes gets violent. So when the barbarian made a barbaric remark—"

"I understand," Mentia said. "I see your tree is looking better—and so are you."

"Yes, thanks to Hiatus," she agreed. "He's off gathering croakusses at the moment."

"Crocuses?" Billy Jack asked.

"Well, he likes to eat frog's legs," Desiree said disapprovingly. "The croaks do cuss when he takes them."

"We must move on," Mentia said, anxious about losing Threnody.

"Do you think the madness will pass soon?"

"This is close to the border now," Mentia said. "It's still slowly contracting. Maybe in another year."

"What a relief!"

They went on, and this time managed to reach the White glade without too much further adventure. Mentia saw Threnody just leaving it, going deeper into the madness. But she couldn't pursue Threnody right at the moment.

Clusters of colored mushrooms sprouted around the yard. Beside each cluster was a small garden of fancy iris flowers. Mentia nodded. She knew that the mushrooms had sprouted from jars of odd Mundane paper money Richard had buried around the yard, and that the irises grew wherever the woman Janet Hines went. If the two ever separated, so would the mushrooms and irises.

She knocked on the door of the neat cottage. A man answered. "Hello, Richard. Remember me? I'm D. Mentia, the temporarily sane demoness. I have brought another Richard fresh from Mundania who I think could use your help."

A woman appeared behind Richard. "Oh, yes, of course we'll help him," she said. "We understand so well."

Mentia turned to Billy Jack. "These folk will help you all you need," she said. "I have to move on now, but you can trust them. They'll get you settled."

"But I'm not staying here!" Billy Jack protested. "I need to find my way home. My wife, my daughter—"

Richard White stepped out and took his arm. "Come inside," he said. "This is my wife Janet. I'm afraid we have unsettling news for you."

Mentia, freed of the temporary obligation her better half's conscience had taken on, moved rapidly after Threnody. She knew what had happened to Billy Jack, but hadn't wanted to tell him. He would not be returning to Mundania. Richard and Janet had been through it already, so would be able to guide him past the madness to his new life.

She caught up to Threnody and Jordan, who had paused in a glade that seemed clear of mad effects. Obviously they were not eager to plunge into more madness, especially since they hadn't succeeded in losing Mentia by coming here.

She approached. "I know the madness better than you do," she said. "I'm Mentia, Metria's worser half. I'm normally a little crazy, but I'm sane here. I suggest to you that you would be best advised to cease this futile flight and take the summons token."

"No!" Threnody cried.

"I think you are unduly hung up on what Metria did four hundred and thirty-eight years ago. You would be better off to forget it, instead of holding an impossible grudge."

"No!"

"Did it ever occur to you that she has a side too?"

"No."

Mentia considered. "Let me offer you a deal. Let's explore the two sides of it, to see which makes more sense. Then I will guide you out of the region of madness and leave you alone."

Threnody was about to say "no" again, but Jordan cautioned her. When it came to wild action, the barbarian had pretty good sense. So she considered. "Guide us out first."

"No. We need the madness for this. But I will give you my word."

"Your word was never any good!"

"On the contrary," Mentia said evenly. "Metria has always told the truth, and so have I. It is one of our foibles."

"That's not true!"

Jordan nudged her again. Barbarians had solid instincts about such things, and though they could be totally foolish about women, they could generally tell whether other creatures were trustworthy. Since the woman Jordan was foolish about was Threnody, he was reasonably objective about Mentia.

"Very well," Threnody said through her teeth. "Two sides. Then you guide us out and leave us alone."

'But her mind is closed!' Metria protested. 'She's just using this to get out of accepting the token.'

'Of course,' Mentia replied sanely. 'But she may change her mind.'

'She'll never change her mind! She hates me.'

'This is the Region of Madness, where odd truths come out. I have had experience. Play it through, and perhaps you both will be surprised.'

Metria, amazed by the assurance and sanity of her crazy worser self, which was not at all true to form, subsided. Mentia had access to all her memories and experience, so was competent to do whatever it was she had in mind.

"First we shall play it through your way," Mentia said to Threnody. "We shall need Jordan's participation."

Jordan jumped. "Mine?"

"You knew King Gromden, didn't you?"

"Yes. Just before he died. He was a good old boy."

"You will play his part."

"I will? I don't know how."

"The madness will guide you. Just go along with it."

Jordan shrugged, intrigued. "Okay. It'll be fun to be a King."

Mentia turned to Threnody. "You will play the Queen's part. You do remember her?"

"Yes," Threnody agreed tightly.

"And I will play the part of the demoness."

"You should be very good at that," Threnody said, with such an edge that Jordan flinched as if he had been cut, though the barb had not been directed at him.

Mentia ignored the thrust. "Bear in mind that we must all reenact the truth as we perceive it. That is, first as you perceive it, second as I perceive it. We will each be true to the scenario we are playing."

Threnody looked sharply at her. "You really believe that something will come of this!"

"Yes. Shall we proceed?"

Threnody shrugged.

"Then I will set the scene," Mentia said. "It is the year of Xanth six fifty-seven, in the countryside near Castle Roogna. Gromden has been King for thirty four years. He is married, but his wife is cold. It was a marriage made for political reasons. He is a good man—"

"A very good man," Threnody said.

"But fallible, as mortal men are. He is not yet aware of it, but there is something missing from his life. That is joy." As she spoke, Jordan postured, emulating the King, and the madness closed in and gave him the aspect of the King: middling-old, pudgy, yet possessed of authority.

"One day as Gromden was out reviewing the kingdom, learning how well things were doing by touching stones and posts and other incidental items and using his talent to immediately Fathom Everything about them, he came across a wretched straggler on the road.''

Now Metria stepped into her part, as the scene of medieval Xanth formed around them. She became the wretched straggler, cloaked and hooded and hunched.

The King paused in the center of the road. He was a stunningly rich figure, in his quality clothing, compared to the creature before him. ''May I help you, good woman?'' he inquired, for he was never arrogant.

The figure looked wearily at him and recognized his status. ''O, your majesty, don't bother with me,'' she said, kneeling and bowing her head. ''I am only a mere outcast from my village, in sore need of help and protection, not fit to bother the likes of you.''

''Come, come, now, my dear,'' he said graciously. ''I'll be the judge of that. What is your problem?''

''O King, my father sought to marry me to the village lout. Rather than suffer that indignity, for I am smart and there are those who call me fair, I fled my otherwise excellent home. But no other family would take me in or give me succor, so I had to depart the village also. It was the same in neighboring villages. No one respects a willful child. Now I am a stranger far from home, who dares not return, and who is grievously weary and footsore from traveling and foraging about the countryside. I wish only to find a compatible place to live, and in due course to find a good man to marry, but in every village it is only the louts who pursue me.''

''You poor girl,'' the King said sympathetically. ''Let me get a look at you.'' He lifted back her cowl, and lo! she was black of hair and eye and fine of feature, a beautiful young woman. He looked at her body, and now saw that under the rough cloak was the stuff to madden a man's mind: every curve and point of her caused his fancy to see the likeness of storks taking wing as if imperatively summoned. She was indeed the loveliest creature he had ever seen. The seed of his undoing was planted in that moment.

She lifted her large eyes to glance briefly at his face, then lowered them demurely. ''O King, I am unworthy of your attention. I will depart forthwith, perhaps to sustenance in yonder field. I apologize for soiling your view with my aspect.''

But the King was generous. "Quite all right, my dear. No need to go to the field. It would have been a shame to see you married to a lout. Far be it from me to see the least of my subjects in dire want. There is a royal station house near the next village which is currently unoccupied. I will install you there until you can find a better situation."

Tears of purest gratitude welled in her perfect eyes. "O, how can I ever thank you for this great kindness, your majesty? Never in my wildest and most foolish dreams did I ever imagine that any such thing would come to pass."

"Tut, none of that," he said, and took her by her delicate elbow and guided her to the station house. It was in a sheltered spot just out of sight of the road, and was well appointed, for normally a small detachment of the King's guards occupied it. But in the past decade the need for such activity had diminished, or perhaps the kingship was losing its power. Gromden was a nice man rather than an imperious one, and had little use for guards or, indeed, for force. Thus this was a relic of a more imperial age. "Make yourself comfortable here, and I will check on you next week to be sure you are all right." He turned to go.

"Oh, but do not leave me so soon!" she pleaded, touching his arm to turn him back. She breathed deeply as she removed her cloak so that her fine bosom heaved. "I haven't yet thanked you for your extreme kindness to me."

"No thanks is necessary," he said. "I am glad merely to have been able to help."

"O my Lord, but you have done so very much for me," she said. "If I may presume—" She stood up on her tiptoes and kissed him with surprising firmness on the mouth.

The King reeled as if clobbered on the noggin—and he had been, in a fashion. He had never before experienced anything half as sweet and potent as this. This girl seemed to be about granddaughterly age, yet there was something compellingly mature about her.

"O King, are you dizzy?" she asked, concerned. "Come, lie down for a moment on this bed, and I will do my utmost to care for you. I would never knowingly cause you mischief."

King Gromden was indeed dizzy, but not from any incapacity of mind or body. Her kiss had simply been so sweet as to awaken in him all manner of notions that had never gotten close to him before. He suffered himself to be brought to the bed and laid upon it, while his newly discovered fancies danced in circles all around his awareness.

"Perhaps your clothing is too tight, your majesty," she said, loosening his collar and then his shirt.

"Oh, no, no need to—" he protested weakly.

But she continued, and somehow he discovered himself under a sheet with her, and she had nothing more on than he did. Then did the storks indeed take notice, for soon such a signal went out as no such bird could have ignored. He had been made deliriously happy.

In the morning, somewhat ashamed for his weakness of the night, King Gromden got up, hastily dressed, and left the lovely girl sleeping in the bed. He had never before done anything like this. He hurried back to Castle Roogna and went about his business with utmost dispatch. He tried to forget the affair.

But such was the illicit appeal of what had happened that in the evening he found himself walking back to the station house, nominally to see how the girl was doing. Love of her burdened his heart, and he simply could not stay away. Yet when he came to the house, he discovered it empty, with nothing touched. It was as if there had never been a woman there. She was gone.

Dispirited, he returned to the castle. Every day for a month he went to the house, but it remained devastatingly empty. He realized that the girl had had whatever she had wanted of him that one night, and would never return. So he resumed his dull kingly life, trying to forget that single dreamlike night of bliss.

Unknown to him, a stork visited the mysterious damsel less than a year after their contact. She had hidden herself, but the canny bird had located her regardless, and delivered its bundle.

Then, when the King was at supper with the Queen and some prominent visitors, the woman appeared, carrying a bundle. "Here is your bastard baby, O adulterous King!" she cried, and dumped the bundle in his lap. "And know, O simpleton, with what you have sundered your marriage vow." She flew into the air, dissolved into a cloud of laughing gas, and vanished as all shocked eyes turned to Gromden. The laughter echoed for a long time as they stared.

Thus did the foul demoness befuddle, seduce, and humiliate the decent King. The slow deterioration of his power swiftened, and before long Castle Roogna was like an empty shell. The Queen, of course, would have nothing more to do with him, and he was a laughing-stock throughout Xanth.

Yet such was his goodness that he made no excuses. He recognized the baby as his own, and set out to raise her as a Princess. Indeed, she became the apple of his eye, the one he loved best, and she loved him. But the Queen, outraged by the situation, finally put a curse on the child: If she remained in Castle Roogna, the castle would fall. So the girl, now about ten years old and as dawningly pretty as her mother had been, fled the castle. She refused to be the undoing of the castle as she had been of her beloved father.

This broke King Gromden's heart. He banished the Queen and lived alone thereafter, with only a maid to tend to the castle. He searched constantly for his daughter, hoping somehow to get around the curse. But she, being half demoness, readily eluded him, though she loved him. Until, years later, she found love in an entirely different story, died, became a ghost, and was revived about four hundred years later to rejoin her lover. Meanwhile poor King Gromden slowly declined into death, and Castle Roogna was deserted. All because of the wicked demoness.

The reenactment ended. "And I still want nothing to do with you, Mother," Threnody concluded. "You destroyed my beloved father with the cruelest of lies, and I can never forgive that."

Jordan was startled. "Metria is your mother? You never told me."

"Of course I didn't," Threnody said, angry tears in her eyes. "I'm ashamed of half my parentage. *That* half." She glared at Mentia, trying to get to Metria.

'See?' Metria said. 'It's hopeless. She will always hate me.'

"Now we shall have the other view," Mentia said firmly. "Back to square one."

"Do we have to?" Threnody grumped through her angry tears.

"Yes. We made a deal for both views. We shall have them."

The scene formed again: King Gromden marching down the road, the cloaked and hooded demoness meeting him. The dialogue played out as before, except that the demoness began to be genuinely impressed with the King's manner and goodness of heart. She lacked soul or conscience, yet was curious about the latter, so what had originally been incidental mischief became something else. She saw how lonely the King was beneath his contented exterior, and resolved to give him some reward for it: one night of the kind of joy only a demoness or a really devoted beautiful woman could give a man. She thought he deserved at least that much.

On the following day he visited her again, so she gave him delight again, for she still respected and liked him, as much as a demoness could. So it continued for some time, in perfect privacy. She was glad at last to have brought joy into his somewhat sterile life. Of course, in time he caught on to her nature, but by then it didn't matter, because he found such delight in her. When, on rare occasion, some mischance threatened to expose their liaisons, she quickly and quietly vanished away, so that there could be no evidence, returning to him only when it was safe. Thus no other person learned of their affair.

But she made one mistake. She forgot about the stork. Normally a demoness prevented the signal from getting out to find the stork, but she was so taken with the nice King that she never even noticed the escaping signal. When she realized, it was too late. Well, she thought, she would just have to find a suitable home for the baby when it came, because a demoness was no fit mother for a human baby. For one thing, the baby would probably have a soul, while she didn't.

When the stork actually brought a beautiful baby girl, the demoness was so taken with her that she almost decided to keep her after all. But she knew that would be folly, and she didn't want her daughter to suffer the neglect that was bound to occur in the company of a demoness. So she did the next best thing: She brought the child to her father the King.

She did this, of course, in decent privacy, so as to avoid embarrassing him. "O King, here is your darling daughter," she informed him, presenting him with the bundle. "I wish I could keep her myself, but I can't, so I trust you to treat her well and give her all the things a precious child needs.''

Gromden was amazed. In the typical manner of men, he had assumed that he had gone through the motions but that the summons would not reach the stork. But one look at the baby captivated him, and he was glad to accept her and recognize her as his own. ''She will be my heir,'' he said, ''for I have no children.'' This was fond illusion, because only a Magician could be King of Xanth. But her magic talent was as yet unknown, so there was always the chance that she would be a Sorceress. Of course, the kingship was traditionally limited to men, for archaic obsolete reasons, and those were the hardest reasons to refute. And she was half demoness, which would complicate her eligibility further. But Gromden postponed those concerns until later, and meanwhile doted on his daughter.

''I think I must not visit you anymore,'' the demoness said to the King. ''For demons are known to be bad influences on children, and your daughter must have only the best influences.''

Sadly, the King agreed. So they kissed once more and parted. The demoness lacked true human feelings, but a few of them had rubbed off on her during her association with the King, and so it would be fair to say she emulated a feeling or two in that time. She would have liked to continue with the King, and did visit her daughter a number of times, taking care never to make her presence known. Thus she was aware of what was going on in Castle Roogna, though she did not interfere.

Gromden named his daughter Threnody, because soon her talent of sad singing showed. He provided every possible thing for her, including tutoring, playmates, and every kind of pastry and pie. She had a nursemaid to look after her. But he could not provide her with a mother.

The Queen took an interest. She was, of course, resentful of the presence of the child, because the child was evidence of the King's infidelity, The Queen had no interest in that sort of relationship with the King, but it was embarrassing to have it generally known that he had found a relationship elsewhere. But for a time she masked her enmity, and Gromden, assuming that others had the same generosity of spirit that he did, did not realize how bitter she was.

The Queen took a hand in educating the child. "The first thing you must understand," she told little Threnody, "is the foulness of your origin. Your father was cruelly seduced by a hideous demoness who somehow made him think she was beautiful. Then she embarrassed him in public by bringing you, so that everyone would know his folly." And the child believed it. "But don't speak of this to your father," the Queen continued, "for he has already suffered more than enough, and it would hurt him to be reminded of it." So the child was careful never to reveal what she had learned to Gromden.

But as the years passed, Threnody showed distinct signs of becoming beautiful. Indeed, she was the juvenile image of the form her mother had assumed to seduce the King. Gromden, of course, treated her exactly the way a father should treat a daughter, not quite realizing the significance of her image. But the Queen couldn't stand it. So finally she acted. She put a terrible curse on the child, forcing her to depart the castle forever. When the King discovered this, he banished the Queen also. But the damage was done.

The vision ended. Gromden reverted to Jordan, the Queen reverted to Threnody, and the beautiful child reverted to little Woe Betide, who then became Mentia.

Threnody seemed shaken. "I remember now. The Queen did tell me that! And I never questioned it. Of course, she had a bad motive. Still, it was wrong of you to seduce the King. My presence did weaken his image. I was his curse."

"No you weren't," Jordan protested. "You were the delight of his later life. His life was empty, until you filled it." He, having just emulated the role of King Gromden, was in a position to know. "The demoness did him a real favor. It was the jealous Queen who made the mischief."

Threnody, having emulated the Queen, now understood that. But the belief of four centuries did not dissipate readily. "I'll have to think about this."

"Now I will show you out of the madness, and depart," Mentia said.

'But she hasn't taken the token!' Metria protested.

'Stifle it, better half. Soft sell does it.'

The demoness led the way out of the madness. During her pauses in the vision, mainly while the Queen was poisoning the mind of the child, she had scouted around and found the best route. "The only obstacle here is the peer pressure," she said. "You simply have to resist it."

Jordan looked around. "A pier? But there's no water."

Then the pressure began. They were squeezed from either side by invisible ramps. "Not pier. Peer," Mentia clarified. "The things of madness are peering at us, trying to make us go their way. They want us to be as mad as they are. They can't touch us physically, but they can peer so hard that it feels solid." She tapped the solid seeming invisible shape beside her, and it made a dull wooden sound. "Just ignore it."

"But it's squeezing the breath from me!" Jordan gasped.

"Peer pressure can be very strong," Mentia agreed. She wasn't suffering, because she had made herself too gaseous for the pressure to affect very much, and Threnody was more slowly doing the same. Threnody could change forms in the manner of a demoness, being a crossbreed, but this took time, so she was under more pressure. "Just say no," Mentia advised them.

"No!"

"No!"

With that the pressure eased, because peering was difficult when the objects of its cynosure didn't cooperate. They were able to pull themselves on through.

They stepped out of the madness and back into regular Xanth. "I'll know better than to go there again," Threnody said, relieved.

"I don't know," Jordan said. "I sort of liked being a King, and making out with that—"

Threnody drew her knife and, with one swift deft motion, cut off his tongue. That silenced him for a while, because though his talent was rapid healing, it took time to grow his tongue back to full size. Things had returned to normal.

5
CURSE

W   ell, it is time for me to depart," Mentia said,
    pausing artfully.
        "Um, wait," Threnody said. "I'm not saying
that I forgive you for the dastardly thing you did, but aren't you
going to try to make me accept that summons?"

'Yes!' Metria said silently.

"No, that wasn't part of the deal," Mentia said.

"But it's crazy not to pursue your advantage, when I'm waver-
ing."

"Thank you. I am a little crazy. I'm sure that mysterious trial will
be able to proceed without your surely significant participation."
The demoness made as if to puff into smoke.

"Maybe—some other deal?" Threnody asked.

"I suppose, if you think that's fair. You know what I want; is
there something you really want?"

"Yes. What I most desire is to be able to return to Castle
Roogna, where I was happy once, without it falling. To walk
through the familiar old rooms, and meet the people who are
there now." A tear formed at one eye or the other. "To remember how it was with my father. To view him on the Tapestry."

That last was ironic, because as a child Threnody could have
viewed recent and current events on the Tapestry, and learned the

truth about her mother. But she had been so sure she already knew
it that she had never done so.

''Very well,'' Mentia said briskly. ''I shall see about abating that
curse. I shall return.'' She popped off.

'What are you doing?' Metria asked as they appeared back at their
home castle. 'How can we abate a four-hundred-year-old curse? That
was a crazy deal to make!'

'Thank you. Maybe there is a way.'

'*What* way?'

'I don't feel free to tell you.'

'What? I'm your better half. I can get it directly from your crazy
mind.'

'Then it wouldn't work.'

Metria, baffled, backed off. She had never been able to conceal
anything from Mentia, but Mentia could hide things from her when-
ever she wanted to. Metria had been grudgingly impressed by her
worser half's handling of the madness and Threnody. Maybe Mentia
actually did know how to lift the curse.

'Yes. Now you must take over the body, and do what I tell you.
Don't question me, just do it.'

Bemused, Metria took over. 'So what do you want me to do?'

'Stoke up your husband for another day's worth, then check for
the least familiar name in your bag of tokens.'

So Metria did both. 'Here's one I don't recognize at all: Phelra.
She's a Witness.'

'Serve her summons next.'

'But she could be way off in some hidden hinterland, and take
more time to locate than any number of regular folk.'

'Good. Do it.'

Metria sighed and held up Phelra's token. It tugged in the general direction of central Xanth. She popped across the terrain in
that direction, appearing in the deepest jungle north of Lake Ogre-
Chobee. She lifted the token again, and its tug was stronger. She
popped off for a shorter hop in its direction, and landed near a
house beside a wooded mountain. The token tugged toward the
house.

So she went to knock on the door. In a moment it opened. A

young woman of undistinguished features stood there. "But I didn't summon you," she said, surprised.

"Should you have?" Metria asked, similarly surprised. Who was summoning whom?

"My talent is to summon animals to help me," the woman explained. "But it doesn't work on demons."

"I came here on my own to summon *you*, Metria said. "If you are Phelra." She held up the token.

"Summon me? What for?"

"For the trial of Roxanne Roc."

"Sorry, I don't summon birds, just animals. Anyway, she's already busy."

"Nevertheless, she is to be tried within a fortnight. Can you get to the Nameless Castle in time?"

"I don't think so. It's not the easiest castle to reach."

'Take her to Castle Roogna first,' Mentia suggested.

"There are some folk going there from Castle Roogna," Metria said. "Suppose I guide you there, and you can go to the trial with them?"

"That would be nice," Phelra said. "I've never been to Castle Roogna, and would like to see it. If you are sure they won't mind."

"I can take you to Princess Ida. She's very nice, and—"

'Don't tell her talent!'

"—will surely see that you are comfortable," Metria finished smoothly. What was her worser half up to?

"Then let's go," Phelra agreed brightly, accepting the token. "I'll summon a large animal to transport us."

"Oh, I don't need—"

'Ride with her.'

"But it does sound like fun," Metria concluded.

Phelra stepped outside and whistled. In a moment there was a heavy clopping sound, and a really weird creature appeared. It looked like an enormous furry comb, with the teeth serving as many little legs, and the head of a cat. It came to the house and stopped, looking at Phelra expectantly.

"What kind of animal is this?" Metria inquired. She thought she had seen just about everything, but this was new to her.

"A catacomb, of course," Phelra said. She caught hold of the tail and climbed up to the top, where the ridge-back widened so that she could bestride it comfortably.

"Of course," the demoness agreed, joining her. "How ignorant of me not to recognize it immediately."

"Take us to Castle Roogna, Comb," Phelra said, and the creature obligingly started walking. It moved surprisingly swiftly, getting through tangles of vegetation without difficulty, leaving no snarles behind. It combed through the forest with smooth strokes.

'Tell her there used to be a curse on Castle Roogna,' Mentia said.

'But there is *still* a—'

'Just do it.'

So Metria did it. "You know, one of the other folk I have to summon had a problem. She was under a curse that Castle Roogna would fall if she ever entered it. So she never would come to the castle."

"But it's okay now?" Phelra asked, concerned.

"Well . . ."

'Don't deny it!'

'But it's not true!'

'How do you know that?'

Metria hesitated. She had always accepted the validity of the curse. She understood that Threnody had once approached Castle Roogna, and that it had started to fall. But that had been some time ago, and it was possible that the situation had changed. Maybe that was what Mentia was gambling on.

"How long do curses last?" Phelra asked. "I thought they didn't last longer than the life of the one who makes them. Is the cursor still alive?"

"No. She died some time back."

"That must be a relief to your friend," Phelra said. "Now she can visit Castle Roogna."

"Maybe so," Metria agreed dubiously. Why should Mentia care what Phelra thought?

The catacomb made excellent time, perhaps because of its many springy legs, and soon they hove into view of Castle Roogna. They dismounted, and the catacomb trotted off, glad to get a chance to comb through new territory.

'Now introduce her to Ida,' Mentia said.

They passed the moat monster, who rose up to challenge the unfamiliar person. "Oh, take it easy, Soufflé," Metria said. "This is Phelra, on my summons list."

"Oooo, hherrr," the monster agreed in an I-knew-that tone, and submerged.

Ida came forward to meet them, her little moon glinting as it caught a beam of sunlight, and Metria performed another introduction and explanation. "Why, of course you can come to the Nameless Castle with us," Ida agreed. "We can ride the two gargoyles up there."

"Gargoyles can fly well?" Phelra asked, surprised, for she had seen how solid the creatures were, and how small their wings were.

"I'm sure they can, for this very special trip," Ida said. "We'll get a flying centaur to make us and them light enough."

And if Ida believed it was so, it was so, Metria knew, for her talent was the Idea.

Phelra looked around. "This is such a nice castle. I'm glad the curse is off it."

"The curse?" Ida asked, and her moon seemed perplexed too, going to half-phase.

"The one that prevented Threnody from coming here," Metria explained.

"Oh, that curse is gone?" Ida asked "How nice! Now Threnody can visit."

Suddenly Metria grasped the crazy logic of her crazy worser self. Phelra didn't know Ida's talent, and Ida didn't know that Phelra had no true source of information. Now Ida believed that the curse was gone—so it was gone, because what Ida believed was true. As long as the source of her Idea was from someone who didn't know her magic. This was such a devious, demented ploy that no one else would believe it, so Metria didn't try to explain it. "Yes," she said. "I will bring her here now."

She left Ida to show Phelra to her room in the castle, and popped back to where she had left Threnody. It didn't take long to locate her, though it was now evening, because Threnody was no longer trying to avoid her.

Jordan's tongue had grown mostly back, though he spoke with a lisp. Threnody was constantly cutting him; it was her way of showing him affection. Metria was sure Threnody had other ways to show him affection, when she chose; she was after all, half demoness. But he was a barbarian, so he related well to tough love.

"I think we have nullified that curse," Metria said. "I think you can visit Castle Roogna now."

Threnody gazed at her. "I am not sure I believe you."

"I'm not quite sure I believe it myself," Metria confessed. "Let's go there and see."

"It will take several days to get there afoot," Threnody pointed out.

And Metria couldn't afford that time. She still had a dozen and a half tokens to serve.

"Maybe a thentaur," Jordan lisped.

That gave Metria a notion. She had two winged centaurs on her list. They were too young to carry such burdens, but if the grown ones helped—

"I'll be back," she said, and popped off to the centaurs' stall.

This was a comfortable house in a glade north of the Gap Chasm. The centaur family was at supper: a winged stallion, a winged mare, and a winged filly. Their huge wings were folded, resembling capes across their bodies. "I would ask you to join us," Chex Centaur said. She was a fine full-figured creature. "But I know you don't eat, Metria."

"Why are you here?" Cheiron Centaur asked directly. He was an impressive centaur, in both his human and equine portions.

"I have summonses for Che and Cynthia."

"Summonses!"

Metria explained the situation.

"Gee," Cynthia said. She was a filly of about ten, not quite verging onto maredom. "I get to serve on a Jury!"

"Che is not here," Chex said. "He is with Chief Gwenny Goblin, at Goblin Mountain. He is her Companion."

Metria already knew about the Companion bit, but had the wit not to say so. "I'll go there soon, to serve him his summons. But meanwhile, there is something else. I wonder if I could prevail on you for a favor."

Chex smiled. "Your soul becomes you, Metria. You are so polite, now. What do you wish?"

"I think we may have abated Threnody's curse, so that Castle Roogna won't fall if she goes there. I need to get her there soon, to see if that's true. If it is, she will accept the summons I have for her. But it will take her and Jordan Barbarian several days to get there by foot. So I was wondering—"

Cheiron laughed. "Of course we'll take them there! I'd love to see if that curse is really gone." He looked at Chex. "In the morning."

"In the morning, when it's light," Chex agreed. "We'll deliver Cynthia there at the same time."

"Thank you." Metria give them directions for Jordan and Threnody's location, though she expected to be there to guide them anyway. Then she popped over to Goblin Mountain to serve Che his token, and tell him where his family was going.

Goblin Mountain looked like a giant anthill. But a pretty one, because the goblins had become aesthetic since Gwenny became their first female Chief. There were flower beds on the terraces, and the guards were garbed in pastel colors.

She landed in front of the main entrance. "Halt, Demoness," the guard said. He glanced around to see if anyone else was within earshot. "And if you know what's good for you, you'll get your smoky posterior elsewhere fast. We don't need your kind here."

"Too bad, snootface," Mentia replied evenly. "I'm here to see the Chief's Companion."

"That piece of horsemeat's overdue for the pot," the guard muttered. "In fact, the Chief should be dunked right in there with him. She's ruining the tribe."

"I'll tell her you said so," Metria said sweetly. "What's your name, big-mouth?"

Suddenly the guard was surprisingly shy. "Never mind. Go on in."

Metria smiled. Goblin men were the dregs of Xanth, mean of spirit and foul of mouth. They hated the notion of having a woman as Chief. But they were stuck with it, and as a result Goblin Mountain and the surrounding territory were prospering. Instead of being a core of outrage, the goblin enclave had become a center of justice and prosperity.

Soon she located Gwenny Goblin, who was at her supper in the main dining hall. Che Centaur was beside her. Metria knew what few others did: Gwenny was slightly lame of ankle and slightly weak of vision—faults that would get her promptly executed if the male goblins ever learned of them. But special contact lenses not only corrected her vision, they enabled her to see dreams, giving her an uncanny insight into plots against her. And her Companion enabled her to conceal any physical or mental lapse. Because Che was a centaur, albeit a young one, his advice was always excellent, and the Chief always heeded it. They were an admirable team.

"Why, hello, Demoness Metria," Che said, spying her. He was careful to introduce any newcomers aloud, so that Gwenny was never embarrassed by missing them.

Gwenny looked quickly up. She was a nice and lovely dark young woman, as most goblin girls were, in contrast to the crude and ugly goblin men. One day she would marry, and make some goblin man undeservedly happy. But so far she had been way too busy reorganizing the goblin property and hierarchy to concern herself with anything like that. She was eighteen; she had a little time yet to worry about her social life. "So nice to see you, Metria," she said. "To what do we owe the pleasure of this appearance?"

"I have to serve Che with a summons, as a Juror," Metria said, and explained. "And you, Chief Gwenny, as a Witness."

"Roxanne Roc on trial," Che said thoughtfully as he accepted his token and read it. "That should be most interesting. It seems hard to believe that she could be guilty of any crime."

"She doesn't know why herself," Metria said. "She's busy hatching that fancy egg, which is due any month now. She hasn't gone anywhere."

"This is certainly peculiar," Gwenny agreed. "Who is charging her with a crime?"

"The Simurgh."

"Now I am really interested," Che said, spreading his wings a bit with excitement. "That big bird is not one for incidental mischief."

"Just so long as both of you are there, in a fortnight minus a day."

"Who else will be there?" Gwenny inquired.

"Just about everyone of any current percentage."

"Any current what?"

"Compensation, indemnification, remuneration, remittance, stipend—"

"Interest?"

"Whatever," Metria agreed crossly. "Magician Trent, Sorceress Iris, Grey Murphy, Princess Ida, Demon Prof Grossclout—"

"Not Princess Ivy?" Gwenny asked alertly.

"She's not on my list. It's Grey as Prosecutor and Ida as Defense Attorney."

"Grey and Ida," Che said thoughtfully, just as her worser self Mentia had before. "Working opposite each other. Suppose she gets an Idea?"

"She wouldn't do that," Gwenny said firmly. Then, less firmly: "Would she?"

"How long have Grey and Ivy been betrothed?" Metria asked.

"Nine years," Che said promptly. Centaurs always had their facts and figures straight. "They were affianced the year after I was foaled."

"Good thing they weren't your parents," Metria remarked innocently, and Gwenny stifled an unchiefly giggle. "Do you think they are ever going to get on with it?"

"No, I think they are waiting for the sun and the moon to collide first," Che said, trying to look serious.

Gwenny made a conspiratorial wink. "Maybe we can encourage them. I understand that Ivy's parents took some time in that respect too—"

"Eight years," Che said.

"—until their friends held a wedding party for them in the cemetery, catching Magician Dor by surprise."

"Are you two thinking what I'm thinking?" Metria asked.

Both Che and Gwenny immediately put on straight faces. "Of course not," Che said. "Centaurs don't conspire."

"But if Professor Grossclout will be there," Gwenny said, "and he's competent to marry a couple—"

"He married me to Veleno," Metria agreed. "Because he wanted to be sure I got what was coming to me."

"Who knows what might happen, coincidentally," Che finished. The expression on his face might have been misinterpreted as smugness, were he not a centaur.

"So anyway," Metria concluded, "Cynthia Centaur will be there too, and your folks are going to take Jordan the Barbarian and Threnody to Castle Roogna tomorrow. I thought you might be interested in joining them."

"Threnody can't go to Castle Roogna," Che said.

"That's what makes it interesting. 'Bye." She popped off. She loved doing that: leaving them with something truly tantalizing. They would have to come to Castle Roogna to see it happen.

She arrived where she had left Jordan and Threnody. They were camped out in the open, barbarian style, beside a perfectly even symme-tree, gazing up at the stars. Metria looked up and saw that some crazy constellations were forming over the Region of Madness. That made sense.

"Cheiron and Chex Centaur have agreed to carry you to Castle Roogna tomorrow," she announced. "They'll be here at dawn. When you see them fly overhead, shout, so they can find you."

"Okay," Jordan said. His tongue seemed to have healed the rest of the way. It was an interesting relation those two had, with her violence and his healing.

'I wonder if she ever cuts off anything else?' Mentia mused. 'When she's indisposed for love.'

Metria popped home and made sure her husband was still suitably delirious. Then she settled down to ponder the remaining tokens. She still had a number of folk to find, and though she had plenty of time, she knew that it could quickly dissipate if even one case turned out to be difficult. So her best course seemed to be to tackle the next most awkward folk on her list: the two Mundanes, Dug and Kim. Assuming she could even reach them. Was there a way? They had entered Xanth before through screens, and—

And there was her way. She would have to approach Com Pewter, the evil machine, next. And hope he cooperated. He was supposed to be a good machine now, but she didn't quite trust that. Fortunately the hour didn't matter; the machine didn't sleep at night.

So she popped off to Pewter's cave, bypassing the invisible giant who helped drive people into the cave. The glass screen was there as usual, propped up amidst pewter and crockery. It certainly didn't look like much.

"Hello, Evil Machine," she said. "I've got something for you."

The screen brightened. Print appeared on it. A GREETING, WORD-IMPACTED DEMONESS.

"Word-whatted?"

BOUND, CONSTRAINED, CONSTIPATED, CONFUSED, CHAGRINED, MORTIFIED—

"Whatever," she agreed crossly.

DO YOU HAVE WHAT I NEED?

"That depends on what you need."

I NEED DIE-ODES FOR MY CIRCUITS.

"You need dead poets for your circus?"

The screen flickered warningly. NO, IGNORAMUS. I ALSO COULD USE A D-TERMINAL.

"What kind of termite?"

The screen flickered again. IT D-TERMINES WHAT I CAN DO. I AM TRYING TO GET UPGRADED.

"Well, don't upchuck on me, machine!"

The screen faded for a moment, while the numbers 1 through 10 zipped rapidly across it several times. Then it got control of itself. YOU ARE THE ONLY CREATURE WHO COMES CLOSE TO ANNOYING ME, DESPITE MY LACK OF EMOTION. WHAT DO YOU HAVE FOR ME?

"That's more like it, Evil Machine. Here's your summons." She held out the token marked "Com Pewter."

DEMONESS CHANGES MIND ABOUT SERVING SUMMONS, the screen printed.

Oops, she'd forgotten how the contraption controlled reality in its vicinity. She withdrew the token, having changed her mind.

But she was no ordinary demoness. Mentia took over the body. She hadn't changed *her* mind. "Listen, you bucket of bolts," she said. "You can't ignore this summons. It's from—"

DEMONESS CEASES DIALOGUE.

And of course, she did. But she had one more chance.

Woe Betide appeared. "O please, O illustrious machine," the tyke pleaded. "The Simurgh will be annoyed if you aren't there. She wants an entity of true competence. Someone completely rational to serve on the Jury, in contrast to the mush—"

The screen flickered. THE SIMURGH?

"Yes, O marvelous contraption. It's such an honor to be selected by her for this trial! Only the very most special folk are on the list, and—"

TRIAL?

"Roxanne Roc is on trial, and—"

WHAT FOR?

"Nobody but the Simurgh knows, O sapient device. But it must be very super duper extra important, because Demon Professor Grossclout is the Judge, and Magician Trent is the Bailiff, and—"

GIVE ME THAT SUMMONS.

The artful moppet seemed to hesitate. "Are you sure, O puissant cipher? I would never want to impose on a thing of your vasty importance."

Com Pewter lost patience. CUNNING TYKE DELIVERS SUMMONS, the screen printed.

Obediently Woe Betide set the token beside the screen. "And do you think you just might, maybe, possibly, consider about helping me fetch in two other summonsees, O astute apparatus? I think only you can do it, O perspicacious mechanism."

The evil machine was evidently not deceived about the child's nature and flattery, but decided to be tolerant. After all, the Adult Conspiracy had its softer aspects, such as treating plaintive waifs with consideration. WHAT TWO OTHERS?

"They are the Mundanes Dug and Kim, who played the game of Companions three years ago."

OH, YES, the screen remembered. HE IS A JERK, BUT SHE IS TOL-
ERABLE. WHAT HAVE THEY TO DO WITH THIS TRIAL?

"They are summoned for Jury duty too, O phenomenal entity,"
the gamine explained. "I must fetch them in, but I can't go outside
Xanth."

The screen reflected for a moment; Woe Betide saw her image
there. THIS IS NOT NECESSARILY FEASIBLE. THE MUNDANES DID AR-
RIVE IN XANTH THROUGH ELECTRONIC SCREENS, BUT THEY WERE
PLAYING THE DEMONS' GAME. THEY STILL PLAY THAT GAME, BUT NOT
OFTEN. IT MAY BE SEVERAL MONTHS BEFORE—

"We have only a fortnight!" the cherub wailed, a large tear forming.

The machine almost seemed to have an emotion. I REGRET I AM
UNABLE TO ENSURE THEIR PARTICIPATION. I CAN CONTROL REALITY
HERE IN MY DEMESNE, AND BRING THEM IN THROUGH MY SCREEN IF
THEY ENTER THAT GAME, BUT I CANNOT MAKE THEM PLAY THAT
GAME.

"Isn't there some other way, O grandiose artifact?" Woe Betide
pleaded, so cute and distressed that her aspect might have melted
silicon.

STOP THAT! the screen printed, blurring around the edges. THERE
MAY BE AN ALTERNATE WAY.

"O thank you, O magnificent creation! What is it?"

THERE IS AN OLD CENTAUR OF MAGICIAN CALIBER WHOSE TAL-
ENT IS TO GENERATE AN AISLE OF MAGIC OUTSIDE XANTH, OR AN
AISLE OF NONMAGIC WITHIN XANTH. IF YOU ENLIST HIS AID, YOU
WILL BE ABLE TO GO INTO MUNDANIA TO FETCH YOUR TWO SUM-
MONSEES.

"An aisle of magic in Mundania?" the tot asked, duly amazed.
"O fantastic intellect, how is this possible?"

HE IS A VERY SPECIAL CENTAUR. THE DISCOVERY OF HIS TALENT
CAUSED HIM TO BE EXILED FROM CENTAUR ISLE, BECAUSE THE CEN-
TAURS THERE DO NOT APPROVE OF MAGIC, OTHER THAN AS A SEPA-
RATE TOOL TO BE USED AT NEED. IN FACT THEY FIND IT OBSCENE IN
HIGHER LIFE FORMS. THUS THEY TOLERATE MAGIC TALENTS IN HU-
MANS, WHICH ARE NOT ALL THAT HIGH ON THE SCALE, BUT NOT IN
THEMSELVES. THIS IS ANALOGOUS TO THE ATTITUDE OF HUMAN BE-

INGS TOWARD STORK SUMMONING. THUS THIS PARTICULAR CEN-
TAUR LIVES ISOLATED FROM HIS CULTURE AND DOES NOT SEEK
NOTORIETY.

A close observer might have detected just a hint of boredom in
the childish mien, as if she already knew much of this. Fortunately
the machine was not observing closely at the moment, being more
interested in showing off his knowledge to the amazed tad. "O
exceptional appurtenance, who is this centaur, and where is he
now?"

HE IS ARNOLDE, AND HE RESIDES SOMEWHERE IN CENTRAL XANTH.
BUT HE IS INTOLERABLY OLD, AND PROBABLY NOT UP TO A JOURNEY
TO MUNDANIA.

"But then he is of no use to me," the little girl said irritably.
Then, catching herself, she added, "O illustrious monitor."

PERHAPS YOU WILL BE ABLE TO PREVAIL ON THE GOOD MAGICIAN
TO REJUVENATE HIM FOR THE OCCASION, AND ON SOMEONE'S CAT TO
LOCATE HIM.

That was what she needed. "Thanks, flatface," she said, and
popped out of the cave, leaving only a dirty noise behind. She reverted to Metria as she appeared by her home castle.

However, it was too late in the night to go after Jenny Elf, who
was the one with the cat who could find anything except home.

The night? It was now coming onto wee morning. Com Pewter
must have jumped time ahead, or put her on HOLD while he considered how to proceed. She had been playing the machine along, but
it seemed that the machine had been doing the same thing back to
her. Well, that was what made such encounters fun.

So she popped across to the brink of madness, where Jordan
and Threnody were just getting up. Sure enough, three winged
centaurs were arriving from the northwest, and another from the
northeast.

They all landed together in the glade beside Jordan and Threnody.
The one from the northeast was Che, and he was carrying Gwenny
Goblin. He was not yet mature, at age ten, but Gwenny was not
very heavy, so he was able to lighten and support her. The others
were Cheiron, Chex, and Cynthia.

In a moment the mature centaurs flicked Jordan and Threnody

with their tails, making them light. Then the two mounted, Jordan on Cheiron, Threnody on Chex. All four centaurs spread their wings and leaped into the air, stroking strongly. They gained elevation, then turned west, toward Castle Roogna. It was a pretty sight—one Metria might not have appreciated, aesthetically, before she got half-souled.

In a time and several moments they reached the castle, and came to land. They stood and watched as Jordan and Threnody walked slowly toward the castle. Princess Ida came to the front gate, garbed in a fittingly princessly robe, and waited similarly. It looked as if her moon had been washed for the occasion. Soufflé the moat monster lifted his head from the brine and oriented on the scene. They all knew the significance of this occurrence. All eyes were on Threnody.

The woman was elegantly dressed, very pretty in a dark gown, her black hair spreading downward and outward like a cape. Her demonly ancestry made it possible for her to assume what aspect she chose, so of course, she was beautiful. But she was also nervous, because for more than four hundred years she had been unable to come near this edifice, lest it collapse. She was plainly in doubt about the abatement of the curse—and so were the others. But there was no way to verify it except to go to the castle.

She came to the end of the lowered drawbridge. She paused, then nerved herself and put one small foot on the bridge.

There was a shudder and a rumble.

Soufflé jumped, craning his head around as if afraid a huge stone was about to fall on it. Metria's half soul sank down to her knees.

"Aw, shucks, it's only an invisible giant," Jordan said. "I can smell him."

Sure enough, the faint stench of giant soon wafted across. The shuddering continued as the giant walked on past, in the near distance, then faded.

Threnody tried again. This time there was no reaction as she put first one foot, then the other on the planking. She walked slowly across the bridge, gazing nervously at the castle ahead.

When she reached the inner side of the moat, Ida stepped up to embrace her. "I just knew it was all right," she said.

"I'm not in the castle proper yet," Threnody said tightly.

"Then come on in," Ida said, taking her hand. The two walked on through the great front door, in perfect silence. Jordan followed, glancing up a bit apprehensively. He had once tried to carry Threnody into the castle, and almost brought it down.

When it was clear that the castle was not about to fall, everyone else took a breath. Then they all hurried to catch up.

"This is the throne room," Ida said, "where—"

"Where my father, King Gromden, used to sit on the throne, and hold me in his lap," Threnody said, remembering. "He told me that one day I would sit there." Her face clouded. "But of course, he didn't know what would happen."

They moved on. "Here is the courtyard," Ida said, "where the Roses of Roogna grow." She paused, but Threnody didn't comment. Metria knew why: Rose of Roogna had brought the magic roses centuries after the castle had been deserted, long after King Gromden's time. So Threnody had never seen them. "The roses represent a test of true love, so great care must be used when invoking them."

They went on, visiting all the historic chambers of the ancient castle, until they came to the one where the great magic Tapestry hung on the wall. "Oh, yes, I spent many happy hours watching this!" Threnody exclaimed. "It shows all the history of Xanth. Sometimes I even dreamed I was there, part of the great adventures of the past."

"Me, too," Ida murmured, and her moon bobbed. She glanced at Threnody, and the two exchanged a smile.

The tour concluded with the room assigned to Threnody. There had been no rumble of protest from any of the stones or timbers. The curse had indeed been abated.

Then Threnody began to weep. Jordan fetched her a handkerchief, somewhat out of sorts; like any barbarian, he had no idea what to do with a crying woman. But they were not tears of pain or grief, but of relief: Threnody had finally returned to the home of her childhood. Her fondest wish had been realized.

Then she turned to Metria, her face shining wet, and held out her hand. Metria put the summons token into it.

But Threnody was accepting more than the token. "Mother," she said, in a way she had never done before. This time the cutting bitterness was gone. She caught Metria's hand and drew her in for a hug. "Mother, I forgive you any wrong I thought you did me or my father. Will you forgive me for my attitude?"

Suddenly the weight of Metria's soul pressed her down—and then released her. For centuries she hadn't cared what her daughter thought, and indeed had seldom if ever even thought of her. But her soul changed all that, and now she wanted more than anything else to have that relationship. Now her own eyes were streaming. "Yes! Yes, my daughter, yes," she said, not caring how foolish it might sound.

Then they were crying together, while the others stood in a circle and watched, and no one was embarrassed. Two curses had actually been lifted: the one on the castle, and the one on their relationship.

"I think we have seen enough," Cheiron said. "Cynthia will remain here until it is time for the trial, but we must return home."

"We will remain here also," Che said. "The trip has already proved worthwhile." He glanced at Cynthia, who, though she was only ten, managed to blush.

Metria had to agree.

6
CONTEST

B ut Metria could not stay to appreciate the joy at the castle; she had plenty of other business to see to. She needed to summons-serve the two Mundanes, Kim and Dug, and to do that she needed to find Arnolde Centaur and get him rejuvenated, and to do that she needed to find Jenny Elf and her cat who could find anything. So how could she find Jenny Elf?

Well, Jenny had served as a Companion in the game that had brought the two Mundanes to Xanth. Metria herself had participated in that game; she remembered the rehearsals and preparations, supervised by Professor Grossclout. After the game, the various parties had gone their various ways. But Grossclout surely knew where every one of them was. So she would ask him. She resolved this time not to let him get to her. She would be her normal indifferent self, no matter what.

No sooner thought than done. She popped across to the demon caves. There was the Professor, breaking in a new class. "But *if* you survive," he thundered at the rows of mushy demon faces before him, "you just may wind up thinking like real demons!" He glowered, evidently doubting that such a thing was possible. The students were obviously cowed, horsed, sheeped, and pigged, daring neither peep nor poop in response. Only Grosssclout was able to manage that; it was his talent to intimidate those who could not be intimidated.

Metria nerved herself and broke the tense silence. "Hey, Prof— where's Jenny Elf?"

The glower cracked around the edges. Wisps of smoke rose from the Professor's glowing eyeballs. "What are you doing here again?" he demanded, shaking with indignity. In fact, the whole classroom shook with it.

Hey—it was working! She was actually resisting his intimidation. But she knew she had to hang on to her attitude, because if she ever lost it, she would never recover it. "Oh, did I interrupt something? Sorry about that." Her conscience required her to apologize when she transgressed, and it was hard to be in Grossclout's presence without developing a feeling of transgressing.

"Come into my office, Demoness," he said, with a calm fraught with such menace as to be terrifying.

"Sure, Prof." She popped in, shoring up her weak knees with metallic bracing.

He popped in after her. "Now, to what do I owe the displeasure of this intrusion, Demoness?" he demanded the moment his glower softened enough to allow the words out. "Even your mushmind must know better than to interrupt one of my classes—which you have now done twice."

She shored up her spine, stiffened her jaw, and spoke. "You know that trial? The one you're going to judge?"

"Of **course** I know that trial, you exasperating creature! I have scheduled it into my calendar."

"Well, you do want all the Jurors there, don't you?"

"I want every creature there who is supposed to be there, of course. Why aren't you out fetching them all in?"

"Because I can't find Jenny Elf. Do you know where she is?"

"Of course I know where she is!"

"Then tell me, and I'll begone."

"Ah, the temptation," he murmured. Then his eyes scowled into canniness. "Demoness, it is not my chore to locate the folk on your list for you. What will you do for me, in exchange for that information?"

Her aplomb dropped and bounced on the floor. She hastily stooped to recover it, stretching her miniskirt tight in the process.

"Why, Prof, I didn't know you cared. You mean all those centuries I flashed my full-fleshed short-skirted legs at you, and my translucent well-filled blouses, weren't wasted? You actually noticed?"

"Of course I didn't! Neither did I observe that you wore a different color of panty every day, including tasteless candy-stripe and polka-dot with no material in the dots, in contrast to the more conservative matching herringbone undergarments you have on now. Why should I deign to notice the apparel of a student who never completed *one single assignment*?"

"Oh," she said, disappointed. "So since you don't want anything interesting of me, what's on your potent mind, Prof?"

His glare focused into a gaze of disturbing intensity. "I have a son," he announced.

She knew that, but had to maintain her pose. "Well, then, you must have looked under the skirt of some student demoness once. Never again, eh, Prof?"

"Cease your ludicrous efforts to bait me, Demoness. You know my son, Demon Prince Vore. He consumes others."

"Yes, I tried to seduce him once, but he ate me instead. He's a real brute. Maybe he mistook my candy-stripe undies for the real thing. What's your point, Prof? It's not like you to be so mushy about business."

She thought he would explode, but instead he deflated. "Touché, Demoness. You may indeed have the ability to accomplish my desire."

"No, I can't harangue a formerly self-respecting class into a mound of quivering mush," she said.

"I am speaking of your propensity for aggravation. I have not encountered any creature to better you in that respect."

"Why, thank you, Prof!" she said, turning pastel pink. "And to think I achieved it without completing one single assignment!"

"And supreme talent must be respected, whatever its nature. I want you to exert yourself on behalf of my son."

"I told you, when I tried—"

"He's young, foolish, and imperative. But it's time he matured. He is, after all, about twenty-three, in human terms."

"Which is twenty-three hundred in demon terms, but who's counting?"

"Precisely. I think the only thing that will settle him down is marriage."

"Now, wait, Prof! I'm already married."

"Yes, I remember. I performed the ceremony."

"And you *knew* I'd get half-souled and develop a conscience, love, loyalty, and all that," she said accusingly. "That I'd be hopelessly tied down by my new awareness of things right, proper, and decent."

"To be sure. And that is what I want for my son."

Her eyes went so round, they bowed out of her face. "Oh, Prof, you play dirty! Your son will rue the day he ever became related to you."

"Naturally. And some century he may even squeeze some of the mush from his skull. He actually does possess some qualities to be recommended. He is honorable, handsome, intelligent, and has fair judgment about things. He merely requires seasoning, to reduce his natural bloodthirstiness. Find me a souled woman for him to marry, and convince him to marry her. That is what I want from you, you impertinent tease."

"All that—in exchange for telling me where Jenny Elf is?"

"To be sure."

"I'd be crazy to make that deal!"

"Ask your worser self."

'Make that deal, blockhead,' Mentia said. 'The Professor always has something devious in mind. You have only to rise to the occasion.'

Metria sighed. Her worser self had good judgment in crazy situations, and she would have to trust that. "Agreed. So where's Jenny Elf?"

"In the naga caves."

"What's she doing there?"

"After she and Nada Naga were released from the Companions game, they found they liked each other. Nada invited Jenny to stay with them, and she accepted. She has been there ever since. Her cat has been useful when the naga wish to locate things, such as plaid diamonds.''

"Now, why didn't I think of that myself?'' Metria asked rhetorically.

"Because your skull is filled with mush. Now I shall expect to see my son ready for marriage within a fortnight.''

"Great expectations,'' she muttered as she popped off.

The naga caves were near the lair of Draco Dragon. The naga maintained reasonably cordial relations with the dragon, having a common enemy in the local goblin horde. Eventually Gwenny Goblin of Goblin Mountain would extend her authority to cover the cave goblins, but meanwhile they were their normal obnoxious selves. Fortunately the naga mutual-assistance treaty with the humans had shored up their resources, and the goblins had not been able to make headway against them.

She popped directly into the throne chamber. King Nabob was there, looking glum. He was in his natural form, that of a large serpent with a human head. He could become a full serpent or full human in form if he chose to, but evidently saw no need to when his natural form was so much better. "Hello, your majesty,'' she said. "I'm Demoness Metria, looking for Jenny Elf. Why so gourd canine?''

He turned his crowned head toward her, seeming unsurprised by her appearance. Probably his daughter had told him about the odd demoness. "Hello, Metria. What kind of emotion?''

"Sadness, grief, affliction, lamentation, suffering, mortification—''

"Melancholy?''

"Whatever,'' she agreed crossly.

He elected to be roundabout, as was the prerogative of senior heavyset Kings. "How is marriage treating you?''

"Actually, that's what brings me her, by a devious route that wouldn't interest you.''

"Well, it might. You see, I'm entertaining the monsters under my daughter's bed while she's out, and they really appreciate a good story.''

"But your daughter's adult! She shouldn't have monsters under her bed anymore."

"True. But Jenny Elf does, and I'm old enough to be in my second childhood, so Fingers now resides under my throne, and Knuckles joins him there at times."

"Oh. May I meet them?"

"Not if you're adult."

Woe Betide appeared. "Gee, I'd really like to meet them," she said, a huge tear welling.

The King nodded. "Certainly; I'll introduce you. Woe, here are Fingers and Knuckles McPalm. Monsters, this is Woe Betide, a childish demoness."

Two hands flickered briefly from the shadow under the throne. Bed monsters were very shy in daytime.

So Metria reverted and told him the story. "And now I need to locate Jenny Elf, so I can serve her with her summons, and borrow her cat. Nada too—she's on the jury list as well."

"They are off hunting plaid diamonds at the moment, but should return soon. Now I will tell you why I am so fruit dog, um, glum. It is because my daughter the Princess is twenty-six years old and unmarried, and my competence is fading. She must marry a Prince who can take over the reins and snows of power, yet she shows no sign of doing so."

"What of your fine handsome son, Prince Naldo? Can't he take the snows?"

"He married beneath him. Mind you, the merwoman is a fine figure of a woman, very fine, especially in salt water, but not fit to be Queen of the naga. So Nada will have to take up the slack, and beguile a suitable Prince soon. Otherwise our people will lose credence, and the goblins will gain confidence and encroach. Unfortunately, Princes do not grow on trees, and she refuses even to consider any who happen to be younger than she is. So she continues to get older, while the naga prospects wane."

Metria began to get a glimmer of the devious notion the Demon Professor had. He had known there was a highly eligible Princess here. "How about a demon prince?" she asked.

"Demons are soulless creatures, capable of any mischief, and not to be trusted."

"Suppose one got souled, or at least half-souled?"

"Why, then he would be eligible," Nabob said, surprised. "But demons seldom have souls, because they avoid them, knowing their consequence. In fact, it may be fairly stated that the only likely way to burden a demon with a soul is by trickery."

"Such as by marrying a mortal with a soul," Metria agreed. "And having one perform the ceremony in such a way that half the mortal's soul transfers."

"Exactly. How did you know?"

"I learned the hard way, when I married a mortal. I thought it was temporary, but I changed my mind when I got souled."

Nabob suddenly was extremely interested. "You know of a suitable demon Prince?"

"Prince Vore, Professor Grossclout's son. Grossclout wants him married within the fortnight. He believes a few decades of marriage would settle the Prince down, and maybe squeeze a bit of mush from his skull."

"This is fascinating news! But I can think of two significant objections."

"Vore and Nada," Metria said. "Neither will want to marry the other."

"Precisely. It is not feasible to apply coercive measures to royal scions. It's bad precedent, and makes for negative family relations. So I'm afraid this won't slither."

"Yet there must be a way. There's always a way to fulfill Grossclout's requirement, however devious. That's how he teaches his classes. It is merely necessary to squeeze the mush out and find it."

"I wonder," he said thoughtfully. "It reminds me of something probably irrelevant—"

"That's also the way Grossclout's examples work. I have seen it hundreds of times, in the course of ignoring his classes. The very thing a mushmind passes over as irrelevant turns out to be the answer."

"This is a story we tell our children about demon interference in human relations. I believe it actually derives from Mundania, where the only magic exists in their imagination. It's called the demons' beauty contest.''

"But demons can assume any form. I am beautiful because I choose to be; my inner essence is as ugly as ever. Any beauty contest among our kind would be meaningless.''

"True. My daughter's human form is beautiful for similar reason. So these demons had a different kind of contest. The male demon chose a very handsome mortal Prince, and the female chose a lovely mortal Princess. Or maybe it was the other way around. The judgement was which of the two mortals was better looking.''

"But demons wouldn't agree,'' she protested. "He would insist that his mortal was best, and she would insist that hers was best. Demons are extremely unreasonable, because their opinions are as malleable as their bodies.''

"Precisely. So they needed a different way to judge the contest— a way that did not depend on the opinions of demons.''

"But what would that be? They certainly wouldn't accept the opinions of mortals.''

"Yes they would. Or they did in the story. They brought the two fair mortals together naked and let *them* judge.''

"This is absolutely crazy! Two mortals who didn't even know each other? They'd both run in opposite directions. Mortals can be very skittish about clothing, or the lack of it. Especially when they are of opposite sexes.''

"It was handled in this manner: The demons caused the mortals to sleep deeply. They put them together, then woke them in turns. So he got to look at her while she slept, and then she got to look at him while he slept. Naturally the two reacted in certain ways, and the one who reacted most to the other was deemed to be the less beautiful. Thus did the demons stage and judge their beauty contest.''

Metria was thoughtful. "This is a most intriguing notion. Are you suggesting that we put your daughter and the professor's son together asleep, and stage a beauty contest? That might be interesting and fun to do, but it wouldn't get them married to each other.''

"Are you sure? In the story the demons satisfied themselves that the man was the prettier of the two, then put both to sleep again and returned them to their homes. But when the two mortals woke, far apart, each yearned for the other, and neither rested until they were together.''

"Because each had had a real chance to inspect the other at close range," Metria said. "That might indeed work. It is certainly worth a try. D. Vore is one terrific catch, and he is a Prince. Nada is Xanth's loveliest mortal female figure. They well might impress each other favorably, especially since both need to marry. But can we put them to sleep?''

"I have a sleeping potion I can slip to my daughter. Surely Professor Grossclout has something similar that will do for his son.''

"Then let's do it!" she exclaimed, gratified.

Soon Nada Naga and Jenny Elf arrived back, with a small bag of plaid diamonds. Metria quickly served them both with their summonses, and explained about the trial, while King Nabob slithered quietly away to make preparations.

Metria popped back to the demon caves to talk to Grossclout again.

"Professor! Something else.''

He paused, midway in a step toward the cowering class. "My patience is being strained somewhat beyond the incendiary point, Demoness," he rumbled.

"You want Vore to marry Nada, right? Suppose you make it a real occasion by marrying Grey Murphy and Princess Ivy at the same time? Nada and Ivy are close friends, and—''

"And it's been nine years," he agreed. "Ivy's mother procrastinated too. Very well.''

Metria smiled. "Thanks, Prof!" Then she told him what else was required.

Within the hour the arrangements had been made. The demons' beauty contest proceeded.

Demon Prince Vore woke to find himself in a strange situation. Wan light filtered down from above. He was in a small chamber whose walls extended well up beyond head height, and there were no doors or windows. Odder yet, there lay beside him a bare girl.

He looked again. This was no girl; this was a fully equipped mortal human-style woman. Her hair was reddish brown, and swirled around her body like a silken cloak. Her face was stunningly beautiful, and so was her body; he lifted her hair out of the way to make sure.

"If this is the creature my father has in mind for me to marry, she'll do," he remarked. "She looks good enough to eat. However, I have no intention of being coerced into anything, or of remaining cooped up here. I am, after all, a demon Prince, subject to the will of just about no one else."

He tried to pop off—but nothing happened. He tried to dematerialize, but again nothing happened. He tried to fly, and could not. His demonly powers had been somehow stripped from him. What had happened?

He checked the circular wall of the chamber. It was firm, without crevice or opening. He pushed against it, but it did not yield. He tried to climb up it, but could find no purchase.

Baffled, he returned to his consideration of the sleeping woman. "Who are you, lovely creature?" he inquired. She did not respond. He touched her slender arm, but she did not react. She was under a spell of some sort that kept her asleep.

A spell! That must be what had happened to him. Some magic had put him to sleep, and the lingering aftereffects still deprived him of his demonly powers. The girl might have been similarly enchanted, but being merely mortal, had not fought even partially out of it as he had.

Now he saw, almost hidden beneath the graceful mass of her tresses, a small golden crown set around her head. She was a Princess!

"Ah, but what a marvel of pulchritude you are, my dear," he remarked. "And a Princess too. I would love to have a tryst with you, were you awake. But as it is, I must let you be, for I am an honorable creature."

He sat beside her, watching her slow even breathing. It was most impressive. Then, suddenly, he knew no more.

Princess Nada Naga woke, surprised. One moment she had been about to retire in the pleasant cave she shared with Jenny Elf, and here she was in some strange chamber.

"Eeeeek!" she screamed, putting at least five *E*'s into it. There was a naked man lying beside her!

She scrambled to her feet, discovering in the process that she was nude herself. She tried to find the door, but there was none. Also no window. Only wan light sagging down from far above. She was in the bottom of a well!

She tried to change to serpent form, but could not. So she tried to revert to naga form, and could not do that either. Something was interfering with her natural shape-shifting ability. She realized that she had probably been put under some kind of spell, and had recovered from only part of it, so that she was now awake, but possessed of no other special abilities.

And this strange man must have been similarly treated. She sat down on the soft bed that filled the bottom of the well, and considered him more carefully. He was a handsome brute, firm of feature and muscular of body. And, as she peered more closely, she saw a light golden crown on his head. He was a Prince!

"I wish I had known about you before," she murmured appreciatively. "I have been looking for a suitable Prince for more time than I care to confess. But of course, you're probably obnoxious, as most males are, when awake." She peered yet more closely. "And you look to be about twenty-three years old. Too young for me, because I am twenty-six."

She pondered, and considered, and thought, and finally decided to take a chance and wake the handsome stranger. She spoke to him, but there was no response. She shook his shoulder, but he did not stir. Finally she tried her ultimate: She got down on her hands and knees, put her mouth to his, and kissed him. But it was no use; he continued to sleep. It was the first time such a thing had happened; she had been able almost to wake the dead with a kiss. Maybe that magic, too, had been stifled by the enchantment on her.

She sighed. Unable either to escape or to wake the man, she would simply have to wait this out. She lay down again beside him, took his hand in hers so that she would know if he stirred, and suddenly she was unconscious.

"So much for the beauty contest," Metria remarked. "Neither one of them really got hot." She was peering through the transparent cloud substance of the confinement tower. Or rather, into the big magic mirror that showed the distant tower as if it were made of glass.

"They're both decent folk," Jenny Elf said. "At least, I know Nada is. I think this plot of yours is crazy."

"They both need to be married," King Nabob said. "That's the point. This is merely stage one."

"I still think it won't work," Jenny said. But Sammy Cat, in her arms, looked thoughtful.

The two prisoners in the well woke together. "Oh!" Nada cried, and tried to change form, for it was not proper to be unclothed in human form with a strange man. But she remained unable to change. So she draped her hair across her torso, covering most of it, though parts of her insisted on poking through.

"You're awake!" Vore said, as startled as she.

"And so are you," she said, not unreasonably, hastily letting go of his hand.

He looked around, then down at his bare self. He tried to fashion clothing around himself, but that power, too, was inoperative. Realizing that there was nothing to be done about it, as his hair was not nearly as long as hers, he made the best of it. "Hello. I am Prince Vore."

"I am Princess Nada." For a reason neither understood, neither gave further identification.

"You are the most beautiful woman I can remember seeing." As a conversational gambit, this lacked finesse.

She, however, took it in stride. "And you are the handsomest man. Even if you are young."

He shrugged. "I am as I am. Do you know how we came to be confined here?"

"I was about to ask you that. One moment I was in my royal chamber; the next, I woke here—beside you. You were asleep."

"Oh? When I woke before, you were the one sleeping."

She pursed her lips, fashioning, if not a moue, at least not a neigh. "I think we have been enchanted."

"My thought exactly. But to what purpose?"

She considered. "I remember a story my father told me as a child, about a demons' contest—but that's irrelevant. Perhaps someone has abducted us, and means to hold us for ransom.''

"But why deprive us of our clothing?''

"So we can't escape without attracting notice?''

"Princess Nada, I think you would attract notice anywhere, regardless of your attire.''

"I presume you mean that as a compliment.''

"I do.''

"Then I thank you. Do you think we can get out of this well?''

He cast about. The soft stuff of which the bed was made seemed malleable. He drew some forth and fashioned it into a cord. "Perhaps, if this is strong enough, I can make a rope that will reach the turret above.''

"I will help you,'' she said immediately.

They got to work on it forthwith, and such was their mutual dexterity that they soon had a fine strong rope forming. Her fingers were nimble for the fine threads, and his hands were strong for the stout rope. She admired his hands, among other things, and he admired her fingers, among other things.

When they had a sufficient length, he made a loop at one end and flung it up so that it neatly caught on a turret. Then he hauled himself up, hand over hand, his muscles straining because he wasn't used to climbing a wall the hard way. He reached the top, sat on the turret, and peered down. "Your turn, Nada!'' he called.

She shook her head. "I'm afraid I lack your strength, Vore. I cannot haul myself up in the forthright manner you did. Perhaps you should go and see if you can win your freedom.''

He gazed at her a bit more closely, and saw that while most of his own extra flesh was in the form of muscles on his arms, most of hers was in the form of curvature on her torso and legs. That would indeed not do for hand-over-hand climbing. "By no means, Nada. Make a loop at the bottom and sit in it, and I will haul you up.''

She did so, and soon he had brought her also to the top. Then they both looked around.

They were perched on the top of a tower, which was part of a formidable castle. The castle was on a white island in a dark blue sea.

"Should we make own way down and then inquire within the castle?" Nada asked.

"I like your trusting nature. But I suspect that whoever or whatever occupies this castle is what has imprisoned us, and we should avoid contact if we possibly can."

"I like your sensible caution. Indeed, you are surely correct, and my notion was foolish. What else should we do?"

For a moment they faced each other, and each became further aware that the other was of wondrously aesthetic aspect as well as possessing trust and caution that nicely complemented each other. But their situation was too precarious to allow them much chance for reflection.

"Maybe we should get down and try to find a boat," she said.

"Agreed. And some clothing. Though I admit it is no great burden to behold you as you are."

She blushed half a shade, becoming twice as pretty, though that was impossible. He might be young, but there was something about him. "I might say the same for you."

Then he lowered her to the ground, and handed himself down. He jerked on the rope, and the loop came off the turret and fell to the ground beside them.

They skulked around the castle, hiding in the shade of the walls. They found what might be a locked boatshed. Vore was going to bash it open, but Nada cautioned him about the noise. Instead she slipped a twisted thread from the rope in through the latch-hole and managed to lift the inner latch. Thus they got inside the boatshed silently. "How can a Princess have developed such skill at thievery?" Vore asked admiringly.

"I once had a certain passion for cookies, which were kept locked up," she confessed. "So I learned how to acquire them without attracting attention."

There was a small airboat inside. Vore put it into the air, and it floated. "I had expected a waterboat," he said, "but this will do."

Nada climbed in, and Vore pushed the boat out the open door, then got in himself. It sank a bit lower in the air because of their weight, but floated well enough. Vore took the oars and stroked, and the little craft moved smoothly in the opposite direction.

There was a noise in the castle. "Oops, someone is stirring," Nada said, alarmed. "We must flee before they spy us."

Vore put his back into it, and the boat fairly shot out from the castle. Now Nada looked down and discovered that what surrounded the castle wasn't water, but sky blue air. No wonder there was an airboat! The castle was floating in the air, on a cloud.

Soon they were able to hide behind another cloud, out of view of the castle. Their escape seemed to be successful.

"But we didn't find any clothes," Vore said, remembering.

"Perhaps I can do something about that," Nada said. "You row us down the ground and see if you recognize any landmarks. I will unravel our rope and try to weave some cloth." She proceeded to do just that, her fingers becoming nimble again.

"You have amazing skills for a Princess," Vore remarked appreciatively.

"Well, as a Naga Princess, I need to. The goblins press us pretty hard, and no one can be slack."

"You are naga?" he asked, surprised.

"Oh, I can say that now," she said, surprised myself. "The effects of that spell must be wearing further off. Yes, I am Princess Nada Naga, once betrothed to Prince Dolph Human but now adrift, as it were. Does that dismay you?"

"There might have been a time when it would have," he said. "But now that I know you, it has the opposite effect. Can you change to serpent form?"

"I will try." Suddenly she was a coiled serpent. Then her human head appeared on the serpent's body. "Yes, my powers are returning." She returned to full human form.

"Then perhaps mine are also," Vore said. "I am a demon."

"A demon!"

"Prince D. Vore. Does that dismay you?"

"Yes, for I was coming to like you."

He puffed into smoke, then re-formed in human guise. "Yes, I can now do demonly things. But why does this dismay you?"

"Because now you will pop away forever in a cloud of mocking laughter, and I will understand how foolish I have been to think you were nice. For a demon has no soul, and therefore no conscience, and cannot love.''

Vore considered. ''Once that might have been the case. But I have come to know you, and I think that since I have been constrained by my father to marry, you are the one I would like to wed. You have qualities I never appreciated in a mortal creature before, and you are a Princess.''

Nada laughed, somewhat bitterly. ''I don't think any male ever noticed qualities in me, only my form. But you would not want to marry me, because then you might get half my soul, and become bound in a way you have never been before.''

''I realize that. But perhaps it would be worth it. Could you spare half your soul?''

''For marriage to a Prince of demons? I think I could. Even if he is young.''

''Well, I am twenty-three hundred years old.''

''Which is equivalent to twenty-three in human terms. I never thought I'd love a younger man.'' She shrugged. ''But these things happen, and allowances have to be made.''

The boat came to rest on the ground. ''Then perhaps our interests coincide,'' Vore said. ''I think we should make it formal, before our captors or pursuers strike again.'' He took her hand. ''Princess Nada, will you—''

A dragon erupted from a nearby cave and launched itself toward them. Nada immediately became a huge serpent, and Vore's free hand sprouted a wickedly gleaming sword.

The dragon hesitated.

''—marry me?'' Vore continued.

The dragon decided to attack after all. But the serpent chomped it on the neck, and the demon thrust the sword hilt-deep up its nose. The dragon sneezed, not being completely comfortable, and backed away.

Nada's human head appeared on the serpent. ''Yes,'' she said.

The sword disappeared. The demon took the serpent body in his arms and kissed the human face. ''We are betrothed,'' he said.

''Agreed,'' she said, resuming full human form. Then they kissed again.

Suddenly several people stood around them. One was the Demon

Professor Grossclout. "I heard that!" he said triumphantly. "I shall perform the ceremony at the Nameless Castle from which you just escaped, right after the trial is over."

Another was King Nabob. "So did I. The wedding will be within a fortnight. There will be an alliance between the naga and the demons."

A third was the Demoness Metria. "And it serves you right," she said. Then she turned to the fourth. "Jenny Elf, I need to borrow your cat."

Jenny was startled. "My cat? Sammy?"

"Yes. The Professor wouldn't tell me where to find you, until I agreed to get his son married. Now that's done, so I can get on with my mission."

Nada and Vore both turned to her. "Mission?" Nada asked, somehow seeming not entirely pleased. "I thought you came to serve Jenny and me our summonses."

"That, too."

"This was arranged?" Vore asked, seeming curiously similarly displeased.

"Sure. It was the demons' beauty contest."

Vore and Nada exchanged a glance fraught with something or other. "We should break the be—" Nada started.

Grossclout fixed her with his patented glare, stopping her in mid-word. "I think not."

"She's right," Vore said. "We should not tolerate such interference in our—"

"Look at her and say it," King Nabob said.

Vore looked at Nada. Nada looked at Vore. He saw Xanth's most beautiful woman, and a Princess. She saw a considerably handsome and talented man, and a Prince. Each saw a truly worthwhile match. Then their respective willpowers melted and they kissed again.

"We shall name the grandchild DeMonica," Grossclout said, and Nabob nodded agreement.

"I guess you can borrow Sammy," Jenny Elf said to Metria.

7
AISLE

W hat is it you need to find?'' Jenny asked, keeping firm hold of Sammy Cat so he wouldn't bound away to find it the moment it was spoken.

''Arnolde Centaur.''

''A centaur? Couldn't you just ask at one of the centaur villages, or at Centaur Isle?''

''I did. The centaurs of Centaur Isle won't even speak of him, because they think magic in a centaur is obscene; I'm sure he's not there. Centaurs in other places haven't seen him in years. They say he must be one hundred twenty-six years old by now, if he's still alive. But Com Pewter says he's still around somewhere. I just have to find him.''

''He must be a very special centaur.''

''He is. He's a Magician who can make an aisle of magic in Mundania. I need him to go after the Mundanes on my list.''

''Mundanes?''

''Dug and Kim. They—''

''Oh, yes! I was Kim's Companion in the game, three years ago.''

Metria paused. ''That's right; I've been doing so many things, I'm forgetting who knows what. And Nada was Dug's Companion. He kept trying to get a glimpse of her panties.''

''And got expelled from the game for it, she tells me,'' Jenny agreed, laughing. "After that he behaved, and became a tolerably good person. Kim was a bit wild too, at first, but settled down. It will be great to see them again."

"We will. I have to get them both to that trial on time, or the Simurgh won't consider my job to be done, and the Good Magician won't tell me how to get the stork's notice."

Jenny cocked her head. "You haven't learned how to do that?"

Metria smiled. "I summoned the stork centuries ago. But I didn't stay to take care of my baby girl. I think after that the stork decided I wasn't a suitable address for deliveries, so it ignores my signals, though I am now married and half-souled and intend to be a good mother."

"Maybe you just haven't sent enough of them. I understand that some messages get lost."

"Seven hundred and fifty in a year?"

Jenny pursed her lips. "I guess you do need some help. The stork has tuned you out." She looked around. "Well, let's get started. Sammy may outrun me, so you will have to keep him in sight. I'll catch up eventually; I always do." She set the orange cat down. "Sammy, we need to find Arnolde Centaur."

The cat was off in a bound, an orange streak amidst the foliage. "Wait for me!" Jenny cried futilely, chasing after him.

Metria didn't wait; she sailed in pursuit of the feline. The cat was fast, but not as fast as a demoness. So they zoomed along through forest and field, upscale and downscale, and across rivers, mountains, and deserts.

Then Sammy paused. There was a creature standing in the way. It was larger and shaggier than the cat, and looked dangerous. It seemed to be some kind of oink. But Sammy didn't seem frightened, just bored.

"And of course, the economics of infrastructure must also be considered," the oink was saying. "These consist of fifteen overlapping conditions that must be predicated on inversely bludgeoning circumstances, with due allowance for rapprochement incentives and integral negations."

"What in Xanth are you?" Metria demanded. "Aside from being the dullest creature I've encountered recently."

The oink glanced at her. "I'm a wild bore, of course. It is my business to bore you to death."

"You don't have to stand for this," Metria told the cat. "Just go on around him."

That broke Sammy's seeming trance of boredom, and he skirted the bore and resumed running.

Jenny arrived. "Wait for me!" she cried.

"Certainly," the bore said.

"No you don't," Metria said. "Go around him."

Jenny obediently moved to the side, where some pretty yellow vines were growing up along the trees. But Metria recognized the vines. "Not that way!" she called.

Jenny pulled back, but the wild bore, barging after her, crashed into the vines. Suddenly there was a thick yellow splatter of fluid, drenching him. "Oh, ugh!" he squealed. "Ammonia!"

"Not exactly," Metria said. "Those are golden showers climbing rose vines." Then she zoomed on after the cat, seeing that Jenny had gotten safely past the bore, who would have to go somewhere to wash himself off.

Then they came to a lake, and in the lake was an island in the shape of a bone. The lake seemed to extend a good distance to either side, so the fastest way to pass it was right across the island, and that was the way Sammy was going. But Sammy did seem to be a bit nervous, and he actually slowed enough to allow Jenny Elf to catch up. Then he walked across a dog-eared bridge onto the island.

"No wonder!" Metria muttered. "This is Dog Island."

Indeed, the island's shore was lined with doghouses, and all manner of dogs were out sunbathing. In fact, they were hot dogs. A stone promontory was covered with Scots on the rocks. The water was filled with dogfish, and old sea dogs, and lapdogs were swimming around and around the island.

Sammy stepped on tippy toes, not making a sound, so as to pass without notice. Metria formed into a haze and surrounded Jenny so she wouldn't be discovered. There was just no telling how these dogfaces would react to this intrusion on their retreat.

The forest inshore was filled with dogwood, dog fennel, dogtooth violents, dog mercury, and dog rose, all of which sniffed the air and growled suspiciously. There was also an occasional have of B-gles. Metria knew that the B-haves could be very bad; because their stings affected people's B-havior.

In the center of the island was a snowy mountain. Anyone who wanted to sleep warmly there would have to snuggle up with an afghan hound. Dogsleds were being hauled up to the top. On the peak was the robot dog, Dog-Matic, who thought he was reciting fine poetry but only spewed doggerel.

They forged doggedly through, and finally traversed a dog's-leg curve leading to a bridge to the far side of the lake, marked "K-9." They had passed Dog Island without getting chewed. Metria was relieved, because though she had nothing to fear from dogfaces herself, Sammy Cat certainly did.

Once safely past the island, Sammy plunged on at speed, leaving Jenny behind again. But now the terrain was becoming vaguely familiar. "Oh, no!" Metria muttered. "Not the Region of Madness again!"

But it was. They were approaching it from a different direction, so wouldn't encounter Desiree Dryad or the White family, which meant that the perils would be unfamiliar. Metria wasn't sure she would be able to protect cat and elf girl here, because the things of the unexplored madness could be truly freakish. Yet the cat was plowing straight on in.

"I'll take over now," Mentia said. "The worse it gets, the saner I get."

Just as well, because it wasn't long before something weird appeared before them. It was a manlike figure, but it looked like a mummified zombie. It reached for Sammy.

Mentia stretched out her arm to three times its prior length, and put her hand between the thing and the cat. Its hand touched her hand—and suddenly her hand and arm stiffened. "What *are* you?" she demanded.

"I am Rigor Mortis," the thing replied in ghastly tones. "I make folk stiff."

For sure. Mentia stiffened her resolve and shoved the thing to the side so that Jenny Elf could pass. Because demons had no fixed forms, they could not be stiffened for long, but it would be another matter for living folk.

Then Mentia zoomed ahead, so as to keep the cat in sight. She wondered how the elf had managed not to lose Sammy in the years they had been in Xanth, because the cat seemed to have no regard for Jenny's convenience.

Beyond the zombielike creature was a grove of angular trees wherein perched strangely thin birds. Sammy Cat plunged right on through it, but again Mentia was rational and cautious, in contrast to her normal disposition. She wanted to know exactly what these odd birds were.

So she inquired, because here in the madness, things were often communicative in ways they wouldn't be normally. "What are you?" she called to the birds.

"We are minus birds," they chorused back. "As you can plainly see, because we live here in the geome-trees."

"I apologize for my stupidity," Mentia said, realizing that flattery was probably better than irritation. "Are either you or the trees dangerous to ordinary folk?"

"No, we don't care about ordinary folk," the birds replied. "All we care about is multiplying."

"Oh—you get together with plus birds to signal the stork?"

"No, we can't find any plus birds, so we multiply by dividing in half." With that each bird split in half, forming two where each one had perched, each new one twice as thin.

Jenny Elf caught up. "Oh, what pretty birds!" she exclaimed. The minus birds preened, pleased.

Mentia jumped ahead again—and was relieved to see an old centaur just making the acquaintance of the cat. Sammy had found Arnolde.

"And what is your oddity, pretty feline?" the centaur asked.

Mentia caused a flowing ankle-length robe to surround her as she approached. "Arnolde Centaur, I presume?"

"And a demoness," the centaur said, surprised. "Make a note, Ichabod: two seemingly normal creatures in as many minutes, which is highly unusual for this region."

Now Mentia saw that Arnolde had a companion, an old human man. The man opened his notebook, and several notes popped out, making brief music. "One mundane cat, no apparent magic," Ichabod said. "One unusually sober demoness."

"That cat's magic talent is to find anything except home," Mentia said. "Now he has found you, Arnolde Centaur, and your nonentitious companion. As for me—I am normally slightly crazy, but in the Region of Madness I am slightly sane. I am not certain about you two, however."

Arnolde blinked, seeming to actually see her as an individual for the first time. "Are you real?" he inquired. "Not a mere semblance?"

Mentia's rationality took hold. "Oh, you think I'm something crazy in the madness? A manifestation, instead of a real creature? That I can appreciate! Yes, I am real, and here comes Jenny Elf, who is also real." For Jenny was now arriving.

"I apologize for mistaking you for part of the local fauna," Arnolde said. "Yes, I am Arnolde Centaur, and this is my friend from Mundania, Ichabod Archivist. We are performing a survey of mad artifacts."

"Hello, Arnolde and Ichabod," Mentia said. "I am the Demoness Mentia, the worser half of the Demoness Metria."

The old eyes brightened with recognition. "Metria! She is notorious."

"She's married now, and has half a soul, so has settled down. Now she's doing an errand for the Good Magician, or for the Simurgh, so she can find out how to get the stork's attention. Seems there was some business a bit over four centuries ago that annoyed the stork, so it won't make any further deliveries to her, no matter how hard or often she signals it."

"I can imagine," Arnolde said. "Do you mind showing Ichabod your legs?"

Mentia knew that the centaur was anything but stupid, even by centaur terms, and she wanted to get his cooperation. So she lifted the hem of the gown and flashed excellent legs at the old man. His eyes immediately glazed over.

Jenny Elf picked up Sammy. "I guess you won't need him now, so we can go."

"Um, maybe better not to depart right now," Mentia said. "It might not be safe. Soon we'll be leaving the madness, and then you can go your way more safely." She let her gown drop back into place, and the man's eyes began to recover. It was clear that he had a taste for attractive legs.

"But this doesn't seem so bad," Jenny said. "Not compared to what it was like when I came here with Dug Mundane."

"Oh, I wouldn't recommend a little girl like you going alone through this region," Ichabod said.

"I'm eighteen, and big for an elf," Jenny said defensively.

"An elf? Why, so you are!" Ichabod agreed, surprised. "But not like one I have cataloged before. Your hands are four-fingered and your ears are pointed, and you don't seem to be associated with an elf elm."

"I'm from the World of Two Moons," Jenny explained.

"Two Moons?" the man asked blankly. "I am certain I haven't cataloged that."

"It's a different magic realm. I came to Xanth following Sammy Cat, who found a centaur wing feather here, but then we couldn't find our way home."

"But surely you have but to ask the cat to find some other person or object in your home realm, close to where you know your home to be," Arnolde said intelligently.

"No, I tried that, but it didn't work. I think he can't find anything anywhere near home, unless he is already at home."

"Then give him some reverse wood, so he can't find anything *but* home," Ichabod suggested.

"No, that didn't work either," Jenny said. "The reverse wood just made him unable to find anything he looked for."

"Reverse wood is treacherous stuff," Mentia said. "That's why they never tried to put it in the Golden Horde goblins' hate spring, to make it a love spring. It might just make everyone hate the water. Same goes for using it to make Com Pewter good instead of evil; it might reverse him in some other way, making him worse."

"True," Ichabod said. "It was hoped that reverse wood would

enable a basilisk's stare to bring dead folk back to life, but it merely caused the basilisk to wipe itself out. They tried to use it to reverse the spell that had transformed people to fish in the Fish River, but instead it turned the fish into water and the water into fish.''

"I remember when a kid had the talent of giving folk hotseats," Mentia said, smiling. "Someone slipped reverse wood into his trouser pocket, hoping it would make him give himself a hotseat, but the next time he tried to use his talent, he got wet pants."

Jenny laughed. "Served him right!"

"That time it worked well," Ichabod agreed. "But not in the expected way. So reverse wood doesn't seem to be the answer for your search for home."

Arnolde frowned, orienting on the intellectual challenge. "Perhaps if you got one of those magic disposal bubbles, and directed it to take you home."

"That neither," Jenny said. "It just wouldn't go."

"It is almost as if your home no longer—" Ichabod started, then stifled it.

"No longer exists," Jenny finished firmly. "I recognized that some time ago. But it could be that my family is all right. If the Holt burned, they would move. But there would be no way for me to find the new home from here."

"Do you dislike it here?" Arnolde asked.

"No. I have been here six years now, and I'm not sure I really want to go home any more. I only wish—"

"That there were others of your particular type," Arnolde concluded. "I know the feeling, being the only centaur Magician in Xanth. I was exiled from my home of Centaur Isle because of that, and can never return."

Jenny looked at him, suddenly warming to him. "Yes!"

"Or being the only completely unmagical Mundane in a magical land," Ichabod said. "Fortunately there are some cheering sights here."

Mentia realized why Arnolde had asked her to show her legs before: for the tonic effect on his friend. She fogged out her gown, showing them again.

"Why did you seek me out?" Arnolde inquired.

"My better half's errand for the Simurgh requires her to round up Jurors for a big trial. Two of them are Mundanes, so—"

"Mundanes!" Ichabod exclaimed.

"Dug and Kim," Mentia agreed. "They visited here three years ago, playing a game, and Kim won a magic talent as a prize. Then they went home to Mundania. Now they are on the list, and must be summoned here to decide Roxanne Roc's fate."

"The big bird in the Nameless Castle?" Arnolde asked. "What did she do?"

Mentia shrugged. "No one seems to know. But once I get all the people summoned and delivered, maybe we'll all find out."

"So you wish me to take you into Mundania," Arnolde said. "To find those two Jurors."

"Exactly. The summons tokens will indicate the way, but I'm a demoness. I can't leave the magic realms. But if I can arrange to take magic with me—"

"And this trial is required by the Simurgh herself?"

"Yes."

"Then it behooves me to facilitate it. I suppose my labor here can wait a while." Then his eye caught something. It looked like a large fly, but it had several buttons on its body. "There's a specimen! Note it, Ichabod."

Ichabod opened his notebook, and several more notes popped musically out. "One buttoned fly," he said, marking it in his book.

"Are they dangerous?" Jenny asked.

"Only when they get unbuttoned," Ichabod replied with an obscure smile.

Mentia changed the subject. "Exactly how long have you been surveying mad artifacts?"

Arnolde exchanged a glance with Ichabod. "About twenty eight years," the centaur said. "Ever since I retired from the kingship of Xanth. I went to Mundania and fetched my friend, who wished to retire in Xanth, and whose archivistic skill complements my specialty of alien archaeology. This is a fascinating region, and until last year, it was expanding."

"Yes, the Time of No Magic voided a confining spell, and allowed the madness to expand,'' Mentia said. ''But we fixed that last year, and now the madness is retreating.''

''*You* fixed it?'' he asked incredulously.

''Well, it was a joint effort. Mainly Gary Gargoyle, but I helped. We were in Stone Hinge.''

''That's a mere ruin, thousands of years old. How could you—''

''Two thousand years old,'' she agreed. ''We visited the deep past in a joint vision. It's a long story.''

Arnolde shook his head, bemused. ''It must be.'' He exchanged another glance with his friend. ''Are you ready to revisit Mundania, Ich?''

''In your company, certainly. Without it, I fear I would soon perish of old age.''

Mentia glanced at Arnolde. ''You're pretty old yourself, centaur, for a mortal. Over a century and a quarter. How is it that you haven't faded away long since?''

''We have wondered about that,'' Arnolde confessed. ''Though I am a Magician, my talent does not relate to age, and of course, Ichabod lacks magic entirely. We conjecture that the ambience of madness has had, if not a rejuvenating effect, a stabilizing one, so that we remain healthy as long as we remain in it. This encourages our continuance of our survey, apart from its value as information.''

Mentia nodded. ''I know some Mundanes who live here, who I think would be dead in Mundania. There's something about the madness.''

''It is, after all, Xanth's most intense magic,'' Arnolde pointed out. ''It may have effects that normal magic does not. We have not been inclined to question this blessing.''

''But if you leave the madness—what then?'' Jenny asked.

''Actually I have on occasion stepped outside the madness,'' Arnolde said. ''I noticed no deleterious effect. My conjecture is that I have become so charged with magic that my aisle in effect extends into Xanth. That is, that I now generate an aisle of madness that keeps me and Ichabod healthy wherever we go. Of course, this could not be expected to last indefinitely, but it will be intriguing to test it in Mundania.''

"Great!" Mentia said. "We can get Jenny out of the madness, then move on toward the isthmus. We'll have to step along, as it will take several days for you folk to traverse Xanth, and we don't have time to spare, but—"

"We may be able to accelerate it, if you can summon assistance for traveling," Ichabod said.

Mentia hadn't thought of that. "I know a giant who was in the madness last year. Maybe if I can locate him—"

Sammy leaped from Jenny's arms and bounded away through the madness. Jenny scrambled after him. "Wait for me!"

"No!" Mentia cried. "You stay here, Jenny; I'll follow him, and bring him back."

Jenny looked doubtful, but stopped running. Mentia floated rapidly after the cat.

This was just as well, because Sammy, still not properly familiar with the madness, was getting in trouble. A huge ant with patterns of stripes on its forelegs was blocking the way. "Company— HALT!" the ant bawled.

Sammy, startled, halted. But Metria didn't. "What are you?" she demanded of the ant.

"I am Sarge. I give the orders around here."

"Well, Sarge Ant, I rank you, because I am a Cap Tain." She formed herself into a large floating cap with the word TAIN printed across it.

"YesSIR! the ant agreed, saluting with a foreleg. "What are your orders, sir?"

"Carry on, Sarge. Just tell me what threats there might be to a traveling cat in this vicinity."

"Just King Bomb, sir."

"What's he King of?"

"The ticks, sir. He's a tick. He has a very short fuse."

Mentia considered. She knew that ticks could be bad mischief in real Xanth, and possibly worse here. Still, a short-tempered tick named Bomb didn't seem too formidable. "What's his given name?"

"Time, sir."

"How can we tell when we're near him?"

"You can hear him ticking, sir."

"Thank you, Sarge. Dismissed."

The ant went his way. So did Sammy, bounding on through the madness. But he paused just a moment, glancing back. "Wait for me!" Mentia cried, catching the hint. Then the cat forged ahead at full feline velocity.

But soon Mentia heard an ominous ticking. They were approaching King Bomb! So she zoomed ahead. Sure enough, there was a tick shaped like bloated sphere standing squarely in the path the cat would take. He looked extremely irritable, likely to explode at any moment.

Mentia came to float directly before him. "Tick King Time Bomb, blow this joint," she said.

The King's tiny eyes glared at her. "Begone yourself, Demoness! I'll have no truck with thee." His ticking got louder.

"That's what you think, Bomb bast. Get out of here before I set you off."

"This is an outrage!" the King declared, growing larger as his ticking intensified.

Mentia discovered an egg plant growing nearby. She picked an egg and hurled it at the King. It splattered on his metallic torso, the white and yoke drooling down.

That did it. The King detonated. The explosion blasted a hole in the ground and sent shrapnel into the surrounding treetrunks, but of course, it didn't hurt Mentia.

Sammy appeared. He bounded across the smoking crater and went on, unconcerned.

Mentia followed. Suddenly the cat stopped. He was before a large dent in the forest floor that was shaped like a human posterior. Mentia knew they were in the presence of a monstrous invisible man, who was sitting on the forest floor. The smell was so bad that she abolished her nose. It was as if a garbage factory with indigestion had burned halfway down.

"Hello, Jethro Giant," Mentia said. "Remember me? I'm the Demoness Mentia. We met last year."

"Oh, yes," Jethro agreed. "Has it been that long? I was just getting ready to get up and go."

"I will gladly show you the way out, if you will help me carry a few people to the edge of Xanth."

"That seems like an amicable deal. Stand back."

Mentia snatched up the cat and floated back. There was a huge grunt and heave, and two monstrous footprints replaced the bottom-shaped indentation. Then an enormous invisible hand came down to take her. "Where are your people?" Jethro asked.

Mentia described the direction, and the giant tromped that way. In only a few steps they arrived at the glade where man, centaur, and elf waited, holding their noses as they turned greenish.

Mentia floated down. "Think of sweet violets," she suggested as she handed Sammy, who looked somewhat green instead of orange himself, to Jenny. "Jethro Giant is a nice guy."

Then the huge hand came down and picked them gently up. "Where to?" the voice sounded from far above.

Mentia floated up to invisible ear level, and directed him toward the edge of madness. In two steps they were out of it. Then Jethro strode rapidly forward toward the edge of Xanth, and the resulting wind blew most of the odor away. The mortals were able to resume breathing.

"Oh, this is interesting!" Jenny cried, peering down through the invisible hand. "Xanth looks just like a map."

"Oops," Mentia said. "I forgot to set you down when we left the madness."

"Don't bother. I know Kim and Dug, and would like to see them again, and Sammy can help you find them. Besides, we're all going to the same place in the end. To that weird trial. It's nice being on a quest, of a sort."

"An elf quest? That makes so much sense, I'll have to ignore it," Mentia said.

"No, just put your uncrazy better half in charge," Jenny said. "I always sort of liked her, even if she did drive me crazy."

"Oh? Why do you asseverate that?"

"Why do I what that?"

"Declare, avow, attest, proclaim, expound, announce—"

"Assert?"

"Whatever!"

"Welcome back, Metria!"

"It's nice to rejoin you, too, odd elf. What are you going to do, now that your friend Nada has found true love, or at least a husband?"

"I don't know. Maybe I should ask Magician Trent to transform someone for me, as he did for Gloha Goblin-Harpy."

"Yes, and in the process I wound up married too," Metria agreed reminiscently.

"You did it to save her from mischief."

"Well, my half soul gave me a conscience, so I had to."

"But didn't you save her before you got your conscience?"

Metria paused, sorting it out. "Yes, I suppose so. But I wanted to find out what love was like."

They looked out across Xanth. "Oh, look!" Jenny exclaimed. "There's a light house."

Metria looked. Sure enough, the house was floating through the air, carried along by the wind. "That's a very light house," she agreed.

"But what's that?" Jenny asked, alarmed, as she looked in another direction.

Metria looked again. "Oh, that's an air plain," she explained. "Where flying centaurs can graze."

Indeed, four winged centaurs were standing on the cloudlike plain, picking berry, bread, and grape fruits.

"And there's an air male," Jenny said, as the centaur stallion waved to her with his wings. "Hi, Cheiron!"

"Wait a half a moment!" Metria said. "How can there be four flying centaurs there? Che and Cynthia are at Castle Roogna until the trial. There should be only Cheiron and Chex."

"Oh, didn't you know?" Jenny asked. "The stork brought two more foals to them last year. Actually centaurs don't use storks, because their foals are too heavy, but—"

"Two more foals?"

"Chelsy and Cherish. Twins. Maybe they were taking their naps when you visited the family."

"Maybe so," Metria agreed doubtfully.

Meanwhile the giant was striding obliviously on, soon leaving the floating plain behind. Jenny looked ahead. "Oops."

Metria followed her gaze a third time. "Oh, it's just a storm."

"Not just any storm. That's Fracto!"

Metria peered at the cloud more closely. "Why, so it is. I remember when he was just another demon, before he specialized in cloud-craft."

"He always comes at the worst time, to mess up whatever others are doing."

"Of course. He's a demon."

"Are you like that?"

"I used to be, as you know. I just had a more delicate contiguity."

"A more delicate what?"

"Concurrence, immediacy, propinquity, proximity, pressure, sensation—"

"Touch?"

"Whatever," she agreed crossly. "Demonesses just aren't as violent as demons, but our mischief is equivalent." She thought of King Gromden and Threnody. Those were the bad old days, when she helped bring down kingdoms with her sex appeal. Windbag Fracto never achieved that.

"Well, maybe he'll fail this time," Jenny said, "because Jethro Giant is too big to be blown away."

"But it should be fun watching him try."

The storm swelled up grotesquely as the giant strode toward it. Dark clouds reached up for the sky, and down for the ground. Thunderbirds and lightningbugs spun in the swirling air currents. Rain splatted against the giant's invisible body, outlining it in glistening water.

"I'll fetch rain coats," Metria said, and popped off. She found an old, ancient, worn-out storm, and took a sheet of its rain, fashioning it into several capes. Because the rain was tired, it no longer had the energy to wet things down, and just hung there inertly.

She returned with the coats. "Put these on; they will keep the wild new water off you," she told Jenny, Arnolde, and Ichabod.

"Oh, a translucent plastic raincoat," Ichabod said, pleased.

"Exactly." Metria didn't find it necessary to clarify the precise nature of the coats.

It was just as well they had the rain coats, because now the giant was striding over Lake Tsoda Popka, and the storm was sucking up water from all the different-flavored little lakelets, so that it was raining popka. Jenny put out her cupped hands and caught some of it, so that she could drink. "Oooo, it's extra fizzy!" she said. "It must have been freshly stirred up."

Ichabod did the same, but as he drank, he jumped. "Who kicked me?" he demanded.

Arnolde laughed. "You happened to catch some boot rear."

They passed over the With-a-Cookee River. Now assorted cookies pelted them. Jenny caught a pecan sandy and threw it away, because she cared to eat neither sand nor the other stuff. But soon she caught a spiraled punwheel and ate that. Arnolde caught some chocolate chip cookie crumbs, and Ichabod a piece of gingerbread. Unfortunately all the fragments were somewhat soggy from the rain.

Fracto stormed on, but could not blow away the giant, who simply forged obliviously on, though his head was in the clouds. They passed a glittering river formed of tumbling crystals, and a huge mattress whose projecting springs were silver. "What's that?" Jenny asked.

"Crystal River and Silver Springs, of course," Arnolde replied. He was good with geography, as all centaurs were.

"Of course," Jenny echoed. "How silly of me not to recognize them. There's just so much of Xanth I haven't yet seen. New things keep surprising me."

Eventually they reached the isthmus. Jethro gently set them down by a tree covered with mouths. "This is as far as I can go," he said. "My head is starting to poke up out of the magic."

Now that they were no longer moving rapidly, the smell was catching up. "That's fine, Jeth!" Jenny called. "Thanks a whole lot!" Then she stifled a gag.

"Welcome." The giant strode invisibly away, and the air slowly cleared.

But the mouths on the tree had taken in some of the stench, and were mouthing gasps. "What kind of tree is that?" Jenny asked.

"A two-lips tree, I think," Arnolde answered.

Then a mouth opened wide. "Repent now!" it preached. "The end is near!"

"My mistake," the centaur said. "Those are apoca-lips."

Metria brought out the token with Kim's name. "That way," she said as it tugged.

They moved along as a group, Metria leading the way. Soon they came to the Interface between Xanth and Mundania. It had been intangible through most of Xanth's history, Metria understood, but since they had recompiled it last year, it had sharpened up considerably, and was now a scintillating zone of intense magic. "We had better hold hands as we cross," Metria said, "so that we'll all return to this same spot when we cross back."

"Correct," Arnolde said. "That will fix us as a party. But I am surprised that a demoness knows or cares about such intricacies."

"I helped fix it," she reminded him. "It's the Interface that confines the madness in the center, as well as keeping most Mundanes out, so Xanth isn't constantly swamped by hordes of dreary unmagical beings."

"So it keeps magic both in and out! We really must talk at greater length, in due course," he said.

Metria shrugged, hardly interested. "Maybe someday."

"However, now that we are about to depart from Xanth, I must caution you that the magic will be limited to a narrow aisle, of which I will be the center." He smiled briefly. "Or the centaur, as you prefer. If you wander beyond that aisle, you will lose your magic, whatever it is. Ichabod, of course, has little to fear, being naturally Mundane—"

"Except that I might suddenly expire of old age," the archivist said.

"But you, Metria, could disappear entirely. So I recommend that you stay quite close to me for this interim." He smiled. "Perhaps we shall have that dialogue sooner than anticipated."

"Whatever," Metria agreed crossly.

They passed through the Interface. There was a slight tingle, and that was all; the land beyond was much the same as regular Xanth. But Metria was keenly aware that she was now dependent for her very existence on the centaur aisle of magic.

8
MUNDANIA

If I may make a suggestion . . . " Ichabod said.

"By all means, friend," Arnolde replied. "This is, after all, your territory."

"I think it would facilitate things if we had rapid Mundanian transportation." He glanced at Arnolde. "You know how they tend to stare at you when they see you, and this time we don't have a spell of invisibility along."

"Excellent point! Perhaps your wheeled vehicle?"

"That was what I was thinking. My pickup truck will carry the full party, and if we put high sides on it, oddities will not be noticed."

"That's right," Metria said. "Centaurs don't exist in Mundania."

"Nor demonesses," Ichabod agreed. "However, if you arrange to be garbed a bit more completely—not that I'm complaining—"

She had left her gown translucent. She opaqued it. "Will this do?"

"Actually, your apparel does not closely resemble that of contemporary Mundania," he said. "Will you accept my instruction in this respect?"

"Maybe I'd better," she said. "But if your hands stray, I'll turn into smoke and choke you."

He smiled. "I'm sure it would be delightful smoke. Please assume a colored blouse, and an opaque skirt extending about halfway to the knees.''

Metria did so. Then she formed the peculiar pointed-heel footwear Mundanes used, and arranged her hair, and reddened her lips. ''I feel like a clown,'' she complained.

''You look like a fine young woman,'' Ichabod assured her. ''And, I might add, a remarkably attractive one.''

Metria, about to say something appropriately sharp, suddenly discovered that her tongue had softened to, as Professor Grossclout would put it, something like mush.

Then Ichabod turned to Jenny Elf. ''No offense, but you could pass for a human child of ten,'' he told her. ''I think you'd do best in juvenile garb, such as T-shirt, blue jeans, and sneakers.'' Then he reconsidered. ''No, you would not appear childlike in such a shirt! Maybe a loose untucked plaid shirt—what's the matter?''

For Jenny was giggling. ''That's the color of Mela Merwoman's—'' She dissolved into more giggles.

''A checkered shirt,'' Metria said quickly.

''That would do,'' Ichabod agreed, perplexed.

''There seems to be something we don't know about,'' Arnolde remarked. ''Perhaps we have been too long in the madness.''

''For sure,'' Jenny agreed as her mirth gradually subsided. ''Plaid sure isn't the way to appear childlike! But I can't just make clothing from my own substance, the way Metria does. I'll have to find some.''

''We're not all the way out of the magic yet,'' Metria said. ''Have Sammy find a shoe tree, and a clothes horse, and I'll fetch what she needs, and a jacket for you, Arnolde.''

Sammy was off and running as she spoke. ''Bring him back with you,'' Jenny said, this time not trying to chase after the cat.

Metria floated after Sammy, who brought her in turn to a shoe tree with a pair of sneakers Jenny's size, a clothes horse with good jeans, shirt, and jacket, and a scarlet ribbon worm that would do nicely to tie her hair. She gathered these up along with the cat and floated back to the waiting party.

Then she formed herself into a high-sided tent so that Jenny could change clothes without suffering the cynosure of three or four male eyes. After all, Jenny was not a nymph.

This accomplished, they resumed their travel in the direction the token had indicated for Kim Mundane. Gradually the terrain changed, with the trees becoming unfamiliar and somehow less interesting, as if ashamed to be without magic. The very air became dusky and less pleasant, losing its freshness.

Ichabod sniffed. "The pollution gets worse every year," he remarked. "Now we shall have to deviate from the true route, because my residence is to the side. Fortunately it is not far, and I believe we can avoid contact with the natives."

Even so, it was a dreary hike. Metria would have popped back to Xanth for a break, but didn't dare try to cross the dread magicless terrain between. She was stuck with the party, in her peculiar outfit, for the duration.

At last they came to Ichabod's house, which was a dull wood and stucco structure beside a broad paved path. Beside it was a funny device with wheels.

But as they approached it, emerging from the forest behind it, a horrible loud monster came zooming along the road. Jenny drew back in fright. "Is it a dragon?" she asked.

"No, merely an automobile," Ichabod replied confidently. "Do not be concerned; it will not leave the highway."

Jenny and Metria looked up, but saw no high way, just the low road. "He means the paved wide path you see," Arnolde explained, realizing the source of their confusion. "There are a number of odd terms in Mundania."

"I will stand behind the house," Arnolde said, "so that I will not be seen. I am uncertain how far my aisle extends now; my long time in the madness may have enhanced it somewhat."

"Let's find out," Metria said. "I don't want to step out of it by accident. Jenny and I can walk slowly to the edge, and when I fade she can pull me back." The prospect made her nervous, but she did want to know the limits. It was a matter of existence and nonexistence for her, which was a new and qualmy sensation.

"Meanwhile I will fetch money and supplies from the house,"

Ichabod said. He alone was free to leave the aisle, unless his age caught up with him.

Metria and Jenny linked hands and walked ahead of Arnolde. "It should extend fifteen paces to the front, and half that to the rear," Arnolde called. "And only about two paces to either side."

Metria looked back. She judged they were a dozen paces ahead of him. She took one more, and a second, getting more nervous as she did.

They were now close beside the paved path. Another noisy block monster zoomed across. But instead of passing on by, it suddenly squealed like a stuck oink and slewed to a halt right before them. Metria, nervous about the limit of the aisle, stood frozen.

The monster whistled piercingly. Then it poked a human head from its side. "Hey, cutie! How about a date?"

"I think it's talking to you," Jenny said.

So Metria responded. "If your dates taste as bad as your air, I don't want one."

The thing whistled again. "Oh, wow, we've got a live one here!" Part of its side opened, and a young man crawled out. "Beat it, kid," he said to Jenny. Then, to Metria, "How about a kiss, sugar-lips?"

Metria was beginning to figure this out. The monster was actually some kind of conveyance, like a magic carpet. The man was the standard obnoxious young human male. She knew how to handle that kind.

"Sure, buttface. Come and get it."

"Are you sure—?" Jenny asked worriedly.

"We'll find out soon enough."

The man came up and put his arms around her. He brought his face down to hers. Just as his mouth was about to touch hers, Metria turned her head into a mound of mush.

His lips sucked mush. His head jerked back. "What the—?"

She poked an eyeball out of the mush. "Yes, loverboy?"

"It's an alien thing!" he cried, pulling away. But her arms were around him, holding him close.

"Then I had better chomp it," she said, her head forming into the snout of a small dragon.

He screamed as it snapped at his nose. "Aaaaahhh!"

"Hold still," the snout said. "How do you expect me to chomp your face off?"

But the man was uncooperative. He hauled himself away so violently that her arms stretched like toffee. He spun about, wrenching free, and leaped into his box. In a moment the box roared, shot out a cloud of gas, and squealed rapidly away.

"I think that thing has indigestion," Jenny said, giggling. "Not to mention the man inside it."

"Well, he shouldn't have tried to get fresh with a demoness," Metria said, resuming her set Mundane aspect.

"I think he won't try it again," Jenny agreed.

But already another vehicle was squealing to a stop. This one seemed to be stuffed full of young men. "Hey, babe!" one called. "How about a smooch?"

Metria found that this sort of thing palled fairly quickly. So she turned her whole body into that of a dragon and roared back at them. This time no door opened, and the vehicle squealed away as rapidly as it had come.

Now at last they could complete their test of the limits of the aisle. Metria took one more step, and remained present. She took another, and still was there. Then she lost her nerve and retreated. "The aisle's strong enough."

Meanwhile Ichabod had gotten his own vehicle loaded. "I stepped out of your aisle several times," he said as he returned to Arnolde. "I felt the difference, but it was tolerable for brief periods. I believe you are correct: We are well charged with magic, and it takes time for it to dissipate. But we had better resolve the current mission expeditiously."

That was his way of suggesting that they hurry, Metria knew. But she wanted to do one thing first. "I was trying to get beyond the front end of the aisle of magic," she said, "but kept running afoul of Mundanes, or foul Mundanes, and lost my nerve. But I think I should find out exactly what happens when I enter Mundania proper. Maybe it's not so bad. Would you guide me where you have been, and bring me back, if—?"

"I understand," Ichabod said graciously. "Rest assured, I would not allow anyone with appurtenances like yours to come to grief if I could help it. Come this way.''

He meant her legs, mainly. She followed him around the back of the house, while Jenny remained with Arnolde, who had not moved. The centaur understood the importance of keeping the aisle exactly as it was, so they could experiment.

''The phenomenon does appear to be significantly more capacious than during its original manifestation,'' Ichabod remarked. ''By perhaps fifty percent. That is, about three paces out, perhaps ten feet. Observe: I scuffed a mark by my back door, here, where I noted the diminution of the ambience.''

''Where the magic stops,'' Metria translated, stopping just short of the line. ''Would you mind, um, holding my hand as I cross?''

''Mind?'' Ichabod said, as if in doubt. ''Dear creature, I would consider it a privilege.''

''Thank you.'' Pleased, she gave him her most fetching smile, then took his hand, nerved herself, and stepped across the line.

Everything turned awful. She was swirling out of control; dissipating in all directions, and losing her mind.

Then, after a yearlong instant, she found herself strewn around Ichabod every which way, in severe disorder. ''Huh?'' she inquired intelligently.

''Are you functional?'' he asked.

She drew in her extremities from around him and got her head together. ''I think so. What happened?''

''You dissolved into a dust devil. That is, a twist of wind, carrying dust and leaves. I tried to push you back into the aisle with my body, but couldn't quite get hold of you, and feared I was merely disrupting you. Fortunately Arnolde realized what had happened, and stepped sideways one pace. That brought the ambience to your locale, and your persona re-formed.''

''A dust devil?'' she echoed blankly.

''At times the wind is channeled into a circular vortex, generating a relative low pressure interior, which sucks in dust. Extreme examples become tornadoes or even hurricanes. But most dust devils swirl for only a few seconds, then dissipate. They have no lasting cohesion. I realized that this was likely to be your fate, if you remained clear of the magic.''

"So you got me back in it," she said. "I think you saved my existence, Ichabod." That explained why she was wrapped around him: She had been no more than energy in the air, and when he tried to push her back, he had simply stepped into the swirl. "Thank you." She shaped her head into its best configuration, made her prettiest face, and kissed him firmly on the mouth.

He looked about ready to faint. Indeed, he sagged somewhat, so that she had to support him. But he was not in discomfort; there was a dazed smile in the vicinity of his mouth, and his eyes seemed to glow. "Thank *you*," he breathed. "But please, if you would . . . ''

"Whatever you wish, friend," she said obligingly.

"Put your clothing back on."

Oh. She had lost that detail, in the confusion of the dissolution. Hastily she re-formed shoes, skirt, and blouse, in that order. Then his eyes dimmed back to medium, and he recovered his equilibrium. He might be old, but his reflexes seemed to be normal.

Arnolde and Jenny were two paces away. "It seems that we now know the Mundane reversion of demons," Arnolde said. "They are the flux that animates the currents of the wind. In Xanth they possess awareness and control, becoming immortal. In Mundania they lack these qualities, so rapidly dissipate.''

"And so a long-standing question has at length been resolved," Ichabod agreed. "Thanks to the courage of the Demoness Metria.''

"Courage!" Metria snorted. "I just wanted to know what would happen if I got out of the aisle. Now I know I'd better not try it.''

"Courage is as one defines it," Arnolde said.

"Um, maybe I should try that also," Jenny said. "I'm not brave, but it does make a difference whether I turn into a regular girl or a swirl of dust.''

"To be sure," Ichabod agreed. "Step this way.''

Metria watched as the two approached the line in the dirt, and stepped across it. The elf girl held her cat tightly in her arms. Jenny did not disappear, or become dust; she simply became a childlike girl, and the cat did not seem to change at all.

"Oh! I have five fingers!" Jenny exclaimed.

"And rounded ears," Ichabod added. "You have become distressingly normal."

"Ugh!" Jenny quickly stepped back into the magic. But then she changed her mind and stepped out again. "The point is to see whether I can safely function in Mundania," she said. "And it seems I can. That's good to know."

"I am not certain that is entirely the case," Ichabod said.

"Why? What's wrong?"

"The Mundanes will not be able to understand you, outside of the aisle. You are speaking the magic language of Xanth, which all humanoids know. But it sounds like gibberish to Mundanes."

"Oh. So if I leave the aisle, I'd better not speak."

"Correct. Your first words would give away your alien origin. That will not be a problem for Metria, who can't depart the aisle, or Arnolde, who carries it with him. But you will have to be cautious."

"In fact, I'd better not stray unless I really have to," Jenny concluded.

"That is my opinion. And the same surely goes for your cat."

Jenny considered that. "I'd better put him on a leash," she decided. "He won't like it, but I don't want us both getting hopelessly lost in Mundania."

"A sensible precaution."

They turned and returned to the aisle. They had not gone far, but there was no doubt that Jenny had been operating well enough outside the aisle. As she crossed back into it, her ears pointed again and her hands (and surely her toes too) diminished to four digits per appendage. A thumb and three fingers. The magic to the World of Two Moons did not apply to Mundania any better than that of Xanth did.

"Now we must travel," Ichabod said briskly. "Since we do not know the address, we shall have to be guided by the summons token. I hope we can proceed without further procrastination."

"Yes, let's move," Metria said.

Ichabod put a crate down behind his truck-vehicle, and Arnolde mounted this carefully and stepped up into the back of the truck, which had now been fitted with high sides. Jenny joined him there. Metria was about to do the same, but Ichabod stopped her. "I must have you in front to direct me, Demoness."

"Oh. Right." She watched him get into the enclosed front portion of the vehicle, then popped into the seat beside him.

"Perhaps it would be better not to move that way," Ichabod suggested. "We do not want to attract undue attention to ourselves."

"Oh, that's right—demons don't exist in Mundania," she said. "Except as swirls of wind. I'll watch my manners."

He took a small key and used it to unlock something on the front side. But no door opened. Instead a dragon growled, so close it seemed almost on top of them. Metria dissolved into smoke, but caught herself before she drifted out of the vehicle. "What's that?" she asked, re-forming.

Ichabod glanced at her. His eyes went opalescent again. "That is the motor starting," he said. "Have no concern. But if you don't mind—your clothing."

Oh. She kept forgetting. It was hard to keep such details in mind when such strange things were going on. She formed the necessary items.

"Understand, I have no objection to your, er, natural appearance," Ichabod said. "In fact, I find it extremely appealing. But I fear I would be unable to drive well with such a distraction, and any other male who perceived your assets would suffer similarly."

"My what?" she asked, glancing down at herself. Then she realized that he had not used a bad word. "You mean if we were alone and nobody else could see, there'd be no problem?" She had a suspicion about the answer. After all, it wasn't as if she were completely inexperienced with human males.

He seemed to hesitate. "I, ah, er, um, that is to say, perhaps not, but that seems an unlikely eventuality."

That was his way of saying that his orbs would burn out. Satisfied, Metria brought out the Kim token and held it before her. She was lucky those hadn't been lost when she stepped out of the aisle! "That way," she said, pointing as it tugged.

Ichabod reached for her knee. Curious, she watched his hand. But it stopped just short, landing instead on the kneelike knob on top of a stick poking from the floor. He wiggled the stick. Then he pushed his feet against pedals on the floor. This was evidently a magic ritual.

The vehicle lurched forward. Metria held her position, and turned her head back to see how the two in back were taking it. They were all right; Arnolde must have ridden in this contraption before, and warned Jenny about it. The two had gotten along very well, ever since discovering that each was isolated from his or her natural species.

"Er," Ichabod said, glancing at her.

She completed the turn of her head. "Yes?"

"You just did a one-hundred-and-eighty-degree rotation of your head," he said. "And then made it three hundred and sixty degrees."

"So?"

"That isn't done among humans."

Oh, again. Of course, mortals had inconvenient anatomical limits. "You mean I shouldn't do that?"

"It might attract adverse attention which we would prefer to avoid."

That meant not to do it. She sighed. "Mundania is a dull place."

"I agree emphatically." Now the truck began to move forward, though he hadn't finished moving his feet or playing with the wheel angled before him. The craft pulled out onto the road, turned in the direction she had indicated, and gathered speed. This turned out to be respectable; it was about as fast as a magic carpet.

"How do you make it mind?" she asked. "You haven't said a word to it."

He smiled. "Now, that would be novel: teaching a Demoness to drive."

"Why not?"

He considered. "Why not indeed! Very well, Metria. I am making the truck respond not by verbal commands, but by the actions of my hands and feet. The key turns on the motor, and the levers connect it to the wheels. I steer it with the steering wheel, here."

"Fascinating!" she said. "It's a mindless machine."

"To be sure. I must guide it constantly, or it will go astray."

She asked more questions, and he, evidently flattered by the interest, explained about the obscure mechanisms of clutch, brakes, steering column, driveshaft, and turning signals. Metria paid close attention. It seemed that Mundania was not quite as dull as she had thought. She could have some fun with a contraption like this, if she ever got the chance.

She checked with the token. It seemed to have no trouble keeping track of its object, though Kim was across a stretch of magicless terrain. The Simurgh must have seen to that, refusing to let her artifacts be limited by Mundane considerations. But now it was tugging somewhat to the side. "We are drifting off-course," Metria announced.

"That is inevitable, given the limits of the highway system. I shall have to angle toward it. Never fear, we shall get there in due course."

He turned at the next intersection, and turned again when the direction still wasn't right. It seemed that it was not possible, in Mundania, to go directly where one wanted to go. So they kept moving, and Metria kept learning about the ways of controlling the vehicle, and at other times gazing out at the changingly dull scenery of the region.

They passed many blocky buildings, and many sections of field between, and sometimes some bits of forest. Other vehicles prowled constantly, on both sides of the road. It seemed that each had to stay on its own side, according to the direction it was going, or there would be an awful crash.

At last the tugs on the token got stronger. "We are coming close," Metria said.

"Excellent. We are approaching Squeedunk. What age is Kim?"

"Nineteen, by now, if folk age at the regular rate in Mundania."

"Then she is college age. She could be at the Squeedunk Community College."

"Community collage? Do they paste unrelated things together to make a picture?"

He smiled. "In a sense, Metria. They try to educate juveniles, which may be about as much of an art."

Soon they came to the SCC campus. The buildings were large and covered with blue glassy squares. Young human folk walked between them, carrying armfuls of books. Some had spread blankets on the flat green sward and were sunning themselves in scant attire.

"They are wearing less than I am," Metria said, pouting.

"They are less endowed than you are," he said diplomatically.

"Less whatted?"

"Healthy, curvaceous, symmetrical, proportioned, statuesque, comely—"

"Stacked?"

"Whatever," he said with a smile. "You would disrupt traffic and classes, so must mask your assets."

There was that word again. "My whats?"

"Charms. Are we going right?"

She checked the token. "That way," she said, pointing to a building.

Ichabod brought the truck around to the parking lot nearest the building. "I hope she lives on the ground floor," he said.

"Why?"

"How will we get to her, out of reach of the aisle?"

"Arnolde will have to go in with us."

"A centaur in Mundania? Better for you to go naked."

Metria sorted that out, and concluded that he meant that it wasn't practical for Arnolde to enter the building. He was probably right. The centaur wouldn't enjoy the narrow steps and halls and landings Metria could see, and might attract more attention than was wise. So it would be best if he remained in the truck.

But that meant that the rest of them would have to stay there too. Except for Ichabod, and maybe Jenny. Jenny couldn't speak outside the aisle, so it would have to be the man. "So you fetch her."

"Men are not allowed in the women's dormitories," he said. "It is one of those archaic regulations that still obtain in the hinterlands." She realized that he was making a funny, but wasn't quite sure about what.

They got out and walked to the rear of the truck. Arnolde's head and shoulders showed above the high side. "We have arrived?" the centaur asked.

"At the girl's dormitory. But we have a problem. She may be out of reach."

They discussed it, but before they came to a conclusion, some students approached. *"Xibu't vq, epmm?"* a young man called to Metria.

Metria looked at Ichabod. "This is Mundane speech?"

"Yes. He just inquired, 'What's up, doll?' He will become intelligible once he enters the aisle."

"Doll?"

"It is an overly familiar mode of address to an unfamiliar woman."

"That's what I thought. Suppose I put on a dragon's snout and bite his head off?"

"I wouldn't recommend it. We don't wish to make a scene."

She had been afraid he would say that. "So how do I squelch this clod of dragon manure?"

"Perhaps I had better handle this." Then, as the youth reached them, Ichabod said, "Were you addressing my married daughter?" Jenny remained out of sight, so this had to be Metria.

"Oops," the young man said, abashed. In three fifths of a moment he was gone.

"That was fun, I confess," Ichabod said.

A young woman approached. "Oooo," she squealed. "Is that a horse in there?"

Metria realized that Arnolde's speckled flank showed through the slats of the side. "Not exactly," she said.

"But I'm sure I saw—yes, that's definitely horseflesh!" the girl said, peering through.

Arnolde looked at her from above the side. "That horseflesh belongs to me," he said. "Would you like a closer look?"

Oops! Metria opened her mouth, but couldn't think of anything to say.

"Oooo, yes!" the girl cried, jumping up and down in her excitement. Metria knew that did interesting things to her sweater, because Ichabod's eyes were starting to shine.

"Then perhaps I might prevail on you for a favor, first," Arnolde said.

"Oh, sure! Anything."

What was the centaur up to?

"There is a young woman we would like to talk with, but of course, we can't go into the dormitory, being male. Would you be kind enough to take a message to her?"

"Sure," the girl agreed, straining to get a better glimpse. So far she had not been able to make the connection between the horseflesh and the talking man.

"Her name is Kim. If you take this emerald disk to her, perhaps she will come out here." Arnolde nodded toward Metria.

Metria was not easy about this, but had no choice but to hand over the disk.

"Emerald?" the girl said. "But it's black!"

"It has become somewhat corroded with age," Arnolde said smoothly.

"Oh." Then the girl made another connection. "But why couldn't you go in to find her?" she asked Metria. "You're about as female as I've ever seen."

"I—I—" Metria said, but stalled almost immediately.

"She has a speech impediment," Ichabod said quickly. "Terrible stuttering. Please don't embarrass her by mentioning it."

"Oh, sure, no," the girl agreed. "Be back in a jiff." She hurried off with the token.

"Suppose she doesn't take it to Kim?" Metria asked, sincerely worried.

"A summons by the Simurgh will travel only to its proper summonsee," Arnolde said. "The girl will not even think of taking it elsewhere."

"How can you be sure of that?"

"I am a centaur scholar."

Oh. Of course. For once Metria wasn't annoyed by the superior certainty of the species.

Soon enough Kim came running out, garbed much as Metria herself was. She had been a lanky girl, somewhat plain; now she had put on some flesh where it counted and redone her hair, and looked more like a woman. Especially while running. "Metria!" she cried, instantly recognizing the demoness. "What on earth are you doing out here, in civilian clothing?"

"How can I understand her from this distance?" Metria asked.

"Because I turned to capture her in my aisle," Arnolde replied.

Then Kim reached Metria, and hugged her emphatically. "I never thought I'd be so glad to see *you*, Demoness! But how is it possible? This is the real world."

"Do you know of the centaur aisle?" Metria asked.

"Oh, sure! But that's old history. There's no longer—" Then Kim caught sight of Arnolde's head. "Oh, no! Can it be? I thought Arnolde faded away decades ago!"

"Reports of my fadeaway have been somewhat exaggerated," Arnolde said, extending his hand.

Kim grasped it. "Oh, marvelous! This is almost as good as visiting Xanth! But what—"

"You will visit Xanth," Metria said. "I brought you your summons. You must return with us."

"But I can't do that!" Kim protested. "I have classes, homework, obligations—"

"They will have to wait," Arnolde informed her. "No one declines a summons from the Simurgh."

"From the Simurgh?" Kim stared at the black disk. "I knew there was something really special about this medal. But I can't get into Xanth, except when I play the game, and I've been too busy even to do that."

"What, even during summer vacation?" Ichabod asked.

"Well, there's Dug," she said, blushing.

Then Metria understood how summers could disappear. Two of her own years had disappeared similarly. "Dug's coming too," she said. "I have a summons for him."

Suddenly Kim's objections faded away. "I'll tell my roommate to cover for me," she said, and dashed off.

Meanwhile the messenger girl had returned. "About that horse . . ." she said.

"Come in and see," Arnolde said.

"Is that wise?" Ichabod asked.

"We made a deal," Arnolde said. "Let her in."

So Ichabod opened the back just enough to let the girl scramble in, then closed it behind her.

There was a breathless pause. Then a faint scream. "Oh, my! Are you *really*—?"

"I am really," Arnolde said. "But please don't tell anyone else, because it would make things rather awkward for me, and I'm rather too old to handle awkwardness gracefully."

"Not so you'd notice," Ichabod muttered. "He's a con artist. There's no counting how many specimens he talked into posing for us, in the madness."

"And who—what are you?" the girl asked after a bit.

"Jenny Elf. I'm too young to handle awkwardness."

Kim emerged from the building, carrying a bag. "My research paper homework," she said. "Maybe I'll squeeze it in, somehow."

The other girl emerged from the truck, looking dazed. "Thanks, Jo," Kim said.

"Any time, Kim." Jo walked unsteadily away.

"Suppose she talks?" Metria asked.

"Who would believe her?" Kim asked. "Come on, let's go get Dug!"

This time Kim got in the front of the truck, because she knew exactly where to find Dug, and since her legs were just as visible as Metria's, Ichabod didn't object. Metria climbed in back with Arnolde and Jenny Elf.

"That girl's face must have been something," Metria remarked as the truck lurched into motion. "She thought she would see a horse, and man, and she saw a centaur."

"She did see a horse and man," Arnolde said primly. "There are both in my ancestry."

"But she did seem about to faint, at first," Jenny said. "I know how it is. I was amazed when I first saw Chex. Fortunately I couldn't see very well, so I didn't realize just how strange she was. Until she got me a pair of spectacles."

"Yes, wings on a centaur would seem extremely strange," Arnolde agreed. "Until the species gets established. Which, of course, may be a problem for the alicentaurs."

"For the what?" Jenny asked.

"Winged centaurs," he said. "If they are to be established as a species, they need a species name. Since a winged unicorn is an alicorn, it is reasonable to call a winged centaur an alicentaur.''

"Alia for short," Metria agreed, glad that for once it hadn't been her in the middle of a confusion of words. "But what's the problem?"

"A winged centaur is not the easiest crossbreed to achieve," Arnolde said. "Chex was the result of a liaisan between a normal centaur and a hippogriph, and Cheiron's origin has not yet been deciphered. Presumably a strategically placed love spring could result in others, but centaurs are generally too intelligent to be deceived, and are opposed to crossbreeding anyway. Since new blood from outside the present alia family is required to make a lasting species viable, prospects for the continuation seem remote."

"No they aren't," Metria said.

Both Jenny and Arnolde looked at her. "I presume you have some insight we lack?" the centaur said in a tone that indicated that she probably didn't.

"Certainly. Magician Trent has been rejuvenated, and his powers of transformation are as good as they ever were. He transformed Cynthia Human to Cynthia Centaur seventy four years ago, and she has now had a bit of rejuvenation herself and is hot for Che Centaur. So Trent can do it again. He can transform humans to alia, or centaurs to alia, or anything else. Probably it would be best to start with centaurs, because they're already smart and know the form; they'd just have to learn to fly, and since the magic of all winged centaurs is similar, making them light enough to fly, that's no problem. They wouldn't have to soil their hands on any other obscenity of magic talents."

Arnolde and Jenny were staring at her. "Out of the mouths of fools and babes . . ." the centaur said, trailing off into some private thought.

"I think she's got it!" Jenny said. "Transformation."

"Who's a fool or a baby?" Metria demanded.

"He said 'babe,' not 'baby,' " Jenny said.

"Oh. Very proficiently."

"Very what?" Jenny asked.

"Suitable, proper, appropriate, felicitous, germane, healthy—"

"Well?"

"Whatever," Arnolde said before Metria could answer, making a cross expression. Jenny laughed, and Metria had to too.

Then the truck clunked to a halt. They looked out, and saw another dormitory just like the first, but with boys mostly surrounding it. Kim got out and walked up to the side until she stood under a particular window. Then she put two fingers in her mouth and make a piercing whistle.

In a moment a head appeared in the window, and a hand waved. "Be right down!" Dug called.

"I thought there was no magic in Mundania," Metria said.

"The magic power women have over men is everywhere," Arnolde explained.

Soon Dug emerged from the building, and Kim brought him over to the truck. He had fleshed out somewhat since Metria had last seen him, and looked stronger and handsomer. "The Demoness Metria has something for you," she told him.

"I don't need it, as long as I've got you," he replied gallantly.

Kim smiled, looking rather pretty in that moment. "It's a summons for Jury duty."

His jaw dropped. "What?"

"Obligation, onus, burden, charge, litigation, trial—" Metria offered helpfully.

"Court case?" Arnolde suggested.

"Whatever!" Jenny, Kim, and Metria chorused, looking mirthfully cross.

"But they don't have that stuff in Xanth!" Dug protested.

"Oh, indeed they do," Arnolde reassured him. "The trial of Gracile Ossein was notorious."

Dug looked at Kim, who nodded affirmatively. She was better versed on Xanth history than he was. "Grace'l is a female walking skeleton, Marrow Bones' wife. She was tried for messing up a bad dream sent to Tristan Troll for not eating an innocent human little girl."

"But that's backwards!" he said. "Trolls shouldn't eat children, and bad dreams should be sent for—"

Kim shut him up by pulling his head down and kissing him.

"Always nice to see proper control," Metria murmured apprecia-tively. "She has certainly learned how to handle him."

"Girls do," Arnolde agreed.

Metria reached down and presented Dug with his token. "But I can't go to Xanth now," he said. "I have homework, papers to write—"

"I'm going," Kim said.

"Let me check out." He hurried back into the building.

"Classes were getting tiresome anyway," Kim remarked. "Though our grades are bound to suffer because of our absence and missed work."

Soon Dug reappeared. Metria was glad that the toughest part of her search was done; all the rest of the summonsees were in Xanth.

9
DEMON DRIVER

K im and Dug rode in the back, discussing old times
with Jenny Elf, so Metria was once again in the front.
They were driving first to Kim's home, because she
absolutely refused to go to Xanth without her dog, Bubbles.

For a time they rode in silence. 'He's looking at your knees,'
Mentia remarked.

'So? They're good knees; I shaped them that way.'

'But I showed them to him first.'

'Well, you didn't show him your panties,' Metria retorted, annoyed.

'Not only would that have freaked him out, it would have violated
the Adult Conspiracy.'

'He's a hundred years old!' Metria thought.

'And in his second childhood.'

She had a point. 'Good thing I had no panties when I forgot my
clothing.'

"Penny for your thoughts," Ichabod said.

"Mundane coins aren't worth much in Xanth."

"I mean that I am curious about what is going on in your mind
that has you focusing so intently, if you care to tell me."

There seemed to be no harm in it, so she told him. "I was talking with
my worser half, D. Mentia. She said you were looking at my knees."

"Well, I was. I have been a connoisseur of distaff limbs since adolescence."

"Of what limbs?"

"The distaff is a long staff for holding wool, flax, or other fibrous material, from which the thread is drawn out when spinning by hand. Since this was almost invariably the work of women, the distaff came to be a generalized symbol of womanhood. Thus I was speaking metaphorically."

"Speaking how?"

"Using a parallel, analogy, correspondence, likeness, affinity, kinship, similarity—"

"Synecdoche?"

"Or more properly, metonymy," he said crossly. Then he did a double take. "How did you come up with that term?"

"I have no idea. Words are strictly accidental with me."

"You are an interesting creature," Ichabod remarked as he drove on toward Xanth. "That is to say, all supernatural entities are intriguing in their separate fashions, but you seem remarkable even for a demoness. What accounts for your, er, unusual way with words?"

"I think a sphinx stepped on part of my demon substance when I was new, and squished it flat. Ever since, some words have been riddles, and my character has been subject to fissioning."

"Oh, is that how you change from Metria to Mentia?"

"And to Woe Betide," she agreed, assuming the form of the sweet, sad child.

"Do other demons have multiple personalities?"

She switched back to Metria, because the question was too complicated for the tyke to answer. "No. Others assume any aspect they wish, but inside they are always the same evil spirits. I'm the only one who takes those personalities seriously. When I'm the child, I mustn't violate the Adult Conspiracy. When I'm Mentia, I'm slightly crazy, except when in the Region of Madness, when I reverse and become slightly sane. When I'm Metria, I have a problem of vocabulary."

"Fascinating! In Mundania, multiple personality disorder—

MPD—usually stems from some difficult event in childhood, such as sexual abuse.''

"Well, getting stepped on by a sphinx distracted by a riddle isn't exactly easy to take.''

He laughed. "Surely so! So you did have a traumatic early experience. As a mature individual you could have handled that stepping on, but as a nascent one you couldn't, so you suffered some subtle psychological damage.''

This was a revelation. "This is true? I mean, do other people really suffer conditions like mine, because of early whatevers?''

"Early traumas. Yes, this does seem to be the case, though psychological opinion is by no means unified. We believe it is the human—and perhaps demon—mind's way of dealing with what cannot otherwise be handled. Or perhaps it is merely the shock of the abuse itself, striking the forming personality like a hammer and cracking it into several fragments. Each fragment then tries to heal itself, forming individual personalities, but never with complete success. Because something broken is simply not as strong as something whole.'' He glanced at her face for a moment. "As is perhaps the case with your vocabulary. You obviously possess a full repertoire of words, but your mechanism for recollecting the particular one you need at a given moment is imperfect.''

"Yes! That's exactly what I have languished!''

"What you have suffered,'' he agreed.

"Oh, Ichy, I could smack you!''

He was taken aback. "What?''

"Osculate, buss, peck, smooch—''

"Kiss?''

"Whatever!'' she said, and kissed him firmly on the right ear. "Now at last I know why I am as I am. I have MPD.''

The truck slewed for a moment and a half before going straight again. "I am glad to have been of help,'' Ichabod said. "But if you ever kiss me again, please do it when I'm not driving.''

"Sorry about that.''

"Oh, don't be! Just be careful in future. It is dangerous for a man my age to suffer such distraction while behind the wheel.''

"I'll try,'' she said contritely.

"This alternate personality, Mentia—you actually have dialogues with her?"

"Shouldn't I?"

"Usually one personality dominates, or the other; they don't hold direct discourses."

"Well, I am usually in charge. But she fissioned off when I did the disgusting thing of getting half souled and falling in love. She's the half without the soul, so she retains the old demonly values. Woe Betide is satisfied to share half my half soul when she's in charge, so she's quarter-souled. But Mentia's curious about just what I get from my soul, in much the way I was curious about the matter before I got it. So she rejoined me, and she takes over when she needs to. Do you want to talk with her?"

"Not exactly. I am merely curious about what the two of you have to have a dialogue about, since both of you must have had much the same experiences in your existence."

"We have. But we place different interpretations on them."

"What would one of your dialogues concern?"

"Love, mainly. She just doesn't understand it."

"Few do, who haven't experienced it! Would it be possible to— to listen to such a dialogue?"

"For sure!" Mentia said. "What kind of idiocy can make a once sensible demoness suddenly become caring, self-sacrificing, and dedicated to making her indifferent husband deliriously happy several times a day? She calls it love, but I don't see anything compelling her except perversity. Who cares whether the man is happy or miserable? He's just a stupid mortal. He doesn't deserve all that attention."

"I don't consider it idiocy," Metria responded. "I get real pleasure myself from making him happy. It's a mutual thing; my desires are defined in terms of his desires. Before I fell in love, my life was empty in a way I never realized; now it is full in a way I never anticipated. Love gives me fulfillment—"

"Fulfillment! Why not chain yourself to a dungeon while you're at it? You delight in your misery."

"It is only your ignorance that makes it look like misery to you. It is sheer joy to me."

"You revel in your humiliation!"

"If your values weren't inverted, you'd know it's exaltation."

"*Yours* are inverted! I'm true to demonly nature."

"I think I get the picture," Ichabod said. "A person without a soul simply can't grasp its nature, and a person without love thinks it's pointless."

"That's right," Metria said. "I was governed mainly by curiosity and mischief, before I got half souled. But my curiosity was in the end greater than my mischief, so I took the plunge and got married."

"I seem to recall Arnolde saying something about a demoness with a soul who married a King, in the past. But when her baby was delivered, the soul went with the baby, and the demoness took off with a rude noise. Will that happen to you?"

"Yes, that was my friend Dara Demoness, who married King Humfrey. Her son Dafrey got the soul. But later she returned to Humfrey, because she discovered that she liked existence with a soul better than existence without a soul. Now she emulates a soul she doesn't have. So I won't give up my half soul when my baby is delivered; I'll share half of it, and hope that a quarter soul sustains me. My child won't have that problem; souls grow to full size when a creature is part mortal."

"You have a generous nature."

"Yes, now."

"When I first saw you, or Mentia, there in the madness, I took you for a variant of a nymph, a creature without much intellectual content. I was mistaken."

She shrugged. "It's understandable. I never cared about intellect before I married."

They reached Kim's home. Her parents were evidently out. Kim dashed in, and emerged leading her old dog. "I left a message on the kitchen table, so they won't think Bubbles was stolen," she announced. Then she lifted the dog into the back, and scrambled in herself. Metria knew that Bubbles would be reassured to find Jenny Elf and Sammy Cat there, because they had been Companions during the game. Metria wondered how it was that the dog could survive in Mundania, as she was very old, but thought that the magic of Xanth could have charged her when she visited there, in effect rejuvenating her somewhat. This excursion should have similar effect, in that case.

They drove for a while in silence. Then Ichabod remarked: "Once we return to Xanth, Arnolde and I will resume our researches in the Region of Madness. But I am curious as to the identity of your next summonsee."

"I hadn't thought about it. I have to guide Kim and Dug to the Nameless Castle, of course, but that will take time, as they can't just pop over there, and we won't have the assistance of a giant. So I suppose I had better travel a meandering course and pick up the remaining summonsees on the way. Beginning with the most difficult."

"And who would that be?"

She opened her bag and checked through the tokens. "Chena Centaur, because I never heard of her."

"Perhaps Arnolde has. He has a centaur's encyclopedic knowledge."

"I'll check." Metria turned smoky and slid through the metal of the vehicle. She emerged in the back. The four folk there were resting comfortably, Arnolde lying down, Jenny Elf leaning against his side, and Kim and Dug snugly ensconced in a corner. "Arnolde, do you know Chena Centaur?"

The old scholar shook his head. "She must be since my time. The name makes no connection."

"Thank you." She slid back to the front seat and solidified. "He doesn't know her either."

"Then I agree: She may be your most challenging remaining summonsee." He shook his head. "I am growing tired; it has been too long since I drove any distance. In fact, I should probably turn in my driver's license after this is done; I have little remaining use for Mundania."

"I can do it," Metria said. "I have learned all the commands."

He laughed. Then he sobered. "Do you know, I believe you could. You have been a most apt student of this art. Perhaps it would be safer trusting your alertness, rather than my failing powers."

"Then let me," she said eagerly.

"Oh, I really wasn't serious. I—"

He lost his voice, for she had fogged out her skirt almost to the panty line. "I'll sit in your lap," she said.

Stunned by the notion, he offered no further resistance.

She sat in his lap, so she could comfortably reach the controls, and operated them. She fogged herself out enough to reduce her weight so as not to be a burden on him, but he showed no sign of complaining. She drove, at first unsteadily, but soon with confidence. The machine responded marvelously to her slightest nudge on the steering wheel or go-pedal. It was like riding a responsive unicorn, except that no self-respecting unicorn would suffer itself to be ridden. This truck didn't seem to mind at all.

Darkness was closing, in its dull Mundane way, as they reached Ichabod's house. "I think we shall be obliged to stay the night here, as it would not be safe for us to drive by night," he opined. "But we should be all right, if Arnolde is properly positioned. So far I am aware of no diminution of his ambience."

"No less magic around him, either," she said. She used the steer-wheel and slow-pedal and got the truck beside the house.

Then it coughed, jerked, and died. "Oh, I killed it!" she said, chagrined.

"My fault. I forgot to remind you to use the clutch. The motor stalled."

"Oh." She had learned about the clutch, but not thought of it in her effort to steer the vehicle just right.

"Have no concern, Metria. It has been a real pleasure."

"Having me drive?" she asked, pleased.

"That, too," he said as she lifted her bottom off his lap.

Arnolde settled down in the center room of the house, so that the aisle reached the length of it and just about to the sides of it. Sammy and Bubbles curled up beside him, evidently thinking of him as more animal than human being, which made him acceptable company. Kim and Jenny checked supplies and found no suitable food; he had been too long away from here. "No problem," Kim said cheerfully. "I'll order pizza."

"Piece of what?" Metria asked.

Dug laughed. "You'll like this. She's going to do some Mundane magic."

Kim did. She picked up a banana shaped item with a curly-tailed line attached, punched some buttons in its belly, and spoke into it. "Falling Blocks Pizza? Two jumbo giant cheesers to this address." She seemed to be requesting something. Then she put the banana back on its stand.

Not long thereafter a vehicle charged up to the house so rapidly, it looked as if it was about to crash. But it squealed to a stop just in time, and a young man scrambled out with two wide, flat boxes. Dug gave him some folding green paper, and in a moment he zoomed away.

Dug brought the boxes inside and opened them. There were two huge flat pies, with surfaces like that of the moon in heavy sunlight: blistering cheese. The five mortals took pie-wedges from them and began eating. "Now, this is what I call responsive mozzarella," Dug remarked, dangling his slice by a stretching string of cheese and bouncing it like a yo-yo.

"Oh, Monster Ella," Metria said, finally recognizing the type. It came from the ella monster, famous for casting long sticky strings of gunk over its prey and smothering it to death. She wondered how the Mundanes had managed to slay an ella; it was a formidable creature. But it tasted wonderful.

This was magic, all right. But since Metria didn't need to eat, she was soon bored. So she explored the house. "What's this?" she asked, opening the curtain to a very small bare room that was behind a less small room.

"That's the shower," Dug said. "You want someone to take it with you? Ow!" Because Kim had kicked him for no apparent reason.

"Take it with me?" Metria repeated. "It doesn't look as if it can be moved."

"I can show you how it—" Dug began.

"*I'll* show her," Kim said as he dodged another kick. She got up, trailing a string of cheese, and approached the chamber. She closed the door to the larger chamber so no one else could see in. Then she turned two handles in the wall of the smaller one. Water gushed from a high nozzle. "Vanish your clothing and step in," she said.

Metria did so, and the warm water struck her bare body. "Hot rain!" she exclaimed. "More magic."

"For sure. When you've had enough, just turn these handles this way, and it will stop. That's how you take a shower."

"It's weird. But nice."

"Exactly." Kim pulled a curtain across and departed.

Metria basked in the shower. She turned smoky and let it pass through her. It was as if she were a cloud, and was raining below. "Move over, Fracto!" she muttered. Then she assumed various shapes, seeing how the water bounced off them. She became a giant pot, and let the water fill it. More fun!

But soon enough she tired, so she turned the knobs and the water ceased. Then she turned smoky so that all the water on her fell away, and re-formed, complete with her Mundane blouse, shirt, and footwear. She stepped back out to the dining room. "I could almost get to like Mundania," she said.

"Mundania would certainly like *you*," Dug said, and Ichabod nodded agreement. Kim looked studiously elsewhere, perhaps because Dug's shin was out of reach of her foot. Metria was catching on to the nature of their interaction; it was as if there were an invisible string of monster ella cheese that Kim used to dangle Dug from. Like most men, he needed to be leashed.

The others finished eating and took turns in the shower, except for Arnolde, who was too big to fit. So he put his front end in, then his hind end, and Dug wielded a hose attachment to get most of the centaur showered.

Meanwhile Kim turned on a box with a picture on the side and voices from within. It was interesting, but seemed to be filled mostly with violence and loudmouthed hustlers. Metria noticed that (blush) panties were openly shown, surely freaking out every male who watched. No wonder Mundane males were such louts!

In due course they settled down to sleep, setting up mats beside Arnolde. Metria didn't need to sleep, so she stayed to watch the magic box. After a while it showed scenes from some far-off land, and became a story, between increasingly obnoxious bouts of hustling. After that was done, there was another story, with different scenes. It was about a young man who fell in love with a young woman, then lost her, then regained her. Metria had never seen such a story before, and marveled at its originality. She wished she were back home with Veleno, making him deliriously happy. For her husband had no other purpose in existence than to be made delirious by her.

She observed the stories interminably, until the others woke. "You watched the movie channel all night?" Kim asked. "You must be worn out!"

"No, it was interesting. I wonder if we could get one of these magic boxes in Xanth. It's almost as much fun as the gourd."

"Maybe Com Pewter could arrange it," Kim said, laughing.

Jenny entered the shower-room. "Oops."

"I don't like the sound of that," Kim said.

"I felt the edge of the magic," the elf explained.

"But the bathroom is well within the ambience," Kim said. "Metria took a shower. Arnolde is exactly where he was yesterday."

"Maybe I'm confused," Jenny said doubtfully.

Whereupon Kim, in exactly the manner of a woman, reversed. "I'm not sure of that. We'd better check."

They looked at Metria. So Metria stepped very cautiously toward that chamber. She extended one arm through the door, feeling a tingling and then a numbness. And the arm dissolved into a swirl of wind.

Jenny squeezed by her to enter the chamber. As she did so, her ears and fingers changed. She faced back toward Metria and walked up to her, pushing the swirl with her body. As it crossed the border of magic, the swirl became a cloud of demon substance, and Metria was able to grab it and merge it into herself. That was a relief, because she had felt diminished without it.

They exchanged a three-way glance. "The aisle has shrunk," Kim said gravely.

"Hey, what's up, girls?" Dug asked, approaching.

They were silent, mutually hesitant to spread the alarm.

"Aren't you going to call me a sexist?" he asked Kim. "Because I didn't say 'women'?"

"The magic's fading," Kim said bluntly.

"Oh, shucks! I thought our love was forever."

"The magic aisle, numskull."

He sobered in a hurry. "How much?"

"The bathroom's out of it now."

He angled his head, which was his way of doing a mental calculation. "Maybe fifty percent. The question is, has it been fading steadily from the time Arnolde left Xanth, or is it just giving out now? We'd better hope that the fading is steady, because that will give us time to get the hell moving before it poops out entirely."

"Yes," Kim agreed tersely.

Both Arnolde and Ichabod remained asleep. In that state, it was clear just how old they were, because of the lack of animation of their features. And maybe fading magic.

"Let's get this organized before we wake them," Dug said. "So there're no wasted motions. Kim and I'll load the truck—has it got enough in the tank?"

"Yes," Metria said. "The magic dial says half of its bloat is left."

"Its what?" he asked. Then, immediately, "Oh—gas."

"Whatever."

"And Jenny and Metria must stay close to Arnolde," Kim said. "For moral support for the elders."

That was one way to put it. Metria had to stay close to maintain her existence, and Jenny to maintain her elfhood.

The two Mundanes loaded the truck efficiently, and set up the box so that Arnolde could climb into the back. "Okay, it's time," Dug said grimly.

Jenny woke Arnolde, and Dug woke Ichabod. Both were slow to be roused, and looked around as if befuddled.

"We were afraid of this," Kim muttered. "Their physical health is tied in with the magic."

"Arnolde, we'll help you up," Dug said, as if things were routine. Then he and Kim helped haul on the centaur's arms, while Jenny and Metria helped steady his rear end as he lurched unsteadily to his four feet. They walked him forward, then half shoved him up into the truck, and made him lie down again with his head toward the front. That was so Metria could sit in the cab, within the aisle.

Then they looked back to the house. Ichabod was tottering, walking erratically away from the truck. "God, he's gone senile," Kim muttered, and jumped down to intercept the old man. Soon she had her arm around his waist, and was half encouraging, half hauling him onto the truck.

"Nuh-uh," Dug said. "He's not fit to drive. Put him in back."

Kim nodded. They got the man in the truck. The dog and cat joined the centaur there, too.

"Now who drives?" Kim asked.

"What kind of shift is it?" Dug asked.

"Stick shift," Metria said.

"That lets me out," Kim said. "All I know is auto."

"Me too," Dug said. "But I guess I'd better learn in a hurry, because we can't wait."

"I can drive it," Metria said.

They both stared at her. "But you're a demoness!" Kim said.

"I had noticed," Metria said. "Ichabod taught me to drive yesterday. I drove us much of the way here."

"This is crazy, but we can't waste time," Dug said. "We don't know how fast the magic's fading. Maybe with a licensed driver up front with her—"

"Me," Kim said. "I won't be distracted by her legs."

"Good point," he agreed. "Let's move out."

They closed up the back, and Metria turned smoky and phased through the truck directly to the driver's seat, rather than risk stepping to the side and maybe out of the narrowing aisle of magic. Kim joined her. "I'll do map duty," Kim said, digging into the panel in front of her seat. "Put on your seat belt."

"But no belt can hold me."

"Put it on anyway," Kim said, buckling hers. "We don't want to attract any traffic cop's attention."

Metria used the key and started the motor, remembering to use the clutch pedal. She knew she had to do everything right, because they couldn't afford any accident. She put it in gear and let the clutch pedal rise slowly.

"The brake!" Kim snapped.

Oh, yes. Just in time. Metria released the hand brake.

"Traffic's clear ahead," Kim said.

Metria pulled the truck slowly in a circle and then onto the road, turning the steering wheel. She was doing it! She got it straight and used the pedals and stick to get it through the gears and up to full speed.

"Keep to the right of the road," Kim said.

Oops, yes. It was just as well that Kim was with her, because there were a number of details to keep track of, and they tended to get lost around the edges.

Kim studied her map and called out a particular magic symbol to look for, which marked the route they needed to follow. Metria hadn't been aware of that; Ichabod had known the area, so hadn't needed any map or route. This business of driving was more complicated than it had seemed.

Then, just as she was getting accustomed to it, something happened. "Drunk driver," Kim muttered. "See that wee-wawing? Stay clear of him."

"What's a drunk driver?"

"Someone who's intoxicated. You know, dizzy, crazy. Liable to do anything. Dangerous, in a car." Kim glanced back. "I hope Jenny doesn't catch on. She'd freak out."

"But what does Jenny Elf know of dunked drivers?"

"Just get the bleep elsewhere, fast."

But the traffic had closed in, so she couldn't get away from the crazy car. So she tried to keep some distance from it, following Kim's advice.

Then it happened. A girl was crossing the road, and the drunk car was headed right for her, not stopping as it should.

"Drat! I knew it!" Kim said, wincing. "If they'd just stop coddling those lushes—"

There was a scream. Another girl ran out in front of the car, getting between it and the first girl, pushing her out of the way. But then the car struck the second girl.

Meanwhile Metria was slewing to a halt, so as not to hit car or girl herself. She saw the second girl lying by the side of the road, and heard the first girl screaming.

"Oh, God, no, we can't stop," Kim said. "It'd be the end of you and of Arnolde, and maybe of Ichabod and Jenny if we get caught up in this. We've got to get out of here!"

But already things were jammed, because of the accident. They couldn't drive on. They had to wait, while a screaming vehicle zoomed up and took the girls away.

"Of all the things to happen!" Kim moaned. "All because of that damned drunk! They should lock them all up forever!"

A Mundane demon garbed in blue came to the truck. "You a witness?" he asked, glancing down at Metria's legs, which were very full and bare below her hiked-up skirt.

"The drunk car aimed for the smaller girl, but the bigger girl pushed her out of the way," Metria said.

"Ixnay," Kim whispered. "We can't get involved!"

But the blue demon was already asking another question. "How do you know he was drunk?" He glanced down her blouse, which happened to be somewhat loose above, showing the fullness thereof.

"He was sliding all across the road," Metria said.

The demon nodded. "Your license, please?"

"My what?"

"Here's mine!" Kim cried, thrusting a small card under the demon's nose.

He frowned, considering it, then nodded as he made a note. "You may receive a summons to appear at court to testify," he said. "Have a nice day, ladies." He took one more glance at Metria's assets, wavered slightly unsteadily on his feet, and moved on to the next vehicle behind them.

"That summons will come to me," Kim said. "Good thing he didn't think to get your identity too, or to look in the back of the truck."

"Well, I did my part," Metria said, lengthening her skirt and raising her decolletage. "I've had some experience befuddling men's minds, and it seems to work about as well on Mundanes as on Xanthians, fortunately."

Kim glanced at her, appraisingly. "Yes, that sort of magic does seem to be universal, for those who have the equipment. I was almost afraid that cop's eyes would bulge out of their sockets. I suppose we're lucky he didn't ask you for a date."

"I could have given him one, but it would have dissolved the moment it left my presence."

"That's date, as in he gets to take you to a meal or movie and run his hands over your body."

"Oh, I wish I'd known! That might have been fun."

"No it wouldn't. Remember, you're married."

"That, too," Metria agreed, thinking of the cop's face on such a date when she made her body smoky and impossible to touch. "But of course, I can't leave the aisle of magic."

"Yes. I hope we get out of here soon. That magic must be fading all the time."

Finally they did get moving. The speed of the traffic became faster in direct proportion to its distance from the cop cars, so that they progressed rapidly toward Xanth.

But all was not completely well. The magic was diminishing. At first Metria felt it in her toes, which were the farthest from Arnolde; they tingled for a while, but then they were turning numb. She looked down, and felt an almost mortal chill. "Kim, my toes are gone!"

Kim looked. "They must be outside the magic. We've got to do something." She knocked on the window to the back, until Dug's face showed. "Get Arnolde closer!" she yelled. "Metria's toes are going!"

There was a scramble in back. Then sensation returned to her toes. They had gotten the centaur moved up as close against the wall as possible, so the magic was back. But she knew this wouldn't last long.

It didn't. All too soon the dread tingling resumed, then the dread numbness. "I'm losing my feet," she said. "I won't be able to push the magic command pedals."

"We can't stop," Kim said. "I'll have to do it. But you'll have to tell me how, because I'm an absolute ignoramus on standard shift."

"Take my place," Metria said.

"We'll have to stop, so we can change."

"No, just sit in my lap and sink through me."

"Oh, yeah—you can dissolve." So Kim scrambled across, and Metria turned smoky, so that she wound up sitting on top instead of on the bottom.

Then she started to drift over to the other seat, but paused when she felt the tingling again. "Oops."

"The aisle!" Kim said. "It's getting shorter and narrower. You can't go that way."

"I'd better go in back, then."

"No, we don't want to alarm them. Can't you curl up in a ball or something, and sit in my lap?"

"Certainly." Metria assumed the form of a lap dragon, curled and snoozing.

But soon Kim had to use the gearstick. "There's a stoplight ahead. What do I do?"

Metria pinched her left leg gently, using a paw with claws retracted. "Push the clutch pedal down." Then she pinched her right arm. "Let me guide you." She curled the tail around it and pushed Kim's hand along the sides of the magic H pattern of the gearshift. By coordinating foot and hand, she got the job done.

"Weird," Kim said. "I don't know how folk ever survived, when all they had was this kind of shift. And that clutch is well named: It makes my stomach clutch, trying to coordinate it." Then she glanced ahead. "Oh, no!"

"What?" Metria asked, resuming curled-up mode.

"This looks like a gang-infested corner. They're holding up cars for money, or worse. And I can't avoid it."

"This is bad?"

"This is awful. A girl can get in real trouble when she's caught by animals like these."

Oh, monsters. Metria knew how to deal with those. "Can you get them to reach in here?"

"I don't *want* them reaching in here! I want to shut those punks out." Then she made the connection. "Oh. Yes, probably." She cranked the window down.

The truck rolled to a stop. In a moment the scene Kim feared began to develop. A young man whose aspect was somewhere between that of a tired ogre and a sick troll appeared. "Hey, whatcha got, chick?" he demanded.

"Nothing for you, snotnose," Kim replied politely. "Now, go away."

"Hey, we got a fresh one here!" he said. "You know what we do to fresh chicks around here?"

"I could care less, sewer-breath."

"We shake 'em down good." He reached in and grabbed the front of her blouse. "Now, cough up some change, or I'll rip this right off you."

"My pet wouldn't like it, punk," Kim warned him.

"Your pet ain't going to get it, girlie."

Then Metria opened her dragon's mouth wide and clamped it on the exposed arm.

"Yeow!" the youth yelled. "Let go!"

"You let go," Kim said evenly. "I warned you about my pet."

He shook his arm, and hauled on it. Metria clamped down harder, and exhaled a small curl of flame. The man screamed with pain.

"I suggest you stifle it," Kim said. "Because noise annoys my pet, and then she starts chewing harder."

The punk took a better look at what had hold of his arm. Metria snorted a demonstration flame through her nose, and winked. He opened his mouth to scream. She clamped down harder, warningly. He managed to stifle it.

"Now, give me your wallet," Kim said.

"Like hell!"

Metria breathed a bit more heat past her teeth, lightly toasting his arm.

The punk reached into his pocket and pulled out his wallet. It was stuffed with money extorted from other drivers.

Meanwhile the way had opened ahead. "Okay, you can go now," Kim said. "I recommend that you not tell your friends what just happened here."

Metria opened her jaws and let the arm go. The punk jerked it out. "There's a damned dragon in here!" he cried. "It bit my arm! It's got fire and everything!"

Meanwhile, with Metria's help, Kim was getting the car in gear. As she pulled it out, the other punks approached.

"They robbed me!" the punk was yelling. "Her and that dragon! Got my wallet!"

Metria assumed the form of the softest, furriest, dearest little cat kitten she could imagine, the feline equivalent of Woe Betide. She put her head up by the window. "Mew," she said sweetly.

The other punks almost fell over laughing. "Some dragon!"

"I did try to warn him," Kim said. Then the truck was out of their range and accelerating.

"Yes you did," Metria agreed with a Cheshire grin.

"That was almost fun," Kim remarked as they resumed normal travel.

"We make a decent team," Metria purred.

But all was not well. The aisle was still shrinking, and Metria had to hunch herself in to avoid the warning tingle. "How far?" she asked.

"Maybe another hour," Kim said. "But you know, there's no road to Xanth."

Metria had forgotten about that. "I don't think we can make it afoot. Arnolde was hardly able to walk before, and Ichabod—"

"I know. So we'll have to drive cross-country and hope we make it. Because without Arnolde—"

Metria knew exactly what she meant. Arnolde was all that stood between Metria herself and a dissolving swirl of dust. "Cross-country," she agreed.

Kim checked her map, then turned off the main road onto a dirt trail. She followed that as far as she could, until it too, went the wrong way. Then she bucked the truck across a field.

"Hey, whatcha doing?" Dug shouted from in back. "You're bouncing us all over the place!"

"Trying to get us to Xanth!" Kim yelled back. "Just hang on!"

"Women drivers!" he said, and shut up.

They found a small winding trail that went approximately the right way. But it was no delight, as Kim zoomed too fast along it. "That's sugar sand ahead," she said. "If I even slow down, we'll be stuck."

"But sugar sand is good to eat," Metria said.

"Not in Mundania it isn't." She plowed into the sandy section, and Metria felt the truck slewing and slowing, but it managed to keep going. "If we don't make it pretty quick, we aren't going to," Kim said grimly.

"Not all of us, anyway," Metria agreed. For the first time in her long existence she felt the threatening fear of extinction. Already the tingling was tweaking her dragon tail when it extended beyond Kim's lap; the aisle was still shrinking.

Then the trail veered whimsically away to the side. "My dead reckoning says Xanth is straight ahead," Kim said. "If I follow the trail, it may take us away from Xanth. But if I don't—"

Metria's dragon ears were starting to tingle. She flattened them down, then changed to Woe Betide, whose ears didn't project as far. "Go for it," she said. "We are about out of time."

"You got it. Get me into low gear."

Woe Betide helped her with the motion of the stick through the labyrinth of the H. The truck slowed, but seemed to have more power.

"Hang on," Kim said grimly. "We're going until we stop."

Metria hung on, hoping that those in back were doing the same. She watched as the scene through the windshield got rough. The truck bucked like an angry unicorn and charged for the trees of the forest. Just as it seemed they would crash into a treetrunk, Kim steered slightly to the right and missed the nearest tree, then slewed to the left and grazed the next. They plowed through thick brush that couldn't be avoided.

The forest, realizing that Kim couldn't be bluffed, gave way, and they ground on slowly toward Xanth. The ride was bumpy but tolerable.

Then they came to a marsh. "Uh-oh," Kim muttered. "I don't know how deep this is. But we'll find out." She revved up the engine and squashed on in.

At first the truck was game. But the farther it went, the slower it got. "The wheels are spinning," Kim said. But they were still moving forward, and ahead the ground was rising. They nudged toward it, and the truck began to lift out of the muck—and then the motor stalled.

"Bleep!" Kim swore. "Wires must've shorted." She tried to start the motor again, but it would have none of it. They were definitely stuck.

10
BOOK OF KINGS

K im sagged in the seat. "We didn't make it," she said. "What now? We can't haul Arnolde through this muck, and he sure can't haul himself. We can't leave him, for two or three solid reasons. And without him . . ."

Woe Betide was only a child, but she knew what Kim wasn't saying. Without Arnolde's aisle of magic, Ichabod would probably die, and she herself would dissolve into a swirl of wind. Only Kim, Dug, and Jenny non-elf would be able to trudge on to Xanth.

So she asked a childish question. "Could Arnolde maybe slide forward to dry land, if the front of the truck wasn't there?"

"I guess. But what would that gain?"

"Could he maybe be pushed, if we had a sledge to hold him?"

"I suppose so. But we don't."

"Could we push it through that rocky tangle ahead, if we had a channel?"

"What is the point of this, Woe? We can't change the landscape."

"Yes we can."

"What are you talking about?"

"Your magic talent."

Kim laughed, bitterly. "I don't have any magic talent! I'm Mundane, remember?"

"The one you won."

Kim reconsidered. "Oh, you mean the talent of erasure I got for winning the game, three years ago. I can use that only in the game."

"Only in Xanth."

"Same thing!" Then Kim did a double take. "We're going to Xanth! I could use it there!"

"What about in the aisle?"

Kim's jaw dropped. "Why—I never thought to try."

"Try," Woe Betide said.

Kim put her hand against the dashboard and stroked sideways, as if washing it. That section disappeared, as if it were part of a picture that had been erased. The brush of the swamp bank showed through that gap.

Kim touched the hole with her other hand. "It's gone!" she said. "The whole front of the truck is gone!"

Then she made a reverse stroke, with her palm toward her. That erased the erasure, and the dashboard was restored.

"So erase what's ahead, and push Arnolde through," Woe Betide said.

"Maybe it would work," Kim said, awed. "As long as the magic lasts. Maybe we can make it after all."

"Sure," Woe Betide said eagerly.

"But this has to be sensible. I can erase the truck, and maybe some of the terrain, but there needs to be something to replace it." Kim erased the front of the truck again, this time using broader strokes, then smoothed her hand across the air that was in the hole. A kind of dull blah substance filled in. "Smeared paints from what I just erased," she said. "Instead of restoring, I smeared it back. That makes a base, I think. Shame to ruin Ichabod's truck, but this is an emergency."

Then she turned around. "This I'd better erase excruciatingly carefully, because I don't want to erase Arnolde too." She moved her hand slowly across the back of the cab.

In a moment and a half the barrier between the front and the back was gone. Dug peered through the hole, with Sammy and Bubbles at his feet. "What are you girls doing?" he demanded. "First you plunge into a swamp; now—"

"Using my talent," Kim replied. "The truck's mired and dead; we need to go on by ourselves."

"Arnolde and Ichabod can't—"

"We have a plan. I'll erase what gets in our way."

"I'm not in your way!" he said, stepping back. Behind him, both Arnolde and Ichabod seemed to be unconscious.

Kim smiled, briefly. "I won't erase you, Dug. We'll need you to push the boat."

"Boat?"

Woe Betide smiled as she took a place almost astride the unconscious centaur. "Ship, craft, vessel, canoe, raft—"

"Stifle it, tyke. *What* boat?"

"The one I'm erasing," Kim said. She had now gotten the rest of the barrier out, and was starting on the back of the truck.

He looked at Jenny. "Does this make sense to you, elf?"

"No," Jenny said.

"So it's not a gender or age thing," he said, shaking his head. "Do you think she's lost her marbles?"

"No," Woe Betide said. "It's an intelligence thing."

"Okay, genius: What is she doing?"

"She's making a boat by erasing everything that's not a boat," Woe Betide explained.

Dug squinted. "I see. But there's a problem."

"Just let me *do* it," Kim said, concentrating on her careful erasing and occasional restoring. She was clearing away the truck from the edges, leaving an intact platform in the center.

Then it stopped happening. She tried repeatedly to erase the side panel, but it resisted, remaining real.

"That's the problem," Dug said. "You can't erase outside the magic, and it doesn't extend far enough out to the sides."

"But if Arnolde turns, so that the aisle angles across the sides—" Kim said.

"Then everyone else will have to turn with him. And even so, it's just a flat platform, not a boat."

Kim paused, considering. Then she resumed her work. "I can carve a boat out of the middle, without erasing what's farther out," she said. "And I can make sides." She demonstrated her newly found smeared-paint technique. "This may not be artistic, but it works."

Dug studied the short smear-wall she had just made. He tapped it with his finger. "Feels like compressed wood or metal. Is it strong enough?"

"I don't know. I'm still learning how to use my talent. Maybe you can find out for me."

"Sure thing." He lifted one foot and brought it down hard on the smear wall. "Ouch! It's strong enough." Then he looked beyond the truck. "But how can you float a boat without water?"

"I hope to erase the land and form a channel, and maybe the swamp water will fill it."

He nodded. "It works for me." He looked around. "Not much I can do here. Maybe I'll scout ahead, see if I can find Xanth."

Kim looked up. "How will you know, without magic?"

"I'll go with him," Jenny Elf said. "When I change form, we'll know."

"Go," Kim said, returning to her work. Woe Betide knew why: They couldn't afford to waste any time. If they didn't get to Xanth soon, it would be too late for half the party.

The two set off, and soon disappeared into the forest ahead. "Don't you worry about your boyfriend and your friend?" Woe Betide asked.

"No. Jenny Elf was my Companion in the game. I know her. And I know Dug."

Answer enough. "Do you think we're close enough to Xanth to make it in time?"

"We have to be. According to my map, we're just about at the Florida border, which for us is Xanth. It must be within a mile or so. And the fringe of magic must extend out beyond it. So any further headway we can make is bound to help." But she looked worried.

Woe Betide knew why. Maps might be wrong, or the party might not be as far along as they thought. A small error could make a big difference. They just had to hope they were close enough.

The boat was forming, but its shape showed their problem: The front was broader than the rear, because in the time it took Kim to erase the connecting truck, the aisle was shrinking. Now it was almost touching the centaur at the sides. Kim also seemed to be working harder, as if the strength of the aisle was weakening as it shrank. Time was really getting short.

Dug and Jenny returned. "We found it!" he called. "Less than a mile ahead. Maybe closer, because it doesn't thin out all at once."

"Thank God!" Kim breathed. Woe Betide saw the suppressed tension leaving her. Then the girl smiled and faced Dug. "Of course," she said, as if there had never been any doubt.

"We've marked out the easiest route," Dug continued. "I mean, there's no point in erasing healthy trees or nice scenery."

"How do I love thee," Kim murmured. "Let me count the ways." Metria was struck by the utter sincerity of her words; under the banter and insults and shin-kicks there was a solid core of real love. Then, louder, "Let's do it. We've got to work fast."

Dug walked around behind what remained of the truck, his feet sinking into the muck. "Must be a rope here," he said. "Or a chain. Got it." He pulled forth a chain from under the truck bed. "I'll just hook this to the boat, and haul it along. Soon as there's a channel."

Kim faced forward. The ground now came right up to the edge of the boat, because the front of the truck had been erased. She brushed her hand across the ground, and it disappeared, leaving a dark hole. She stroked her hands back, and the hole spread. She wiped it out to the sides, and now some water seeped in.

She reached farther forward, but couldn't erase the land there; the aisle was now too short. So she did what she could close to the boat, while Dug tried to hook the chain on. "Need a hole," he muttered. So Kim wiped one finger there, and made a hole. He passed the chain through, then tried to tie it.

"Here," Kim said. She erased part of one link, set the end of the chain there, and unerased the link. Now the chain was firmly anchored.

Dug looked at that. "That's a more versatile talent than I thought."

"It's close to Sorceress level, properly exploited," Woe Betide said.

Dug braced himself and hauled on the chain, but couldn't budge the boat. "Too much weight on it," Kim said, stepping off. "And not enough pull. I'll help." She joined Dug.

"You know, a fellow could get to like you, if he tried," Dug remarked.

"Don't get fresh, just pull," Kim retorted, smiling.

But though the boat wavered, it didn't actually move. Jenny joined them, but still it didn't work. It seemed to be caught on something below.

"I can help," Woe Betide said. She turned smoky, sank through the boat, and spread out into a sheet immediately below it. She could do this because she was still close to Arnolde, within the aisle. In fact, she could now resume full volume and be Metria again. She felt the snags on the bottom of the boat, where Kim had not been able to reach, and solidified her substance around them, smoothing them out. Then she turned her bottom side slippery.

Suddenly the boat lurched forward. It splashed into the erased hole before it—then out of it and onto the land. Metria had made it so slippery that it moved readily, no longer actually needing a water channel.

The others did not question a good thing. They kept hauling on the chain, and so Metria maintained the slippery bottom, and the craft fairly whizzed along over the ground. It left the peculiar wreckage of the truck behind. Years later, perhaps, Mundanes would discover it, and wonder whether a monster had chomped a boat-shaped bite out of it. They would surely never guess the truth.

The trees passed, and the forest thickened. The boat sloshed in irregular curves as it followed the route Dug and Jenny had prescribed. Progress gradually slowed, because the haulers were getting tired, and because Metria was beginning to tingle on her underside. She thinned her body, but knew that soon she would have to withdraw to the top of the boat or lose her substance. That would make it that much harder to haul. Were they losing their race against time after all?

Then the tingling faded. Was she turning numb? If so, she had to quit right now. But it didn't seem like that. It seemed almost as if she was gaining strength. How could that be? Well, as long as it lasted, she would do as much as she could. She made her under-surface even more super slippery, and felt the boat pick up speed. The others were pulling harder, doing their last-gasp bit too.

Arnolde lifted his head. "What is going on?" he inquired.

Metria poked a mouth up through the boat. "We're hauling you to Xanth," she said. "Before you poop out entirely."

"Poop out? I was just resting. You don't need to haul me anywhere."

"Yes we do, because—"

"Look at Jenny's ears!" Dug exclaimed. "They're pointed."

"We're in Xanth!" Kim cried. "Oh, I'm so glad, I could kiss someone!"

"Well, if you feel that wa—" But he was cut off by her hurtling kiss.

Metria floated up through the boat. She extended an arm cautiously to the side. She reached beyond the prior limit, and felt no tingle. It was true: They were now surrounded by magic.

"I could kiss someone too," she said. She floated to Ichabod, who was just beginning to stir. "I think I'll wake the sleeping prince." She put her head down, solidified her face, and planted Xanth's most poignant kiss on his mouth.

The man came awake as if electrified. He seemed to float. "I thought I was dying," he said. "Now I'm in heaven."

"Would you settle for Xanth?" she asked.

"Same thing."

Dug and Kim and Jenny closed in. "You made it possible, Met," Dug said. "We couldn't budge that thing, until you iced it. You were the difference."

"You're a great person," Kim said, and Jenny nodded agreement.

Metria opened her mouth to say something clever, but it dissolved instead. She had never anticipated such a reaction. She melted into a puddle.

They crossed the Interface and were back in Xanth proper. Sammy found them a pie tree, and they feasted. It was such a relief to be back in Xanth! Even the animals seemed to like it; Sammy lived to find things magically, and Bubbles was becoming more lively than she had been. Evidently she, like the centaur, needed magic to restore her vitality.

"Now we must organize," Kim said. "Arnolde and Ichabod need to return to the Region of Madness, and Dug and I and Jenny have to get to this Nameless Castle, and you, Metria, have your other summonsees to summons. Do we just split up and go our separate ways?"

"No," Metria said immediately. "It's my job to get all the summonsees there safely, so I can't just turn you loose. And I should make sure that Arnolde and Ichabod get to the madness safely too, because it was to help me fetch you that they left it, at great discomfort and risk to themselves."

"Then perhaps we should travel together for a while longer," Arnolde said, seeming undispleased.

"It works for me," Dug agreed, similarly satisfied. "Maybe the rest of us can help her fetch in the remaining summonsees."

"If my new talent can be useful—" Kim said.

Metria laughed. "It was your talent that saved us! It can surely help again."

"But without Arnolde's aisle of magic, I couldn't have used it," Kim said.

"And I couldn't have existed," Metria added.

"There is enough credit to go around," Arnolde said. "I think it is fair to say that we have come to respect each other, by profiting from the abilities each brought to the mission. Ichabod provided the house, truck, and knowledge of Mundania, without which the effort would have foundered. Dug and Jenny explored for the most expeditious route and provided most of the hauling strength. Each person's contribution was vital at some point."

The others passed a glance around. The centaur did have a point. Suddenly they all felt better about themselves.

"Then let's travel," Kim said briskly.

Dug shook his head. "You're a bit hyper, know that? All the rest of us are tired from physical exertion, or wrung out from a siege of low magic. And you are too, if you had the wit to know it. We need to rest, or we'll blunder into real mischief. Xanth isn't all that safe for distracted or dull folk. Tomorrow we can find an enchanted path and travel well. Today we'd better just recover.''

Another glance circulated. It was another valid point.

''I'm sorry,'' Kim said. ''I'm being pushy again. Yes, I'm tired too, and sort of dazed about being back in Xanth. I never thought I'd get here outside of the game. But it's great. I'll shut up.''

''That's the way I like my women,'' Dug said. ''Quiet and submissive.'' He dodged her first kick. ''And beautiful.'' That stalled her second kick in midair. She lost her balance and fell into him, so he kissed her soundly. Actually Kim wasn't beautiful in the standard sense, but it seemed that Dug knew a bit about girlfriend management too.

''I'd better check on Veleno,'' Metria said, remembering her husband for some irrelevant reason. ''Will you folk be okay here for a while?''

''We should be,'' Arnolde said. ''This close to the edge of magic, there shouldn't be any bad monsters.''

''And we can simply step back through the Interface if there are,'' Jenny said. ''We can go where they can't.''

So Metria popped off home, where Veleno was just beginning to run out of delirious happiness. It had been, after all, more than a day. She bustled him back to the bedroom and dosed him with another day's worth. She would have liked to stay longer, but she had an obligation to the traveling group to see it safely to its destinations. Her new conscience was a strict mistress, but she didn't mind.

When she returned, the group was relaxing under a weeping willow tree, cheering it by their company. Arnolde was discoursing on some of the problems of archivism. ''Old documents are invaluable,'' he was saying. ''Even those deemed to be of little worth by their perpetrators. A scribbled note to stay out of the honey pot informs us that they did have honey pots in those days, and that they had writing. Unfortunately some key documents have been lost to history. As a centaur, I naturally know the list of the human Kings of Xanth, but there are some distressing lacunae.''

''Lacuna,'' Metria said. ''She's still around. She was retroactively married, and—'' She paused, seeing their stares. ''Did I say something stupid?''

Arnolde smiled. ''No, of course not, my dear. I was merely using the word in its linguistic capacity, meaning a gap or omission. Perhaps we expected you to say, 'A distressing what?' and we could then have had the dubious pleasure of redefining the term.''

''Oh. Whatever.'' She still felt out of sorts.

''At any rate, I was going on too long,'' Arnolde said. ''I wish there were some forgotten tome listing all the missing Kings, felicitously turning up. But of course, Good Magician Humfrey would have found it already if any such existed.''

''Unless it got lost during his distraction of wives,'' Ichabod said. ''Then he might have overlooked it.''

''Say,'' Dug said. ''I wonder if Sammy could find such a tome.''

The cat had been snoozing beside Bubbles, but suddenly woke and set off running. Jenny Elf scrambled after him. ''Wait for me!''

''Now look what you've done, idiot!'' Kim told Dug.

''I'll track him!'' Metria said, glad for something to do to make up for her conversational gaffe. She floated rapidly after the cat.

It turned out to be no long chase. Sammy ran up to a small structure bearing a plaque with the words BOOK STORE. Metria lifted its lid and peered in. It turned out to be a solidly constructed box wherein books were stored. The top one was a tome titled BOOK OF KINGS. So she took that out, set the lid back in place, and opened it. She was holding it backward, so she saw the last page first. There was a crude scrawled entry: STOLN BY TH OGRE ACHEVER, OGRE AN OGRE AGIN.

She considered. That did look like the writing of an ogre. Ogres were justifiably proud of their stupidity. But how could any ogre have stolen such a (presumably) important book once, let alone over and over again? Even an overachiever among ogres would have trouble stealing a book; few ogres even knew what a book was.

Still, this one obviously did. He was actually a literate ogre, perhaps the only such in the mottled history of ogredom. So he had evidently done it, and was proud enough of his achievement to record it in the very book he had stolen.

She turned back another page. This one listed Magician Aeolus, the Storm King, assuming the throne in the year 971.

That was all. The rest of the page was blank. No other Kings were listed.

Since there had indeed been Kings thereafter—she could think of Magician Trent the Transformer, Magician Dor who talked with the inanimate, and about eight brief others in between—she knew that this book had been stolen during the Storm King's reign. That wasn't surprising, since the Storm King had become rather dim in his declining years, able to blow up hardly more than a breath of wind, and not much stronger intellectually. He had probably lost or forgotten the book, and the ogre achiever had found it, and given himself credit for stealing it. Thus all that it contained had been lost to Xanth history.

Assuming that it contained anything much. So she turned some more pages, and saw that more Kings were indeed listed. In fact, they went right back to the beginning of Xanth Kings. This book must have been passed down from King to King over the centuries, each one filling in the end date for his predecessor and his own year of ascension.

Good enough. She closed the book and carried it back to the waiting group. ''I think this is it,'' she said, presenting the tome to Arnolde.

''Why, so it may be,'' the centaur said, amazed. He opened the book and read its title page. ''Human Magician Kings of Xanth.'' He looked up. ''Astonishing! Where did Sammy find this?''

''In a book store.''

''A book store—in Xanth?'' Kim asked. ''Did you have to buy it?''

''No, it's just a box where books are stored.''

''There are other books?'' Ichabod asked alertly. ''If they are of similar rarity and quality, that may be an informational fortune! We must examine them.''

''Sure,'' Metria said. ''Right this way.''

But when she returned to the place she had found the box, there was nothing there. There did not seem ever to have been anything there, either; it was just an undisturbed rocky region in the forest.

"Maybe Sammy—?" Dug said.

But this time the cat was indifferent. "I don't think there's anything to find," Jenny said. "He can find anything but home, except when there isn't anything. Then he just ignores it."

"But there *was* a box!" Metria protested.

Ichabod cogitated. "Perhaps it moved—and the cat is unable to find a given object a second time, that being, as it were, a home base, something already found. I think we shall have to relinquish any notion of finding those other books."

"Oh, fudge!" Metria swore. "I did it again! I should have grabbed them all."

"You are not a scholar," Ichabod said, excusing her. But a cloud of disappointment hovered near him.

The ogre achiever had stolen it over and over again, she remembered. Did that mean that each time the book store disappeared, he hunted it down again? Or that he had finally hidden it in this foolishly obvious place, and it had turned out to be a better hiding place than it seemed? If so, they had caught the book store just at the right time, before it moved. That made her feel a smidgen less worse.

They returned to Arnolde, who was engrossed in the *Book of Kings*. "This is absolutely fascinating!" he exclaimed. "I can vouch for its accuracy by the entries relating to what I already know. But there are many more. This is indeed an invaluable lost tome of information."

"What's so exciting about a list of Kings?" Kim asked. "I mean, that's what makes British history so absolutely, totally, completely boring, not to mention dull."

"Well, there are also the dates of the Kings," Ichabod said, looking over his friend's shoulder.

"Maybe I didn't make myself quite clear," Kim said grimly. "If there's one thing worse than lists of names, it's lists of dates. Not only are they boring and dull, they're impossible to remember, and you flunk if you make a simple little mistake, like putting the wrong name with the right dates."

"Yeah," Dug agreed. "I remember when I listed Henry the Eighth for 1909 to '47. You'd have thought the sky was falling!"

"You were precisely four centuries off!" Ichabod exclaimed, shocked.

"So what's four centuries between friends?" Kim asked.

"I certainly wouldn't want to bore anyone with unwanted lists of names and dates and talents," Arnolde said. "I shall be happy to commit this volume silently to memory." He pored over the book with much the same intensity that Magician Humfrey did with his own tomes. "Oh, my! The Sorceress Tapis was once married? That explains so much! And the Zombie Master was actually the son of a King, but alienated because of the nature of his talent. I never suspected! This will revolutionize Xanth history."

"Or at least the current rendering of it," Ichabod agreed. "It does seem that there were some dark secrets in those early days."

"Exceedingly dark," Arnolde agreed.

"Actually, I'm curious," Metria said. "Maybe I knew some of those Kings."

Dug and Kim started to laugh, then stopped as they saw that neither Metria nor Arnolde was. "That's right," Dug said. "Demons live forever, or as close as makes no nevermind. Maybe she *did* know some Kings."

"I did," Metria agreed. "But I got close to only two, Gromden and Humfrey. The others didn't interest me."

"That's right," Kim said. "Humfrey was King once. You tried to distract him from his studies at the Demon University. But what's this about you and King Gromden?"

"I seduced him. But it got complicated."

Kim reconsidered. "Maybe I *am* interested in some of those Kings. If they were real living people, I mean, not just dates."

"Gromden must have been a hot date," Dug said.

She ignored him. "Let's hear about some Xanth Kings. You've got my curiosity going."

"And she's dangerous when she's curious," Dug said, dodging another kick.

So they settled back and listened to Arnold's recital of Kings, old and new, as augmented by the *Book of Kings*.

"The uninterrupted human population of Xanth began with the

First Wave, its arrival defined as the year 0. For the first two centuries there were no Kings. The savagery of the early years may have prevented the human folk from achieving sufficient unity. Then King Merlin, whose talent was Knowledge, became the first in the year two-oh-four, just in time to try to help organize the women to kill their rapist husbands of the Third Wave and bring in better men, the so-called Fourth Wave.''

As he spoke, Jenny Elf settled by his flank with Sammy and Bubbles and hummed a little tune. Metria, interested in information about the old Kings that she hadn't paid much attention to at the time, listened with complete attention. She realized that her half soul was giving her a new perspective, so that now the events had meaning. She remembered the brutal Third Wave largely exterminating what had been the brutal Second Wave. But the Fourth Wave had been something else, and that one had built the foundation on which the human kingdom became significant.

Then she saw old King Merlin vacating his throne, separating from his wife, the Sorceress Tapis, and going to Mundania on some kind of business only he could understand. Tapis was so annoyed, she never remarried, and never spoke of Merlin again. She did tolerate her daughter the Princess, but neither spoke of their connection because both had written the memory of the King out of their lives.

''Well, Merlin did have business in Mundania,'' Ichabod remarked. He was standing beside her, watching King Merlin depart Xanth. ''There was a lad named Arthur he had to educate to be King.''

''That was more important than governing Xanth?'' Jenny asked. She was standing on Ichabod's other side.

The old Mundane shrugged. ''There are those who thought so.''

''Hey, here comes Roogna,'' Kim said from Metria's other side. ''But this is starting to get cluttered with dates.''

Then in 228 Magician Roogna, whose talent was Adaptation, assumed the throne. Eight years later the Princess suffered a change of plans and married him, with her mother's blessing, because he really was a decent man. He built Castle Roogna, with the help of centaurs.

''Naturally, the centaurs,'' Arnolde said. ''No other species had the expertise.''

King Roogna died fighting the Sixth Wave. It was an ugly scene, because the invading Mundanes were so brutal and ignorant of magic. Ichabod, Kim, and Dug winced in unison, ashamed of their heritage. Roogna's place was taken by Xanth's first female King, the Sorceress Rana, whose talent was Creation, in 286. When she died in 325, Magician Reitas, whose talent was Solving Problems, took over. Unfortunately he seemed to generate almost as many problems as he solved, because there were always unintended complications. When one of those complications killed him in 350, ending Reitas' reign, Rana's son Magician Rune became King. His talent was evocation. "Too many dates," Kim muttered.

That lasted until 378, when Rune died fighting the Seventh Wave. The people, desperate for leadership that could save them, persuaded the zombie Jonathan to assume the throne.

"The Zombie Master!" Kim cried. *"He* was King of Xanth?"

Metria popped out of her dream. She was back in contemporary Xanth. "But demons don't dream," she protested.

"Yes you do, when you have a soul," Jenny said. "You were sharing my dream just now; I saw you there, watching the parade of Kings with me. We all were there."

"That's right—I can dream now," Metria said. "Mentia dreamed with Gary Gargoyle last year. That was really ancient history."

"Sorry I jogged us all out of it," Kim said. "Anyone who isn't paying attention can enter one of Jenny's dreams, when she's humming. That's her talent. But it's easy to startle folk out of it. I should have kept my big mouth shut, as usual. But this business of the Zombie Master being King of Xanth—how come he never mentioned that?"

"Well, zombies don't have very good memories," Arnolde said. "Because their heads are filled with—"

"Never mind!" Kim said. "I get the picture. But how could a zombie govern?"

"I remember that," Metria said. "That was one King I *didn't* try to seduce! He couldn't be killed, so anyone who attacked him just got frustrated, until Jonathan caught up to him and threatened to turn him into a zombie too."

"But he couldn't turn living folk into zombies," Kim said.

"They didn't always know that. And of course, he could have arranged to have them killed first. So they didn't give him any lip, or any other parts of their bodies. They did exactly what he told them to do, so that he would stay away from them. And he did, as long as they behaved. He was actually a very gentle man. That's why his reign lasted a whole century. He finally got fed up with the rotten job and abdicated. He was more interested in chasing after Millie the Ghost anyway."

Kim shook her head. "You were right: there are wrinkles to Xanth history I never suspected. The Zombie Master is a nice guy, now that he's alive."

"He always was. It was just that other folk couldn't stand his talent. So he was somewhat isolated, until Millie loved him."

Night was threatening by now, so Kim erased a nice place on the ground, making a pit, then smeared a top across it, so that they had a safe underground chamber to sleep in. Sammy located a pillow bush and blanket tree, and they made comfortable beds.

"You know, a single bed would do for the two of us," Dug suggested hopefully.

"Sorry—I'm already sharing mine with Bubbles," Kim informed him. Dug didn't argue. They had evidently discussed this before.

Metria didn't need to sleep, but she did settle down to dream again, as Jenny started humming. She dreamed of Magician Vortex becoming King in 478 after the Zombie King abdicated. Vortex's talent was Summoning Demons. How well she remembered! He had summoned her once, but not for anything interesting; he was merely curious about her impediment of speech, as he put it. She tried to distract him by seducing him, but he had a policy against being seduced by demonesses. That was when she learned that sometimes it was best to conceal her nature, and that caution was to stand her in good stead two centuries later with King Gromden. But it took her a good five minutes of seductive effort before she realized that it wasn't working with Vortex. She was about to do her ultimate, by showing him her panties, when—

"Wow!" Dug exclaimed. "Now, that's what I call a hot scene!"

"Get out of this dream!" Kim snapped at him, and he vanished, but the interested look remained on his face.

So it was the group dream again. That was all right; Metria found that she rather liked the company. Jenny Elf's talent was a lot of fun.

"Thank you," Jenny said.

The dream continued through the next name on the list, King Neytron, whose talent was Bringing Paintings to Life; he didn't need any sexy demonesses either, because all he had to do was paint the type of woman he desired, and she would be his. He also painted elaborate furnishings for Castle Roogna, and, when times became lean, supplies of food for the people. It occurred to Metria that Kim's talent was the reverse of this. Then there was King Nero, who animated golems, and they were very good for getting work done. They planted a much larger orchard, so that the local folk would never again have to be concerned about their food supply.

Then came Gromden, in 623. She concluded her dream with him, though there were a number of other Kings of Xanth to follow him. Including a second female King, Elona, in 797, whose talent was longevity for herself and any others she chose. She governed for a long time. Today, Metria thought, folk believed that there had never been female Kings of Xanth, historically, but that was ignorance. And the Ghost King Warren, who had also been lost to history. But after that came King Ebnez, with his talent of Inanimate Adaptation, followed by Humfrey, the Storm King Aeolus, Trent, and Dor. She would dream about them some other time.

"That was definitely not fit for Dug to see," Kim said. "He already has too many big ideas."

"You don't like them?" Jenny asked.

"Not when they're about other women."

Jenny laughed. The effort was too much for the dream, and it faded out, leaving Metria awake.

Oh, yes, she had toyed with history, in her fashion. Now, with her soul, she regretted some of it. But not much.

Then she snapped alert. There was someone with her, and not one of the regular party. "Who are you?" she demanded abruptly.

A horse figure reared back, startled. A night mare!

"Not so fast, equine!" she said, puffing into smoke and surrounding it. "How is it that you're trying to give a bad dream to a demoness?"

The figure tried to run away, but her smoke surrounded it, so that it couldn't get away. So it projected a little dream figure of a man. "I thought you were mortal," the man said. "What are you doing with half a soul?"

"You're male?" she asked, astonished.

"I'm a night colt," the dream man said. "They wouldn't let me take out any dreams. So I stole half a soul and went out on my own. I sniffed out some impromptu dreaming here, so I came to see if I could get in on it. I don't have much experience, you know."

"That's obvious," Metria said, realizing that it had been Jenny's powerful group dream that had attracted the colt's attention. "You can't just go anywhere with dreams; you have to bring them from the gourd, to assigned people who deserve them."

"But I told you, they won't let me have any of those."

"Then maybe you had better just explore Xanth, and not mess with dreams at all."

"No, I'm a dream creature; I have to associate with dreams. Since I don't have a cargo of my own, messing with others is all I can do."

Metria considered. "Then maybe you can make something of it. Why not enter ordinary dreams and make the folks in them do things they'd never do on their own? That could be fun, correctly done."

"I hadn't thought of that. Thanks, Demoness!" he galloped off, and this time she let him go.

It was good to be back making some mischief, even in such a small way.

Then she thought of something else. Jenny Elf's group dream had attracted a night colt. What would the Night Stallion himself think of her dreaming ability? The stallion could, of course, assume any shape he wished, being master of the dream realm. He could become a handsome man—or an elf of any size. Suppose he got interested in Jenny's talent, and then in Jenny herself?

Nah, she thought. Jenny's future was surely in regular Xanth. Or in her realm of origin, the World of Two Moons.

11
Chena

In the morning, refreshed, they set out to locate Chena Centaur, the mystery token. Kim passed the back of her hand across the surface of the nether chamber, and restored the ground the way it had been. "No sense leaving a mess," she explained.

"That is one powerful talent," Ichabod remarked. "Sorceress level, perhaps."

"I don't know," Kim said. "I'm still learning how to use it. I don't know its limits."

"It would be wise to ascertain them."

They moved on. Soon they came to a river that looked too deep to wade across. "Maybe I can erase a section," Kim said. "So we can walk across dry. Then I can unerase it after we're across."

Arnolde looked thoughtful. "I wonder."

Kim squatted by the riverbank, and passed her hand across the surface of the water. There was a ripple, but it didn't disappear. "I don't understand," Kim said. "Why isn't it working?"

"Because the water fills in the gap as soon as you make it," Arnolde replied. "I thought that might be the case. It would be remarkable were it otherwise."

Kim nodded. "I guess so."

"Perhaps it is just as well that there is some reasonable limit on it,'' Arnolde continued. ''It would be dangerous, otherwise. I think I feel more comfortable this way.''

''Me, too,'' Kim confessed. But she seemed a bit disappointed, too.

''Now how do we get across this river?'' Dug asked. ''It's too deep to wade, and I don't like the look of those shark fins in the center.''

''Loan sharks,'' Kim agreed. ''They'll take an arm and a leg if you let them. Let's not let them.''

''Maybe you could carve out another boat or raft,'' Jenny Elf suggested. ''That worked well to get us to Xanth.''

''I suppose I could. But it wouldn't be easy to navigate, because I can't get under to make a keel. We could haul it across with ropes, if we could get the ropes anchored on the far side of the water.''

''And who'll swim across with ropes!'' Dug said.

''I can do that,'' Metria said. ''I can't float with heavy things, but I can with light things, and hemp feels light.''

''It can make men light-headed,'' Ichabod agreed.

So they sent Sammy Cat to locate some hemp with suitable ropes, while Kim found a fallen log and made a dugout boat by erasing a hole in it. There were some cracks in the wood, but she smoothed those over with finger-smears, making it watertight. It wasn't Xanth's prettiest boat, but it seemed serviceable. And, contrary to her expectation, she had been able to shape a crude keel, by having the menfolk roll it over so she could work on the bottom of the hull. Small selective erasures could do a lot.

When the craft was ready, and they had the necessary rope, Metria floated across the river, carrying the end of the rope. The sharks leaped up and snapped at her with their red, green, blue, and white teeth, and sometimes they did catch a piece of her, but she just dissolved that portion into dirty tasting smoke and they were left with no interest, though they continued to make efforts on principle. She made sure to float low enough to tease them well. Her soul was a hindrance when it came to mischief against nice folk, but loan sharks gave her no problem at all.

She tied the rope to a stout A-corn tree and floated back, almost touching the water, but the sharks now knew they couldn't get a real piece of her and didn't try. "Ready," she said, tying the other end to a similarly stout B-corn tree. She yanked on it, to be sure it was tight; that shook the trees, and a few ripe cobs fell, but the rope held.

They hauled the boat to the water, and Arnolde stepped carefully in and lay down. Sammy and Bubbles joined him. That filled the boat. They would have to make two trips.

Kim had shaped two paddles by carefully erasing most of the wood from two logs. Metria took one, while Arnolde took hold of the rope and hauled himself and the boat along across the river. He wasn't strong for a centaur, but he was able to haul his own weight. Metria paddled to help move the boat.

A loan shark, sniffing mortal meat, forged up to the boat. This one was yellow, and shaped like a submarine sandwich. Its tongue was like hot pepper, and its teeth like despair. It opened its mouth just about wide enough to take in an arm or leg. Sammy hissed, and Bubbles growled, but the big fish was undaunted.

Metria struck it on the tender snout with the paddle. It hastily submerged, and they moved on across the river unbitten. The centaur got out, clearly relieved to be back on terra firma. Metria formed herself into a pulley connecting rope and boat, and pulled the boat back across.

Now Ichabod, Dug, Kim, and Jenny climbed into the boat, Dug and Kim taking the paddles. Ichabod and Jenny took hold of the rope, not so much pulling the boat along as making sure it didn't get carried away by the current. Metria settled in the center, keeping an eye out for mischief.

Mischief wasted no particular time orienting on them. This shark was huge and dark, with teeth capable of crunching through their boat in short order. It charged up, jaws open for a horrendous chomp. No swat on the snout would dissuade this monster!

So Metria became a big mass of stink-horn-flavored toffee, and thrust herself into the oncoming maw. The shark clamped down— and tasted the flavor, which was Xanth's very filthiest, stenchiest, disgustingest tang. Arnolde caught a whiff, and remarked as his face turned a trifle bilious: "Of this nefarious horn it has been said that if a sphinx with a clogged snout sniffed it once from a distance, through a thick filter, the poor creature would turn to putrid green stone for a century, and never clear its nose of the degradation.''

The shark, of course, tried to spit the loathsome mass out, but the stuff stuck to the once clean teeth and festered on the roiling tongue. The putrefaction dripped into the mouth, sending up nauseating fumes. The shark tried to wash it out with water, but the surrounding river turned an obscene shade of noisome hue and threatened to curdle. Finally the shark plunged under the surface and swam away as fast as inhumanly possible, leaving a swath of bubbly retchings behind.

Metria turned smoky and floated up through the water, leaving just enough flavor behind to guarantee that the shark would not soon be free of it. Stink horn was one of her favorite last resorts, reserved for only the most deserving opponents. Usually it was sufficient merely to blow the horn, and its foul smelling sound would drive most creatures away. But she had felt that the shark deserved more intimate treatment.

Meanwhile the boat was wending its way across the river, and a courteous breeze was clearing the air of the lingering bouquet. The passengers were starting to look as if the miasma was, after all, bearable.

Ichabod faced Metria as she returned. ''Demoness, if you please—next time a monster threatens to engulf us—let it do so in peace.'' But he managed a sickly smile.

They reached the far bank and clambered to shore. The boat still reeked of horn, so they turned it loose to float disconsolately downstream. The vegetation along the banks wilted temporarily while the boat was passing.

They set off across a field of posies that opened out before them. Each flower puffed itself up as they passed, enhancing its color and stiffening its petals, posing.

Then a girl appeared before them. No, it was two children, the other a boy: evidently twins. ''Who are you?'' the girl asked boldly.

Metria popped across to stand before the children. ''I am the Demoness Metria, passing through on business. Who are you?''

''I'm Abscissa,'' the girl replied. ''I travel along the X axis, because I have the X chromosome.''

''Along the what?''

"Horizontally." A line appeared, and the girl suddenly jumped a brief distance to the side, without moving her legs.

"I'm Ordinate," the boy said. "I travel along the Y axis, because I have the Y chromosome." A line appeared, and he jumped backwards without moving his legs. "Vertically."

"Geometrically and genetically speaking," Ichabod remarked, intrigued. He brought out his little notebook. "These are most interesting talents. Whose children are you?"

The two zipped back together. "We were supposed to be Grey Murphy and Princess Ivy's twins," Abscissa said.

"But they took too long to marry, so the stork dropped us off at an orphanage," Ordinate said.

"Well, shame on them," Kim said. "I knew they were taking too long about it."

"And they should marry any time now," Metria said. "Even if they don't know it."

The others glanced at her curiously, but the glances bounced off her without penetrating, because she wasn't paying attention.

"Does the orphanage treat you well?" Arnolde inquired.

"Oh, sure," Abscissa said.

"Of course, it can't keep us if we want to go out," Ordinate said.

"Together we can go anywhere we want to," Abscissa said.

"By projecting our coordinate map," Ordinate said.

"This is most interesting," Ichabod said, making another note. "Instant travel by geometry."

"Where can you go?" Jenny asked.

"Anywhere," Abscissa said.

"Such as to that tree?" Jenny asked, pointing to a distant nut and bolt tree beyond the flower field.

"Sure," Ordinate said. "Watch."

The two children concentrated. Lines appeared, marked X and Y, stretching all across the field, intersecting each other, forming a grid. A dot appeared beside the distant tree. The two children took each other's hands, and suddenly they were standing by the tree.

Metria popped over to them. "It is really you?" she asked.

"Sure, Demoness," Abscissa answered.

"Who else could it be?" Ordinate asked.

"It might be an illusion."

"No, we don't have that magic," Abscissa said, frowning cutely.

"But it might be fun if we did," Ordinate said.

Metria popped back to the group—and found the children already there. "Say, you're good," she said.

"Of course," Abscissa said. "We're always good."

"But we'd have been better with a family," Ordinate said.

"Maybe we'll find a family that needs twins," Kim said.

"Gee, that would be nice," Abscissa said, clapping her hands girlishly together.

"Will they let us eat eye scream every day and have pillow fights?" Ordinate asked.

"More likely they'll make you eat pillows and have eye scream fights," Dug said.

"Dug!" Kim exclaimed indignantly. "Don't tease them like that."

But the children seemed thrilled with the notion. "That's better yet," Abscissa said.

"Food fights are great," Ordinate agreed.

"Now see what you've done," Kim said to Dug. "You've given them a wicked notion. You're lucky you're not held in contempt of the Adult Conspiracy."

"Sorry 'bout that," Dug said, not looking overwhelmed with remorse.

"Well, we have to go now," Abscissa said.

"Because you folk are getting dull," Ordinate said.

"This is the nature of adults," Ichabod said. But already the coordinate map was forming, and by the time he finished speaking, the twins were gone.

They moved on. The token began tugging more strongly, so Metria knew they were getting close. Indeed, they spied some hoofprints, and followed them.

"Young filly centaur," Arnolde said.

"How can you tell?" Jenny asked. "Couldn't it be a unicorn or something?"

"No. Centaurs are especially heavy on the front feet, and tend to set them down farther apart, to brace the bodies for the use of the hands. Also, the configuration of the prints is distinct from that of unicorns.''

All hoofprints looked alike to Metria, but it was clear that Arnolde knew what he was talking about. When one set of prints crossed another, he immediately pointed out the fresher ones, before Metria confirmed it with the tug of the token.

Soon they found a bedraggled young filly centaur. Her blond hair hung lankly around her shoulders and juvenile breasts, and there were curse burrs tangled in her tail. She was eating bitter fruit, and looked miserable.

''If you stare, you'll reveal yourself as an ignorant Mundane,'' Kim whispered to Dug.

''Uh, sure,'' Dug agreed, dimming down the intensity of his stare. Like many young men, he seemed to be fascinated by nude nymphs and centaur fillies.

''Chena Centaur?'' Metria called.

The filly heard her, looked—and bolted. In half a moment she was gone.

''Hey!'' Metria exclaimed. She floated after the creature. ''I have a summons to serve.''

But the centaur fled blindly, paying no attention. Finally Metria popped to a place in front of her, and assumed the form of a centaur. She didn't have the substance of a centaur, so was mostly smoky, but it did get the filly's attention and bring her to a halt.

She stood there, panting, looking wildly about, ready to bolt again the moment she spied a feasible route.

''Chena Centaur?'' Metria asked again, sure that it was.

''Why don't you leave me alone!'' the filly demanded tearfully.

''I can't. I have to serve you with this summons.'' Metria held out the token.

''Summons?''

''For a trial. You see—''

Chena whirled around and bolted back the way she had come. But that soon brought her up against the following party. She turned again to face Metria, her eyes showing desperate white. ''I didn't mean any harm!''

Arnolde stepped forward. "My dear, the trial is not of *you*. You are being summonsed as a mere Juror."

The filly's head turned back and forth between Arnolde and Metria. "But—"

"See, it says 'Juror' on it," Metria said, holding the token up. "And your name. I must gather all the Jurors for the trial of Roxanne Roc. If you come with me, I will see that you get there safely. Several of these others in my party are similar summonsees."

"Me," Kim said. "And him," indicating Dug, "and her," indicating Jenny Elf.

The filly began to relax. "All right. I'm Chena." She took the token.

The day was getting on. "Let's find a place to camp," Kim suggested. "Tomorrow is another day."

Metria realized that this was mostly to help get Chena settled, as the filly still looked pretty wild. So while Kim erased a shelter for the night, Jenny worked with a comb to get the tangles out of Chena's hair and tail, and to brush her coat down. It seemed funny to hear Jenny's muttered cursing, but it was the only way to get curse burrs off. Sammy Cat located food for them, and Dug brought it in. Arnolde and Ichabod talked with the filly, and began to get her story. Then Jenny started humming.

On Centaur Isle a filly named Chena was foaled with a magic talent. The cursory magic inspection which all foals were given did not pick it up, so she lived for some time in blissful ignorance of her critical liability.

Chena had a loving sire and dam, two older colt brothers, and many peer-group friends. She was contented in a completely normal way: She groused about having to spend so much time in centaur school, she was furious at herself when she missed the bull's-eye once during bowmanship practice, annoying the bull, and was mortified when one foot got sore. "Dam, I have foundered!" she cried as she limped home.

"Don't use language like that," her dam reproved her. "Laminitis. Say it correctly. Night mares founder; centaurs suffer inflictions of laminitis."

"Yes, dam dear," Chena replied obediently.

"Now, go to the doctor for some enchanted balm of Gilead to put on it."

"Enchanted!" Chena said, appalled. "But isn't that magic?"

"Magic in itself is a useful and sometimes necessary thing," her dam said sensibly. "In fact, it can even be endearing, in lesser species. Just so long as it is not too closely associated with a centaur."

"Oh." Chena had thought, from the attitudes of her siblings and friends, that magic was somehow dirty. Now she understood the distinction between using magic and possessing magic, and realized that her friends were actually somewhat ignorant about it.

So she went to the centaur doctor. "I need a bomb of Gilead," she told him. "For my sore foot."

He smiled in that annoyingly superior manner of adults everywhere. "Which digit do you need detonated?"

"My right forefoot," she said, lifting it.

"Indeed," he said, examining it. "Well, here's the bomb." He rubbed some thick fragrant ointment on it, and the pain exploded outward and dissipated.

"Oh, thank you, Doctor!" she cried, dancing on the pain-free foot.

"And here is some more, in case the infliction of laminitis returns," he said, giving her a vanilla envelope.

Apart from routine things like that, Chena was a happy camper and homebody. Her main hobby was magic rocks, now that she knew that it was all right to use magic things. Some stones were pretty, and some were useful, but to her the most fascinating ones were magic. Some were known to everyone as magical, but were difficult for most folk to activate, such as charmstones and hearthstones. Others didn't seem magical at all, but Chena was able to divine their hidden powers.

In fact, she didn't know it, but she had a magic talent. It was the ability to activate magic rocks. It was not her words or insights that did it, but her hidden talent.

So she became a collector of magic stones. She always wore a pouch around her waist filled with different kinds of gems and pebbles. Rolling stones, for example, rolled without being pushed; they also, for some unknown reason, played music. Rock music, of course, and Stone Age melodies, and pebble tunes. They refused to be put in the same pouch as moss agate, not because it was soft and green, but because rolling stones gathered no moss. Then there were ope-als, which opened doors, and sapph-fires, which burned with blue fire, useful for igniting wood. Rubies would rub against her, and spinels would spin in dizzy circles.

One rock in the pouch was neither lovely nor useful. It was grayish and ordinary, and seemed to have no magic. Chena kept it because she felt sorry for it.

Then one unlucky day a centaur Elder saw Chena playing in the street with her pebbles. "Filly, what are you doing with those rocks?"

"I'm studying them," she replied, in some surprise. "I want to be a mineralogist when I grow up, and classify all the magic stones of Xanth."

"Magic stones?"

"Yes. I am very good at recognizing them and figuring out how they work. See, here is a gall stone."

"A gall stone?"

She held it up, and the stone made a galling remark. "What's it to you, horseface? You got a sore on your rump?"

The Elder did not know very much about stones, but he did know something about magic. He took Chena at once to the Building of Magic Inspection to have her reexamined. The magic detection tool they had there was the kind that responded only to active magic. Naturally her talent was active only when she was around magic rocks, which was why it had not registered before. This time she had the stones in her pouch.

"Show them your gall stone," the Elder told her.

She brought it out, and it made another galling remark. "I resent the implication, founderfoot," it said bitterly.

The instrument hummed, pointed directly at Chena, and indicated the use of a magic talent.

That was enough. That same day, Chena was exiled from Centaur Isle for obscenity. She gathered her few possessions, bid tearful farewell to her sire and dam and siblings, who tried to pretend that she had not deeply shamed them, and quietly left. She held her head high, refusing to let any emotions show, because she was, after all, a centaur, even if she was a filly of tender years.

Once she had been rafted to the mainland and was entirely free of the Isle and alone, she paused to release her pent-up emotions. To her surprise, she discovered not grief but anger. "I *like* my magic talent," she said defiantly to the forest. "They can humiliate me in public and even exile me because of it, but they can't make me ashamed of it!" Suddenly the young filly's anger exploded in one sentence: "I wouldn't go back there even if I could!" But there was just a suggestion of a trace of a tear in an eye and a thought of a tremble on a lip. She was, after all, only eleven.

Chena began to adapt to the wilderness, little by little, or even tiny by tiny, in the course of the next few hours, venturing slightly farther inland from the coast. She knew enough to avoid tangle trees and carnivorous grass—there were, after all, such things even on Centaur Isle, carefully fenced off and labeled as examples of what life was like elsewhere—and to be alert for stray dragons. With the aid of a chunk of magic searchstone, which her talent had enabled her to recognize and activate, she managed to search out pie trees and other food-supplying plants.

She also discovered the full range of her talent, now that she no longer had to hide it from herself. For example, when she accidentally cut herself on a thorn bush, she was able to use a piece of bloodstone to stanch the blood. If she wanted to go fishing, she could use a garnet to net gar. If she was thirsty, and didn't trust the local groundwater (love springs and hate springs weren't common, but why take chances?), she could get lime juice from a limestone, olive juice from olivine, or several quarts of milk from milky quartz. Gradually Chena came to realize that her talent was more powerful than the Centaur Isle Elders had suspected. It wasn't Sorceress or neo-Sorceress level, but it was still an excellent talent to have in the uncharted Xanth wilderness. They might have thought she would soon perish, alone, thus enabling them to get rid of her without having to execute her themselves, keeping their dirty hands clean. They would be disappointed, maybe.

Chena did not take unnecessary chances. She was, after all, a centaur, and possessed of excellent intelligence and judgment. She stocked up on pies at the first pie tree she found, lest she not find another soon. That night she ate a banana cream pie, because it was too squishy to last long in her knapsack, and a key lime pie, which was already getting overripe. She carefully picked the keys out, leaving the limes alone, and was about to throw them away when she decided to save them. She might need those keys later. Ope-als couldn't open everything, after all.

Now where was she to go? She had no idea. It wasn't as if she had planned this excursion. She couldn't stay long in this vicinity, because centaur hunting parties came here regularly. She didn't even dare use their trails, because she would be killed if any Isle centaur saw her. Unfortunately, she was sure that the farther she got from the Isle, the more dangerous the land would become. She had been allowed to take no weapon, which made her situation that much worse. She might be able to fashion a crude staff or club, but what she really needed was a good knife or bow.

"I wish I had a really good bow and arrows," she murmured. "And I wish I knew what to do."

Then she heard something. It sounded like trotting. Was it a unicorn—or a centaur? She quickly concealed herself in a place few folk would even think to look: behind a tangle tree. She could do this because she could see by the fresh bones that the tree had recently feasted. That meant it should be quiescent for another day or so. It was a nervy thing to do, but not as nervy as remaining in sight for a centaur archer to spot.

And it was a centaur coming. She peeked out between the listless tentacles of the tree. In fact, it was her eldest brother, Carlton Centaur! That terrified her, because when they played hide-and-seek, he had always been able to find her, no matter how cleverly she hid.

He galloped right toward her, and for a moment she was sure he saw her, but then he went on by. Then he turned and trotted back, and halted. Again she was sure he had seen her. What was he going to do? They had always gotten along well, but if there was one thing stronger than a centaur's marksmanship, it was his honor, and he would be honor-bound to execute her if he ever saw her again close to Centaur Isle.

Carlton stood near her tree, but faced to the side. "Now I don't see anyone," he said to the forest. "And I don't expect to. But it occurred to me that if anyone happened to be lost around here, he might be able to use something, so I'll leave it, just in case. And I might also remark that probably the best place for a person in doubt to go is to the human Good Magician, and ask a Question, any Question, because the Good Magician requires a year's service for an Answer, and I understand that querents are well cared for while performing such service." He set down a long package. "Of course, any lost person is surely greatly missed by his folks, even if they aren't able to say so, and I'm sure their best wishes go with him. But there's no sense in talking any longer to myself, so I will depart and not return." And he walked away, not looking back, and was soon gone.

The scene blurred, and Chena realized that there was no longer any mere hint of a tear in an eye, but a copious flow in both eyes. Her dear brother had known she was there, and brought her a gift, and some excellent advice, and gone his way, not even able to remain for her thanks.

She came out and checked the package. It was a fine bow, and a dozen perfect arrows, and one very sharp small knife. With these she could defend herself from most predators, and do some hunting. She lacked the muscle to kill a dragon at long range, but she could certainly score on small game at intermediate range, with an excellent weapon like this. She knew that Carlton had not acted alone; their parents must have supported it, though they would never say so. They couldn't stop her exile, but they did love her.

She donned the harness, so that the bow and quiver of arrows lay across her human back. The bow was so long that its ends came close to the ground and well up beyond her head; she would have to stay clear of tight squeezes. But it was wonderful having it. She strapped the sheath of the knife to her human waist, where it was readily in-reach. She felt so much better, with such equipment—and because of what it told her about the true sentiment of her family.

And what of the advice? Well, it made sense to her. Go ask the Good Magician a question, and have a year to learn how to get along in the big uncivilized world of Xanth. Not only did it give her somewhere to go, it would give her a year's leeway before she had to make a decision about the rest of her life. The Good Magician wouldn't care that she had magic; all human beings did have magic, so they saw little or no shame in it. That was, of course, part of what made them lesser beings.

So she would do it. She set her face to the north. "Thanks, Carlton," she said. "Thanks, family." Then she started on her long journey.

As dusk came, something dark and snarly loomed ahead. Chena brought her bow about and nocked an arrow. The thing hesitated, then charged. It looked like a robert cat. She loosed her arrow, but the cat saw it coming and dodged to the side. The arrow caught it in the flank instead of in the heart, so wasn't fatal. But the cat decided that this centaur filly wasn't as helpless as she seemed, and bounded away, leaving a trail of blood, but, unfortunately, taking the arrow with it. Chena hated losing an arrow, but it was better than losing her life.

She found a reasonably safe niche by two intersecting wallflowers, and settled her rump there. Then she set her bow and three arrows on the ground before her, and lay down. If anything came in the night, it would have to come from the front, and she could put an arrow or three in it before it got close. She slept, keeping her ears attuned to anything unusual. But she was in luck; nothing came.

Sometime in the night there came not a predator, but a realization: Her brother Carlton had magic too; he could find things. That explained so much! But of course, he could not admit it. He had used it to find her, so he could give her the bow, knife, and advice, but could never demonstrate it elsewhere, lest he, too, be exiled. She would certainly keep his secret.

So it was, in the next few days as she traveled north. She encountered a small mean dragon, but two arrows dissuaded it. She regretted this, because again she lost the arrows, and they were irreplaceable. But at the same time she appreciated how very much worse it could have been, without the bow. There was all the difference in Xanth between an unarmed centaur and an armed one.

It turned out to be a long way to the Good Magician's castle, especially since she didn't know exactly where it was. Every so often she would inquire of some creature, and learn that she still wasn't far enough north. So she continued, gradually and reluctantly expending her valuable arrows.

"I wish I could have at least a brief dialogue with someone friendly," she said wearily.

Chena longed more than anything else for companionship. Her rocks couldn't take the place of friends, and the only halfway intelligent person she met (other than brief glimpses of harpies, ogres, goblins, and other unsavory characters) was a more or less human child close to her own age. He had brassish-browning hair, gray eyes, and a brass-colored suntan.

"Hello," she said, pausing with her hand not far from her knife, just in case, though he didn't look dangerous. "I am Chena Centaur, age eleven. Who are you?"

"I am Brusque Brassie-Ogre," the lad replied. "Also age eleven. My father is part ogre and my mother is all brassie. That's why I'm so handsome."

"You certainly are," she agreed, realizing that by the standards of his crossbreeding, he was probably the only and therefore the handsomest of his kind. "I didn't realize that ogres crossbred with brassies."

"It started with my grandfather Smash Ogre," he said proudly. "He made the acquaintance of my grandmother Blythe Brassie, and they liked each other well enough."

"Oh, so they married."

"No. He married a nymph named Tandy, and she married a brassie man named Brawnye."

Chena was perplexed. "Then how—

"Smash and Tandy's son was Esk Ogre. Brawnye and Blythe's daughter was Bria Brassie. They married, and I'm their eldest son."

"Oh," Chena said, feeling uncentaurishly stupid. "Of course. So you are half brassy and—"

"And a quarter human, if you count Curse Fiend as human, and one-eighth ogre and one-eighth nymph," he concluded. "I'm a crossbreed's crossbreed. My talent is to make things hard and heavy, or soft and light."

She couldn't think of a suitable comment, so she changed the subject. "Is there a place for ex-Isled centaurs near your home?" she asked shyly.

"No, I live in the Vale of the Vole. No centaurs there I know of. My father has a centaur friend, but she doesn't visit much anymore, now that she has a family of her own."

"Yes, I suppose families do keep folk busy," she said, thinking of her own lost family. "Do you know where else I might find a centaur community? Preferably one of those who have magic, or who are tolerant of those who do."

"Oh, sure! The centaurs at Castle Roogna do magic, I think. Or maybe they're nearer the North Village, across the G—oops, Mom's calling me!" Indeed, there was the distant sound of a brass cymbal. "I gotta get home. Nice meeting you. 'Bye."

"'Bye," she echoed as he ran off. She was delighted with the information, but sorry that she hadn't quite learned what the North Village was beyond. Still, she could find out, by continuing north. So she did. Maybe she wouldn't have to ask the Good Magician a Question, if she found compatible magic-talented centaurs like herself.

Several days later, Chena was still trekking through the wilderness. She had one good meal one day: She caught some lox in a salmon stream (or maybe it was light pink), and smoked them over a piece of smoky topaz. They were locked, of course, so she opened them with some of her lime-pie keys. She looked for something to eat them with, and found a bagel bush, then searched through a creamweed for some cream cheese. She found it, but not until after she'd found egg cream, buttercream, shaving cream, light cream, dark cream, cream of the crop, cream soda, whipped cream, chocolate cream, marshmallow cream, and eyes cream in various ice-cold flavors. She scooped up the latter four to make a wonderful eyes cream Mondae for dessert.

This was the last good meal she had for some time. She was now passing through an area with very few feed-bearing plants. She carefully rationed the amount of pie she could eat each night, as well as her quartz-milk and limestone juice, which she called her "rock food." Chena was tired, hungry, lonely, and growing desperate.

Her original determination to survive and possibly even prosper, to find magic-wielding centaurs who would accept her, or to ask the

Good Magician a Question and be well cared for for a year while she performed her service—all these notions faded in the face of her growing desperation. Now she appreciated just how difficult the realm of untamed Xanth could be. To make it worse, she had reluctantly expended the last of her fine arrows, in the course of discouraging passing monsters who showed too great an interest in her tender flesh. She was now almost defenseless. She was tempted to gobble down her last two squished pies, instead of rationing them, so that at least she wouldn't be so hungry today, regardless what happened tomorrow.

"I'd almost rather be eaten by a monster right now and have it over with," she whispered miserably.

Suddenly she heard an ominous rustling, and then a slavering sound, followed closely by a loud roar. "I didn't mean it! I take it back!" she cried as a catawampus burst into view. This was an enormous feline creature, three times Chena's size and vaguely resembling a catamount. The most frightening thing about it was that it seemed to be entirely crazy. Like its bearish black and white cousin, the pandemonium, and its sheepish cousin, the bedlamb, it brought chaos wherever it went.

Chena whipped her bow around and cocked her fist, drawing back the string. She was bluffing, because she had no arrow, but maybe the monster wouldn't realize. But the catawampus was too demented to be bluffed. Its eyes rolled wildly in its head as it tore at the grass in front of it, cackling and snorting before it remembered it was supposed to roar. It uprooted a tree and shredded it into splinters. It fought its own tail, tearing out several hunks of fur without feeling any pain. It coughed, and spat out a fur ball. Then it extended its claws, showed its teeth in a wicked grimace, and advanced toward Chena.

She ran, as any normal person would. The monster pursued her. She stayed out of its reach for a little while, but she was too hungry and tired to keep up the pace for long. Gradually the catawampus gained on her; she could hear the closer thudding of its hugely clawed feet, and the blasting bellow of its breath.

She saw a clearing ahead. She used her last burst of speed to race for it, hoping that there would be something there to save her. But as she reached it, she shrieked with pure horror.

She was at the edge of a huge chasm. It stretched as far as her tired eye could see, to both sides, and was dreadfully deep and wide. She had to screech to an emergency stop, lest she run right into it.

The catawampus rushed toward her, cranking up its claws for pounce mode. She had a quick decision to make: Should she die by leaping into the chasm, or by letting the monster tear her apart? She decided that the chasm frightened her less. So she leaped, screaming again, as if that would do any good. "I wish something would save me!" she cried despairingly as she began her fall into the dusky depths.

Someone grabbed her hand. A tail slapped against her flank, making her feel strangely light and free. She opened her eyes, looking down, and discovered that she was suspended above the chasm, being pulled to safety. She looked back, and saw that the catawampus was growling on the brink, unable to catch her here.

She looked up—and there was a winged centaur colt of about her own age, or maybe a year younger. He was flying in place, and somehow supporting her whole body by his hold on her hand. How could this be?

"Who—how—?" she asked.

"I am Che Centaur," he said. "I made you light so I could hold you up, but I shall have to bring you back to land soon, because the effect fades with time."

"I am Chena Centaur," she said. "I didn't know that winged centaurs existed!"

"We're a relatively new species. We call ourselves alicentaurs. Will it be all right if I set you on the far side of the Gap Chasm?"

Chena looked down again. There was a small cloud passing beneath her. It looked worried that she might drop a clod on it. Of course, she was now so light that any such clod might simply float away, but she could nevertheless appreciate the cloud's concern. She tried not to giggle at the thought of clouds being peppered by flying centaur manure. "Yes."

Che pumped his gorgeous wings more forcefully, and towed her across the yawning gulf of the Chasm. She wondered whether the Gap was falling asleep, and whether it would close its mouth after it yawned.

He brought her safely to the far rim. She was glad to feel her feet firmly on land again, and was sure that Che was glad too, because she had been gradually gaining back weight and he had had to work hard to keep her aloft. They paused to rest and talk. She learned that Che had been trying out his flight feathers, using the warm updrafts of the Gap Chasm, when he had abruptly spied her in trouble. He had managed to reach her just in time.

She offered him one of her squished pies, which he gravely accepted, and she ate the last one herself. She was so relieved by escaping the monster and finding a friendly centaur that she hardly cared about what she would eat tomorrow.

"We had better walk to my home," Che said. "Actually I'm not living at home right now; I'm with Gwenny Goblin, who is camped not far from here. The goblins are doing an exercise."

"Goblins!" Chena cried, horrified. "They captured you?"

He laughed. "That was five years ago. We're firm friends now. I'm Gwenny's Companion."

This was too strange for her to assimilate. "Don't goblins hate all other creatures? Especially beautiful or smart ones, like centaurs?"

"Yes and no. Most goblins are like that, but the goblins of Goblin Mountain are ruled by Gwenny, the first female Chief, so they are becoming halfway decent. So it's safe for other folk to visit them. You'll like Gwenny; she's nice."

Chena remained confused. "If this gobliness is their chief, why does she want a centaur around? I don't mean any offense to you. It's just that she must have important things to do."

"She does have things to do. I help her. She can't fly, of course, and she's not as intelligent as a centaur, so I can scout for her and give her advice. It works well enough."

Chena almost suspected that he wasn't telling her everything, but it wouldn't be polite to pry. "I'm sure it does," she agreed.

They came to the goblin camp. Ugly goblin warrior men charged up at the sight of them, but Che merely held up his hand. "A visitor for the Chiefess," he said. "Inform Moron." So instead of attacking, the goblins fell in around them as an approximation of an honor guard, while one of them dashed off.

Chena would have been really uneasy about this if Che weren't so plainly at ease. "Who is the moron?" she whispered.

"He's Gwenny's Head Honcho. Think of him as the chief of staff."

"But you shouldn't call him names."

"That is his name. All the goblin males have ugly names."

"Oh." Perhaps that did make sense.

They stopped at a prettily decorated tent. Che assumed a serious mein as a vile-looking goblin approached. "Moron, this is Chena Centaur, here to visit the Chief."

Moron turned to face the tent. "Chief, Chena Centaur is here to see you."

The tent flap was pushed aside, and a pretty goblin girl emerged. She looked very young, but Chena realized that was because she was so petite. She was probably seventeen or eighteen years old. She had a mental picture of herself embarrassing them all by treating a mature Chief as a child.

The gobliness smiled. "It has happened," she said.

Chena was astonished. Had the girl read her thoughts?

"I rescued Chena from a monster by the Gap Chasm," Che said. "May we come in?"

"Of course," Gwenny said.

The tent was surprisingly large inside. When the three of them were alone, Che turned to Chena. "Gwenny can see dreams," he explained. "I thought I saw Mare Imbri pass by; she must have left you a day dream."

"Mare Imbri?"

"You are not from these parts," Gwenny said, smiling.

"No. I'm from Centaur Isle. But I was exiled."

"She has a magic talent," Che explained. "She's looking for other centaurs like her, or perhaps she will go to the Good Magician."

"But she will need to recover her strength first," Gwenny said. "I can see that she has suffered privations on the way here."

Thus began what was to be one of the most pleasant interludes of Chena's young life. She remained for a fortnight with the goblin camp, during its exercises. Che and Gwenny were usually together and often busy, but Moron saw to it that Chena was courteously treated. He introduced her to his friends Idiot, who was in charge of intelligence, and Imbecile, the goblin foreign relations officer.

They seemed like ordinary goblin males, apart from their titles: ugly, stupid, and foul-spirited. Yet not bad people, as she got to know them, and no other goblin bothered her as long as one of the three was anywhere near.

Chena managed to make herself useful, by finding magic stones and invoking their properties. Some goblins were worried about getting injured in battle, so she gave them guardstones. Others feared they weren't ugly enough, so she gave them uglystones. Some wanted to express themselves more effectively, so she gave them cursestones. These were very popular, even if they weren't allowed to use them in the Chiefess' presence.

Then it was time for the exercise to end. The goblins had learned to march in disciplined formations, and to sing tunes as they did. That would enable them to make a good impression when they guarded the lady Chief on an official visit to another species. Every one of them wore the same uniform and stepped to the same beat. Chena had watched their practice sessions, and had to admit that they were impressive. Such a formation would quickly abolish the notion that all goblins were undisciplined hordes. This was a disciplined horde.

But something else had been happening in this period, and now that it was time for the goblins to go home and for Chena to go her way, she realized what it was. She had been falling in love with Che Centaur. He was such a decent creature, and so handsome when he flew.

When the time came for the goblins to go home, Gwenny approached Chena. "You are welcome to join us at Goblin Mountain," she said. "Your magic talent is useful, and I'm sure you would be well received."

Chena hesitated. "I—how does Che feel about it?"

"Oh, Che likes you too. He says you are excellent company. He has missed associating with centaurs during his stay at Goblin Mountain, so you have given him something valuable."

This wasn't quite what Chena wanted to hear. "Is that all?"

"All? I don't understand."

"I—I think I love him."

Gwenny sat suddenly down. "Oh, my!" She did not look pleased.

"I know he's very busy being your Companion, and all, but if there is any chance that he might feel the same about me—"

Gwenny looked sad. "Chena, I never suspected! It hurts me to have to be the one to say this. But you are not of his species. He must grow up and marry a winged centaur female, so as to perpetuate his species."

"But if there is no such female—"

"But there is. She is Cynthia Centaur, once a human girl, who was converted to winged centaur form some time ago by Magician Trent. She is living with his sire and dam while he is with me at Goblin Mountain. It is understood that they will marry when they are of suitable age."

"Oh!" Chena cried, mortified. "I didn't know!"

"There seemed to be no reason to mention it," Gwenny said. "I'm sure he would have, if—"

"Oh, please don't tell him what I told you!" Chena cried. "I must depart immediately, so as never to embarrass him."

"No, Chena! That is not necessary. I'm sure that if you just explain—"

But Chena, hurt and humiliated by her own misunderstanding, couldn't bear to face Che again. Desolate and despairing, she could think of only one thing to do. She gathered her meager belongings and fled.

Now she was back in the jungle, this time north of the Gap Chasm. But she had learned much more about the nature of the backwoods, for the goblins were expert foragers. She could feed herself, and she also had some replacement arrows for her quiver, not as good as the originals, but they would do. And—she had learned of a region to the north, called the Void, where a person could enter but never leave. That was what she needed now.

The Void proved to be farther away than she had expected, and harder to find. But she kept looking, meanwhile staying clear of both human and centaur settlements. She didn't want to associate with anyone; she just wanted to enter the Void and disappear. So she had become a hermit centaur, always hiding, always searching—until the summons party had run her down.

"Oh, Chena," Jenny Elf said. "Che is my friend! I know he would never have hurt you, had he realized."

"I know it too," Chena said. "That's why I had to go."

"Now I wonder," Arnolde said. "Are you sure you came to the correct conclusion?"

"I did what I had to do," Chena said. "And if I have to face Che again, I don't know what I'll do."

"Che is another summonsee," Metria said.

Chena made as if to bolt again.

"There is no need for that," Arnolde said. "I am a centaur with magic myself; I understand your position. I merely suspect that you have misunderstood a key aspect of it."

"I can't embarrass Che!" Chena said. "He was so nice to me, never suspecting."

"I want you to picture what you most desire," Arnolde said. "See, here is Mare Imbri with a day dream for you."

He was right; Metria saw the flicker of the mare.

"But what I truly want isn't right," Chena protested.

"It may not be what you think it is," Arnolde said. "Accept the dream."

Jenny Elf began to hum. Metria ignored her. What did Arnolde have in mind? Centaurs were never frivolous; he surely had some phenomenally sensible conclusion to make, but she couldn't guess what.

Chena stood still, and the day mare passed and delivered the dream. And Metria found herself in Chena's dream.

It was of a lovely valley, with flowers growing all around. The filly was standing there alone. But she was changing. From the juncture of her human and equine torsos grew nubs, and from the nubs sprouted feathers, and the feathers expanded to wings. She stood as a winged centaur.

And that was all. The dream faded, taking the wings with it. All was as before.

"Where was Che?" Arnolde asked.

"Che?" Chena asked, confused.

"He wasn't in your dream."

Chena was silent, evidently not knowing what to say.

"Your dream was of becoming an alicentaur," Arnolde said. "That is your true desire. You are in love with the idea of becoming like Che—rather than with Che himself."

"But I can never be like Che!" Chena wailed.

"Are you sure of that?"

She looked at him blankly.

"Trent!" Metria exclaimed. "Magician Trent! He could change her. They need more flying centaurs."

Dawn was rising in Chena's face. "I could be changed?"

"We may not need Magician Trent," Arnolde said. "Take the gray stone from your pouch."

Blankly Chena obeyed. She reached into her pouch and brought out the stone.

"Now dream again of your fondest desire," Arnolde said. "Speak it aloud."

Mystified, Chena held the stone and closed her eyes. "I wish I were an alicentaur," she breathed.

For a moment nothing changed. Then the dream repeated, and the wings appeared.

"And that, I think, is the end of your talent with stones," Arnolde said. "It was the price of your conversion."

Chena opened her eyes. "My conversion?"

"Make a mirror, Demoness," Arnolde said. Metria became a wide, flat surface, reflective on the side toward the filly. Chena looked—and almost fell over. "My dream remains!"

"Because this time it wasn't a dream," Arnolde said. "This time you used your wishstone."

"My—?"

"When you wished for a good bow and arrows, you received them," he said. "When you wished for a friendly dialogue, you got it. When you wished to be consumed by a monster, one came. When you wished to be rescued, Che did that. And when you wished to become an alicentaur, that, too, was granted. Now you have your desire, and no longer need your power over stones. Your magic is now to make yourself light enough to fly. Try it."

Chena flicked herself with her tail, as she had seen Che do so many times to himself, and to her when he brought her across the Gap Chasm—that most glorious experience. Then she spread her wings, and pumped them—and lifted into the air.

The six spectators broke into applause.

12

SCRAMBLE

W ho's your next summonsee?'' Kim asked.
Metria opened the bag. There were ten tokens
remaining. ''I don't see how I'm going to serve
all of these in time,'' she said. ''I've already used up several days,
and the others are scattered all over Xanth.''

''And what you have already accomplished along the way is remarkable,'' Ichabod remarked. ''If I understand what I have heard
correctly, you have enabled Princess Nada Naga to marry a Prince,
shown the way to resolve the problem of a viable alicentaur species,
reconciled a four-century alienation from your daughter, abolished
a longtime curse on Castle Roogna, and discovered a significant lost
history of the Kings of Xanth—and you haven't yet finished your
job. This reminds me of the type of chess problem I used to see in
the newspaper, wherein the challenge is for White to win one pawn,
but along the way occur casualties of rooks, bishops, knights,
queens, and threatened checkmates. But the pawn is won.''

''What's a pawn?'' Metria asked.

''I think it's a type of shrimp,'' Jenny Elf said.

''That's a prawn,'' Arnolde replied with a face too straight.
''However, it may do.''

''A pawn is a chess piece, generally regarded as insignificant,''
Ichabod said, with a reproving glance at his friend. ''Though at times

it becomes a key element in the game. My point is that sometimes amazing things occur as the result of what seems like a rather simple task. It may be that the Simurgh is using you as a vehicle to accomplish a variety of significant things that are in need of accomplishment.''

"In short, the demoness may indeed be a pawn," Arnolde said. "In the human sense."

"I'm not human!" Metria said indignantly.

"To be sure," Ichabod agreed. "Though you certainly appear so when you choose to." He glanced at her legs. "At any rate, I believe it would be in order for us to facilitate your project with a bit of advice."

"I could use advice how to fetch in all the remaining summonsees in one day," Metria said. "So I could relax with my job done, and get my Answer from the Good Magician."

"Not to mention getting the summonsees in this party to the Nameless Castle," Arnolde said.

"And the two of you back to the Region of Madness," Jenny Elf said.

"Precisely," Ichabod agreed. "Would you like that admonition, Metria?"

"That what?"

"Counsel, guidance, recommendation, suggestion, advisement—"

"Advice?" she asked.

"Whatever," he said crossly.

"Yes."

"Pop over to Castle Roogna and ask Princess Electra if she would like to have her husband Prince Dolph out of her hair for a day or two. She will surely agree. Then ask Dolph to assume the form of a roc bird, so he can carry the summonsees directly to the Nameless Castle as you serve them. The process can be accomplished in a day, if you are able to locate them that rapidly, and if they are ready to go then."

"Now, why didn't I think of that?" Metria exclaimed, striking her head with the heel of her hand, which assumed the form of a heel of a shoe for the occasion.

"Because you're not a scholar," he replied.

"I'll be back," she said, and popped across to Castle Roogna.

Electra was out in the orchard, trim in blue jeans and freckles, as usual. She didn't look very princessly, but the folk of the castle had gotten used to that. She was watering some of the smaller plants, using a hose connected to a tap root. Her four-year-old twins, Dawn and Eve, were playing in a small house plant. When it was fully grown, it would be big enough for full grown-ups to use, but right now it was just child-sized. Lady bugs and gentlemen bugs were sitting around it, because the children evidently wanted their play-house to be in a city. There was a fast food chain draped around it, in case they got suddenly hungry. Metria realized that the children were using their talents to find the best things for their play, because Dawn could tell anything about any living thing, and Eve could tell anything about any inanimate thing.

But it was Electra she had come to see. "Would you like to have Dolph out of your hair for a day or two?" she asked the Princess.

Electra's normally sunny visage dimmed. "Don't you have something better to entertain you, now that you're married?" she asked.

Metria realized that there was a slight misunderstanding. The girl evidently recalled when Metria had teased Prince Dolph, threatening to show him her panties. Odd that such a minor thing could be remembered so long. "I'm not trying to vamp him," she said quickly. "I'm on a mission for the Simurgh, and I need to transport a number of people to the Nameless Castle, from all parts of Xanth. I thought he might become a roc bird and carry them for me."

"Oh, yes, of course. Che and Cynthia are here, and Grey and Ida and Threnody will be going too. Everyone is curious what Roxanne Roc could have done to warrant being tried. If it will help resolve that mystery, by all means borrow my husband." There was a slight stress on the last two words, indicating that Electra would not look kindly on any display, or threatened display, of panties.

"Got it," Metria agreed. "Thanks, Princess."

She popped into the castle, where Prince Dolph was doing house-work. That made her pause. "What's this with woman's work?" she demanded.

He looked abashed. "Electra wanted to clean things up, but she had to go water some plants in the orchard, so she asked me to do it."

"And she's got you wrapped around her little finger."

"Yes."

Metria nodded. "That's exactly as it should be. But how would you like a one- or two-day break from such chores?"

"I'd love it! But Electra—"

"Has given permission. I need you to become a roc bird and haul scattered folk to the Nameless Castle for me. Will you do that?"

Dolph became a baby roc, because a grown one wouldn't fit in the castle. "Squawk!" he said emphatically.

Good enough. "First we have to go to north Xanth, to move some folk. Make yourself into something very small, and I'll take you there."

He became a hummingbird. "Humm-humm-humm-humm," he hummed in four notes.

She put one hand carefully around him, then popped back to the party in the Northwest. She opened her hand, and Dolph resumed his natural form.

"This is Prince Dolph," she said. "He will transport you to the places you need to go.

"Hello, Prince Dolph," Kim said. "I'm so glad to meet you at last. I'm Kim Mundane."

Dolph looked puzzled. "Mundane?"

"Dug and I were in Xanth three years ago, playing the 'Companions' game, but we didn't get to meet you then."

"Oh, the game Nada was in," he said, remembering.

"And Jenny Elf," Kim said. "As our Companions. I suppose it wasn't important to the regular folk of Xanth, but it made a big difference to us." She took Dug's hand possessively.

"Well, let's take Arnolde and Ichabod back to the madness," Metria said briskly. "Thanks for your help, folks."

"You're welcome," Ichabod said wryly. "It has been an interesting experience."

"Quite interesting," Arnolde agreed. "It will be good to get back to the madness, where things seem more settled."

There was a perplexed look on Dolph's beak as he assumed roc form. His giant bird body now took up most of the glade they were in. He picked the two up carefully with his talons, spread his monstrous wings, and took off. One wing clipped a tree, ripping off a branch; then he was in the open and gaining altitude. He spiraled up high in the sky, turned south, and accelerated. There was a thundery sound.

"What was that?" Jenny Elf asked.

"Sonic boom," Dug replied. "Those big birds fly pretty fast."

Kim squatted and stroked her hand across the ground. A swath of smear followed.

"What are you doing?" Dug asked.

"I'm making a cabin," she said. "A thing for us to ride in, so we won't have to risk falling between the big bird's talons when it picks us up."

He nodded. "Good point."

"I could fly there myself," Chena said hesitantly.

"If you know the way," Kim said. "If you could keep up with the roc. Better to ride with us."

"Yes," the centaur agreed, relieved.

By the time the roc returned, Kim had shaped a basketlike structure large enough for herself, Dug, Jenny, and Chena. "A gondola," she said with satisfaction. "That will give us a more comfortable ride."

"Do you want to go directly to the Nameless Castle," Metria asked, "or to Castle Roogna, where you can stay in comfort with illustrious figures of Xanth until it is time for the trial?"

"Well, since you put it that way, I'd love to see Castle Roogna," Kim said. She looked around. "Anybody object?"

"I've been there," Dug said. "It's a great place, and that orchard is something else."

"It's fine with me," Jenny said. "Especially since Che and Cynthia are already there."

"Che—?" Chena asked, stricken.

"You're winged now," Kim reminded her. "You don't need him to fulfill your dream."

"But I still do like him, even if—"

"So?"

"The other female—Cynthia—"

"Had a crush on Magician Trent," Metria said, catching on to the filly's concern. "As did Gloha Goblin-Harpy. These things don't always work out, but friendships do. Gloha was my first friend, and she's Cynthia's friend too. They'll all be at the trial. Don't worry about it." Actually she wasn't at all sure how Chena and Cynthia would get along, but the last thing she wanted was to have Chena fly away now.

"And maybe you can use the time to visit the centaur villages and ask if any other centaurs would like to turn winged, as you do," Kim continued. "You're experienced in that respect. For you, the perfect companion would be a male who just turned winged." She smiled. "A handsome one."

Chena nodded thoughtfully. "And there will be time to get to know some, because I'm young yet."

"Right on," Kim said briskly. "So you'll stay with us, until you get comfortable with others. We're all going to that trial, remember."

"Yes," Chena agreed, relieved.

They climbed into the gondola. The roc picked it up. This time Metria squeezed in too, as it was easier than trying to pace a roc in flight.

"This reminds me of my flight home in the bubble," Kim said, holding her dog Bubbles, whom she had found in a bubble. "But it's more fun this time, because I'm not on my way out of Xanth."

"You floated home in a bubble?" Dug asked. "I just blinked, and I was back in my own room. How did you rate?"

"I won the game," she said. "Actually, toward the end we passed back through the screen, same as you did."

"Oh, yeah. But I got your number."

"You sure did," she said, and kissed him.

"I'll be back," Metria said, and popped off home. It was time to dose Veleno with another charge of sheer bliss. Something about the gondola ride had reminded her.

*   *   *

When Metria left home again, the party had long since reached Castle Roogna. As she zeroed in on it, she saw two winged centaurs flying out from it. So she zipped over to check on them. And was surprised.

"Chena and Cynthia!" she exclaimed.

"Oh, hi, Metria," Cynthia said. "I'm showing my friend Chena around. Things look different from above, and I wouldn't want her to get lost."

"Your friend?" Metria repeated somewhat dumbly.

Cynthia smiled. "Comrade, associate, colleague, acquaintance, companion—"

"But what about Che?"

"He's with Gwenny Goblin," Chena said. "They're playing a game of people shoes. She suggested that we go flying together."

"We have much in common," Cynthia said. "Both of us were transformed from other forms. I knew the moment I saw Chena that we would be friends. Che had told me all about her, about how nice she is, and how sad he was when she left. And now she has wings! It's wonderful to have company. I'm trying to talk her into joining me with Che's family, after the trial."

Metria remembered belatedly how Electra and Nada Naga had been close friends, though both betrothed to Prince Dolph. Apparently something similar was operating here. "That sounds nice," she said.

"You explained to me about friends," Chena said happily. "About Gloha and Cynthia and Magician Trent. And you were right. We have a lot in common. We're both converts from other forms, which makes us special regardless how we look."

"Magician Trent," Cynthia echoed, a look of fond nostalgia crossing her face. "Now, there's a man! I know exactly how Gloha feels."

"She's on my list," Metria said. "I'm going to serve her next." Because suddenly she wanted to see her friend again.

"Go ahead," Chena said. "We're fine, and Dug and Kim and Jenny are fine too. Electra's showing them around the castle grounds."

"Where's Dolph? I need him."

"He's around," Cynthia said, turning her head. "Yes—there." She pointed at a shape in the distant sky.

"Thanks." Metria popped across to that shape.

It was the big bird, playing with the updrafts. "Squawk?" he asked.

"Right. I'll take you." Metria reached out and grabbed on to the tip of the roc's tiniest huge talon.

Then the hummingbird was there. She closed her fingers carefully around it. Then she popped off to Gloha Goblin-Harpy's nest. This was in a gan-tree, which was one of the weirder trees of Xanth, looking like a tall network of metal beams. Gloha resided there with her husband Graeboe Giant, another converted winged monster.

"Metria!" Gloha exclaimed, flying out from the nest to embrace her. "How's Veleno?"

"I left him with a heavy dose of delirious happiness, because I have a job to do. How's Graeboe?"

"The same. What job?"

"I have to serve summonses for a big trial. Here's one for you." She brought out Gloha's token.

"Oh, I couldn't go without Graeboe!" Gloha protested.

"I have one for him too." She produced the other token.

"Oh. Very well, then." Gloha took the second token. "We'll be there. Where and when is it?"

"At the Nameless Castle, in two thirds of a fortnight."

"The Nameless Castle! Isn't that where—?"

"Where Roxanne Roc will be put on trial. You're on the Jury."

"Because we're winged monsters," Gloha said. "She has a right to be tried by her peers. All right; we'll be there."

"I wish I could visit longer, but I have eight more summonses to serve."

"We'll see you at the trial," Gloha said.

Metria realized that she was still holding Dolph. Well, no problem. She checked her next token: MELA MERWOMAN—WITNESS. So she popped over to the east coast of Xanth where Mela lived.

But Mela wasn't there. Instead, where a river emptied into the sea, she found a different merwoman. "Who are you?" she asked.

"Who wants to know?" the other replied.

"I'm D. Metria, on business for the Simurgh."

"Oh. In that case I'll answer. I'm Merci Merwoman." She reached down into the water and hauled up a human head. "And this is Cyrus Merman. He was playing with my tail."

Now Metria remembered that liaison. "What are you doing here in brackish water?"

"It's the only water both of us can stand," Cyrus explained. "I'm a freshwater creature, and she's saltwater, so we get together at the fringe."

"However, our children are tolerant of both waters," Merci said proudly.

"That's interesting. But I'm looking for Mela Merwoman."

"Oh, Mother's with Prince Naldo Naga. She showed him her panties, and—"

"I know that. Where are they?"

"In his princely estate in the naga caves. He had salt water piped in for her."

"Oh. Thanks." She popped back to the naga caves, where she had found Jenny Elf and Nada Naga. Soon she delved down and found the salted caves.

There was Mela Merwoman, sporting in the water. "Eeeek!" she cried, exactly like an innocent young thing, though it was clear that no female with her endowments could ever be innocent.

"It's just me, D. Metria," the demoness said.

Mela looked at her. "Oh, I didn't see you."

"Then why did you scream?"

"Naldo's playing with my tail."

Like daughter, like mother: Both had irresistible tails. "I have to serve you with a summons."

"Oh? What for?"

"You're a Witness in the trial of Roxanne Roc."

"That big bird? What did she do?"

"I don't know. But I hope to find out at the trial."

"So do I! I'll be there." She took the token. "Where is it?"

"In the Nameless Castle."

"How do I get there?"

"Prince Dolph will take you." Metria held up the hummingbird.

Prince Naldo's head broke the surface of the water. "That's a rather small bird to carry my wife anywhere."

Dolph assumed roc form and hunched at the edge of the water. "Squawk!"

"But I might be mistaken," Naldo conceded. "May I go too?"

"You're not on my list, but I suppose you can be a spectator."

"Then let's go," he said, assuming full human shape. "As soon as we don some clothing."

Mela split her tail into legs, climbed from the water, shook herself gloriously dry, and donned plaid panties. The roc's eyes bulged dangerously.

"Maybe a bit more clothing," Naldo said reluctantly.

So she put on a reasonably sexy dress, and he put on a princely robe. "We'll meet you on the surface," Naldo told Metria. "Your roc won't be able to fly from here."

True. Metria put out her hand, and the roc became the hummingbird. She popped to the surface, where they waited for the others to make their slower way through the labyrinthine naga passages. "Haven't you seen panties by now?" she asked the bird.

Prince Dolph appeared. "Only Electra's, of course. They're nice, but—"

"But nobody fills panties the way Mela does," Metria finished. "As I recall, she even almost freaked you out without them, when you were nine."

"Yes. I never forgot."

"Nor should you," she said primly. "She would have been in violation of the Adult Conspiracy had she shown you her panties then. That's why I never showed you mine."

"I know. It was most frustrating."

"Well, that's the point of the Conspiracy. What would Xanth come to, if children got to see anything they wanted to, or if they never realized that things were being kept secret from them?"

"I understand that now. But then I didn't."

"Because children aren't *supposed* to understand. They have to be kept in agitated ignorance, suspecting what they're missing. Otherwise what would be the point?"

"None," he agreed.

A stone hatch opened, and Mela and Naldo climbed out. "Let's go," Naldo said.

Dolph assumed roc form, and took them gently in his talons, and launched himself into the sky. But he forgot, and took them to Castle Roogna instead of the Nameless Castle.

"Well, that's all right," Mela concluded. "We'll wait there until the trial. I can visit with my friends, and Naldo can hobnob with royalty."

"It works for me," the Prince agreed. "Maybe I can meet that Demon Prince my sister's hot for. I worried about her, but she came through in the end."

Metria resisted the temptation to advertise her part in that, because she had to keep moving on her summonsing. So she saw them safely to Castle Roogna, then oriented on her mission again.

The next token was for Okra Ogress. That should be no problem; Okra lived in the deepest darkest jungle with Smithereen Ogre.

She popped across, and knew she was in the right region because of the small trees tied into pretzel knots, large trees with wary looks about them, and the furtive ways of medium-sized dragons. The presence of an ogre did that to a neighborhood. Okra had charmed Smithereen Ogre despite being insufficiently ugly, stupid, or strong, but it had worked out because he had more than enough of all three qualities for both of them. She owed her success, she thought, to her achievement of Major Character status, because no really bad things happened to one of those folk.

Sure enough, there was a bashed-wood house in the center of the devastation, where a not-very-ugly ogress was wielding a length of ironwood, pounding chestnuts on a mossy stone. The chest she was working on was tough, but she had it between her rock and a hard place, and was slowly getting at the nut inside.

"I have a summons for you," Metria announced. "You have to be a Witness at the trial of Roxanne Roc."

"I don't think I can go," Okra said. "I have to get this nut out, so Smithereen can eat it and be fortified for his evening of dragon intimidation.''

"Couldn't he bash that chest open faster himself?''

"He could, but then he'd lose most of the nut. It tends to fly into widely scattered fragments when he bashes it.'' She smiled fondly. "He's just such an ogre. So I do it, because I have a gentler touch.'' She whaled away with the club, chipping away another corner of the chest. "Anyway, he's helping.''

"He is? How?''

"By providing the support for the chest, so I can bash it. It takes a really dense block to hold one of these.''

Metria looked. Now she realized that what she had taken for a low mossy ridge was actually an ogre lying down, and the rock on which the chest rested was his head. "That's as dense as anything is,'' she agreed.

"Yes. I couldn't do it without him.'' Okra clubbed the chest one more time, and it finally cracked open. She pulled apart the sides and lifted out the big nut inside. She heaved it up, her limited muscles bulging. "Open your big mouth, dear,'' she gasped. "This is one tough nut!''

The face of the rock cracked open like a mountain fissure. Okra let go of the boulderlike mass, and it dropped into the hole. A tongue appeared as the ogre chewed, and sparks flew where the great teeth battled the hard nut. It would evidently hold him for a while.

"The trial isn't for a while yet,'' Metria said. "But maybe you could bring your husband along. He might find it interesting, in a dim-witted way. It's at the Nameless Castle.''

"Oh, I remember that!'' Okra said. "Yes, he would probably like it there. He could chew on that extra tough solidified cloud material. He's always been curious about clouds.''

Metria was surprised. "I thought true ogres were too stupid to be curious about anything.''

"Oh, that's not true!'' Okra protested loyally. "It is rumored that clouds are even more stupid than ogres, and since that hardly seems possible, naturally ogres are curious about it. Smithereen could do a great service for ogredom by investigating the matter.''

"I could take you both there now," Metria said. "But remember: He mustn't bash the castle down. Just the surrounding cloud."

"I'll keep an eye on him," Okra promised.

"Good enough. Dolph?"

The hummingbird she held became the roc. The roc fastened one set of talons around the ogre's feet, and the other around the ogre's head, and looked around. So many trees had been bashed down here that there was clearance for takeoff. The bird squawked.

"Do what?" Metria asked, perplexed.

"Squawk, squawk, squawk, squawk, squawk—"

"Squawk?" Okra suggested.

"Whatever," Metria agreed crossly. "Get on."

But Okra was already climbing onto Smithereen's body, following her own suggestion. The roc spread his wings and launched into the air, carrying the stiff ogre flat, with Okra riding it like a platform. The big ogre mouth shill chewed on the tough nut.

They winged it to the Nameless Castle, where they deposited Smithereen on a suitable outcropping bank of cloud. Dolph returned to hummingbird form.

Smithereen sat up and poked a finger at the cloud, intrigued by its toughness; this was not ordinary cloudstuff. He put his face down and took a bite of it. The stuff resisted, yielding only very slowly. "Ugh!" he remarked, disappointed.

"Well, it depends on which part of the cloud you bite dear," Okra said. "This evidently isn't the part that contains thunder or lightning. But keep biting; that section is bound to be somewhere."

Metria nodded. There was enough cloud here to hold his attention for some time. "I'll let you know when the trial actually starts," she told Okra.

"That's fine," the ogress said, turning to admire the towering castle in the center of the cloud isle.

"Don't wander too close to the edge. It's a long way down."

"I know. I remember." Okra waved as Metria popped off.

After a quick check on Veleno at home, to verify that he was still floating blissfully somewhat above the bed, she brought out her next token. This was for Stanley Steamer.

This could be tricky. But if she had to, she'd get his friend Princess Ivy to ask him. How they were going to keep him from steaming and eating the other Jurors during the trial she didn't know, but her job was just to get him there.

She popped across to the Gap Chasm. Suddenly the steep walls rose on either side of her, and she looked across the reasonably pleasant base of the valley, where small fur trees fluffed themselves out and a stray sick-a-more tree waited for a victim. She couldn't resist teasing it. She sashayed right toward it. "Ha-ha, sicko; you can't make me sick. I'm a demoness."

Then she heard a faint retching. Oops—it was the hummingbird. She had forgotten about Dolph. She hastily popped across the valley, well out of the sick range of the tree. "Sorry about that," she said. "I forgot I was holding you."

Dolph resumed his normal form. He looked as if he had just succeeded in not quite retching. "Shnake," he gasped.

"What?"

He swallowed. "Reptile, serpent, viper—"

"Snake?"

"Whatever," he said weakly, looking better. "It's on your leg."

Metria looked down. There was a garter snake swallowing her left leg. She had inadvertently landed beside a hose bush, and the snake had come out to enclose her leg up to the thigh, as was its wont. Given time, it would digest the leg below its fastening on the thigh.

"Ugh." She puffed into smoke, and the snake dropped. She reformed to the side. She should have watched where she landed. Such a snake could not hurt her, of course, but it was embarrassing.

"Is that Stanley?" Dolph asked, peering down the valley.

"It does look like a serpent," she agreed. "But not like Stanley."

The serpent approached them. A human head appeared in place of its reptile head. "Hello."

"A naga!" Dolph said.

"Yes," the naga said. "Perhaps you could help me. I seem to be lost."

"Of course," Dolph said. "I always liked the naga folk. I'm

Prince Dolph, of the human folk, and this is the Demoness Metria. What can I do for you?''

The figure assumed human form. She was a young woman, attractive in the way of those who could craft their appearance to suit their desire. She lacked clothing, because in her natural state she wore none. Dolph's eyes did the usual male thing, trying to bulge out of their sockets. It occurred to Metria that the human male form was badly designed: Its eye sockets were too small.

''I'm Anna Conda,'' the naga said. ''I am traveling to the northern naga caves via the underground route, but I don't recognize the terrain.''

''That's because you're in the Gap Chasm,'' Metria said. ''You came up too soon.''

''Oh, the Gap! I forgot all about it!''

''It happens,'' Dolph said. ''Some wisps of the forget spell that was on it for eight centuries may still be around, and you ran into one. Just go back into the caves and bear north and you'll get there.''

''I will. Thanks.'' She shifted rapidly to full serpent form, slithered into a hole, and disappeared.

Prince Dolph shook his head. ''I'm happy with Electra, of course,'' he said. ''But sometimes I wonder how it would have been with Nada Naga.''

''She doesn't love you,'' Metria reminded him. ''Electra does.''

He nodded. ''That, too.''

As with most young men, he could hardly see beyond a girl's physical form, especially when it happened to be nude. That was what made human men such easy prey for demonesses. ''Well, let's go find Stanley.''

''Sure thing.'' He glanced once more at the hole down which the naga had vanished, as if almost tempted to assume serpent form and go after her, then became the hummingbird.

She took him in her hand and floated up high enough to get a better view of the chasm. Then she took the token in her free hand and heeded its tug. She zoomed along in the correct direction.

Soon enough she spied the Gap Dragon whomping along. Stanley was now full grown, a long, sinuous, slightly winged green dragon with six legs. The legs were too short for real velocity, which was why he whomped: lifting up his foresection, hurling it forward, landing it, and bringing the rest of his body along in a following arc. It looked awkward, but it got him where he was going in a hurry. Hardly any animal caught in the Gap escaped, once the dragon went after it. Those that were just out of reach of the teeth could still be brought down by a searing jet of steam. The Gap Dragon was one of the most feared creatures in Xanth.

Except for certain folk. Metria was one, because she was a demoness. Prince Dolph was another, because he could assume dragon form if he chose, and because he had known Stanley Steamer since childhood and they were friends.

So she glided down. "Ho, Stanley!" she called.

The dragon paused, lifting his snoot. There was a puff of steam.

"Now, don't get steamed," she said. "It's me, Metria. And Prince Dolph." She opened her hand, and Dolph assumed his human form and dropped to the ground.

Stanley recognized him. Dolph threw his arms around the dragon. They rolled, wrestling and tickling. It was an embrace almost nobody else in Xanth would have risked. But they had been young together, for all that it was Stanley's second childhood. He had been youthened more or less by accident over three decades ago in a slight mishap. Stanley had become Princess Ivy's pet, until it was time for him to resume his job guarding the Gap.

There were three basic types of dragons in Xanth: fire breathers, smokers, and steamers. The fire dragons were the most feared, but actually the smokers were more dangerous, because their smoke could blind and suffocate others, especially in closed places. The steamers were the least common, but were to be respected in their regions.

When the two settled down, Metria held out the token. "I have a summons for you, Stanley," she said. "You are to be a Juror in the trial of Roxanne Roc."

The dragon's ears perked up, startled. One ear was slightly shorter than the other; that dated from the time that Smash Ogre had chewed it off, and even the rejuvenation hadn't repaired it entirely. His snout assumed a perplexed aspect.

Dolph took the form of a small dragon and growled at him. Metria wasn't strong on dragon talk, but knew that Dolph was explaining the situation in greater detail.

Stanley growled back. Then Dolph resumed man form. "He says he'll have to ask his family."

She couldn't say no to that. "So let's go ask."

Stanley led them to a deep side shoot of the main chasm. There was another grown dragon, and a baby dragon. Metria had known nothing of this. She felt slightly jealous. Even dragons could get the attention of the stork, while she couldn't. But the baby was cute.

"His mate Stella Steamer, and their son Steven Steamer," Dolph said, chucking the baby under the chin. Steven puffed out a bit of warm vapor that couldn't be rated as steam, but showed promise for the future.

"Stanley is on my summonsing list, but I don't know that the whole family would be welcome in the Nameless Castle," Metria said doubtfully.

"Stella says someone has to patrol the Gap," Dolph said. "They take turns, with the off-duty one taking care of Steven. If Stanley goes to the trial, he'll have to take Steven along, because Stella can't both whomp and baby-sit."

Metria considered. "Let me see the tyke," she said.

Dolph picked up the little dragon and handed him to her. She held him, and the little snoot caressed her neck with warm vapor. Suddenly she lost control. "Oh, you little darling!" she cried, and hugged Steven close. She so missed the baby of her own she had not been able to get.

"I think Steven will get along okay at the trial," Dolph remarked. "If your reaction is typical."

"I guess he will," she agreed, kissing Steven on the cute snoot. "There's nothing much cuter than a baby dragon. When can they go?"

Dolph consulted. They decided to bring Stanley and Steven just before the trial date, so as to minimize disruption.

Metria set down the little dragon with reluctance. "I still have more to summons," she said, noting that dusk was beginning to think about arriving. "It's a real scramble."

"Who are they?" Dolph asked.

She checked the five remaining tokens. "Marrow Bones and Sherlock Black next, I think."

"They're both family men. You'd better go after them tomorrow."

"I suppose you're right. I do have several days remaining before the trial."

"Then if you don't mind, I'll fly home to my wife," he said.

"See you tomorrow," she agreed.

He became the roc, spread his wings, and stroked up toward the band of daylight above the Chasm.

Metria waved farewell to the steamer family, and popped back home. She didn't need any rest, but it would be good to relax anyway.

This job didn't seem so bad after all. Tomorrow she would complete her summonsing, well ahead of schedule.

13
MPD

In the morning she took care of routine details, stoked her husband up for another day's worth of bliss, and checked her tokens.

She paused with surprise. She had thought there were five left, but she hadn't been counting carefully. There were four: for the walking skeleton, the black man, and the Simurgh herself. Plus the mysterious unmarked one. But now that fourth one was marked. It said MPD. And on the other side, WITNESS.

So the blank token was finally identifying itself! Well, she had better attend to that immediately, because she had no idea who MPD was, which meant that he or she or it might be hard to find.

She held up the token to see which way it tugged. There seemed to be a firm direction, north, so she put it away and popped over to Castle Roogna to fetch Prince Dolph.

He was rubbing sleep from his eyes. "Last day, huh?" he asked blearily. "I'll be glad of that."

"So will I," she agreed. "This has been an interesting experience, but I'll be glad to have it done."

"I forget," he said. "Did you ever tell me why you're doing this? I mean, sure, for your Service to the Good Magician. But what was your Question?"

"How to get the stork's attention," she said. "I know the motions, but the stork has been ignoring me."

"Oh," he said, looking reasonably embarrassed. He was twenty-one, and married, and a father, but retained a certain fetching naïveté. "Well, let's go get Sherlock and Marrow."

"Something's come up," she said. "I had a blank disk. Now it has a name. MPD, a Witness. To the north."

"Who's MPD?"

"I have no idea. But the token should lead us to him."

"Then let's go." He became the hummingbird, and she took him, and popped north.

She landed safely north of the Void—and now the token tugged south. Hmm—that could be bad news. Nothing left the Void except night mares. She was a demoness, but even she didn't dare risk passing the Void's event horizon, because then she would have to give half a soul to a mare to carry her out, and half a soul was all she had. She was not about to give it up.

But as she approached that dreadful line, the token tugged down. Down toward a gourd. That was almost as bad. Normal folk entered the gourd realm by looking in a peephole, and though their bodies remained outside, their souls were locked inside for as long as the eye contact remained—and they could not break it themselves. So anyone visiting the dream realm needed a friend to put a finger over the peephole at an agreed time, freeing the visitor. But this didn't work for demons, who had no permanent physical bodies; their whole selves entered, and they could not leave without the permission of the Night Stallion. Trojan, that Horse of Another Color, was not particularly partial to demons. So what was she to do?

Well, she was on business for the Simurgh, so she would just have to tell the horse that. Meanwhile, it would be interesting exploring the dream realm.

"Dolph, it seems I have to enter the gourd," she said. "So maybe you had better go home, and I'll return for you when this is done."

"I don't know," he said, assuming his human form. "The gourd's a pretty tricky place, even for demons. Maybe I better go in with you."

"But your body would be left out here," she reminded him. "And you would be unable to break contact."

"Actually, I have a pass for the gourd; the Stallion lets me visit when I want to. But it's true I don't want to leave my body exposed." He looked around. "But maybe if I assumed a safe form, it would be all right."

"A safe form?"

"Some creature no one will bother. Like maybe a snake."

"A what?"

"Serpent, viper, reptile—"

"I *know* what a snake is! But someone could step on you."

"Not if I become the right kind of snake. Like maybe a bushmaster."

"Oh. Yes, maybe so."

"I'll change; you orient the gourd for me." He became a bush with reptilian scales and poisonous foliage. No one would bother him in that state.

She turned the gourd around until its peephole faced one of the bush's eyes. When the bush went rigid she knew it had taken. Then she turned vapory and carefully insinuated herself through the peephole, careful not to interfere with Dolph's line of sight.

It was dark and wet inside. She couldn't see anything, so she formed a light bulb on the end of her nose. The bulb absorbed darkness, leaving the light behind, so that the scene became dimly visible.

She was floating in some deep brine green sea. There might be a surface somewhere far above, but it seemed too distant to bother with. There was no sign of Dolph, but since he could change form here as well as in normal life, he might be a fish exploring ahead. There did seem to be a sea floor, and on it was a large decorated vase. She wasn't sure what it might contain, so she made a knuckle and rapped on it.

A head popped out. "Eh?" it inquired. "Who patted my urn?"

"Sorry," Metria said. "I didn't know it was a pat urn."

He stared at her. "What manner of creature are you?"

"I'm the Demoness Metria."

He looked disappointed. "Oh. One of those."

She bridled. "What's the matter with me?"

"Nothing, except that you're only half what I wished for. But that's the way it always is."

Her curiosity, never far beneath her surface, surged up. "You always get half your wish?"

"Yes. I'm Hal Halfling, a bit player for bad dreams. It is my fate to get only half of what I wish for, no matter what it is. This time I wished for decent company, and I got you."

Metria nodded. "I'm indecent company, for sure. Not only am I not a real person, I have only half a soul, and I'm not staying."

"Exactly. I thought I could outsmart it by wishing for Xanth's most lovely and accommodating woman, figuring that I could settle for an ordinary one, but once again it halved it in such a way as to leave me no benefit. I had such Xanticipation." He sighed.

"Well, this is your Xanthropology lesson," she said. "I could assume the form of Xanth's loveliest woman, but I don't care to. I study men, but I try to please only one, and it isn't you."

"Obviously. I don't know why I keep making wishes, since they never work out well."

"What was your first wish?"

"I wanted to be a wit."

"That explains it."

He looked sourly at her. "I would wish you to depart, but—"

"But half of me might remain to pester you," she finished. "I see your problem. Actually, I do plan to depart, once I locate my partner and figure out a way to travel conveniently in here."

"Yeah, sure, leave me already," Hal said, grimacing.

"Isn't that what you wanted?"

"No. What I wanted was good companionship." He reached up and tore out a hank of hair. "Why can't I ever have what I want?"

"Maybe you should have wished for control over your emotions," Metria suggested.

"I did. I can control them only halfway."

"Too bad you can't control the emotions of others."

"I'd just get the wrong halves of their emotions."

She paused, having a notion. "Maybe you should make a wish for me."

"You'd get only half of it."

"I wonder. Limited wishes may have their uses. Wish for my ship to come in."

He shrugged. "Suit yourself. I wish for your ship to come in."

A light showed in the blurry distance. It forged nearer. It turned out to be a sort of ship, but it sailed well below the surface of the water. "What is that?" she asked.

A hatch opened. "It's a yellow submarine," Dolph said, in human form. "I was in fish form, looking for a better way to travel, and I found this just lying where someone discarded it, so I brought it in. We can travel in comfort in this."

"See?" Hal said. "That's a half ship. Halfway sunk."

"So it is," Metria agreed, floating into the hatch. "Say, how is it we can talk normally here underwater?"

"This is the dream realm," Dolph reminded her. "It doesn't follow regular rules."

"That's right, I forgot." She settled on the interior floor of the submarine, and Dolph closed the hatch. It was miraculously dry here, and portals looked out on the sea around them. The interior looked lived in, as if several not-quite-housebroken entertainers had spent time here. There was a picture of a beetle on one wall.

"Where does your summons token point?" Dolph asked.

She brought it out. "That way," she said, pointing.

He steered the submarine that way. It accelerated, forging through the sea.

Then the sea dried. It didn't end, it just thinned into air. The submarine didn't care; it floated on through the air. "This is a pretty nice machine," Dolph remarked. "I can't think why anyone would have thrown it away."

"There's a man out there," Metria said. "Don't run him down."

The airship slowed, but the man became a dragon and snapped at it. "Oh—a were-dragon," Dolph said. He opened the portal. "Hey, don't snap at us! We're just passing through."

The man reappeared. "Ooops, sorry about that. I thought this was an invader from Mundania."

"That's okay," Dolph said. "I'm Prince Dolph of Xanth. Who are you and what do you do?"

"I'm Jay. My father was human, my mother a firedrake. I wasn't quite comfortable in either society, so I got a job supporting bad dreams. I listen to the instructions in my human phase, then perform in my dragon phase. It's a living.''

"Do you know anyone here named MPD?''

Jay scratched his head. "There are some pretty strange folk here, but I don't recognize that one. Maybe the cyborg would know.''

"Cyborg?''

"He's part animal, part machine. Really weird. I think he's reducing flowers today. Just keep on going the way you are, and you'll find his dung pile soon enough.''

"Thanks.'' The submarine floated on.

They came to a sign: HUNG DEEP.

"Better turn aside,'' Metria advised. "I don't think we want that.''

The submarine veered to the left. There was another sign: ROWING GONG.

Metria looked around, but saw no gong. "This doesn't seem right either.''

So the submarine moved to the right instead. This time it encountered a sign saying ROT NIGHT.

"I told you this was an odd place,'' Dolph said. "We'd better ask again.''

They saw a woman painting a sign. Dolph opened the hatch. "Hello—I'm Prince Dolph, from Xanth. I think we're lost. Can you help us?''

"I'm Miss Pell,'' she replied. "Of course I can help you. Why should I?''

"Because the sooner we find what we're looking for, the sooner we'll be out of here.''

Miss Pell nodded appreciatively. "That does seem worthwhile, Drince Polf. Simply correct my signs, and you should be successful.''

"Drince Polf?'' he echoed blankly.

"Miss Pell!'' Metria exclaimed. "Misspell! That's what's wrong with the signs!''

He brightened. "Oh, okay!'' He closed the hatch, and guided the submarine back the way they had come.

"NOT RIGHT,'' Metria read, correcting the third one. "GOING

WRONG,'' as she saw the second. "And DUNG HEAP. This is where we were going!''

Sure enough, there was a machine man with a piece of wood, surrounded by beetles. He was touching them with it, and they were in turn turning flowers into dung. There were not many flowers remaining, and the pile of dung was quite large.

Dolph opened the hatch. "You must be the cyborg," he said. "But why are you destroying those flowers?"

"They were part of the last set," the cyborg explained. "Several dreamers were pushing up daisies. Now we need to recycle them, so I'm using reverse wood to enable the dung beetles to turn them back into dung."

"That must make sense, for dreams," Metria said. "But I think I see one of a different species." She floated out and picked up a bug. "I'll bug his ear," she said to Dolph. Then she put the bug in the cyborg's ear and whispered something.

"Why, of course!" the cyborg said. "Right that way." He pointed.

Dolph set the submarine in motion. "What did you do?"

"I dropped a hint," she explained. "That was a hint bug I found. Once I bugged his ear, he had to tell me the truth."

They moved on. The landscape faded into a sort of fuzzy nothingness with colored ribbons curling through. The tug of the token got stronger.

At last they came to a man sitting on a loop of ribbon, surrounded by music. He had a huge shock of hair swept back from his forehead, and wore a suit that trailed almost to the ground behind him. He had no instrument, and his mouth was closed, yet the music was clearly governed by his will, because he was nodding to its beat and moving his hands as if to accent some aspects while smoothing down others. When Metria approached him, he looked up, and it faded. "Yes?"

"Are you MPD?" she asked.

"I am No One." Somewhat wary violin music sounded.

"I think you are MPD, because this summons token is nudging right toward you. You must appear as a Witness at the trial of Roxanne Roc."

The music rumbled, with drums ascendant. "Where is this trial?" No One asked.

"In the Nameless Castle, in Xanth proper. We're here to take you there."

A bassoon made a dirty noise. "I can't leave the dream realm. I can't go."

"But this summons says you have to," she said, holding out the token.

No One brushed it away. "Forget it, Demoness." The woodwinds whistled as he dropped off his loop of ribbon and fell into the depths below.

She dived down after him, but the bands of ribbon became numerous and convoluted, obscuring her view and her way. MPD had disappeared.

"So it's going to be *that* type of a serving," she muttered. "Well, I won't be balked." She held up the token and heeded its tug.

She threaded her way through the ribbons, and they became thin bands of candy, then thickened into flavored, colored cotton. The cotton formed into threads, and then into fabrics, and the fabrics wound their way into items of clothing. And there, amidst the hanging suits and dresses, sat a young woman with fair hair, pressing sections of cloth to each other. They adhered where they touched, and she twisted the free sections around and pressed them together again, and they stuck together again, forming the configurations of clothing.

"Yes?" she inquired as Metria floated up.

"I'm looking for MPD. Have you seen him?"

"Who?"

"His name is MPD. He has a big shock of wild hair, and he makes music just by thinking of the instruments."

"Oh, that's Maestro No One. Maybe Me Two can tell you. He's that way."

"Thank you." Metria floated hurriedly in the direction indicated. The racks of clothing became blobs of goo. She weaved around them, and soon they became blocks of charred wood. She lifted the token again, and it tugged her in a new direction. She followed it.

She came across a short, stout man with fiery red hair standing in a smoking pit. A blob of goo appeared before him. He stared at it, and it burst into flame. It burned vigorously for half a moment, then settled into a moderate glow for another moment, and finally became another charred lump.

He looked up as she floated close. "Yes?"

"Me Two? I'm looking for MPD."

"Who?"

She described the maestro. The man frowned. "Who told you that was the one you wanted?"

"I know, because my token indicated him. But a fair-haired young woman told me to come this way, because Me Two would know."

"That was She Three. She shouldn't have told you that."

"Why not? Don't you know where MPD is?"

"I know where Maestro No One is, but she shouldn't have told you."

Metria was beginning to be annoyed. "I think you folk are giving me a runaround. Now, tell me what you know."

"No. Go away, Demoness; we don't want your kind here."

"Listen, burnbrain—" she started angrily, then realized that he was baiting her. Since she really didn't need him, she refused to let him waste more of her time. She lifted the token—and it tugged right toward him.

"What's that?" Me Two asked.

"It's a summons token for the trial of Roxanne Roc, in mainland Xanth. And it seems to be tugging toward you," she said, perplexed.

He squinted at her—and suddenly she was a mass of flames. He had spontaneously combusted her!

"You dirty noise!" she swore, becoming water. The flames hissed out. But the distraction had been effective: Me Two was gone.

She lifted the token and zoomed along the path it indicated. The charred blobs became polished blocks of wood, and then polished metal, and then polished glass. Reflections were everywhere. And there among the reflections were a host of little old whiskery men with collections of small objects.

Metria knew the difference between a real figure and a reflected one. She zeroed in on the original. "Where is MPD?" she demanded.

The man looked up. "Who?"

"The maestro! Did he pass this way?"

The little man lifted a glistening red bottle. He put his two hands around it, and drew them apart, and lo! there were two glistening red bottles. "No."

She was getting about as fed up as a noneating demoness could be. "No you won't tell me, or no he didn't pass this way?"

"No neither."

"Who are you?"

"I am Who Four. I duplicate inanimate objects, as you can see. I am busy at the moment, as you can also see. Now, go away, Demoness."

Metria was getting more crafty. She lifted the token—and it tugged right toward Who Four. "Are you MPD?"

"I don't know what you're talking about." He lifted a small puzzle box, put his hands around it, and separated them, holding two small puzzle boxes.

"Well, I'm going to serve this summons on you, Who Four," she decided. She floated toward him.

Who Four jumped. The action was so sudden that it caught her by surprise. He sailed right up past a mirror-beam and disappeared. She followed, but all she found were dozens of reflections of herself. So she faded into invisibility, and then there were dozens of reflections of nothing. But Who Four was gone.

Now she was getting good and irritated. "There is something very odd about this," she muttered. She lifted the token and followed its tug once more.

This time it led her away from glass column and beams, and past a forest of upside trees, to the blank wall of a massive rock cliff. There was a door set in it, marked GOURD STORAGE DEPT.: **NO ADMITTANCE.**

"Fooey on that foul noise," she muttered, and floated through it.

For a moment she wished she hadn't, because something fearsome rose up before her. She screamed and retreated halfway back into the wall. Then she got hold of herself, putting one hand on a shoulder and the other on a knee, and hung on tight. "You're a demoness,

Metria!'' she reminded herself. "You aren't afraid of anything, because nothing can hurt a demoness."

Then there was a small swirl of leaves and dust before her. She screamed again and popped right out of there.

But in two thirds of a moment she took stock. "That is the storage place of fears," she realized. "No wonder it's scary." And her worst fear was of stepping beyond the magic in Mundania and dissolving into a mindless swirl of dust. But this was the gourd, the dream realm, one of the more magic aspects of Xanth; she would not fade out here. All she had to do was conquer her unreasonable fear and follow the token. This time she would not let whoever or whatever it was she found escape. Because a remarkable suspicion was lifting its pointed head partway into her consciousness.

So she nerved herself, and walked back through the cliff wall. The dust swirled up again, but this time she addressed it with what boldness she could muster: "You are merely a fear from my memory of Mundania. I am not dreaming. You have no power over me."

"Aw, shucks," the swirl muttered, subsiding.

Metria smiled. Dust did not normally speak in human fashion, unless King Dor was around, but this was the dream realm, where the rules were as the Night Stallion made them. She had won a small victory.

Now, where was that person hiding? She lifted the token and followed its tug. The Simurgh had good magic, because these disks worked in Xanth, Mundania, and the dream realm. Which stood to reason, because Metria wasn't sure that any entity had more power than the Simurgh, except perhaps the Demon $X(A/N)^{th}$ himself. That reminded her of the root of this endeavor: Whatever could Roxanne Roc have done to warrant such a prominent trial, with the threat of enormous punishment? The Simurgh must be really annoyed!

Well, she would find out when the trial came. Meanwhile, she merely had to serve the last three summonses, then report back to serve the Simurgh herself. Of course, her job wouldn't be quite finished, because she still had to make sure that every last summonsee arrived at the Nameless Castle. But she was confident she could handle that, because once served, no summonsee could really decline.

She walked onward through the Storage Dept. of Fears, seeing things that were surely fearsome to normal folk. Slavering dragons, hissing snakes, quivering tentacles, things going bump in the night, hairy-legged spiders, rent collectors, and a long hollow stick.

She paused. "What's so fearful about you?" she asked the stick.

"I am from the stem of a plant known as rye," the stick answered. "I am full of my seeds, which are very solid."

"And that terrifies dreamers?" she asked with a hint of a suggestion of a sneer she knew would annoy it.

"Yes—when someone points me at such folk, and threatens to shoot out my seeds," the rye full replied. "I think it's the loud bang I make as they go, because I don't like losing my seeds."

Metria shrugged and moved on. Mortal folk chose funny things to fear. Soon she came to an eye land. It was shaped like a giant eyeball gazing up at the sky. She remembered that big eyes in the night frightened some folk. The token tugged toward it. But it was surrounded by water, as most eye lands were, for some reason; maybe the water cooled their chafing orbs as they shifted in their sockets. She could float across to it, but preferred to walk, so she wouldn't miss anything low. That made the water a problem.

Well, she would just have to wade. She put a foot to the water— and discovered it was solid. She could walk on it!

"What kind of water are you?" she asked it.

"I am hard water, of course," it said.

"Oh, of course," she agreed, feeling stupid. "What's fearful about you?"

"Folk fear drowning in me, especially when my surfs are revolting. They can get pretty violent, especially during a storm."

All of which she should have realized on her own. She walked on across to the eye land. There she saw an eyeglass bush, which was, of course, made of glass, with glass eyes in lieu of flowers. The eyes glared at her in frightening fashion, so she could appreciate why this plant was stored here. There certainly seemed to be a good many props; no wonder the dream crews had no trouble crafting bad dreams for all occasions, every night. It amazed her to realize how many bad dreams were needed; since they went only to those who deserved them, there had to be a great many imperfect people. If it was like this in Xanth, how much worse must it be in Mundania!

The token tugged her on. She came to a rocky section of the eye land. She paused at a big rock. "What's so scary about you, rock?"

It opened an eye. "That's roc, Demoness, not rock. Haven't you learned the difference?" It shook out a wing, which she now saw was folded around it, making it as featureless as a boulder.

"Sorry about that," she said, amused. "But you still don't seem very petrifying to me."

"Very what?" the stone-hard bird asked.

"Appalling, dismaying, horrifying, alarming, consternation-ing—"

"Frightening?"

"Whatever," she agreed crossly. "Why should any dreamer fear you?"

"Because of what I do," the roc said. "Like thus."

Suddenly Metria was rock hard. She had become a statue!

She puffed into smoke, nullifying the effect. "Why, you putrescent excrescence!" she swore. "You turned me into a rock!"

"That's what I do," the rock agreed. "Folk are terrified of being petrified."

She gazed at the sharp tip of its beak as it spoke. "You have a point," she agreed cuttingly, and went on.

She came to an ugly tree with uglier fruit. It was a bag tree, growing every kind of bag. She touched one, and found it was full of trash: a trash bag. Another contained a sandwich and bottle of juice: a lunch bag. One almost put her to sleep: a sleeping bag. A fourth one grabbed at her: a grab bag. So she made like a punching bag, and punched it in the mouth. "Get out of here, you old bag!" it told her.

The token led her to a bookshelf, and stopped. When she tried to walk on, the token tugged back. When she went to the side, the token tugged toward the shelf. But there was no one there. So she considered it more carefully.

On it were several books, scattered and tumbled. There were parts of pictures on their spines. "Someone didn't put these away properly," she said, disgusted. So she stood the books up and set them together. But the picture segments on their spines formed a jumbled mess. "This won't do," she said. So she rearranged the books, with an eye to the picture segments, and they began forming a proper picture.

When it was complete, the picture was of a comfortable chamber, wherein a man snoozed on a couch. He was a fairly handsome human male, obviously just resting between stints of work; an open book was on the table beside him. The picture, now properly assembled, was surprisingly realistic.

And the token tugged right toward it. Toward the snoozing man.

"This is weird," she muttered. But she reminded herself yet again that she was in the dream realm, where weirdness was routine, and in a private section of it, where fears were stored for future use. There seemed to be nothing fearsome about this scene, but she didn't yet understand all its implications.

So she turned smoky, then shrank into the scale of the scene, and entered it. She found herself in the room, beside the couch. "Are you—" she began.

But she stopped, because the man wasn't there. He must have gotten up as she was phasing in. He was standing to the side, near the door. "Who are you?" he asked.

"I am D. Metria, here with a summons for MPD," she said. "And I think you must be him." She stepped toward him with the token extended. "You have to report to the Nameless Castle as a Witness."

But he had already moved away. "I have no reason to accept such a summons," he said.

She whirled on him. "Then tell me who you think you are."

"I am Take Five," he said. "And I was doing that, as is my wont, when you intruded into my home."

"What is your talent?"

"I can see five seconds into the future. That is why you will not be able to serve me with that summons. I will be five seconds elsewhere."

"I am a demoness," she said evenly. "I can float or fly at any speed. Suppose I take out after you and simply pursue you unremittingly, no matter how fast you flee? You may see it coming, but you will not be able to prevent my serving you with this summons eventually. You won't even be able to sleep, unless you can do so in naps less than five seconds each.''

He pondered, evidently realizing that she was not bluffing. There was a limit to his talent. ''How much do you know?'' he asked.

''I don't know anything for sure, but I think that you are a person with multiple personalities—and each personality has a different magic talent.''

He nodded. ''How did you catch on?''

''In part because I have the same complaint myself. I am Metria, and Mentia, and Woe Betide.'' She shifted briefly into the two other forms as she spoke. ''It's a nuisance, but it has its points. So I'm not condemning you. I just have a job to do.''

His attitude softened. ''I see. You do have a similar complaint. I took you for an impersonation.''

''A what?''

''Counterfeit, bogus, fraudulent, pretense, semblance, substitute—''

''Fake?''

''Whatever,'' he said, smiling. ''I couldn't see why anyone would summons an entity who exists only in the fear storage of the dream realm. I have many personalities and forms and talents because I am a general-purpose substitute. When they don't have the proper character for a dream sequence, I fill in as well as I can. My mind is deemed irrelevant. So I assumed you were another joker sent to disturb my equilibrium.''

''They play jokes on you?''

''Sometimes. It seems it gets boring between scenes.'' He shrugged. ''Nevertheless, I can't go outside the dream realm, because I have no reality in the real world. So I think that however sincere you may be, your summons is not.''

''It's from the Simurgh.''

''That may be. But unless she is prepared to lend me a soul, I may not leave here. I lack the solidity of the walking skeletons or brassy folk; I would simply fade into oblivion, like any other figment.''

"Maybe the token can handle it," she said doubtfully.

"Very well. Let's test it. I will know if it provides support for the external realm."

She handed him the token. He took it and paused. "No, this has no animation for me. It's dead. In fact, it seems to be blank."

She looked. Indeed, the disk was blank on both sides. "I don't understand. It said 'MPD—WITNESS' before, and it led me right to you. To all of you."

"Something is amiss. Try it again." He handed it back.

She lifted it—and now the words were back. It tugged toward him. "It's working again. See—there are the words." She held it up so that he could see."

"True. So it works when you hold it, and not when I hold it. Maybe I just happen to be the wrong personality."

"So let's try the others."

No One appeared. The token tugged, but faded when he took it. Me Two appeared, with no better result. The same happened with She Three and Who Four.

"Well, maybe one of my alternates," Take Five said.

A new form appeared, in the uniform of a nurse. "I'm Pickup Six. My talent is to take pain away by touch." But the touch of the disk did nothing for her.

Another form appeared, a very friendly-seeming character. "I am Roll Seven. My talent is making friends." But there was still no reaction.

Yet another appeared, a young man vaguely reminding Metria of Grey Murphy. "I am Eight Late. My talent is dehancement." Still nothing.

A mischievously smiling young woman appeared. "I am Nine Line. My talent is to tickle at a distance." She gestured with her hands, and suddenly Metria exploded into helpless laughter, because she was being terribly tickled. She had to form a layer of impervious shellac all over her body before she was able to withstand it. Then the tickle started in her throat, making her cough.

She lost track of the other variations. The token answered to none. "I don't think it relates to any of your aspects," she said at last. "I don't understand this. It was blank until today, and then it suddenly brought me here, and now it doesn't seem to want to be served.''

"Is it possible that someone else enchanted it?" Take Five asked, resuming form.

"Who could interfere with something the Simurgh set up?"

He nodded. "That is an excellent question. But perhaps it isn't interference, merely illusion. You say that's a blank token, so maybe there is no magic on it. If someone made it look as if it had a name, and made it seem to tug, that might not be overriding the Simurgh's magic, merely sliding past it.''

Metria considered. "That seems possible. But who would bother?''

He shrugged. "I can't imagine. But it seems like a possibility to be investigated.''

"Yes." She put away the token. "Then I won't bother you anymore. I apologize for chasing after you.''

"A demoness apologizes?''

"I'm half-souled. 'Bye." She popped off.

She returned to the region she had last seen Prince Dolph. He was in the submarine, playing with a creature he had found somewhere. It had big heavy flat feet that smashed constantly against the floor. He looked up as she popped in. "This is a stampede," he explained. "It stamps nickelpedes into flat squares of paper." Indeed, there were several such squares before him, each marked "5¢": five-cent stamps. "So did you nab your summonsee?"

"It was a bum lead," she said. "Let's get out of here.''

The submarine got into motion, taking them back. While it traveled, she explained what had happened. "Too bad I had to waste a day finding out that this was a wild duck chase.''

"Goose?''

"If you do, I'll tell your wife!''

"We had better have Eve check that disk," he said. "She should be able to tell if anything has been done to it.''

"Good idea." His twin daughters were only four years old, but were full Sorceresses.

They reached the exit region, and Metria slid out. She knew that she probably wouldn't have been able to do it, if the Night Stallion objected, but her mission for the Simurgh gave her authority. Then she put a finger between the bushmaster's eye and the peephole of the gourd, breaking contact, so that Dolph's attention returned to the regular world of Xanth. It was now late in the day.

He resumed his human form. "Every time I enter the gourd, it's different," he remarked. "This wasn't as wild as sometimes, but it was interesting. I liked that submarine. And that stampede could be useful out in real Xanth." Then he became the hummingbird, and she took him and popped back to Castle Roogna.

They explained the situation to Electra, who took them to the twins Dawn and Eve, who were in their playroom, playing with their pet eight-legged kitten, Octo Puss. Then Metria showed Eve the token.

The child's eyes went round. "Something awful strong did this," she said. "But I don't know who, 'cause she never touched it."

"Someone enchanted it?" Metria asked. "From a distance?"

"Yes. It's s'posed to be blank." Eve lost interest and returned her attention to the kitten.

Metria shared a glance with Dolph and Electra. "So there was interference. And I can ignore it after this."

"Do we have time to serve the last two?" Dolph asked.

"Let's go!"

They went after Marrow Bones first. He lived in a house made of bones, with his wife Gracile Ossein and their eight year old son Picka and daughter Joy'nt.

"So how do you like your eight souls?" Metria inquired. She had been present when Graeboe Giant had given Marrow Bones half his soul, enabling the walking skeleton to remain permanently outside the gourd. Marrow, of course, had shared with his wife and children. Now each of them had an eighth soul, because souls didn't regenerate in nonliving folk.

"It's odd," Pick said.

"Odd," Joy'nt agreed.

"But nice," Grace'l said. "Now we do nice things naturally, instead of having to figure them out."

That was the thing about the Bones family: They had always been nice despite having no souls. Metria had not noticed or cared before she got her own soul, but now she found it remarkable. Marrow and Grace'l had been two of the most decent creatures in Xanth—while believing that they were not. It made Metria wonder whether souls really were the origin of goodness.

"I have a summons for Marrow," she said. "To be a Juror at Roxanne Roc's trial." She explained the situation, as far as she knew it.

"I shall be glad to attend," Marrow said, accepting the token. "Though I find it hard to believe that such a bird would do anything culpable, or that I should be competent to judge her in such a matter."

"It's one monstrous mystery to me too," Metria confessed. "I have always been curious, and this has pulled my curiosity so tight, it's about to snap." She assumed the form of a giant rubber band, tightly stretched.

"Do you think Grace'l and the bonelets could come to watch?" Marrow asked. "I am sure they would find it educational."

Metria resumed human form, and shrugged. "We can bring them along, and see whether there is any objection. It isn't my job to exclude anyone, just to make sure that every person on my list is there."

The two little skeletons jumped up and down, clapping their bony hands with a rattling sound. "Goody!" they exclaimed. "We get to see the Nameless Castle!"

"Are you ready to go now?" Metria asked. "It's early yet, but I'd like to get folk there early rather than late. I have just one more token to deliver, and if you don't mind sharing the trip—"

Marrow and Grace'l exchanged an eyeless glance. "We are ready now," Marrow said.

So Dolph assumed roc form, and Marrow bent over, and Grace'l kicked him on the tailbone. He flew apart and formed into a basket of bones, and the others climbed into this basket, and Dolph hooked three talons into it, spread his wings, and heaved it up.

"OoOo, this is fun!" Picka cried, peering down through the bone-bars of the basket.

"It looks just like a map!" Joy'nt exclaimed.

Metria found herself enjoying the flight through their eyes, as if experiencing it for the first time. Maybe this was another fringe benefit of having a soul.

"Squawk!" The big bird was circling high, getting his bearings.

Oh, she had forgotten! "Go to Lake Ogre-Chobee," she called to Dolph's huge head. "The Black Village."

The bird oriented and winged swiftly for the lake. "OoOo!" the children repeated as the land slid by below, showing off its fields, forests, rivers, mountains, and settlements. The outlines sharpened, because the land, too, was responsive to appreciation, and wanted to make its best impression. Even the small passing clouds brightened their silver linings, looking pretty. Most clouds were sweet-spirited, in contrast to stormy Fracto.

They spiraled down toward the Black Village, which was in the center of a nicely landscaped section beside Lake Ogre-Chobee. Dolph landed in the central square, released the basket, folded his wings, and resumed man form.

A cheerful black man approached. "To what do we owe the pleasure of this visit, Prince Dolph?" he inquired. His eyes passed across the skeletons. "I see you come in style."

"The Demoness Metria has something for you, Sherlock," Dolph replied.

"A summons," Metria said, and explained.

Sherlock considered. "I suppose I could go. This is a quiet time. During tourist season it's another matter. Let me go post my name on the black list." He walked away.

The little skeletons were looking at the village. Everything was black, from the houses to the black-eyed peas growing around the square. A black cat eyed them from atop a black post, and blackbirds sat in the edge of the black hole that was the village well, surrounded by blackberries. A black snake slithered across the black peat. In the village men were playing blackjack, and they could see the school where black magic was being taught. There were letter boxes for black mail. In a nearby field black sheep grazed among black-eyed Susans.

"What a neat place!" Picka said, awed.

"Yes, everything's a dull bone white where we live," Joy'nt agreed.

"Black is beautiful," Grace'l agreed. "Let's go get some black paint, so we can turn our house and boneyard black."

Delighted, they went with her along the black brick road to the black market at the other side of the village.

Dolph kicked the bone cage, so that the bones flew apart, and reformed as Marrow. "This is already proving to be worthwhile," the skeleton remarked.

Sherlock returned, wearing a black hat, showing that he was now dressed for duty. "I got a black look when I said I'd be away, but I showed them this black beryl token and they knew it was legitimate." He looked around. "Uh-oh—are they shopping at the black market? That can be dangerous for the inexperienced."

"Why?" Marrow asked. "Are the proprietors blackhearted?"

"Not exactly. It's just that too many things are available."

"All they want is black paint."

Grace'l and the children returned. They carried a can of black paint, but also a black bag with black bread and black silk cloth, and a Black Pete doll, and the children wore blackface as they chewed on black licorice sticks.

"I think my common sense blacked out," Grace'l said, abashed. "There were so many nice things—"

"Point taken," Marrow muttered. "Black markets are dangerous."

Marrow resumed basket form, and the others crowded in. Dolph resumed roc form and lifted them up. They were on their way to the Nameless Castle. Metria's job was almost done.

14
PROSECUTION

S o you are the last one I am serving,'' Metria told the Simurgh, offering her the token with her name on it.

OF COURSE, the Simurgh agreed, accepting it. YOU HAVE DONE WELL, DEMONESS.

"But there is one token remaining. It's blank, so I can't serve it. Do you want it back?"

The Simurgh cocked a huge eye at her. NO. IT MEANS THAT YOUR JOB IS NOT YET FINISHED.

"At one time it had a name, but that was an error."

The eye remained fixed on her, so Metria told the Simurgh about the MPD misadventure. "Do you think someone is trying to interfere?" she concluded.

The Simurgh sighed. I HAD HOPED THIS WOULD NOT HAPPEN IF I EMPLOYED AN INSIGNIFICANT PERSONAGE. IT SEEMS THAT THE OPPOSITION DID IN DUE COURSE REALIZE WHAT IS GOING ON.

"You mean someone *is*—?"

YES.

"But who would dare try to interfere with something you wished to accomplish?" Metria asked.

ON OCCASION THE MAJOR DEMONS HAVE CONTESTS BETWEEN THEMSELVES, IN THEIR ENDLESS QUESTS FOR ENHANCED STATUS. THREE YEARS AGO THE DEMON E(A/R)th CHALLENGED THE DEMON

$X(A/N)^{th}$ FOR DOMINION OVER THE LAND OF XANTH, AND THEIR IN-
STRUMENT OF DECISION WAS THE COMPANIONS OF XANTH GAME AS
PLAYED BY TWO IGNORANT MUNDANES. NOW THE DEMONESS $V(E\backslash N)^{us}$
IS CHALLENGING THE DEMON $X(A/N)^{th}$, AND IT SEEMS THAT THEIR IN-
STRUMENT OF DECISION IS THIS TRIAL.

Metria was amazed. "You mean the way Roxanne's trial is decided will decide the fate of Xanth?"

SO IT SEEMS. THIS WAS NOT MY PURPOSE IN INSTITUTING THE TRIAL,
BUT THEY HAVE NOW FIXED ON IT FOR THEIR OWN PURPOSES. I HAVE
NO POWER OVER THE SENIOR DEMONS, NOR DO I KNOW IN WHAT WAY
IT WILL SETTLE THEIR ISSUE.

"But don't you know everything?"

EVERYTHING EXCEPT WHAT IS IN THE MINDS OF SENIOR DEMONS.
THEY ARE LAWS UNTO THEMSELVES.

"But then how do we know which side we're on?"

WE DO NOT KNOW. BUT IT SEEMS LIKELY THAT IT IS THE DEMON-
ESS WHO WISHES TO DISRUPT THE TRIAL, BECAUSE THE DEMON
COULD HAVE CANCELED IT AT THE OUTSET HAD HE CHOSEN. IT MAY
BE THAT THE LIKELY DECISION IN THE TRIAL WILL FAVOR THE
DEMON, SO SHE HOPES TO PREVENT THAT DECISION FROM OCCUR-
RING.

"Then we need to make sure that the trial proceeds as scheduled," Metria said.

EXACTLY, GOOD DEMONESS. BUT I HAVE NO POWER TO ENSURE
THAT, AS I AM AT THIS STAGE MERELY A WITNESS.

"Then who—?"

The eye merely gazed at her.

Oh, no! "But my job is merely to fetch in the witnesses!" Metria
protested.

YOUR JOB IS TO SEE THAT ALL THE CHOSEN PERSONNEL ARE PRES-
ENT FOR THE TRIAL AT THE APPOINTED TIME.

"I can't do anything to stop an entity as powerful as the Demon
$X(A/N)^{th}$ himself!"

PERHAPS YOU CAN. THERE ARE CONSTRAINTS. BECAUSE THE DE-
MON $X(A/N)^{th}$ EVIDENTLY WISHES THIS TRIAL TO PROCEED, THE DE-
MONESS CAN NOT INTERFERE OPENLY. DEMONS NEVER OPPOSE EACH

OTHER DIRECTLY. SHE MUST ARRANGE FOR THE TRIAL TO BE DIS-
RUPTED BY SOME SEEMINGLY COINCIDENTAL FACTOR, OR INTRO-
DUCE SOME ELEMENT THAT WILL CHANGE THE VERDICT. THIS WAS
SURELY HER INTENTION WHEN SHE CAUSED AN ERRONEOUS DESIG-
NATION TO APPEAR ON THE THIRTIETH SUMMONS DISK. IT MAY BE
THAT HER INPUTS ARE LIMITED, PERHAPS TO THREE, AND THAT YOU
HAVE NULLIFIED ONE. YOU MUST BE ALERT FOR ANY DISRUPTION OR
UNWARRANTED CHANGE, SO THAT THE TRIAL PROCEEDS AS ORIGI-
NALLY SLATED. ONLY IN THIS MANNER CAN YOU BE ASSURED THAT
XANTH WILL NOT BECOME SUBJECT TO THE WILL AND MAGIC OF A
FOREIGN ENTITY.

And such a change might well be the end of Xanth as they knew
it, because a foreign demoness would have different priorities. The
Demon $X(A/N)^{th}$ allowed the Land of Xanth to function without
interference, and that was the way most residents preferred it. The
Demoness $V(E\backslash N)^{us}$ might similarly let it be, or might decide to
change everything, just to spite the former proprietor, or perhaps
from simple whimsy. Metria, as a demoness herself, had no confidence in the motives of the type. It would be better—infinitely better—to remain with the present administration.

Metria swallowed, which was a sign of stress, because she had
no saliva to swallow. "I will try my best," she said.

DO THAT, GOOD DEMONESS.

Then it was time to go, so she popped back home. She saw to
the routine chores with only half a mind; in fact, her worser half
Mentia saw to most of them, realizing that this was not the occasion
for mischief.

What was the Demoness $V(E\backslash N)^{us}$ going to do next, and what
could Metria do about it? She had no idea, and no idea. Yet she had
to be ready.

So she circulated constantly, making sure that all of the summonsees were ready, and that they would report to the Nameless Castle
at the right time. She encouraged them to go early, because once
they were there at the Castle, they couldn't depart until the trial was
done. Fortunately the Nameless Castle had accommodations for
everyone, and was a fine place to stay. The Trial Personnel, and

Prospective Jurors, and Witnesses, and their families and friends, had a fine time associating with each other. They were all under the aegis of the castle, so tender morsels like Jenny Elf or Mela Merwoman had no fear of the dragon Stanley Steamer or the reality-changing Com Pewter. In fact, they were having a great time. Rapunzel and Threnody were learning weird games like bridge and poker from Kim and Dug Mundane, which were actually played with decks of cards; they had little or nothing to do with rivers or fires. The children of the Bones family were playing dice with Okra Ogress and Stanley Steamer; somehow the children kept winning, and claiming their prizes of ogreback or dragonback rides. Princess Ida was in a deep discussion with Com Pewter about whether changed realities were believable. Kim's dog Bubbles and Jenny's cat Sammy were playing tag-tail around cloud hummocks with little Steven Steamer. The two gargoyles provided a steady stream of guaranteed fresh water, which pooled in two depressions of the cloud, so that Nada Naga could swim in one, and Mela Merwoman could swim in the other, after it had been appropriately salted. When they swam, by some coincidence, all of the unattached males got interested in watching. Possibly their preference for swimming in bare human form had something to do with it. In short, a good time was being had by all.

It wouldn't last.

The Day of the Trial came. They assembled in one of the main halls that did not connect to Roxanne Roc's chamber, for she had been left alone by the Simurgh's decree. "All rise," Magician Trent said.

Most of those present stood. Two of the winged ones flew up higher, before realizing that this wasn't required. The dragon lifted his head high. One child wasn't paying attention, so Trent walked over to him and transformed him to an infan-tree. Then he changed him back, having made his point: The Bailiff could enforce his directives.

Demon Grossclout appeared with a great noxious flair of brimstone and called the proceedings to order from the lofty rampart of his Bench. "I realize that there remains an inordinate quantity of mush in your heads," he said politely, "but if you really concentrate, maybe, just maybe, you will get through this procedure without utterly disgracing yourselves." However, he looked extremely doubtful about that. "Now, do we have the Prosecuting and Defense Attorneys present?"

Magician Grey Murphy and Princess Ida stepped forward. "Yes, Your Honor," they said almost together.

Grossclout frowned, though this was hardly distinguishable from his normal expression. "You have flies, Princess Ida?"

"No, just a little moon." She tilted her head so that the moon swung up for a clearer view. Now the others in the courtroom noticed it, and were impressed.

He glowered forbiddingly. "And have you prepared your cases?"

"Yes, Your Honor."

"Be seated." He glared around. "And is the Court Bailiff present?"

Magician Trent stepped forward, looking about as young and handsome as he ever could be. "Yes, Your Honor."

"And the Special Effects person?"

Sorceress Iris stepped up, young and pretty. Her recent rejuvenation became her, though she was probably enhancing her appearance as well. "Yes, Your Honor."

"And the Court Translator?"

Grundy Golem stepped forth. "Present, Your Honor."

"Be seated." Judge Grossclout's terrible gaze forged across the remaining people and creatures. "And the eighteen Prospective Jurors?"

"Here, Your Honor!" they chorused.

The Judge frowned horrendously. "I heard only seventeen responses."

One was missing? Metria's soul almost sagged out of her body. She had thought she had everyone!

"Identify yourselves," Magician Trent said. "Grundy, count them off as they do."

The Prospective Jurors stood in turn, lifting their summons tokens and speaking their names, and the golem counted them off. When they were done the count stood at seventeen.

Meanwhile, Metria made her own count. She had served seven Trial Personnel tokens, seventeen Juror tokens, and five Witness tokens. That was twenty-nine of the thirty tokens she had been given.

And there was the key. "Say, I know what—" she started, but was almost immediately stifled by the collision of Judge Grossclout's glare. "I mean, if it please the court—"

The glare became insignificantly less forbidding. "Speak, Demoness."

"Seventeen Juror summonses was all I served. All I had. I have one token left—but it's blank. That must be for the eighteenth Juror."

"Approach the bench."

She approached, holding up the blank disk. Grossclout took it and frowned on it for a generous moment. Then he looked up. "Is the Simurgh present?"

PRESENT, YOUR HONOR, the Simurgh's powerful thought came. OCCUPYING ANOTHER CHAMBER OF THE CASTLE.

Even the Judge's forbidding mien seemed just a trifle daunted by that puissant presence. "Why is this summons disk blank?"

IT IS A SPARE, TO BE INVOKED AT A LATER TIME.

Grossclout's eyes looked as if they would have rolled somewhat in their brooding sockets, had the response been from any lesser creature. But he put a lid on it as he returned the token to Metria. "The Prospective Juror roster is complete at seventeen. Are the five Witnesses present?"

"Here, Your Honor."

The Judge nodded. "This is to be the trial of Roxanne Roc for Violation of the Adult Conspiracy."

There was a mixed gasp. Some were amazed by the seriousness of the charge; others that such a creature could have done it. Roxanne had not even been near a child in centuries.

The awful brows lowered. "We shall now impanel the Jury." The grim gaze focused. "Bailiff, Prosecution, Defense, perform your roles." The Judge closed his eyes, seemingly going to sleep.

Magician Trent called the first name. "Threnody Barbarian."

Metria's beautiful daughter, the half demoness, stepped up and took the interrogation chair. She had done her hair for this occasion, and looked stunning in her short skirt, especially when she crossed her legs.

"Do you understand that you are under oath?" Grossclout asked her.

"Sure. You want me to tell the truth."

Prosecutor Grey Murphy approached her. "You are a barbarian," he said.

"By marriage," she replied. "I'm an asocial half demoness in my maiden state."

"Do you care about enforcing the Adult Conspiracy?"

"I think it's hilarious!"

"Is that a yes or a no?"

"That's a laugh."

The Judge's left eye cranked open. "The Prospective Juror will answer the question with an affirmation or a negation."

"What?"

"That means yes or no," Grey said.

"Oh." She considered. "No."

"You don't care about enforcing the Adult Conspiracy?"

"Right. I think it's crazy. I mean, what's so bad about using hot words or showing your panties to a child? The kids all know about them anyway."

Grey frowned. "I challenge this Juror, on the ground that—"

"The Juror is excused," the Judge said.

"What, just because I told the truth? I thought you wanted the truth."

"We appreciate the truth," Grey said carefully. "We just don't feel that you are suitable for this Jury."

"Well, if you feel that way, I don't want to be on it!" Threnody got up, almost showing her panties in the process, and went to join the audience.

Suppose those panties had shown? Metria wondered. There were some children in the audience. Would the Judge have called a mistrial? Or merely tossed Threnody off the cloud for contempt of court?

The Bailiff called out the second name: "Rapunzel Golem."

Rapunzel took the chair. She was as lovely as Threnody, but in a much safer, more demure way. She agreed that the Adult Conspiracy should be enforced, lest childish minds be corrupted. The Prosecution accepted her.

But the Defense did not. "Do you have any affinity with the Defendant, Roxanne Roc?" Princess Ida asked.

Rapunzel frowned. "I don't know what you mean. I don't even know her, except by reputation."

"Have you formed an opinion about her guilt in this matter?"

"Well, there must be some reason for her to have been charged. I'm ready to listen to the evidence and decide."

Ida's moon swung meaningfully around. "Suppose *you* were charged with such a violation?"

"Objection!" Grey called. "The Juror is not being charged."

"This relates to her attitude and belief," Ida responded.

The Judge shrugged. "Overruled. The Juror will answer."

Rapunzel was shocked. "Why, I would never, ever—!"

"But you are prepared to believe that a bird you don't know *would*?" Ida demanded, and her moon looked bleak.

"I didn't say that! But if the evidence—"

"Objection," Grey said. "Counsel for Defense is badgering the Juror."

The Judge rapped the counter with his gavel. The sound was explosive. "Approach the Bench."

Grey and Ida went to the Bench. "What is your point, Defense?" Grossclout asked.

"My client has the right to be tried by a Jury of her Peers," Ida said. "Rapunzel is certainly a nice person, but her perspective is that of an ordinary Xanth citizen, not that of an isolated roc. So she is not a Peer."

The Judge actually looked faintly impressed. "What do you consider to be qualification for a Peer?"

"To be a winged monster, or isolated from mainstream Xanth."

"But that would exclude almost everyone!" Grey protested.

"No, I could find twelve or more qualified Jurors in this group."

Grossclout nodded. "Point taken." He glanced at Grey. "Do you have any objection to a Jury consisting of winged monsters and isolated others, provided there are a sufficient number?"

Grey shrugged. "No objection, Your Honor. Provided they accept the Adult Conspiracy as valid."

"Very well. This should facilitate the selection process. Proceed."

But at that point the castle shook. There was a faint howling sound, and the floor slowly tilted.

"What is going on?" Grossclout demanded irritably.

"I'll check!" Metria said, and popped outside.

It was an ugly storm brewing. Dark clouds were scudding around the castle in a malignant pattern, and the winds were rising. Because the Nameless Castle stood on a floating cloud, it was subject to destabilization by high winds.

"Fracto!" Metria exclaimed.

She was answered by a menacing roll of thunder. It was the evil cloud, for sure. Fracto had probably been sent to do this mischief by the Demoness V(E\N)^{us}: her second effort to disrupt the trial. That meant that the storm could not readily be stopped.

She popped back inside. "Cumulo Fracto Nimbus is attacking," she said.

"Why, that impertinent pip-squeak!" Grossclout snapped. "I remember when he flunked out of my Ethics of Magic class a mere century ago."

"Well, we'll have to find a way to stop him, and soon," Metria said. "Before he huffs and he puffs and he blows our castle down."

"I could transform a number of folk into roc form," Magician Trent suggested. "So they could flap their wings and blow him away."

"Objection!" Ida said. "Anchored to the castle, their backdraft might turn it right over."

And if she believed it was so, it well might be so.

"We need something fast and gentle," Metria said. She felt responsible, perhaps because she had been forewarned by the Simurgh.

"A person in the audience has the talent of making a force field," Magician Trent said. "Perhaps that could stabilize the castle."

"No," Sorceress Iris said. "It merely keeps anything in or out. It wouldn't stop the castle from being turned over entire."

Meanwhile the storm intensified, shaking and tilting the castle worse. People were holding on to their chairs, but the chairs were starting to slide.

There was a squawk of alarm from Roxanne's chamber; she was trying to protect the egg in this increasingly treacherous situation. Normally, being between a roc and a hard place was quite safe, but the egg could crack against the stone nest if jogged or rolled too violently. HOLD ON! the Simurgh's thought came. Then, to Metria: DO SOMETHING.

But what could she do? She was an insignificant demoness. It would do no good for her to go out and insult Fracto, who would just get worse.

Her despairing gaze saw the winged monsters flying above the others, achieving stability by having no direct contact with the heaving castle. Among them was Chena Centaur, the most recently converted one.

Chena! Metria popped across to her. "Chena—I need your wishstone. Will it work for me?"

"I'm not sure. No one else has tried it."

"It has to. Give it to me."

Distracted, the centaur reached in her pack and brought out the little stone. Metria took it and popped outside the castle. The clouds were roiling closer, and worse, forming obscene blisters about to burst and spatter the castle with their juice. The castle was in the center of a turbulent wall of gray-black cloud that formed a complete circle and extended up and down, making an awful tube. That tube was contracting, and the clouds were moving faster as it did, like a stone winding up on a whirling string. When that tube got small enough, the castle itself would be whirled around and probably hurled right out of Xanth. Fracto was doing his very worst ever this time. And the Simurgh couldn't stop it, because she couldn't directly oppose the Demoness V(E\N)^{us}. That was why Metria had to find another way.

She lifted the stone. "I wish Fracto would go away," she said.

The storm hesitated. The wish was taking effect!

But then the motion resumed. Metria's wish wasn't enough to stop the effort of two demons: Fracto and Venus. Now what could she do?

A light bulb flashed just over her head. 'Mentia, make your wish!'

Mentia took over the body. She was a little crazy, but not crazy enough to support the possible destruction of all Xanth. She held up the wishstone. "Fracto, go away!" she wished.

Again the evil storm hesitated. Two wishes were stronger than one. The funnel of dark clouds lost cohesion and began to expand.

But then it pulled itself together again. Fracto was so ornery that even two wishes were not enough to turn him aside.

'Woe Betide!' Mentia said.

The innocent tyke took over the body. Woe Betide's big soulful eyes brimmed with fetching tears. She held up the wishstone. "Please, Fracto, go away!" she wished.

This time it was too much. The wish of an innocent child was the strongest of all. *Curses! Foiled again!* The wall of cloud fragmented, and the fierce winds died. The storm fell apart into a great mess of brownish blobs, like diarrhea fouling the sky, and faded into impotent drools of mist. Fracto was gone.

GOOD WORK, GOOD DEMONESS

Metria resumed control. She was, if not overwhelmed by the compliment, at least generously whelmed. But she knew her job was not done. There could still be one more effort to disrupt the trial, and she had to guard against it.

She popped inside. The castle had stopped rocking, and the creatures were settling down. Judge Grossclout spied her. "You had something to do with this?" he asked around a glower in her direction.

"Yes, Your Honor," she confessed, abashed as always by his direct attention.

"You may yet lose a bit of mush from that idiot skull," he said, turning away. And she felt deeply flattered again, because the Demon Professor's faintest favor was a thing rarely granted to any creature.

The impaneling of the Jury continued. In deference to the nature of the Defendant, who was a winged monster, half the selected Jurors were winged monsters: Gloha and Graeboe Giant-Harpy, Gary Gar and Gayle Goyle, Stanley Steamer, and Che Centaur. The others were objective aliens, on the assumption that this would enable them to understand the viewpoint of a bird who had been mostly isolated from Xanth for several centuries: Dug and Kim Mundane, whose contact with Xanth had been limited; Sherlock Black and Jenny Elf, who had come from far lands not all that long ago; Marrow Bones from the gourd realm; and Com Pewter, who never did relate well to ordinary Xanth reality. Cynthia and Chena Centaur were seated Alternates, in case something should happen to any of the impaneled Jurors; each of them had become winged monsters after being something else, so they should understand both perspectives. Overall it was an unusual but well qualified Jury.

The Judge wasted no time. "Is the Prosecution ready?"

"Yes, Your Honor," Grey Murphy said.

"Proceed."

Now the wall separating the trial chamber from Roxanne Roc's nesting chamber slid back, making one huge central chamber. Metria was surprised; she hadn't realized that this was a feature of the nameless Castle. The big bird was now in the full view of all the assembled trial personnel. She seemed oblivious, neither twitching any feather nor making any sound. She merely sat, as she had for centuries.

Grey took the center stage. "The Prosecution will demonstrate that the Defendant, Roxanne Roc, egregiously violated the Adult Conspiracy by uttering an Adult Word in the presence of a minor, and thereby may have prejudiced the future of Xanth."

A murmur passed across the group. Roxanne's near eye opened. "Squawk!" she protested.

The Judge's loud gavel banged. "There will be order in this court. Defense will have its hour in due course."

But this was the nub of it, Metria realized: How could Roxanne have done any such thing, when there had not been any minors in this castle in all the centuries of her confinement here? This was one of the most protected places in all Xanth; before the trial, few creatures had even known of the Nameless Castle's existence, fewer had visited it, and the roc had not spoken any bad words to them. So the charge seemed baseless. Yet Grey Murphy evidently took it seriously, and he was nobody's fool. His talent was to nullify magic, and he seemed to be able to nullify foolish notions too. If he thought the big bird was guilty, it seemed likely that she was.

Grossclout oriented on Grey Murphy. "Resume."

"First the matter of the Adult Word. The Prosecution calls Phelra Human to the Witness Seat."

Phelra stood and came to the Witness Box. Grundy Golem approached her. "Do you swear to tell the truth, no matter what?"

"Sure."

"The Witness is duly sworn," the Judge said, with more than a hint of annoyance at the informality.

Grey approached the Witness. "Where do you live?"

"I live in a mushroom in the deepest jungle north of Lake Ogre-Chobee."

"What is your talent?"

"I summon animals to help me, or those I want to help."

"Have you ever interacted with the Defendant, Roxanne Roc?"

"Yes, once, about two years ago."

"State the full nature of that interaction."

"Well, it was an accident, really, and nothing much happened, just—"

"Objection!" Ida said, and her moon bobbed. "The Witness is offering a conclusion."

"Sustained," the Judge said.

Grey grimaced, then came at it another way. "Did you have a dialogue with Roxanne Roc?"

"Yes. But it really wasn't—"

"Objection!"

"Sustained."

"But I need to establish the context of this encounter," Grey protested.

The Judge was unsympathetic. "Find a way that doesn't cause the Witness to offer a conclusion about the Defendant."

Grey considered. Then he faced the Judge. "Prosecution requests the assistance of the Court Special Effects Officer to animate this testimony, and the Court Translator to represent speech, without invoking any conclusions of the Witness.''

''Granted.''

The Sorceress Iris came to the stage, followed by little Grundy Golem. ''What scene do you want?'' Iris asked.

''Start with her home, and animate her description for the Jury and audience.''

Iris stood beside the Witness, and listened to her words, which were now spoken faintly, so that the Jury did not hear. After two and a half moments, the illusion picture formed. It started with an aerial scene, similar to that seen by creatures being carried through the air by a roc. It showed Lake Ogre-Chobee, with the chobees basking at its edges. South of it was the Curse Fiends' Thunder-Dome, and west of it was Black Village. Then the view slid to the north, moving down until it intersected the ground.

There was a deep jungle there, through which the Kiss Mee River wound. The river had been very friendly, until the demons pulled it straight, making it into the Kill Mee River. But later its friendly curves had been restored, and once again those who drank of it became kissing friendly. In fact, some of those who partook of its fresh water became quite fresh.

Metria, watching, found herself becoming part of the scene, and came to understand the impressions and feelings of the woman whose scene this was. It was her half soul that was doing it, she knew; she never used to care about feelings.

This became a problem one day for Phelra, when a man called Snide happened by. He spied her giving directions to her pet catalog, and made sarcastic remarks about the cat. ''You think that moth-eaten fur ball will remember your directions?'' he demanded sneeringly. ''You must be as stupid as it is.'' The image was Snide, but the voice was that of Grundy Golem, who was doing the dialogue. It didn't matter, because Grundy had a natural talent for insults.

Now, Phelra was not a person to take offense without cause, but something about the man's attitude annoyed her. For one thing, he was wrong about the cat, who could indeed take orders competently. ''Oh, go have a drink!'' she said, which was just about as close as a nice girl could get to swearing. Then she wanted to swallow her tongue, because she remembered the effect the river water had on folk who weren't used to it. The last thing she wanted was to have Snide get too friendly.

So she retreated into her mushroom and closed the door. The house was, of course, somewhat mushy, but was the best she could afford. She was afraid Snide would come after her, and that the mush would just make him even more inclined for what she didn't want.

She peeked out the window, and her fear was confirmed: Snide was drinking. In a moment he would be not only snide but fresh. She had to escape!

Maybe if she could find her friend Alias, she could get away. Alias' talent was to make everyone around him answer to wrong names. When there was a crowd of people, it could get so complicated that they had to compile a list to get them all straight again. Snide would never find her in such a crowd!

But Alias was elsewhere today, and anyway, there was no crowd of people to help confuse things. So what about her friend Tom, who could conjure a small cloud and pluck any tool or weapon he needed from it? Of course, he had to return the tool to the cloud before he could get any other tool, but it was a pretty strong talent. If he were here, he could pull out a sword and tell Snide to go lose himself in a boggy swamp.

But Tom wasn't here either. None of her friends were close. So she would just have to flee for it, hoping that Snide would give up the chase. She would invoke her power to summon an animal to carry her rapidly away. What animal would be best?

Now Snide was approaching the house, and he looked really super awful fresh. His hands would be all over her the moment he got close. She had to summon an animal immediately.

Maybe a Rocky Mountain Goat, because it would carry her swiftly up the nearest rocky mountain, and she would be able to hide behind the rocks if she needed to.

She opened her mouth as she exerted her summoning talent. ''Roc—''

Then Snide crashed through the wall of her house. Actually ''crash'' wasn't a good description; it was more like a squish, ripping a sagging hole. The suddenness of it startled her, so that she didn't complete her word. Besides, Snide was already reaching for her, and he smelled sickeningly fresh. It was probably time to scream.

But her talent had been invoked, and it oriented on the nearest animal of the type she had named. Unfortunately she hadn't named an animal, but a bird, and she didn't do birds because a peculiarity of her talent was that—

Too late. Suddenly she was flying. She sailed right out through the hole in the mush wall and up into the air. She knew what had happened: She had attempted to summon the wrong kind of creature, so instead of bringing it to her, she was being brought to it. Because it was a type of bird, she was flying to it. It was her own messed-up magic doing it. She just had to hope that wherever she landed was not worse than being caught by a fresh man.

Lo, she found herself flying right up into a cloud. Her talent had never backfired this badly before. But of course, she was going to wherever the nearest roc bird was, and it must be flying high above the clouds, as they tended to do, so that the magic of perspective would make them seem like much smaller birds. For reasons she wasn't quite clear on, the big birds tended to conceal their presence, so that human folk seldom encountered rocs close by.

Then, astonishingly, she saw a building on the top of the cloud. A castle in air! And she was flying right into it. What a misadventure!

She came to light in a huge inner chamber, before a roc bird sitting on a huge stone nest. The bird was fearsomely large, but seemed as startled to see her there as she was to be there.

"Squawk?" the bird inquired.

Phelra didn't understand bird talk, but took this as a question. She started to explain how her talent had gotten fouled up, bringing her involuntarily here.

"Squawk!" the bird said, evidently miffed.

"Freeze that frame," Grey Murphy said.

The scene stopped where it was. Grundy turned to the Witness, who was sitting right where her illusion self was standing. "Repeat exactly that Roxanne Roc said to you."

"She said 'Squawk?' and then 'Squawk?' and then she—"

"Those were the very words?"

"Yes. And then—"

Grey turned to Grundy. "And what do those words translate to, in human terms?"

"The first is 'What?' and the second is 'Darn!' " the golem said.

"Are you sure?"

"Of course I'm sure! I speak and understand the language of all living things. That's what I was made for, before I achieved living status."

"And what is the nature of the second word?"

"Objection!" Ida cried. "Conclusion!"

Grey turned to the Judge. "This is in the Translator's line of expertise. He is qualified to define the word."

The Judge nodded. "Overruled. The Translator may answer the question."

"It refers to the process of mending torn cloth by means of rows of stitches," Grundy said. "The process is tedious, and the result tends to be unsightly, so is usually not appreciated. A darned item is neither as pristine nor as valuable as the original. Thus when anything is accused of being darned, or when anyone is told to darn—"

"Get to the point," the Judge rumbled.

"It is considered an objectionable word," Grundy said. "One not suited for the delicate young ears of small children."

"A word not suited for small children," Grey repeated with emphasis. "One which would be a violation of the Adult Conspiracy if uttered in the presence of a very young child."

"Exactly. Of course, it's only a mild transgression—"

"Thank you." Grey turned to the Judge. "I am done with this Witness." He stepped away.

"But what's the relevance?" Metria asked. "There wasn't any child there!"

The Judge's glower swiveled to cover her, but she passed her hand across her mouth, leaving it visibly zipped shut, and he let it pass. She knew she had better not speak out of turn again.

Ida approached the Witness. "Was there a translator present when you encountered Roxanne Roc?" she asked.

"No. I didn't understand her squawks."

"So you did not realize that she had spoken an unfortunate word."

"That's right."

"In fact, until this time you had no notion why you were summoned to be a Witness at this trial."

"Objection!" Grey said. "Irrelevant, immaterial, and beside the point."

"Sustained."

"What happened then?" Ida asked.

"Objection! Relevance."

"It's relevant to my Defense!" Ida snapped, with unusual asperity for her normally sunny nature. Her moon looked similarly annoyed, though not actually eclipsed.

"But this is a Prosecution Witness."

"Sustained."

"Then I'll call her when my turn comes," Ida said, walking away.

"The Witness may step down," the Judge said.

Phelra returned to the audience, evidently somewhat bemused. The scene faded.

Grey smiled grimly. "Second, the matter of the presence of a child. The Prosecution calls the Simurgh to the Witness Seat."

There was a murmur of awe at this, causing the Judge to issue a general-purpose glower that silenced the sound.

THE SIMURGH REQUESTS PERMISSION TO RESPOND IN PLACE, OWING TO THE LIMITED SIZE OF THE STAGE.

Grossclout almost smiled. "Granted. The Special Effects Officer will generate a small illusion to be addressed in the Witness Box."

Sorceress Iris nodded. A small image of the Simurgh appeared, perched on the back of the Witness Chair. If anyone thought such a representation humorous, he had the sense to stifle his reaction.

Grundy Golem approached. "Do you swear to tell the truth, no matter what?"

I DO. The answer seemed to come from the bird in the Witness Box.

"The Witness is duly sworn," the Judge said.

Grey Murphy approached. "What is the nature of your employment?"

"Objection," Ida said. "Relevance."

Grossclout frowned. "Is there relevance?"

"Yes, Your Honor. It will be apparent in a moment."

"Then proceed. The Witness may answer."

I AM THE OLDEST AND WISEST CREATURE IN THE UNIVERSE. I HAVE SEEN THE DESTRUCTION AND RESURRECTION OF THE UNIVERSE THREE TIMES. I AM AMONG OTHER THINGS THE GUARDIAN OF THE TREE OF SEEDS.

"Do you find this tiring?"

AFTER A FEW MILLENNIA, IT DOES GET DULL.

"Are you considering any way to alleviate that dullness?"

I HOPE IN DUE COURSE TO PASS ALONG SOME OF THESE CHORES TO MY SUCCESSOR, WHO WILL EVENTUALLY BE AS WISE AS I AM.

"And who is your successor?"

MY UNNAMED CHICK.

"Where is this chick?"

IN AN EGG BETWEEN A ROC AND A HARD PLACE, HERE IN THE NAMELESS CASTLE, WHICH WAS ESTABLISHED FOR THIS PURPOSE.

"And where precisely is the egg now?"

UNDER ROXANNE ROC.

There was a murmur in the chamber, despite the Judge's glare. This was news of enormous import.

"How long will it take your chick to hatch from the egg?"

SIX HUNDRED YEARS.

"When was the egg delivered to you?"

SIX HUNDRED YEARS AGO, IN THE YEAR 495.

"Then it must be due to hatch this year."

YES.

"What is the state of the chick?"

THE CHICK IS SENTIENT AND SAPIENT.

"That is, alive and intelligent," Grey said. "Can the chick hear words that are spoken in the nesting chamber?"

YES.

"So when Roxanne Roc spoke that forbidden word, the chick heard."

YES.

Roxanne, listening in the adjacent chamber, jumped. It was clear this was a revelation to her. That wasn't surprising; there was a glare-stifled murmur in the audience, and a muted exchange of glances in the Jury Box.

Grey turned away. "Your Witness."

Ida approached the image, and her moon inspected it curiously. "Since you are the wisest creature in the universe, why didn't you anticipate this infraction and prevent it?"

WISDOM DOES NOT EQUATE TO FOREKNOWLEDGE. PHELRA'S VISIT TO THE NAMELESS CASTLE WAS ESSENTIALLY A RANDOM ACT THERE WAS NO WAY TO ANTICIPATE. THE DAMAGE WAS DONE BEFORE I COULD ACT.

"So you did nothing?"

I INITIATED THE SEQUENCE OF EVENTS LEADING TO THIS TRIAL.

"Even though you knew that the Defendant had no awareness of her violation?"

"Objection! Argumentative, conclusion."

"The Simurgh knows everything," Ida said evenly. "She is qualified to give an opinion."

"It's still argumentative," Grey argued.

The Judge pondered briefly. "Rephrase your question."

"Do you believe the Defendant was aware of her infraction?"

NO.

"Then why did you—"

"Objection! The Witness is not on trial."

"Sustained. The Witness does not have to answer."

I WILL RESPOND NEVERTHELESS. I REQUIRED THIS TRIAL BECAUSE IGNORANCE IS NO EXCUSE. A VIOLATION HAS OCCURRED, AND IT MUST BE DEALT WITH.

"Even though—"

"Objection!"

"Sustained."

Ida shrugged, not looking frustrated. Metria understood why: The members of the Jury, both human and monster, understood the nature of the unvoiced objection, and were being swayed by it. "I am done with this Witness," she said.

"The Witness may step down." The small image faded from the chair.

Grey Murphy stood. "The Prosecution rests," he announced.

He had called only two Witnesses, but they had been enough: They had established that the Defendant had uttered a Forbidden Word, and that a minor had heard it. Roxanne Roc was in deep dung.

15
DEFENSE

The Judge's devastating gaze swept across to Princess Ida. "Is the Defense ready?"

"Yes, Your Honor."

"Proceed."

"The Defense calls the Simurgh to the stand."

"Objection! She said she was done with that Witness."

"I was done for cross-examination. Now I want her as *my* Witness. That's a different matter."

The Judge rolled one eye expressively, but allowed it. "Overruled."

The image of the Simurgh reappeared on the chair. Ida addressed it. "You have stated that your egg was delivered six hundred years ago, and that you arranged to set up the Nameless Castle for its incubation. When did you assign Roxanne Roc as eggsitter?"

THE YEAR 500.

"So that was five years after you received the egg?"

YES.

"You had to take care of the egg yourself in the interim?"

"Objection! Relevance."

"I am establishing the importance of the Defendant's duty. This relates to her character."

Grey shook his head. "Importance and character have no necessary interconnection. Prosecution will stipulate that the job is important. So important, in fact, that any default is a most serious—''

''Objection! The Prosecution's case has already been made.''

Judge Grossclout's dour mouth quirked in a hint of a suggestion of a thought of a faint unfrown. ''The Defense's objection is sustained. The Prosecution's objection is overruled. But do not try the limited patience of this Court with too free an interpretation of your mission.''

Ida smiled sweetly at the Judge. Metria realized that she looked very nice when she did that. Probably she believed that she was making a marginally favorable impression, and so it was true. Even her little moon seemed to glow. That was bound to have more of an impact when she addressed the Jury. Then she returned to the Witness. ''You took care of—''

YES.

''Was it difficult to eggsit while also guarding the Tree of Seeds on Mount Parnassus and attending to your other duties?''

YES.

''So you decided to get an eggsitter?''

''Objection! Defense is leading the Witness.''

''This Witness can't be led against her will,'' Ida retorted.

''Overruled.''

YES.

''Was the egg important to you?''

There was a ripple of mirth through the audience as the Simurgh answered YES.

''So you did not seek just any creature to do the job.''

TRUE.

''In fact, didn't you seek the most qualified creature available for that most important task?''

YES

''And that creature was Roxanne Roc.''

YES.

''So by your judgment, which is by definition the most authoritative one available, Roxanne Roc was a highly qualified bird. In fact, a creature of excellent competence and character.''

YES.

"And did she perform in the manner you required?"
YES.

"For almost six centuries."
YES.

"And does she remain so qualified today?"
YES.

"So your pursuit of this infraction does not imply that the Defendant is in any way deficient in competence or character."
AGREED.

"And you still trust her to sit your egg."
YES.

There was another subdued murmur in the court. The words and action of the Simurgh herself were the best possible endorsement of Roxanne Roc's character.

"Thank you." Ida turned to smile at Grey Murphy. It was a *try to dispute THAT* expression, but her moon brightened prettily. Metria worried about its effect on a man who had been too long betrothed without result. "Your Witness."

Grey approached the chair. "But the Defendant did violate the Adult Conspiracy."
YES.

And there was the crux, Metria realized. It hardly mattered how great a person Roxanne was; she had done the deed. And it hardly mattered how fetching Princess Ida became; Grey's talent nullified that magic.

He nodded significantly at the Jury. "Thank you. I am done."

The image faded. Ida faced the audience. "I call Gwendolyn Goblin to the stand."

The pretty little lady Chief of Goblin Mountain stood and came to the stage. She was duly sworn in.

"Have you encountered the Defendant?" Ida asked her.

"Yes, once."

"State the circumstances of that encounter."

"Well, I was rivaling my bratty little brother Gobble Goblin for the Chiefship of our tribe, and he arranged for me to have to fetch what was between the roc and the hard place." As she spoke, the Sorceress Iris animated it, so that the scene in Goblin Mountain appeared. Gwenny Goblin was with her Companion Che Centaur and her friend Jenny Elf, both of whom were now on the Jury. The three of them struggled to grasp the meaning of the requirement, and realized that they would have to somehow find their way to the Nameless Castle in order to fetch the precious roc's egg.

The scene shifted past the complicated route they took to reach the Nameless Castle. It was in fast forward, so it looked as if they were feverishly dashing across Xanth and scrambling upward toward the Castle. They reached the main chamber where Roxanne sat on the nest. Gwenny used her magic wand to lift the supposedly sleeping bird off the nest, exposing the beautiful crystalline egg. Then Che touched it.

And Roxanne squawked. "Stop!" Grundy translated. "That's the Simurgh's egg!" And on her command the entire castle was suddenly sealed shut, so that the intruders couldn't escape.

There followed a chase, as the big bird sought to catch and confine the three, and they sought to escape. They managed to get Roxanne into one of Jenny Elf's shared dreams, and had a dialogue with her, and learned how she had run afoul of the Simurgh and lost her power of flight. She had finally petitioned the Simurgh for release from her grounding, and the Simurgh had assigned her to community service in the Nameless Castle, where she had to remain until she hatched the egg stored there. She did not know that she had actually been chosen for this important labor; she thought it was a rebuke rather than a privilege, but she did her best regardless, because she was that kind of person.

And there she remained for almost six centuries, guarding and warming the egg. She was allowed to eat only those intruders who threatened the egg, and since she didn't want to make a mistake, she was very careful. In this case she had waited until one of the intruders actually touched the egg. Then she had acted.

Metria remembered. She had passed that scene at that time, while on game-duty for Professor Grossclout, and seen Jenny and Che in the cage the roc had put them in. Gwenny Goblin had been fending off the bird with her magic wand, so it was an impasse, but it didn't look good for the intruders.

"So the Defendant defended the egg loyally," Ida concluded.

"Oh, yes!" Gwenny agreed. "She was a terror. But we came to understand that she was just doing her job, and we came to respect her for that. In the end we reinterpreted our requirement, and took one of Roxanne's old shed claws, because it had fallen into the nest beside the egg, so was also between the roc and the hard place."

Ida next called Okra Ogress to the Witness Stand. She testified that she and her friends Mela Merwoman and Ida Human had been sent by the Simurgh to rescue the stranded trio, and had done so, with the help of a Seed of Thyme and some negotiation. Because Roxanne had been out of circulation for several centuries, she had not learned that Che Centaur was to be protected by all winged monsters, so that he could in due course change the history of Xanth. Once she learned this, she honored it.

There was another murmur in the audience as the animation showed Ida herself in the scene, along with two of the members of the Jury and three Witnesses. But an all-purpose glower by the Judge stifled it, as usual.

Okra agreed that Roxanne had acted in an honorable manner, and had certainly protected the egg to the best of her ability.

Mela Merwoman, the next Witness, was wearing her legs instead of her tail. She took time to settle her comely posterior in the Witness Chair so that the males in the audience could complete their gawking, then endorsed the ogress' testimony. In the end they had given Roxanne the Seed of Thyme, and the big bird had not used it to destroy them, as she readily could have done.

"So the Defendant proved to be a creature of her word," Ida concluded.

"Yes. She's a good person."

Phelra was the next Witness. "So you heard the Defendant squawk, but did not at that time know the meaning of her exclamation," Ida said. "You were not aware that she said a word that was forbidden in the context she didn't know existed."

"Objection!"

"I'll rephrase. It was just a squawk to you."

"Yes," Phelra agreed.

"Perhaps an exclamation of surprise or dismay, when she realized that you had arrived there accidentally and that it might be a chore to get you clear of the Nameless Castle."

"Yes. That is the way I understood it."

"And indeed, that is exactly the way she intended it. She could understand your speech, because most animals take the trouble to learn human speech despite being unable to speak it themselves, in contrast to the ignorant attitude of most humans. Her frustration was that she was unable to explain to you how to return to your home."

"Yes."

"In fact, she might even have made an analogy to a sock that had been torn, that would need tedious and imperfect mending, because the sock doesn't understand the problem."

"Why, yes," Phelra agreed, brightening. "In that sense, it wouldn't be a bad word at—"

"Objection!"

"Sustained. Jury will disregard that comment."

The Jury, however, looked as if it wasn't sure it wanted to forget the comment. Ida was doing a remarkably apt job of swaying the members of the Jury, perhaps because of her talent of belief. She probably had the Idea that she could save Roxanne, and what she truly believed always came to pass, because she was a Sorceress.

"But she did get you safely home, didn't she?" Ida continued.

"Yes. She had a chip of reverse wood. I held it, then exerted my talent to summon the roc again. It reversed the thrust, and sent me flying right back the way I had come. It was exactly what I needed. In fact, it even helped me get rid of Snide. I'm sorry that I never had the chance to thank her, or to return her chip of wood."

"So the Defendant, once she understood the situation, treated you with helpful courtesy."

"Yes. She was great. She could have eaten me, but she didn't."

Metria could see that this made another impression on the Jury. By rights, Roxanne could have chomped Phelra, for intruding where she didn't belong. But the bird had acted compassionately rather than viciously. But still, she *had* uttered the bad word.

Ida was finished with the Witness, and Grey had no further questions; the damage to his case was already quite enough.

"The Defense calls Roxanne Roc to the Witness Stand."

Judge Grossclout spoke. "Are you aware that if the Defendant testifies on her own behalf, she will become fair game for the Prosecution, who may cause her to incriminate herself?"

"Yes, Your Honor." Ida's moon looked serious. "But I feel the risk must be taken."

"Proceed. The Witness may answer from her present location."

Ida faced the other chamber. "Roxanne, please relate what befell you during the Time of No Magic."

There was yet another muted murmur. The Time of No Magic had occurred in the year 1043, fifty-two years before, and a number of the participants of this trial had not been on the scene at that time. To them it was History, and therefore boring. What relevance could this have to the present case?

But Grey Murphy did not object. Either he saw some relevance, or he was curious himself.

Roxanne began squawking. Grundy Golem translated, and the Sorceress Iris animated the scene. It was of the Nameless Castle on its cloud, floating serenely above the Land of Xanth. Roxanne herself was snoozing, as she sometimes did during the somewhat tedious centuries, and in that state she looked as if she were a great stone statue.

Then, abruptly, the magic ceased. This was because Bink Human, participating in an aspect of the Demon X(A/N)th's reality, had given the Demon leave to depart. The Demon had done so in half a trice, going somewhere far from Xanth, and taking his magic with him. For all of Xanth's magic stemmed from the ambience of the Demon, representing that trace that leaked out, much as the heat of an animal's body leaked out to the surroundings. Some magic remained for a while, in the manner of some heat, slowly diffusing from Xanth's larger concentrations, but it was so scant as to be virtually unnoticed.

Immediately the cloudstuff of which the castle was made began to soften, and the cloud itself lost its buoyancy. It sank rapidly toward the suddenly bleak land. Roxanne had no idea of the background cause, but did realize that the cloud and castle would crash and be destroyed if she didn't do something quickly.

She leaped off the nest and ran outside. She peered down past the fragmenting brink. There lay Xanth, spread out much as usual, but twice as dreary as usual. It looked almost as bad as Mundania. Not far away was Lake Kiss Mee, looking as if it had been kicked instead of kissed.

Maybe she could get the castle to splash down into the lake, instead of wrecking on land. It would still be one awful collision, but the cushioning effect of the water might enable her to save the egg. That was all that mattered.

She dug her talons into the loosening cloudscape, stood up straight, and spread her giant wings. She couldn't fly, because the Simurgh had deprived her of her power of flight for the duration, but her wings still could beat the air and make a strong backdraft. If she could just push the castle toward the lake . . .

The castle moved—in the wrong direction. Of course; she was facing the lake. She angled her wings, and caused the cloud isle to spin around until she was facing away from the water. Then she pumped as hard as she could. Already the castle was much lower, because it had continued falling. But there was still a chance to slant it down to the lake.

She pumped until she thought her heart would burst, watching the land rush up beneath her. She couldn't see the lake now; was she going in the right direction? She must be, because forward was the one way she could not see.

But she couldn't let the egg take the shock by itself; it could be cracked open. So as the tops of the trees loomed close beneath, she let go, turned, and launched herself back into the incubation chamber. She was diving for the nest—just as the castle struck the water.

There was a horrendous swish. Walls of water sailed up all around, visible through the higher windows. The castle came to a sudden but not calamitous partial halt—and bounced back up. It was skipping across the water like a clumsy stone! Because she had succeeded in angling it forward at a faster rate than it was falling. She overshot the nest, because everything but her was slowing down drastically. She scrambled to turn around, so as to get back on the nest and protect the egg.

The bounce reversed, and the castle descended again. The egg sailed out of the stone nest. Roxanne leaped at it, and caught it in her talons, oh-so-carefully, so that it would not fall back against the stone. But she was falling now, too. So she pushed her wings down, hard, to break her fall and keep the egg clear of the hard nest. Normally the safest place in Xanth was between the roc and the hard place, but not in this circumstance.

The castle skipped again, rising a second time. It came up hard under her. Her wings took the shock, and she was able to land in the nest and lay the egg gently back in it. But she felt a terrible shock of pain, and knew that one of her wings was broken.

But she had no chance to be concerned about that. The castle was still bouncing across the water, in diminishing hops, rattling the egg dangerously. She wrapped her wings down under herself and the egg, cushioning the contacts with the hard nest.

At last the awful motion ceased. She breathed half a sqawk of relief—then realized that there was still some motion. A slow settling. The castle was sinking in the lake!

She left the egg, secure for the moment, and scrambled back outside. Water was covering the surface of the cloud and lapping at the base of the castle itself. The castle was light, but the cloudstuff was getting waterlogged, so that in the end it would sink to the bottom. How deep was the lake? She didn't know, but feared it was way beyond the height of the castle. The egg would drown at the bottom of the lake.

Unless she could do something to shore it up. If she could make it float—

She clawed at the cloudstuff of the cloud-island's rim, hauling it up. A fragment tore out, leaving a gap. She quickly jammed it back down, but at an angle, so that part of a rim formed. One advantage of the deteriorating nature of the cloudstuff was that it was now malleable; she could shape it to her whim.

She moved around the edge, turning it up and jamming it in place. Soon she had a boat of sorts, or raft. But it was waterlogged, and still slowly sinking. So she formed a channel-ramp, low inside, high outside, set herself at the low side, dug in, and began flapping her wings again. Pain shot through her left wing with every stroke, but she gritted her beak and forced the motion through. She was directing her backdraft across the water, by the crude channel.

As she pumped harder, the wind pushed the water along the channel, and off the cloudbank. More water seeped in to fill its place, and this, too, was forced along the channel and out. Soon she had a weak fountain of water forming, squirting off the edge of her island, and the level on the island was dropping. As it did, the island became more buoyant, and the castle slowly lifted. She was succeeding in making it float!

At last the cloud surface was mostly dry, and she was able to relax. Her broken wing was smarting something awful, and the rest of her was almost worn out. But she had succeeded in saving the castle, and with it the egg. That was all that mattered.

She checked on the egg, and it was secure. She didn't have to sit on it all the time; it was large enough and dense enough to hold its heat for some while. Still, it wouldn't hurt to—

The castle shook. She scrambled back outside to check. There was a ship trying to collide with it! A big boat, filled with annoying-looking people. Its side was banging into the cloudwall, threatening to dent it and let the water pour back in.

"What are you doing?" she demanded angrily. "Get away from here!" But all that came out, of course, was two squawks, which she knew from experience were indecipherable to ignorant human folk. Indeed, they were standing at the rail of the ship, staring stupidly at her.

Then she saw the name of the boat: RELATIONSHIP. This was the craft that carried all the relatives! Naturally folk hated to see its approach, because relatives tended to be a pain, particularly those of one's spouse. These were probably kissing cousins, because this was Lake Kiss Mee. Right now they looked quite sour, though, because the magic was gone.

She braced one foot against the ship, and hooked the other into the cloudstuff, and managed to shove the ship away. It drifted onward, toward whatever fate any relationship was doomed to suffer.

Now she had time to ponder. Obviously the magic had departed, for what reason she wasn't competent to wonder. The Nameless Castle had lost its enchantment, and surely the spell that denied her the ability to fly was also gone—except that the magic of rocs was the ability to fly, because no other creature their size could do it. So the loss of the magic had the same effect on her as the null-spell. And of course, her broken wing would have prevented her from flying anyway. The question was, would the magic return? She had to assume that it would, because otherwise she and the castle and the egg were doomed. The proper place for them was in the sky, where it was safe; down here on land or water, it would be only a matter of time before land monsters attacked, or a storm blew it over.

But she had no control over that. All she could do was wait—and hope. And keep the precious egg warm.

She went back to the nest and sat on the egg. She tried to sleep, but her wing was too painful. She wished she had access to a healing spring, but realized that the healing elixir wouldn't work without magic. So she simply steeled herself against the pain and waited.

Every so often she went outside and repaired the deteriorating rim. She judged that if the magic stayed away more than a day, there would be nothing more she could do to preserve the castle, because the cloudstuff continued to sag. It would founder, and disappear under the water.

Unless she could guide the castle to land, so that at least it couldn't sink. Yes—that was her best course.

She anchored her feet and pumped her wings again. The pain flared awfully, but she kept at it, until at last the soggy floating island bumped up against land. She nudged it as far up as she could, then rested. Now it wouldn't sink, at least.

She returned to the egg, and sat on it, warming it with her body. It took her a while to snooze, because of her pain and fatigue—and when she did, more trouble came.

There was a horrible howling near the castle. Some monster was coming; and it sounded dangerous. She scrambled out to assess the situation, because she did not want to be surprised on the nest. The big disadvantage to perching the cloud isle on land was that it was now exposed to the depredations of land creatures, which could be about as bad as the sea creatures. Worse, really, because surely there had been no unfriendly ceatures in the Kiss Mee lake.

It was something that might once have been a dragon, but now was a crazed obscurity in the night. It snapped at the fringe of cloud-stuff, tearing out huge gobs. It lurched toward the castle itself.

Roxanne gave a squawk for challenge and charged it. She could not let it chew up the softening fabric of the castle and perhaps get at the egg itself. She was in no condition to fight, but she had to protect what remained of her charge, in case the magic ever came back.

The monster hissed and whirled on her. Its eyes glared balefully. It was confused and maddened by the loss of magic, but it was large and vicious. Maybe it was the remnant of a sphinx. All she wanted was to make it go away, but she feared that it would feel no pain and would not be bluffed.

She was right. The monster snapped and clawed at her, gouging out feathers and flesh. She retreated—away from the castle. It followed, intent only on viciousness. So she continued to hold its attention, luring it away from the castle. She could have fled, and saved herself a beating, but she wanted to be sure it was far enough away so that it would not blunder into the castle again. So she endured the unrelenting attack, though hardly any part of her body escaped laceration and bruising.

When she was finally satisfied, she backpedaled faster, escaping the nearly mindless thing. But now she was so worn and battered that she wasn't sure she could straggle back to the castle herself, let alone defend it from other predators. She wanted simply to collapse and expire.

But she didn't. She dragged herself in what she thought was the right direction. After a time the deadly fatigue overwhelmed her and she sank down on the ground, unconscious. But after more time she recovered a bit, and resumed dragging. She couldn't leave the egg vulnerable!

She had no idea how long she dragged and collapsed, dragged and collapsed, but certainly time was passing. Her concern for the egg grew; when would it cool too far? She had to get there, and collapse on top of it, so that it would have its best chance, regardless what happened to her. Even if she died, her body would take time to cool—perhaps time enough for the magic to return. Then—

Then what? The egg needed her protection with magic as much as without it.

Her consciousness was dimming, but she realized that she had to do more. She had to find a way to get the castle back in the sky, where it and the egg would be safe. If the magic returned, the castle might recover, and float again. But she had to be with it, warming and protecting the egg.

But what could she do? She was so far gone that just getting to the castle might be more than she could manage, and then she would be unable to do anything more useful than warming the egg.

She pondered, and slowly came to some conclusions. First, if the magic did not return, all was lost; the egg, Roxanne herself, and all Xanth. Second, if the magic returned, there was a way to help. But first she had to help herself, because otherwise the egg would be lost anyway. And if the magic returned, there was a way.

She had to find a healing spring. And she remembered that there was one in this vicinity; it was one of the numerous springs that fed the Kiss Mee lake. For there was healing in kissing. Where was it?

She struggled with her memory, and concluded that the spring was no farther from her than the castle was. So she changed her course and dragged toward the spring. If the magic did not return, it would be no good, but since in that case everything would be lost anyway, it didn't matter. If the magic did return, it could be the salvation of the egg.

At length she reached the place she remembered. There was an indifferent pool, but the growth of vegetation around it was good, suggesting that normally it existed in supreme health. This had to be it.

She would need to take a quantity of it with her. So she labored to fashion a watertight container. She gathered leaves and twigs and clay, and tediously pieced together a bag, drawing on bird lore that was older than magic. Now, if the spring ever resumed its power, she would be ready.

She stood at the brink of it, and relaxed. She had done what she could. As she relaxed, she lost her balance, and fell forward into the spring. She landed with a great splash, and sank down below the surface of the water, too tired to try to climb back out. She knew she would drown, but her last physical resource had been expended making the bag; now she could not save herself.

Then something happened. She was feeling better! The pains and rawnesses of her mangled body had faded, and she saw that her plucked feathers had been restored. But that was impossible, unless—

The magic had returned!

But why hadn't she drowned, even so? She was floating beak down in the pool, not breathing.

Then she realized that it was impossible to drown in a healing spring, because it constantly healed whatever damage the body suffered. The magic had returned in time to save her. Or maybe it had returned after she had drowned, and restored her. It didn't matter; she was suddenly fit to proceed. She was no longer horribly fatigued, and her broken wing was whole.

She hauled herself out, and filled her bag with the precious elixir. Then she charged for the castle, at a phenomenally faster rate than before. In two and a half moments she was there—and saw the castle walls stiffening. Magic gave them their hardness.

But more was required. She lifted the bag and held it over the gouged rim of the cloud isle. If this worked—

The rent healed. The cloudstuff had just enough life in it to respond to the healing elixir. Her desperate ploy was working.

She walked all around the isle, carefully dripping elixir on every wound. Then she went inside, and dripped more elixir on the castle's injuries. These, too, healed. Finally she came to the nest, and the egg, which was shivering with cold, and dropped the last drop on it. The shivering stopped; the egg, too, had healed.

She climbed on top of it—and felt the castle move. It was floating again! It lifted from the ground, at first slowly, then more swiftly, as the healing elixir penetrated to the last of the damaged crevices.

She had done it. She had saved the egg. That was all that mattered. All was well again.

*   *   *

"The Defense rests," Ida said as the illusion image faded. "Your Witness."

But for some reason Grey didn't choose to question Roxanne further.

"Proceed to the summations," Judge Grossclout said.

Now Grey Murphy took the floor and addressed the Jury. "You have just one thing to decide," he said grimly. "Did Roxanne Roc violate the Adult Conspiracy? Her personality does not matter; the Prosecution concedes that she is a fine bird. Her intent does not matter; the Prosecution concedes that her violation was inadvertent. Only one thing matters: *Did she do it?* The evidence shows that she did. You have no choice but to find her guilty as charged." He sat down again.

Ida approached the Jury. "It is not that simple," she said. "Intention does matter. Perhaps it can't entirely excuse the infraction, but it can mitigate it. You must weight the balance of what Roxanne Roc did. Suppose she had not been there: What would have been the fate of the egg? Would it have been better off without her? This is the context in which you must judge her."

She paused, marshaling her arguments, and her moon got focused. "Imagine that you were passing innocently by a region you didn't know was forbidden, and suddenly found yourself grounded, as she was, and punished by being required to sit on an egg for centuries. Wouldn't you feel a trifle rebellious?" Now the power of her sorcery was coming into play. Her talent was the Idea, and what she believed came to be true, provided that no one who knew her talent originated the idea. Could there be some members of the Jury who didn't know her talent? Metria doubted it, but wasn't sure.

"Suppose you nevertheless served that penance honorably, though it meant almost complete isolation from your kind, and from all others, except for unwarranted intruders? So that your only contacts with others were hostile ones, though you yourself were naturally friendly?" Metria saw Jenny Elf nodding, and Graeboe Giant-Harpy, and Sherlock Black. An impression was being made.

"Then suppose that your chance came to escape, because the enchantment that bound you was gone, in the Time of No Magic? Would you have done it?" Stanley Steamer nodded, and Marrow

Bones. "But Roxanne Roc did not. She remained true to her mission, though in great pain and peril. She went to extraordinary lengths to preserve the egg, and succeeded when many another creature would not have." Kim Mundane nodded, and Gayle Goyle.

"Then suppose you made a trifling inadvertent error, merely exclaiming in frustration when you realized that you were unable to explain to an accidental intruder what the situation was. Would you ever have suspected that a chick who had been silent in the egg for more than five centuries was listening? That it would understand?" This time only three did not nod: Com Pewter, whose screen couldn't nod anyway, Stanley Steamer, and Che Centaur, who as a centaur was probably smarter than all the rest of them.

"And suppose that for that inconsequential infraction you were hauled up on a charge of Violation of the Adult Conspiracy? That despite all your loyalty beyond the call of duty, you faced punishment for breaking a rule that many feel is a pointless infringement on the rights of children?" Now Com Pewter's screen showed a pattern of dots that formed into an exclamation point: his way of agreeing. And Che Centaur, the youngest Juror, nodded. So did Cynthia and Chena Centaur, in the Alternate Juror section.

And so did Ida. "You have to know, when you think about it, that sometimes the law is a donkey. Sometimes it is not the person, but the law, that needs correction. When extreme honor and loyalty are punished on a technicality instead of being rewarded, you have to know that something is wrong." Che Centaur nodded again, and so did several others. So did most of the audience.

Now there were tears in Princess Ida's eyes, and her moon clouded over. "Roxanne Roc gave the best years of her life doing the very best she could in a sometimes extremely difficult situation. She made one tiny mistake. Who among us all would have done better? Who among us all has not made at least as bad a mistake at some point in our lives? How can anyone condemn her for being, in the end, not quite perfect? That egg could not have had a finer guardian, other than the Simurgh herself! How are we to reward this devoted servant of that egg, who did so much to preserve it, and who would never have had the chance to commit the infraction had she failed to safeguard that egg so well?" The tears were reflected in Kim's eyes, and Jenny's, and Gayle's, and Gloha's, and the Alternate Jurors', and the others looked uneasy.

"If this is the reward of virtue, what hope is there for any of the rest of us? You must decide whether you can in conscience convict Roxanne Roc in a case that shames the standards of Xanth. You must decide what is right. Otherwise what point is there in even being here?"

Ida turned away, and her moon hid behind her head as if disgusted with the proceedings. There was silence in the court. Metria felt the way she was sure most of the others did: that the trial was, in the end, ludicrous.

The Judge focused both grim eyes on the Jury. "It is not your business to determine the fairness of the law, only whether it has been violated. The evidence and arguments have been put before you. I want you to understand that I expect a suitable decision in this matter. I do not expect to have a hung Jury. However, if that turns out to be the case, I will deal with it as needs be. Behold." He gestured, and one of Iris' illusions appeared behind him. It was an economy-sized gallows, with twelve hangman's nooses turning slowly, slowly in the wind. "I trust I make myself sufficiently clear."

The Jury made a collective gulp and nodded. There would be no hung Jury.

Judge Grossclout banged his gavel. "The Jury will be sequestered for deliberations. This court is in recess."

The Jury and Alternates went to a private room, and a murmur of relaxation rippled across the audience. The trial was almost done.

Metria hoped that the Jury would come to the right decision. But she had a soul-sinking feeling that there was no certainty of that.

$$\underline{16}$$
VERDICT

M ela and Nada were back in their pools, splashing each other and screaming and bouncing as each was struck by drops of salt or fresh water, and assorted males were watching just as if this were the most interesting show in Xanth. One would never have known from watching them that both were mature Princesses, or that one had a daughter almost as well endowed as she was. Cute Steven Steamer was being adored by any spare ladies in the vicinity; when Ida picked him up he snapped at her moon, but the moon was elusive. The little skeletons were playing tag around the chairs in the courtroom. Others were feasting on the refreshments provided, including a considerable puddle of boot rear left over from somewhere.

Metria went to talk with Roxanne Roc, who remained at the stone nest. "They can't convict you," she said. "The whole thing is facetious."

"Squawk?"

"Ridiculous, droll, farcical, funny, absurd—"

"Squawk?"

"Whatever. It would be ludicrous to convict you after six centuries of such loyal service."

But the big bird did not look reassured.

"Metria." It was Bailiff Magician Trent. "The Judge wants to talk with you, in his chamber."

"Oh. Thanks." She popped off, leaving Trent to converse with Roxanne.

Grossclout's glower was unchanged. "Metria, fetch Princess Ivy here."

"But I can't carry a full person," she protested.

"Then get Prince Dolph to do it. In fact, you might as well bring Electra and the twins too. And King Dor and Queen Irene."

A bulb glimmered over her head. "Ooo, Grossie, is this what I think—"

"Don't call me Grossie, you impertinent spook!" When he saw that she was sufficiently cowed, he continued: "And don't say anything about any conjecture you may have. Just tell them that I wish them to attend the conclusion of the trial."

"Yes, Your Honor!" She popped off to Castle Roogna.

Soon enough the entire royal family was traveling in a basket carried by Prince Dor in roc form. Metria popped back to the Judge's chambers. "Mission accomplished, Judge," she reported.

"Good. Now go with the feline."

"The what?" But then she saw Jenny Elf's cat Sammy approaching her. "Oh, he must be lost. I'll take him back to Jenny." She picked him up and walked to the Jury's chamber.

Jenny Elf was waiting. The other Jurors were seated in a wide circle. "Thank you, Metria," she said. "Now, please sit here and watch what we do."

"But I only brought the cat back," she protested. "I'm not supposed to stay in here."

"Yes you are," Jenny said evenly. "I asked Sammy to find the one most suitable for our purpose. He found you. It seems appropriate, since you are half-souled. Judge Grossclout understands."

"But what—?"

"We do not wish to be a hung Jury, but we have found ourselves unable to agree on a Verdict. Therefore we have agreed to find another way to do it. We have a show for you."

"A what?"

"Demonstration, exhibition, array, display—"

"I know what a show is! But why show me anything, when you're supposed to be deliberating?"

"We will explain that in due course. It is important to us that you not know immediately."

"I have no idea what this is about!"

"Excellent. Now, please watch, and I will explain as it goes."

"As *what* goes?"

"The play about the dream of souls."

"The—?"

"Whatever. Now, there once was a young woman called Donna, but you may think of her as anyone you wish to." At this point Kim Mundane stood and stepped into the center of the circle. "She was wooed by a very handsome, sensitive, thoughtful, and likable young man." Dug Mundane rose and joined Kim, taking her hand and kissing it. Kim looked thrilled.

"He had a pair of lovely winged centaur steeds who took them wherever they wished to go," Jenny continued, her voice assuming a humming quality as Che and Cynthia Centaur joined them. "He took her to nice places. They did many interesting things together, and Donna was falling deeply in love with him, and believed that he loved her too. He just seemed to have more than the normal amount of soul."

Metria watched, bemused. What was the point of this irrelevant little skit?

Then a scene filled in around the two people and the steeds. They were no longer in the castle chamber, but in an amusement center having fun. She saw Dug tease Kim (Donna) by inviting her to step on a pretty rug. When she did, the rug threw her off, so that she landed in a bed of feathers. "That's a throw rug!" she exclaimed with happy indignation.

He laughed and stepped on the rug himself. It promptly threw him after her. They wound up in a tangled heap on the bed. Kim squealed and kicked her feet as he tickled her, obviously enjoying herself.

A light illuminated them. Kim quickly sat up straight and tried to straighten her hair, afraid that someone would think she was doing something private in public. "What's that spotlight doing here?" she demanded, picking a feather off her skirt.

"That is not a spotlight, it's a searchlight," Dug informed her.

"What's the difference?"

"The searchlight hasn't yet found what it's looking for."

Kim grabbed a feather pillow and whammed him over the head with it. They had another pleasant bout of tickling and squealing. But Metria noticed something slightly odd: Dug did not look when Kim's skirt flew up to show too much of her legs, and did not let his hands stray when he tickled her under her arms. These were opportunities any normal young man would take automatically. It was almost as if he had some purpose other than normal.

Then they entered the castle's dining hall. Kim reached for a large, pretty, but oddly shaped fruit. The top part of it was transparent, and there were moving bubbles inside.

"I wouldn't recommend eating that," Dug said.

"Why not? It looks good."

"It's a perk-U-later fruit. It tastes fine, but later it makes you wide-awake, so you can't sleep."

"Oh." She set the fruit down, and its perking subsided. "I'm already beginning to get tired; I don't want my sleep disturbed."

"Here," he said, bringing out a small metal object. He used his thumb to flick a little wheel on it as he touched it to her arm.

"What's that?" she asked.

"It's a lighter. It will make you light, so you won't be tired."

"Oh, yes, I feel much lighter now," she agreed, and indeed her step became bouncy.

They walked into the courtyard. There was an icy wall with odd formations on it. Dug reached out and took one. "What is that?" Kim asked.

"An I-cycle. Shall we have a race?"

"How do we do that?"

"We each get on an I-cycle and pedal it as fast and far as we can before it melts."

"Oh, this sounds like fun," she said. She took an I-cycle of her own.

They both got on and put their feet on the cold pedals. The cycles enabled them to race through the courtyard and on out into the garden. The loyal steeds ran after them, seeming strangely subdued, as if none of this fun meant anything to them. Again Metria felt a tinge of concern.

There was a friendly barking sound as several of the flowering plants leaned toward them. "Oh, how cute!" Kim said. "What kind of flowers are those? They remind me of dogs."

"Those are cauliflowers," Dug said. "When they are young, they are collie pups. They grow into dogwood trees." Actually they looked and sounded more like the two gargoyles, But Metria didn't care to quibble with the dream animation.

Kim laughed, loving it. But neither Dug nor the steeds did. Dug seemed quite serious, when not actually playing up to Kim, and the centaurs seemed depressed.

They zoomed toward a lady with a musical instrument. She looked just like Jenny Elf, and the instrument looked like Sammy Cat. She began to sing, but then cut off. "What's the matter?" Kim asked, concerned.

"I am Marcia the minstrel. I just realized it's too early for me to sing," the singer replied.

"Oh—you must have the pre-minstrel syndrome," Kim said sympathetically.

"Yes. Soon I'll be singing the greens and blues, instead of the reds and oranges."

They raced on through a series of arches. But there was a man with a sledgehammer knocking them down. He looked like Graeboe Giant-Harpy. "Why are you making falling arches?" Kim asked him.

"I have to. I'm an arch-enemy."

"This is one weird place!" Kim exclaimed as they raced on into a sheep pasture. But now their I-cycles were melting. Soon both dissolved into puddles, on which the breeze raised very small waves. In fact, they were microwaves. That left Kim and Dug standing on their feet in the pasture.

"You won," Dug said. "You cycled farther than I did before yours melted."

Kim looked around at the sheep, laughing. "That depends on your point of ewe." She didn't notice that neither Dug nor the centaurs laughed.

Then they saw the beautiful sunset. "Oh, this has just been the most wonderful day of my young life!" Kim cried. "I'm so excited I could burst! I think my soul is ready to float away in pure happiness."

"Yes," Dug agreed. He took her in his arms and kissed her deeply. The centaurs flinched.

Something was wrong. Kim seemed to shrink, to dwindle, to fall away as if struck. "Oh, I am undone!" she cried. "You have sucked out my soul!"

"Right," Dug said, satisfied. "And a fine soul it is, too." He walked away, whistling. The centaurs followed, downcast.

"He what?" Metria asked. She realized belatedly that she was in one of Jenny's dreams, and so were the others.

"He sucked out her soul," Jenny said. "He is a soul vampire."

"That's awful!"

Jenny didn't answer. Metria watched in horror as Kim staggered away, barely finding her way home. She looked despondent, hopeless, empty, and wishing she could die. But, Jenny explained, Kim discovered that scattered bits of her soul remained, clinging to her deepest loves, such as her pet green steamer dragon who came out looking for her and helped her struggle the rest of the way home. These pieces came together to keep her alive, but they were only a shadow of what had originally been hers.

Kim was now mostly soulless, and with this emptiness came the baser emotions. She had been happy; now she was depressed. She had loved life; now she had the urge to kill. She was bent on revenge. She got a sharp knife and made a concealed sheath for it, so she could keep it with her all the time.

"No, no!" the inadequate fragments of her soul cried faintly. "This is not right!"

Because those fragments were precious to her, Kim tried to heed them. She went to a wise and gentle man to ask for help. This man was Graeboe Giant-Harpy, no longer knocking down arches. "My child," he counseled her, "do not seek revenge. Stay home and let yourself recover; your soul may regenerate in time from the fragments you still possess."

It was good advice, but she lacked enough soul to take it seriously. Vengeance was an easy concept, and forgiveness a difficult one, for a person with too little soul. She had thought Dug loved her, and he had only been after her soul. He had played her along, until her happiness of the occasion had lightened her soul and loosened its moorings, so that he could more readily steal it. He had callously taken her most precious possession. She had to make him pay for it.

In fact, she wanted to kill him. Yet she was also afraid that he might return, realizing that he hadn't gotten quite *all* her soul. She didn't know how she would react if she saw him again, because the main remaining fragment of her soul was what had loved him most deeply. She was afraid that if she somehow found him, she wouldn't be able to destroy him, because of that little bit of love that remained in her, and that he would then finish her off, cleaning out the last bits and pieces of the remnants of her soul, leaving her entirely barren. So she wasn't certain whether she should kill him, or if she could. She battled the monsters in her mind, trying to come to a firm decision.

In the dream, those monsters appeared, resembling two gargoyles and a walking skeleton. Kim fought them, but her knife had no effect on stone or bone, and she had to retreat.

She realized that she wasn't the only victim. Dug must have done this to many other girls before her. Ooo, that made her furious! Maybe she could, after all, kill him.

Then Dug reappeared. She knew what he wanted: the rest of her soul, which had regenerated a little bit. She knew what she should do: stab him. But he was so handsome, and so much fun to be with, and his two sad centaur steeds were so nice. He brought her a Q-T pie, guaranteed to make her cute. He promised to take her to see the bottle-nosed purpose, one of Xanth's most helpful marine creatures. He said they could even go to Washing-town, where they washed folk utterly clean. He spoke of eating the special fruit that hung from bendy branches and tasted so good that anyone who tasted it was ready to have a party; it was called the dangling party citrus. It all sounded so wonderful!

In this manner he wooed her again, and though she knew better, she felt herself giving up. She wanted to believe it was true, that she could share joy with him as she had before, that her loss of soul had been only a bad part of the dream. She wanted to love him. At the same time she knew that she was being utterly foolish, and that she should kill him. She fought to get her hand on the hidden knife, to bring it out and up, to stab him, but her willpower was feeble and fading.

Dug took her in his arms and brought his lips down to hers. He was going to do it! He was going to suck the meager rest of her soul out, and leave her completely void.

She made one final effort. Her knifepoint came up partway. She wasn't able to stab him, just to prick him through his clothing.

And he exploded like a burst balloon. Souls flew out everywhere. Some were fresh, some decayed; some were in good shape, some hideously shrunken. Most were in between. Hundreds, maybe thousands of them—and in his greed he had wanted yet more. He had been so full of souls that he was ready to burst, and her tiny pinprick had done it. She had, after all, managed to kill him.

Kim remained seriously shaken, not to mention appalled and disgusted and afraid, but she had the common sense to grab her own soul before it floated away, and draw it back into her. It was one of the good ones; it had not had time to get degraded. She was whole again!

The two centaurs grabbed at their own souls similarly. Then their sadness faded, and they smiled. "You have saved us!" they told Kim. "You are a heroine." They spread their wings and flew joyfully home, no longer bound to the one who had stolen their souls and exploited them.

So Kim went home, feeling better, though she was sorry about losing such a handsome suitor.

Unfortunately, there was a wannabee in the neighborhood. This bee liked to assume characteristics that didn't belong to it. This time it assumed the mantle of Public Citizen. It had seen her prick Dug, and reported her to the Better Business Bureau. She was arrested and brought to trial. Since there was no delectable corpse, they charged her with something else, because it wouldn't do to have a false arrest.

The Judge was a machine with a stern monitor screen who looked just like Com Pewter. The Prosecutor was a fierce black man resembling Sherlock.

"We shall demonstrate that the Defendant violated the Adult Conspiracy," the Prosecutor said.

"But she didn't mean to," the Defense Attorney protested. She looked like Gloha Goblin-Harpy.

"Who says I did it?" Kim demanded.

"I do," a winged monster replied. "I am the Simurgh. With my omniscience I saw that when you rolled in the feathers with that man, you were careless about how your skirt hiked up, and a baby mouse looked out of its hole and saw your panties. That is a violation."

"But this is ridiculous!" Kim protested. "I never even knew the mouse was there."

SILENCE, the Judge's screen printed. HOW DO YOU PLEAD?

"This is crazy!" Kim said. "Here I have just survived having my soul stolen, not to mention losing my boyfriend, and all you care about is—"

IRRELEVANT STATEMENT DELETED, the Judge printed, and it was as if it had never been spoken, for reality was changed.

"I don't care what the Defendant knew or when she knew it," Sherlock said grimly. "I am prepared to bring the mouse in to testify to the crime."

"But the Defendant is a person of good character, from a far land," Gloha said. "She had no knowledge of any such violation."

"Ignorance is no excuse," Sherlock insisted.

"And she restored lost souls to many folk," Gloha said. "I am prepared to bring in two centaurs to testify to that. Surely the good she has done outweighs any inadvertent evil."

"She did the crime," Sherlock said.

"She's a good person," Gloha replied.

The Judge's screen flashed. THE CASES HAVE BEEN MADE. THE JURY WILL NOW RENDER THE VERDICT.

Suddenly Metria was the cynosure of all eyes. This was weird, because she wasn't even slightly sure of anything, let alone cyno sure. "Who, me?" she asked.

YES, YOU.

"This is all just a crazy dream!" Metria exclaimed. "This whole thing is just a house of cards. I'm getting out of here." And she broke her way out of Jenny's dream.

Only to find herself in the middle of the Jury Room, still being watched by at least a dozen pairs of eyes. NOW YOU MUST DECIDE, FOR WE CANNOT, AND WE MUST NOT BE A HUNG JURY, Com Pewter printed, the image of a hangman's noose appearing on his screen. IS THE DEFENDANT GUILTY?

"I'll do no such thing!" Metria said. "I'm not even on this Jury."
DEMONESS CHANGES HER MIND.

Metria found herself with her mind changed. "Yes, of course I'll decide," she agreed. "Just let me ponder a bit."

OTHERS RELAX WHILE DEMONESS PONDERS. Musical notes appeared on Com Pewter's screen, and Jenny Elf began to hum again. Soon a new picture formed, with all the members of the Jury at the fancy castle, dancing in the ballroom. Marrow did the *Danse Macabre* with a fine rattling of bones, while Gloha and Graeboe did pirouettes in the upper dome. Stanley Steamer kept the beat by clacking his teeth, and the two gargoyles made stone circles around each other. The rest formed a fine square dance, drawing Marrow in to make it complete, and then a round dance, followed by a triangle dance. In this dream Dug was handsome in a formal suit, and Kim lovely in a flowing dress, and the rest looked great too. They were all having a wonderful time.

But not Metria. She was stuck with the Verdict. They couldn't decide, so they wanted her to do it for them, and Com Pewter had changed her reality so that she couldn't refuse. She was supposed to decide whether Kim was guilty of showing her panties to a baby mouse, but she knew that this was just a Suppose story. The real Verdict would be on Roxanne Roc, who had just as innocently erred.

How could a responsible Jury abdicate its responsibility like this, by assigning the decision to a slightly weird demoness? This was a plain violation of its whatever.

In fact, this was a demons' beauty contest. The issue would be decided not by those who had the debate, but by an innocent person who hardly knew what was going on. That person was Metria herself. "Hoist by my own petard!" she muttered angrily.

'Lift up what?' Mentia inquired. 'Did you say something dirty?'

'I'm caught in my own kind of scheme. I helped arrange a marriage by setting up a demons' beauty contest, and now the Jury is making me decide their Verdict similarly.'

'I wonder what gave them that notion.'

A light bulb glowed. The Demoness V(E\N)^{us}! This was her third effort to mess up the trial! She had caused the duly appointed Jury to abdicate in favor of an unqualified creature. Metria understood this now—but still couldn't change it, because of Com Pewter's stricture. It might be wrong, but she still had to do it.

Well, there was a way out. She could just pop back to Judge Grossclout and tell him what had happened. Com Pewter wasn't watching her at the moment; she could escape before he overwrote her decision.

But what would happen then? Grossclout would declare a mistrial—and that would probably represent the victory of the Demoness V(E\N)^{us}, who was trying to disrupt the proceedings. There had to be a Verdict—or the Demon X(A\N)th would lose, and all Xanth would pay the price. So Metria had to do it—even if it resulted in an unfair Verdict.

But not alone. 'Mentia! Woe Betide! You are in this too. *You* decide.'

'Sure,' soulless Mentia said. 'The law may be crazy, and I'm crazy, and I say she showed her panties and she's guilty.'

'No she isn't!' Woe Betide protested. 'She's a good girl who was led astray by a bad man. He pushed her, he made her roll in the feathers. *He* is the guilty one.'

'But he's not on trial,' Mentia said. 'Maybe they're both guilty. We have to decide about her, no one else. And she did it.'

'But there were ex—ext—exten—' Woe Betide stalled, unable to handle such an adult word.

'Extenuating circumstances,' Metria said.

'Yes. So she's innocent.'

Mentia and Woe Betide were on opposite sides, making another hung jury. So it was up to Metria after all. She couldn't let all the others get hung.

The case, as presented to her, was against Kim Mundane, who had been deceived, led astray, deprived of most of her soul, and arrested when she fought back. Instead of charging her with the crime of killing an evil predator, they had trumped up a ludicrous incidental indictment they thought would be easier to prove. Because Kim had acted in self-defense, and helped many others recover their souls, so should be praised rather than condemned. So she was on trial for something irrelevant, because someone wanted a conviction. The tactic reeked.

And Roxanne Roc had given almost six centuries of loyal service, doing as well as any creature in Xanth could have. Yet instead of being requited as she deserved, she was put on trial for a trifling technical violation. Why? So as to avoid the need to reward her? That gross unfairness was surely what had hopelessly divided the Jury, and it divided Metria too. She wanted to praise Roxanne, not punish her, but the situation had been so crafted that she couldn't. She had to decide on the basis of the limited technicality. Oh yes, the Jury had re-created the situation, in the guise of a different story, so that no one could say that an unauthorized person had made the decision about Roxanne. But in fact, they had dumped the outrage into Metria's lap. She had to decide.

Why had the Simurgh done this? Why did Grossclout and the others go along with it? Where was there any fairness in any of this business? Metria had only half a soul, yet she could see that this entire thing was a travesty. The Jury saw that too. Why couldn't the Simurgh? She was supposed to be an extremely fair-minded and wise bird. Was she actually just a mean-spirited creature determined to welsh on a deal?

But the Simurgh was not on trial. Roxanne Roc was. Metria had to address the issue before her, not the issue she wished she could tackle. Maybe the Demoness V(E\N)^{us} figured that the Jury would refuse to address that issue, and would win if that happened. And if Metria herself refused, what mischief might she be doing to all Xanth?

She struggled, going round and round, but finally she came to an unwilling conclusion. "It's crazy, it's wrong, it's ludicrous, it's a blot on us all, the law is a mule, but technically Kim is guilty of the charge against her," she said.

The dance abruptly stopped. All the living Jurors looked stricken. But it was clear that they had made a deal, and were honoring it.

SO BE IT, Com Pewter printed. DEMONESS, INFORM JUDGE GROSS-CLOUT THAT THE JURY HAS REACHED ITS VERDICT. YOU WILL SAY NOTHING OF THE MANNER OF IT. And the others nodded grimly. This was their secret—and hers.

Had she just saved Xanth—at the expense of a noble and really innocent bird? Metria was much afraid that she had.

She popped out. Grossclout scowled at her. "The Jury is ready," she said grimly. And wished she could sink into some other realm.

The Judge called the court to order. The various celebrants ceased their efforts and quickly returned to the main chamber. The audience had swelled in size, because of the arrival of King Dor, Queen Iris, and the rest of the Castle Roogna personnel. Even the Good Magician Humfrey and the members of his household were here now. Metria was amazed. She had delivered Grossclout's general summons, but it was still astonishing to see it honored so completely. The Good Magician almost never left his gloomy study.

The Jury returned to its Jury Box. Metria saw that several of the female members were dabbing their faces with handkerchiefs, and several males looked unhappy. They had not liked their decision any better than Metria had. Only Com Pewter looked smug with a smiley-face on his screen. He must have been the only one to insist on guilty, forcing them all to face the threat of being hung. And Metria had sided with him. What a disgrace!

"Have you reached a Verdict?" Judge Grossclout inquired rhetorically, through a glower.

"We have, Your Honor," Sherlock said. He was evidently the foreman. "We find the defendant, Roxanne Roc, guilty as charged."

There was a gasp of dismay from the audience. Princess Ida looked stunned, and her moon turned its bright face away, becoming dark. In the adjacent chamber Roxanne's beak dipped; if she had hoped for better, it had been in vain.

Yet somewhere distant there was a sinister vibration as a powerful demoness cursed and departed. Metria thought she knew who that was. CORRECT, DEMONESS, the Simurgh's thought came. YOU HAVE SAVED XANTH. THE DEMONESS V(E\N)^{us}' BET WAS THAT ROXANNE WOULD NOT BE CONVICTED. SHE BELIEVED THAT NO JURY COULD BE FOUND TO DECIDE STRICTLY ON THE BASIS OF THE EVIDENCE.

She had indeed saved Xanth. But at what price? Metria's half soul was hurting.

Judge Grossclout nodded. "Roxanne Roc, you have been found guilty of violation of the Adult Conspiracy to Keep Interesting

Things from Children. Because this may prejudice an extremely important chick, I sentence you to a continuation of your obligation to care for this bird until such time as the Adult Conspiracy no longer applies to it.''

"Objection!" Ida cried. "That could be centuries!"

The Judge ignored her. "You will continue to place the welfare of this creature before all others, until it is grown and independent. No other desire or obligation will take precedence over this mission." He glared in her direction. "Do you understand and accept this sentence, Roxanne Roc?"

Slowly her head lifted. "Squawk."

"She understands and accepts," Grundy Golem translated. "She will do her best."

"So let it be," the Judge said, banging his gavel on the desk. The sound was so sharp and loud that it made the entire castle reverberate. Then he turned to face the Jury and audience. "The supreme importance of this mission made it necessary to verify the constancy of the one selected to perform it. A pretext was established for this purpose. I have five rhetorical queries and a statement to issue."

He paused a moment. It was surely for effect, because the Demon Professor never had any hesitancy about anything. "Here is the statement: No other desire or obligation in all Xanth will take precedence over this mission."

His baleful near eye fixed on the Jury Box. "You, Che Centaur, will in due course be summoned to tutor this chick in all the things needful for it to know and understand. It is for this purpose you came into existence: winged so as to be able to fly with it, a centaur so as to command sufficient intellect for it. You will for a time share its destiny. Do you understand and accept this mission?"

Che Centaur's mouth had fallen open, as had those of the other Jurors. They were beginning to realize that the Verdict they had just rendered had more significance than they had thought. "I—I do," Che said. His word was, of course, inviolate, because he was a centaur. Yet he was dazed; he had just learned the purpose in his life.

The Judge focused on Grundy. "The chick and roc will on occasion need to communicate with other creatures. You, Grundy Golem, will provide your service as translator as required. Do you understand and accept?''

For a moment even the big-mouthed golem was flustered. ''Yeah, sure,'' he agreed, looking quite flattered.

Grossclout's terrible gaze swung toward the audience, which collectively blanched. It fixed on the Good Magician. ''And toward the successful completion of that mission, your resources will be made available to Che Centaur and Roxanne Roc at need, without impediment. Do you understand and accept, Magician Humfrey?''

''Of course,'' Humfrey said, seeming unsurprised. Metria realized that there had been considerably more purpose in the Service he had required of her than she or anyone had guessed.

The Judge's gaze swung toward the chamber where the Simurgh perched. ''And yours. Do you accept, Simurgh?''

YES. There was no surprise there, either. It was, after all, her chick.

The gaze moved to another creature Metria hadn't noticed before, perhaps because it became visible only now. It was a great horse, black as the midnight sky, with the small bright lights of the stars shining from it. It was the Night Stallion, the lord of the realm of dreams! ''And yours. Do you accept, Trojan?''

I do. The Horse of a Different Color faded out.

Now that gaze swung back to the Defendant, whose beak lifted to face him. ''To facilitate the further obligation you have acquired, Roxanne Roc, your power of flight is hereby restored and magnified beyond that of any of your kind. You are granted the freedom to travel anywhere in Xanth in the performance of your mission, without impediment. No creature or thing will hinder you in any manner, on pain of being banished to the realm of dreams and subject to the extreme ill will of the Night Stallion and his night mares.'' There was a groaning murmur through the hall; there could be no worse fate than to be locked into perpetual bad dreams. ''You will take any step you deem appropriate to secure the safety and welfare of your charge, and will preempt the services of any creature or thing of Xanth toward that end, as necessary. For the chick about to hatch—'' Grossclout glanced at his left wrist. ''—in three quarters of a moment is destined to be the successor of the Simurgh, when she retires. It must have the best upbringing and education available, and the most constant guardian and governess, in fair times or adversity. This court is satisfied that you are qualified for that duty.''

There was a murmur of awe through the audience and Jury. Metria realized that Roxanne Roc had just been promoted to Xanth's most powerful position, because of the importance of her job. Her sentence was not a punishment, but a reward for her extremely loyal service. None of the members of the Jury had suspected!

''And because this mission may indeed require some additional centuries, the enchantment that has preserved your youth will continue for the duration. You will not age until your job is finished.'' Judge Grossclout's gaze lifted. ''Now it is time.''

The gavel banged again, shaking the castle. There was a loud crack, as if something extremely hard had sundered. Roxanne squawked and jumped off the nest.

''Oh!'' Grundy translated.

The egg was cracking open. It fell into two segments. As it did there was the whirring of wings, and a stork flew in, bearing a bundle. It landed on the nest Roxanne had just vacated, set down its bundle, and removed from it—a fluffy towel. It set this towel in the open egg and used it to dry off something inside. Then it released the towel.

Metria watched in bemusement. If the stork brought birds, what was the point of eggs? And how could the chick have been inside the egg, to overhear the bad word? Then she realized that this was probably a courtesy call, to attend to the hatching and make sure all was well. For of course, this was not just a routine hatching.

From the towel stepped The Chick. It scintillated with twice the colors of the rainbow, sparkling like a collection of brilliant faceted gems. It was, taken as a whole, the most beautiful and precious chick anyone had ever seen.

It blinked, and caught sight of Roxanne. ''Cheep!'' it exclaimed.

''Nanny!'' Grundy translated.

The chick stepped toward Roxanne, who quickly returned to the stone nest and spread a wing protectively over it. It was obvious that the two would get along.

The partition returned, closing off the scene. "Now there is other minor business," Grossclout said. "Is the wedding party ready?"

Magician Trent stood. "Yes, Your Honor."

"Proceed."

The Sorceress Iris stood, turning to focus on the chamber. It became a festively decorated room, with the audience appropriately garbed. There was even a stork in attendance, for the one who had come to dry off the chick had remained for the other ceremony. This was unusual, but of course, everything about this occasion was extraordinary.

Trent walked to the side, and brought back the Demon Vore. "Stand here," he said. Then he walked to the other side, and brought back Magician Grey Murphy. "Stand here."

"But I'm not—" Grey protested.

"Yes you are."

There was a crash somewhere outside. Everyone jumped, and Ida's moon looked alarmed. "What was that?" Grey asked.

"The sun and the moon just collided," Che Centaur said, and Gwenny Goblin tittered. "Fortunately no harm was done."

Metria remembered how they had joked that this was what Grey and Ivy were waiting for, before they married. Now their last excuse for delay was gone.

Then the music started. Metria looked toward its source, and was surprised to see Maestro No One sitting in a pit marked ORCHESTRA, conjuring a series of musical instruments to play the theme. Apparently he had been able to leave the gourd for this occasion, perhaps because the Night Stallion himself was attending.

Now a great organ manifested, and played with enormous authority. It was the wedding march.

Two young women appeared at the back, in twin wedding dresses. Princess Nada Naga and Princess Ivy Human. They had been friends since both were fourteen. Now they were getting married together. Metria recognized the wedding dress first used by Electra, now restitched to fit Nada, making her magically beautiful, though of all the women in Xanth, she needed it least. Ivy wore a pale green dress her mother must have made, which did much the same for her. The two began their long walk down the aisle toward the two handsome males waiting at the front. Nada was accompanied by King Nabob Naga, and Ivy by King Dor Human: Naturally their two fathers were participating, after waiting so long for this occasion.

Metria's eyes blurred. Now that she was married herself, and had half a soul, she cried at weddings, and this was a double wedding, so she cried twice as hard. Her tears washed out most of the details, but it did seem to be a nice, if blurry, event. Before she knew it, it was done, and the happy couples were slicing the monstrous cake someone had made. Individual groups were forming, as folk with common interests chatted. Magician Trent was talking with Che, Cynthia, and Chena Centaur, probably about the prospect of transforming some regular folk to winged centaur form. They would need to search for suitable volunteers, and surely some normal centaurs would be interested. Rapunzel was talking with the Bones family; no telling what mutual concern such folk had. Metria found herself sitting alone amidst a pile of wet hankies.

She was dimly aware of a dialogue between Dug and Kim as they settled nearby to eat their wedding cake. "I dread going back to Mundania, after this," he said. "I wish I could stay and play the game again. Grossclout let slip that the next winner's prize is the talent of creating things. That would go nicely with your talent of erasure."

Kim ruffled his hair. "Maybe next time, Dug. The trial was more important, and the wedding was divine. At least we get to keep our summons tokens as souvenirs, though I guess no one would believe us if we ever told the truth about them. And I shouldn't tell you this, after the way you stole my soul—"

"Well, you got back at me!" he retorted. "You pricked me into burst nothingness."

"You deserved it. Anyway, the Simurgh told me that instead of being docked for skipping classes, we'll both get A's. It seems that Com Pewter has a connection to the college database for grades. It's sort of our reward for Jury duty."

"That's great! I can't think of much of anything I want more than an easy A."

"What, not anything?"

He looked at her. "Well—"

"Nuh-uh! That stork is entirely too close for comfort." Bubbles perked up, glancing at the stork, which was standing by a wall as if asleep. It was a curious business, having a stork remain, Metria thought; maybe it was on call in case there was an emergency with the chick.

Dug sighed. "You know, you'd look good with a moon like Ida's. Then maybe I'd know by its phases whether you—"

Kim stomped on his toe, but not hard. "You may kiss me, if you promise not to suck out my soul again."

"Done."

Metria realized that she hadn't seen her husband in several hours. She had more than kisses in store for him. Then she remembered something else. She stood, shedding hankies, and started to cross the hall.

"Metria."

She jumped. It was Grossclout. "Yes, Your Honor?"

"Forget that. My duty is done. Where are you going?"

"To the Simurgh, to return the extra summons token."

"Is your skull still entirely filled with mush? The Simurgh doesn't want it back."

"But then what—?"

"What do you think, Demoness? You have completed your assignment, and by enabling the trial to proceed and a proper Verdict to be achieved, you have spared Xanth much mischief. The Simurgh intended you to have your reward when that was done. Now you must serve that last summons and go home to your husband."

"But who is there to serve it on? It's blank."

"Is it?" His tone said *mush*. "Whose attention or attendance have you most wished to compel? You know that creature will not wait here forever."

She brought out the last token and looked at it. Now it said THE STORK. The other side said DELIVERIES.

'Well, now,' Mentia remarked, while Woe Betide stared in childish awe.

"Oh!" Metria exclaimed, a brilliant bulb flashing. Then, with determination and excitement, she marched in the direction of the long-legged bird.

The Demon Grossclout almost smiled. Fortunately he was able to stifle the miscreant expression.

Author's Note

X anth is a funny place, and it has some funny origins. It has grown gradually more adult over the nineteen years of its existence, as befits its age, while never losing its punniness or naughtiness. But on occasion there is a bit of seriousness in its hidden background. Last time it was the death of Lester del Rey, my former editor at Del Rey Books, whose efforts did so much to put Xanth on the fantasy map. This time it was several events in the lives of readers, including a death. I am sensitive to death, being depressive, as so many humorists are.

I attended a convention in Panhandle Florida—yes, near the entrance to Xanth—just as I started writing this novel. The convention was called HurriCon—most fan conventions in this genre find clever ways to fit the word "Con" in—and it was a normal example of its kind, which is to say, it would be weird to any outsider. In the bustle of this and that, a woman approached me, with her little girl. She explained how they had been planning to attend as a family, but two weeks before the Con, her husband was killed by a drunk driver. That was all, but it was enough. Readers of this series will know that I have certain sympathies and certain peeves, and drunken driving scores on one of each. In too much of America a bottle and a car represent a license to maim or kill with virtual impunity. Jenny Elf came to Xanth when twelve-year-old Jenny was struck, put into a months-long coma, and left almost completely paralyzed by a drunk driver. That story is told in the Author's Note for *Isle of View*, and in the book *Letters to Jenny*. She is now seventeen as I write this novel, and doing well enough, considering her continuing paralysis, and I still write to her every week. I completed the non-Xanth fantasy novel of Robert Kornwise, *Through the Ice*, after he was killed at age sixteen by another reckless driver who had been drinking. But there are other cases that don't involve alcohol. Janet Hines was taken by a long-term, wasting illness that first paralyzed and blinded her. Richard C. White died in a suspicious accident. They were fans of Xanth, and they came to Xanth when they left Mundania. And so Richard (Billy Jack) Siler came to join them, in Chapter 4.

But it isn't all negative. When I got home from the convention there was a pile of thirty-five fan letters to answer, and one was from Mariah Spencer, age twelve. On Jamboree 24, 1994, Mariah was about to be run down by a drunk driver. But her sister, Andrea Spencer, age fourteen, saw him coming and pushed Mariah mostly out of the way. But Andrea got hit herself, and suffered a hematoma, a blood clot on the brain. She had brain surgery, and they had to shave her head. She did okay, but maybe you know how important hair is to a girl; it wasn't a fun time. So this time someone who isn't a fan of Xanth gets mentioned—because she saved a fan of Xanth. The incident appears in Chapter 9, where Metria couldn't remain as a witness, so didn't learn the details, and Mariah didn't see Metria passing by.

And sometimes it gets downright nice. I heard from Samantha Pendery right after that Con too. She had had a rough year, with a nasty divorce in which she lost her dog and her son via "parental kidnapping." But the child proved to be more than his father could handle, so early one OctOgre morning, son and several months' worth of dirty clothes were dumped on her doorstep. Life is like this, in drear Mundania, and of course, men don't know that clothes have to be cleaned every so often. So it was off to the Laundromat. Since this promised to be an all-day adventure, she suggested that her son bring a book. He chose *Isle of View*. That's the one that starts with Chex Centaur's darling son Che being lost, appropriately. No, I can't say for sure that it was Samantha's collection of Xanth novels that brought her son back, though it's tempting. The magic dust between the pages can have unpredictable effect, as we shall see. Then, in the throes of handling all that laundry, he forgot the book, and it was left behind. He rode his bicycle to retrieve it, but it was gone. Disaster! But remember about that magic dust. Samantha had had the sense to write her name and phone number inside the cover of the book, just in case, because of course, a Xanth novel is too valuable to risk losing. So about a week later a man called: He had found her book, and would have called earlier, but he had opened it and gotten instantly addicted by that magic dust, and was a very slow reader. He just had to finish it before returning it. He asked whether there were any other books like it. Well . . . Since this was obviously a man of taste, Samantha agreed to meet him at the Laundromat. Laundry led to coffee, coffee led to dinner, dinner led to sharing Thanksgiving, and to sharing Hanukkah. There was more, but I trust the general nature of the progression is clear. She wrote to tell me that they would be getting married. All because of the magic dust, and maybe because someone said the title *Isle of View* aloud. One does have to be careful, around Xanth.

Apart from special cases like those described here, I don't use real people in Xanth. But sometimes associations develop, as with the Good Magician and Lester del Rey, or the Gorgon and Judy-Lynn del Rey; I don't choose them, they choose themselves. One long-term association was between the Princess Ivy and my daughter Penny. Ivy, over the years and novels, reflected the stages of Penny's growing up. But such associations have their liabilities, because things may happen in one realm that aren't reflected in the other. Ivy got betrothed and was ready to marry—but Penny didn't marry. Thus poor Ivy was caught in a social limbo. So finally I had to divorce Ivy from Penny, so that Ivy could get on with her life. The instant I did that, Ivy married Grey, and of course, her friend Nada Naga got married too. *Then* Penny got married. Um, no, I'm not sure where that leaves her twin Princess Ida, who argued so eloquently for Roxanne Roc's acquittal but couldn't quite believe that the big bird was technically innocent. Ida came onto the scene when Penny discovered a friend exactly her age, and acquired a moon when the asteroid Ida was discovered to have a tiny moon—in the middle of the writing of this novel. Maybe there is some magic in Mundania.

Now we're coming to the reader-suggestion list. Notions have been coming in faster than I can use them up, and well over a hundred have been used here. I have mostly caught up on them through the year 1993, and used the majority of them for the first three months of 1994, but some still have to wait their turn, because they concern things like the children of Grey and Ivy. So if you incorrigibles insist on sending me notions, bear in mind that it may be years before you ever see them in print. Many suggestions are rejected, because they duplicate ones already used. As it is, there have been so many that I can't be sure I haven't reused some old ones, crediting them to new folk.

Laurel Kristck pointed out that probably I had an inadequate notion of trilogies. Instead of being 3×3, they should be 3^3. That is, 3 cubed, or 27. Thus this novel, #19 in the Xanth series, would be leading off the last third of the trilogy. Now, why didn't I realize that before?

The others I'll simply list without much additional comment, though some are for incidental notions and others are for major segments. Those who find such lists boring may quit reading at this point. I hope to see you again at the next novel. I do have a number of further titles in mind, such as *Yon Ill Wind* and *Faun & Games*, and readers have suggested some phenomenal future notions and characters.

A female doing daring things—Janet Godsoe (Metria's trying!). Fire cracker plants—Ben Smith. Sand worm, Sugar Loaf Mountain, grass hopper grass—Trista Casey. Come-quat, go-quat, hard water, surfs revolting, stampede, singing the blues and other colors, fisin' plant for electrici-trees, hippo-crate—Paul-Gabriel Wiener. Sour grapes with attitude—Justin Dossett. Wing nuts, light house—Tom Boyer. Kill a June-bug and lose a month—Troy Winslow. Moat filled with boot rear, illusion ceiling—David Lee. Building blocks— Kevin Shiue. Quarterhorse—Meghan Kwist. Demoness Helen Back—Ross Fabricant. Simurgh replacing the universe—Emily Ashcroft. Chain letter—William Sherry. Hell toupee—Katie Woolsey. Night light, timber wolf, air plain, air male, light bulb—David M. Gänsz. Hare used as wig—Evie Trester. Mara—Marie Manus. Talent of bird calling, wild bore—Matt Cannington and Heather Miller. Sprinkle Ida with Lethe water to restore her talent—Jeremy Gray, Melissa Barshop. Trial for violation of the Adult Conspiracy, Xanthropology lesson—Michael A. Weatherford. Re, who re-does things—Marie Isert. Rock in chair—Jessica Grider. Mood swings, Nada Naga marries a demon prince—Amanda Findsey. Cat or pillar, mine—Steve Killen. Croakuses, golden showers climber—Ron Leming. Threnody as Metria's daughter—Bill Talley. Peer pressure—Mark A. Hickenbotham. Phelra, who summons animals to help her—Krishawn Smith. Ivy and Grey want the sun and the moon to collide at their wedding—Scott Patri. Threnody's curse removed—Roger Brannon. Catacomb, Human Magician Kings of Xanth, catalog—Trevor Boylan. Princess Ida as a major character—Jeremy Billette. Symme-tree—Brendan Mathis. Die-odes—Esther Undercoffer. D-Terminal—Alex Feely. Demon Vore—Joel R. Vore. Fingers & Knuckles McPalm—Eric Cromwell. Nada Naga loves a younger man—Jennifer Cleckley. DeMonica—Aimee Caldwell. Dog Island puns—Stephen Sandford. Rigor Mortis—Nichole Adkins. Minus (mynah) birds—John & Sara Potter. Note book—Anne Petersen. Sammy Cat finding something in the home world—Holly Layton, Melissa Barshop. Sammy Cat with reverse wood: nothing *but* home—Adam Ranciglio, Melissa Barshop. Reverse wood in hate spring—Louis King. Other reverse wood notions—Judah Nagler & Aaron Lehr. Magic bubble to take Jenny Elf home—Vicki Kunz. Buttoned fly—Chris Anthony. Sarge Ant—Nick Bergeron. Tick King Time Bomb—Donna Vincent. Egg plant—Michael Kyle Leneski. Chelsy Centaur—Carl Kushinsky. Thunderbirds and lightningbugs, tap root, house plant, lady bugs and gentlemen bugs, fast food chain—Conrad, Ed, Walt & Pete Kolis. Rain coat, dung beetles with reverse wood—Malcolm Jones. Raining tsoda popka—Lexi Bond. Crystal River, Silver Springs—Davida Klinger. Two-lips tree—Beth Hamlin. Apoca-lips—David Abolafia. Alicentaurs—Philip Iredale. Ogre achiever, ogre and ogre—Lenna S. Hanna-O'Neill. Reitas' reign—Kevin Anderson. Night colt—Dawn McClain. Dreamwatcher—Brendan Murphy. Erasure talent can't

erase a river—Vicki Kunz. Jenny Elf's dreams compatible with
dream realm—Stephanie Erb. Abscissa and Ordinate—Travis Hodg-
don. Chena Centaur's history—Adam Shain & Christy Woodman.
Brawnye Brassie: Blythe Brassie's husband—Xanth Xone via Becca
Parker. Flying centaur manure—Carrie Ogawa. Merci and Cyrus'
offspring tolerant of both fresh and salt water—Alyson Dewsnap.
Sick-a-more tree—James Riley. Garter snake—Josh Anderson.
Anna Conda—Sarah Kramer. Steven Steamer—David Lee. Pat
urn—Kevin Shiue. Half wishes—Rem Haft. Talents: making wishes
come true to a limited degree, making music by thinking of instrument; sees five seconds into the future—David Forrest. Xanticipation—Carl Kushinsky. "Someday my submarine will come"—
Cricket Krishelle—one of the meaningless moments of her life. Talent of controlling emotions—Matthew Brennan. Jay Were-dragon—
Justin Savanah. Cyborg in Xanth—Shawn Henley. Miss Pell—
Christopher Rans. Dropping a hint—Joy Appel. Man with five personalities and talents—Matt Gillmore. Talents: making objects stick
together, take pain away by touch—Janet Godsoe. Talent: making
things spontaneously combust—Ki-Ki. Talent: duplication of inanimate objects—Paul Smaldino. Gourd Storage Dept. of Fears, rocs
turn others to rocks—Troy Winslow. Rye full—Shirwyn Dalgliesh.
Eyeglass bush on an eye land—Marie Daniels. Bag tree—Wesley
Pope. Picture segments on book bindings—Jason E. Smith. Talent:
making friends—Joy Appel. Talent: dehancement—David Lee. Talent: tickle from a distance—Katie Morein. Octo Puss, point of
ewe—Dianna Woolsey. Force field—Catherine Coleman. Fresh
water—John Surber. Snide—Mark A. Hickenbotham. Alias—
Lakaya Peeples. Pluck any tool or weapon from a cloud—Tom
Koonce, Roger Brannon. Problems of the Nameless Castle during
the time of No Magic, interruption of Roxanne Roc's grounding
spell—Jennifer Roscoe. Relationship—Louigi Addario. Can't drown
in a healing spring—Paul Gladis. Dream of souls—Donna Etzler
(whose four-year-old daughter had bad dreams, until the nature of
night mares was clarified; after that she set out apples for the mares,
and had no more bad dreams. Of course.) Throw rug—W. G. Bliss.
Spotlight versus searchlight—Dawn Lisowski. Perk-U-later fruit—
Jeremy Fuller. The lighter—Alan Little. I-cycle—Josh Anderson.

Cauliflowers with collie pups—Kirsten Slotter. Pre-minstrel syndrome—
Jean Lamb. Arch enemy—Cheryl-Anne Thornton. Microwave—Daniel
McBride. Q-T pie—James Riley. Bottle-nosed purpose—Rebecca
Robinson. Washing-town—W. E. Jorgens. Dangling party citrus—
Tim Cummings. Wannabee—Doni Rose Hyden. Search for volun-
teers to become winged centaurs—Joseph A. Rausch. Talent of cre-
ating things waiting for Dug to win—William Kelly.

And there were two thirds of a slew left over! Some that weren't
used this time have been saved for more significant treatment in the
next novel.

For those of you who haven't yet caught on, Xanth now appears
first in hardcover, followed a year later by the paperback edition. So
if you enjoyed this novel in paperback, and simply can't wait for
the next one, you don't *have* to . . .

> For a sample newsletter and catalog of
> Piers Anthony books, call ''troll-free''
> 1-800 HI PIERS.